A SINISTER QUARTET

D1563605

Also available from Mythic Delirium Books
mythicdelirium.com

Novels

Latchkey
Nicole Kornher-Stace

Story collections

Bone Swans
C. S. E. Cooney

The History of Soul 2065
Barbara Krasnoff

Snow White Learns Witchcraft
Theodora Goss

In the Forest of Forgetting
Theodora Goss

Unseaming
Mike Allen

The Spider Tapestries
Mike Allen

Aftermath of an Industrial Accident
Mike Allen

Poetry collections

Songs for Ophelia
Theodora Goss

Hungry Constellations
Mike Allen

Anthologies

EDITED BY MIKE ALLEN

*Clockwork Phoenix: Tales of Beauty
and Strangeness*

*Clockwork Phoenix 2: More Tales
of Beauty and Strangeness*

*Clockwork Phoenix 3: New Tales
of Beauty and Strangeness*

Clockwork Phoenix 4

Clockwork Phoenix 5

EDITED BY MIKE
AND ANITA ALLEN

*Mythic Delirium:
an international anthology
of poetry and verse*

Mythic Delirium: Volume Two

A SINISTER QUARTET

MIKE ALLEN   C. S. E. COONEY
AMANDA J. McGEE   JESSICA P. WICK

Mythic Delirium
BOOKS

mythicdelirium.com

A Sinister Quartet

Cover art © 2020 by Jason Wren, jasonwren.crevado.com

Cover design and interior designs and illustrations © 2020 by Brett Masse, brettmasseworks.com

Release date: June 9, 2020

ISBN-10: 1-7326440-3-9

ISBN-13: 978-1-7326440-3-8

Published by Mythic Delirium Books
Roanoke, Virginia
mythicdelirium.com

This book is a work of fiction. All characters, names, locations, and events portrayed in this book are fictional or used in an imaginary manner to entertain, and any resemblance to any real people, situations, or incidents is purely coincidental.

Our gratitude goes out to the following who because of their generosity are from now on designated as supporters of Mythic Delirium Books: Saira Ali, Cora Anderson, Anonymous, Patricia M. Cryan, Steve Dempsey, Oz Drummond, Patrick Dugan, Matthew Farrer, C. R. Fowler, Mary J. Lewis, Paul T. Muse, Jr., Shyam Nunley, Finny Pendragon, Kenneth Schneyer, and Delia Sherman.

CONTENTS

INTRODUCTION

The fountain bubbles. You presume it is a fountain, though no water spews up from the center of the round basin. Odd, that whatever mechanism aerates the fountain remains active well after sunset. The noise it makes separated from the ambient mix of insect churring and the hiss of passing cars when you stepped onto the cobblestones penned inside the balustrade. Likely the stone amplifies the sound.

Come closer, peer over the basin's lip, and ponder the reflections fragmented by the disturbance in the water. The mystery deepens as you lift your head to regard the sky, a sheet of deepest black perforated with pinpricks that let starfire shine through. When you return your gaze to the fountain, nothing in the firmament explains the bright shapes you find there, prevented from coalescing by the agitated surface.

You think of crystal balls and scrying pools.

You glance around the misplaced plaza, a curious monument to lost elegance planted in the midst of an otherwise unremarkable neighborhood park. Only a short stroll away, jungle gyms, swing sets and slides flatten in silhouette into a single incomprehensible machine, its moving parts dormant. The stones set in the ground beneath your feet and the waist high balustrade limning the plaza with its uprights molded as Ionic columns project a relic from an antique era, perhaps the last remaining portion of a larger structure long since razed.

The murmur from the fountain grows richer in its variety. At first you're uncertain that you actually detect musical notes amid the swash, but you lean closer and have your suspicion confirmed. Though faint, these notes bite quick and sharp, layered in a chaos like hard rain. Yet you detect motifs, deceptive in their jittery complexity but more evident the longer you listen.

The movement of the forms blurred on the surface matches the tempo of the melody frothing from the water. You sense that if only you could hear better, you could identify the instruments -- wind, you think, or string.

You lean closer, and what's before you is no longer a pool but a circular arch comprised of gleaming basalt wedges. No water muffles the music now. You have passed through the arch and taken several steps further before your mind registers the discrepancy, because so little else changed on first glance, with the major exception that you have company. Beyond the balustrade the park has blurred, but your focus is on the figures who share the plaza with you.

They are a quartet, seated in filigreed chairs. Their backs are to you. Their limbs move with the cadence of these deep, bright harmonies. Their limbs at first glance seem too numerous. You shake your head to clear up the mirage.

Such glorious music. The tempos have slowed, every note drawn out into an ache. You still cannot pinpoint what instruments produce such pure tones, their voices so widely ranged, deep as magma and piercing as ice crystals in the stratosphere and ascending and descending many scales in between, yet these elements that should be incongruous lock together in harmonies of clockwork perfection.

Each figure projects a potential energy, as if they could at any moment turn their heads and reveal their profiles to you. Yet they do not, and the need to see drives you to hurry around them.

You gasp. You collapse to your knees.

You cannot fit the musicians into your mind with vision alone. They are wonders. They are terrors. They are one with the instruments they play.

Relative to you, they are positioned so that their chairs mark the four corners of a diamond. The one in the forefront cradles a cello between their legs, or so your first glimpse tells you. The object has the right girth, but the constant movement of light and shadow teases piping in the curvature of a contrabassoon.

Flickers of motion swath musician and instrument alike, underpinning the wordless bass chanson with a wasp-flight whine, blurring the outlines of arms, legs and sound chambers. The fluttering growths could be beetle wings or long-lashed eyelids, but you can no longer mistake the eyes peering out from underneath, eyes of all kinds, arthropod and vertebrate, looking in every direction from every surface, more of them focused on you with each new note. Some of those eyes glow in soft golds and deep blues, creating new constellations every time they wink.

Your fascination overpowers any instinct to flee. Your senses are snagged in conflicting directions by the congeries of grotesque and gorgeous on exhibit.

To your left, more movement like a flurry of wings, on a much larger and more feathery scale, but you can't be certain what you glimpsed in the corner of your eye, as when you turn to look straight on this musician gleams crisp as silver moonlight. The gown they wear could be made of marble, as if the sitter was carved in that place, yet somehow its folds flex, and the viola-sized instrument tucked under the musician's chin is made of masks, renditions of beaked monsters and human faces with the eyes closed as if sleeping or blank as if entirely unreal. The musician's face too is concealed behind a mask, which changes from one fantastic creature to another each time you look, each transformation erasing the memory of what came before.

Whatever peers from the eyeholes is pitch dark yet glistens like dew, projecting a hunger that makes your heart lurch.

To your right, a gleam of white distracts you. The sound this player produces, rising and falling scales of purity and pain, comes from an ivory instrument that appears to combine string and woodwind. The fabric of the musician's three-piece suit, even the skin visible beneath the spiny green moss of their hair, cracks constantly, like warming ice.

A further illusion spreads cold to the pit of your stomach. For a moment the complicated instrument resolves into a pair of skeletal arms, that emerge from the musician's torso and struggle to retract themselves, but the musician's grip can't be broken, forcing the bones to tangle together, torturing notes from their friction. But your mind has tricked you. Surely this is an intricate, alien mechanism, not something alive and screaming.

Tearing your eyes away brings you to the final musician in the quartet, whose visage gives you no comfort, their scalp bald and leathery, their face a patchwork, as if a dozen different skins have been snipped into squares with scissors and recombined in a single quilt. The instrument they press to their chin pulses as if grown from the neck like a tumor.

The musician's face has no mouth, but mouths open all over the tumorous growth, the source of the crystalline choir harmony that provides the highest notes of the composition they all play. More mouths open above the final musician's exposed collarbones, on the backs of their hands.

How have you gotten this close, to perceive such detail? You are not kneeling before the quartet, but in our midst, a bewildered bystander caught inside the diamond like a summoned demon.

You have arrived to join us in response to our invitation. Your entrancement, your trepidation, your fatal curiosity is our delight. The prelude has ended, and we open out our secret symphonies to engulf your senses, to welcome you.

—The Sinister Quartet

THE TWICE-DROWNED SAINT

C. S. E. COONEY

BEING A TALE OF FABULOUS
GELETHEL, THE INVISIBLE
WONDERS WHO RULE THERE,
AND THE APOSTATES WHO TRY TO
ESCAPE ITS WALLS

In Memory of Gene and Rosemary Wolfe

With thanks to Magill Foote

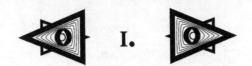

I.

ANALEPSIS: PORTRAIT
OF A CHILD SAINT

There were two things every Gelthic citizen knew.

One: only saints could see the angels who ruled us.

Two: Alizar the Eleven-Eyed, Seventh Angel of Gelethel, had no saint. He hadn't had one for a long time.

Now I will tell you what the angel Alizar looks like. I can do that—because I was the saint no one else in Gelethel knew about. I was the Seventh Angel's best kept secret.

And he was mine.

The angel Alizar sometimes looked like a human-shaped paper lantern, or a sudden release of soap bubbles, or a cloud. He glowed on the inside as if he'd swallowed a hive of horny fireflies, and on the outside, he looked as if a toddler with a glue gun had gone wild with the craft buckets containing outrageous feathers, and twining golden vines, and trumpet-like flowers, and thin, prismatic insect wings.

Alizar also had the ability to spontaneously produce eyeballs whenever and wherever he fancied, though I'd never seen him sport more than eleven at a time, hence his name.

When he was in his human/lantern shape, two of his eyes were pretty much where you'd expect them—affixed to the center of his head—only his eyes were elongated ovals, perfectly symmetrical, of a deep, unending, twilight blue. No pupils or sclera or anything; Alizar the Eleven-Eyed couldn't be bothered with minutiae. Higher up on the center of his forehead, he had one all-black eye, glossy as a wolf spider's. Another eyeball resided where his nose should have been: yellow and slit across the center like a goat's. Three smaller eyes, robberfly-green, beaded the lower part of his face like a mouth. (He had no mouth otherwise.) A torque of three round red eyes opened like cabochon carnelians right above his collarbones, if he had collarbones, which he didn't. One great golden eye blinked sleepily from the curve of his breast, bright amidst a nest of pale down.

He loved to be admired. He was very vain and always preening—but good-naturedly, willing to see beauty in everyone else around him, too. His problem was, of course, that only a handful of saints could see him, and they were all wrapped up in their own angels.

I was supposed to be the one who devoted my whole attention to him—only I'd refused his offer when I was eight years old, and that was three decades ago.

As my saint, you could have everything you ever wanted, he'd sang to me that day, in that way angels have of singing (which was a little like having your head held under water and your feet set on fire, while being tickled) (and also a little bit like being licked by a giant oyster tongue, only on the inside of your body). I shook my head.

"Gross," I'd said, very softly, so no one else in the Celestial Corridor could hear me.

Alizar pulled back a bit on his singing, and the overwhelming urge to pee and giggle and vomit left me.

He said coaxingly: *If you confess your vision of me to the Heraldic Voice, they will know you have tested true. We can have you crowned, gowned, and cloistered before lunchtime. You shall live your life emmewed with thirteen others of your kind: one saint per angel, appointed till death does us part. You'll been given every luxury: a closet stuffed with fabulous clothes, all the jewels of the treasury, the finest foods, a host of servants, the best education, and unlimited access to the Hagiological Archives of Gelethel. All you'd have to do in return is never leave the walls of the Celestial Cenoby. Ever.*

"No thanks," I'd muttered under my breath. "I'm going to grow up and be like my bad uncles. Or maybe like one of the Zilch, and ride around the desert on a viperbike. Or maybe, like, I'll run away and be a movie star or aeroplane pilot or something."

Oh, you like movies, do you? Alizar seemed very interested, which made me more interested.

"Oh, sure!" I said, and then we got to talking for a while about our favorite films, and the whole conversation ended quite amiably, with both of us agreeing to look the other way and pretend that this whole thing had never happened. Only it had. Irrevocably.

Mind you, Ish, you're still my saint—whether anybody knows about it or not, Alizar warned me. *That's not something I have any control over. It just happens.*

"Just don't tell anyone. I don't want to be stuffed in a cell to pray all the time."

I won't tell if you won't. Alizar batted all eleven of his eyes at me, even going so far as to grow extra eyelashes for greater effect.

And anyway, he mused with typical angelic obliqueness, *it might be better, after all, if no one knows about you—for now.*

II

INTERIOR: THE CELESTIAL CORRIDOR

I n fabulous Gelethel, we citizens of the Angelic City operated on a fort-nightly calendar: fourteen being the perfect number. Each day was a feast day named after one of the fourteen angels. Each feast day had its own bespoke rituals and miracles.

And then there was the fifteenth day.

Officially, it didn't exist. But everyone observed it anyway. Gelthic citizens reserved fifteenth days for our most distasteful chores—in memory of Nirwen the Forsaker, the Fifteenth Angel. She'd abandoned Gelethel about a century ago, ascending the impenetrable blue serac that surrounded and protected our city, and shook our dust from her feet.

This royally pissed off the other angels, who proclaimed Nirwen's memory disgraced forever. They scorched her face out of every wall mural, scratched it off every bust and statue. All references to Nirwen the Artificer (as she'd once been known) in the Hagiological Archives received a black slash through it.

Not that Nirwen cared. As far as we knew, she'd picked up and left the day her last saint died, and she'd never looked back.

Petition days in the Celestial Corridor were always on the fifteenth day.

My earliest memories of petition days were of pilgrims coming from out-side Gelethel to beg the boon of citizenship from the angels. The Holy Host would lower a long bridge from the ramparts of the serac, and then a small group of pilgrims—chosen by lottery in Cherubtown—would ascend and enter Gelethel.

Usually, they'd bring gifts with them. Something precious and particular. Something that meant a great deal to the pilgrim personally, which they would then offer to the angels in hopes of winning their favor. That was how my dad gained his citizenship—as well as Quicksilver Cinema, Gelethel's only movie palace, which he ran for many years.

I'd practically grown up in the Quick, and now I owned it. I'd also grown up with a soft spot for pilgrims, because, well . . . *Dad*. That was not true for most citizens of Gelethel.

These days, petitions were less about gifts and more about sacrifice. They'd become sort of a spectator sport for Gelthic citizens—with pilgrims acting as unwitting gladiators and angels playing the dual roles of monsters and referees.

Dad had stopped attending petition days years ago, when the war in the Bellisaar Theatre had grown so bad that Cherubtown, once a small shrine out-side the serac for pilgrims seeking congress with the angels, swelled into a refu-gee camp with a population double the size of Gelethel.

They came to be safe: everyone knew that the Angelic City, protected by its fourteen Invisible Wonders, was the only safe haven left in this part of the world. Dispossessed families came by the thousands wanting in.

Impregnable Gelethel! Immaculate, untouchable. Where the war could not hurt them anymore.

They came with very little to offer, these new pilgrims. Some offered nothing but themselves, in exchange for citizenship for their children. Some offered the lives of their aged parents, or superfluous orphans, or an enemy they'd made in Cherubtown.

And the angels, who rarely refused a sacrifice, were hooked.

It was like nothing they'd ever tasted before, the death offering of a human being. Oh, the jolt of it! The juice! The effervescent intoxication! No longer could the Invisible Wonders who ruled Gelethel rest content with a steady snack of life-long worship from their long-lived worshippers. And why should they, when they could just mainline pilgrims instead?

So bright, so foul. Such meat to feed on.

Thus, every fifteenth day, we let the bridge down. We invited the pilgrims, in groups of fourteen, into Gelethel. Seven of these would be hand-picked by the self-designated sheriffs of Cherubtown—officials on the take from our Holy Host, willing to do us favors in exchange for goods passed to them over the serac. The chosen seven were quietly given to know that the angels were happy to hear their petition for citizenship, but would require a sacrifice—of the human variety. Cherubtown's sheriffs left it up to the pilgrims to choose whom they would bring over. The unlucky seven usually never saw what hit them.

Alizar the Eleven-Eyed, alone among the fourteen angels, did not partake of the sacrifices. He attended petition days, but recused himself of the feast. Some of his colleagues looked at him askance, some scoffed, but in the end, they allowed him this eccentricity; after all, it meant more for them.

Every time I asked him why he refused his sup, Alizar gave me a different answer: *I do not want to be beholden to strangers.* Or, *I'm saving myself for my true love.* Or, *Some habits reward one with diminishing returns.*

The Seventh Angel may have been gentle and vain, may have liked pretty, silly things—but he was not a liar, and he was not stupid. His reasons for abstention, vague though they may have seemed to me, made sense to him—and, I have to admit, it was a relief to be spared sharing the feast. Bad enough for me to catch the ricochet when the other angels fed. But if I had to experience it directly, through him? I wouldn't have remained his secret saint for long.

I knew this much: angelic politics were vicious. Alizar had been out of favor with the other thirteen angels ever since Nirwen the Forsaker left Gelethel. The two of them had been the fastest of friends. Her disgrace had also been his, and Alizar bore it proudly, held himself aloof and lonely. A few of his former allies among the angels tried coaxing him back to the fold from time to time. Others, like Zerat and Rathanana, thought him weak.

Alizar longed for Nirwen—but he took comfort in me. I, in turn, had Alizar and my family and that was it. It wasn't that saints couldn't make friends. It was just, as I got older, I found our secret too burdensome for intimacy. Alizar saw how it weighed on me, kept me isolated, disinclined to engage with my peers. To make up for it, he did his utmost to be all things to me: friend, confidante, beloved. He rarely asked me for favors.

Except, that morning, he had.

Like Dad, I tried to stay away from petition days whenever possible. But today, the Seventh Angel let me know—even before my eyes came unstuck from sleep—that my presence in the Celestial Corridor was requested.

Something is about to happen, he'd told me in his inimitable way, humming behind my eyelids and in the pits of my teeth.

Something is coming from beyond the serac, he said. *Something I was promised a long time ago. And, Ish*—he'd added cheekily—*I am going to need an extra pair of eyes.*

"**Y**ou," said the Heraldic Voice, pointing at a pilgrim—one of a dozen there to petition the angels for citizenship that day.

"Herald," replied the young man standing right next to me.

"Step forward and state your petition," said the Heraldic Voice.

They were resplendently dressed in voluminous purple silk, with wide sleeves that covered their hands, and filigreed cuffs adorning the tips of their ears, proclaiming their position as official interpreter for the angels. Set against the backdrop of the Celestial Corridor, which was vast enough to engulf several city blocks and white enough to write on, they looked properly imposing.

While not themself a saint, the Heraldic Voice, through long exposure to the divine and rigorous study, could take all of those pressure-cooker, biting-on-foil, blood-on-the-boil, icicles-in-your-organs sensations that were the sound of angels singing, and translate it into words for the laity. It was a thankless job—which was why the saints did not do it. It may also have been the reason that the Heraldic Voice's face was so stern and set. They were like the Celestial Corridor: as hard, as dazzling—as if they, too, were composed entirely of bricks of compressed salt.

The Heraldic Voice stood at a podium at the foot of the Hundred Stair Tier, around which the dozen or so pilgrims from Cherubtown had been corralled. The rest of the Celestial Corridor was crammed full of Gelthic spectators, there for the best entertainment Gelethel had to offer. The Invisible Wonders watched over the proceedings from fourteen empty thrones at the top of the stairs. Between them and us stood rank upon rank of the Holy Host.

I was among the bystanders—as close to the pilgrims as I could get. After all, Alizar had told me to keep my eyes open.

The boy upon whom the Heraldic Voice had called now shuffled forward a few steps, dragging with him what appeared to be a sack of rags and ropes. He stood hunched, head bowed, as if it would take too much effort to straighten up. None of us in the Celestial Corridor were allowed to sit. Sitting was for angels, who didn't need to.

Typical pilgrim fare, this one. Fresh from Cherubtown (which was to say "fetid"), where conditions were rife with drought, starvation, lawlessness, crime, and disease. A stunted gangle, more marionette than flesh. Short on chin, long on nose, snappable at wrists and ankles, desiccated as a desert corpse. His eyes were pitfalls. He had a brow on him like a pile of rock at the point of collapse: the brow of a powerful but perhaps not very thoughtful man, a brow he had yet to grow into. His skin and hair might once have been a handsome bronze; now he seemed to be flaking all over into a friable rust. He smelled oddly sweet beneath his stale sweat, a little like fruit, a little like yeast, though from the look of him I couldn't imagine he'd been anywhere near food like that for fortnights on end.

"Herald," the boy rasped into the waiting silence. "I am Alizar Luzarius."

I shivered inwardly at his forename and took a cautious step closer. Was he the one the Seventh Angel was anticipating. The promised "something" from beyond the serac? His name couldn't be a coincidence—could it?

"I have come," continued the boy in his flat whisper, "to offer sacrifice to the Invisible Wonders who rule Gelethel and to petition them for citizenship."

He had the words exactly right, by rote—but he'd mispronounced Gelethel, a point against him. You can always tell a foreigner by the way he pronounces the name of the Angelic City. He softens the "g" almost to a "zh". His first syllable holds the accent, making his "zhgel" rhyme with the third syllable's "thel." Natives of Gelethel know that the "g" is hard, that the accent is on the second syllable "leth," and that in "thel" the vowel is swallowed.

Dad, who wasn't a native, says it makes more sense the way natives say it; the Angelic City, he says, deserves no poetry.

Between the boy and the angels stood a thousand shining warriors of the Holy Host. They stood, ten to a stair, a hundred stairs to the vertex, shields locked, spears sharp, white-eyes shining and mouths smiling like benevolence itself. From the polished bronze and boiled leather of their armor to the jaunty tips of their plumes, the Holy Host was the dedicated force of Gelethel, trained up at the Empyrean Academy from adolescence to adulthood, and dedicated— body and soul—to the objectives of the angels.

The boy's tarpit-on-fire gaze lingered lovingly on the ranks of the Holy Host before lifting and peering beyond them.

He could not, of course, see the angels. But he could see the fourteen vacant thrones, each carved and bejeweled with the various aspects of the angel who sat upon it.

His face shone with a ferocious light—ah! An ascetic. Having grown up with Mom, I knew the signs.

We had our cynics in Gelethel: Dad, my bad uncles, and myself among them. But there were others—devout and pious types—who, after years of careful observation, might be rewarded for a lifetime of worshipful attention by fragments of angelic discernment. The lightning flash of an eye; the scintilla of a pinion; one wet ruby heart beating mid-air, two separate hands skewering it on long silver fingernails; a rotund belly like a great fissiparous pearl swollen to the splitting place; a capillary-popping pressure on the ears and eyeballs that meant the angels singing.

It was the most anyone but saints ever perceived of the angels. Some people spent their whole lives pining for a single glimpse. Some hated the saints for being so blessed. Others worshipped the saints as second only to angels, even petitioning them as intermediaries for their deepest concerns. I didn't know which this kid might be: saint-hater or saint-prater. I only that knew he wasn't a saint.

The sack at his feet, on the other hand...

A buzz in the back of my skull alerted me to the Seventh Angel's interest in that sack. So while the Heraldic Voice was asking the boy all the usual questions ("Tell the Invisible Wonders of *Gelethel*," stressing the correct pronunciation, "why they should choose *you* for their citizen, Pilgrim Luzarius?"), I sidled in for a closer look.

It was a person. A girl.

She'd begun to stir, then to writhe, when the boy had first begun dragging her forward—probably just waking up from the clout or drug that he had used to knock her cold. A pointy chin emerged from the sacking. A compellingly large nose, wide mouth.

I pegged her for the boy's sister, maybe cousin. Of the same too-skeletal, too-sunburnt, too-seldom-washed pilgrim type, she nevertheless seemed more lively than her upright counterpart. Even lying there, trussed and gagged, she bore a greater resemblance to a stack of dynamite than a lamb for slaughter. Her hair was short but heavy, nearly black at the roots, glinting red at the tips. It curled around her head like a nest of vipers. Her skin was that same starved-to-rusting dark, but her eyes were light. If lucid were a color, that would be the color of her eyes.

Her gaze was fixed, unerringly, upon the Seventh Throne. She was a saint.

What's more, she was *his* saint. Alizar's. Like me.

"Shit," I said aloud.

The Heraldic Voice tripped on their tongue and turned bespectacled and accusatory scowl upon me. "I beg your pardon?"

"Sorry," I whispered, offering no further excuse for the Heraldic Voice—and therefore the angels—to examine me too narrowly.

As I sweated in my coveralls, the Heraldic Voice went on to grill the boy. "Pilgrim Luzarius, you claim that your father was a citizen of Gelethel."

I turned from the girl—the saint—to look at the boy. I'd somehow missed that part. But hey, you can't catch everything when you're in the middle of a *divine revelation*. Right, Alizar?

"My, my father was born in Gelethel," the boy stammered his reply. "He t-told me I was named for the Seventh Angel himself, that citizenship was, is, my birthright . . ."

The Heraldic Voice interrupted him. "This morning, you arrived with the other pilgrims from Cherubtown—from outside the Gelthic serac—did you not?"

The boy nodded.

"Those who come from outside the Gelthic serac have no rights in Gelethel. *Citizens* of Gelethel never venture beyond the serac, for they know that to do so means their citizenship shall be revoked, and they shall be named traitor unto the angels who succored them—"

Here the boy interrupted him: "My father was no traitor! He was born a citizen of Gelethel—he said so! He was named for the Seventh Angel, and I am named for him too. He told me I was entitled—"

"He told you lies," snapped the Heraldic Voice. "You are entitled to nothing but what all pilgrims who come to the Celestial Corridor are offered: a chance to humbly beg the boon of offering sacrifice unto the angels, who may, if pleased, decide to grant you leave to stay in fabulous Gelethel."

Their inflection promised nothing, hinted at grave doubt. I watched the boy struggling to decide whether or not to argue. Or perhaps he was just gathering his strength.

And then I stopped watching him, because an eyeball popped open on the back of my hand, right under my knuckles.

It looked up at me imploringly. My mouth filled with the taste of ghost pepper and ozone. My ears began to ring.

Oh, bells.

Fucking angel bells.

Furtively, I cast a veiled glance up at the Seventh Throne. It was hard to miss, decorated as it was with eleven jewels cut into the shapes of eyes. But those gleaming gems was lost to me today; I had eyes only for the Seventh Angel—who'd apparently gone totally lathernutted.

A green-gold glow beaconed out from his paper-lantern skin. Each little insect wing and bird-like bit of him was fluttering with adoration and distress as he divided his attention between preening for the new girl—who was staring at him open-mouthed—and pleading with *me*. One of the cabochon eyes that grew in a collar about Alizar's throat was missing. Because it was on my hand.

Nirwen sent her, Ish! Alizar told me excitedly. *Nirwen sent her here to me! She's the sign I've been waiting for! We must help her!* A pause. *Don't let the other angels see you do it, though.*

"Fine," I breathed—not so much speaking as grinding the chewy gong of Alizar's entreaty between my teeth. Unobtrusively as possible, I scooted closer to the girl. Reaching for the penknife in my pocket, I carefully palmed it, unfolded it, cut a hole in my canvas pocket, and let the knife drop down the length of my leg.

It slid soundlessly off the side of my boot and onto the floor, spinning to a stop near the girl's right ear. Distracted by the movement, the girl turned her head and met my gaze. Her limpid, cunning eyes narrowed. Her gaze went right to my hand and the glossy red eyeball protruding from the back of it. It rolled at her in bright excitement, then blinked gratefully up at me, then disappeared.

A moment later, on the Seventh Throne, the Seventh Angel pulsed vividly, all eleven of his eyes restored to him.

Meanwhile, the other Alizar—Alizar Luzarius—had decided to escalate his argument with the Heraldic Voice after all.

"When I am a citizen," he rasped, "I mean to serve as warrior in the Holy Host." The real Gelthic citizens let out a corridor-wide gasp at his audacity. "My father was a soldier. Like him, I am strong and able," he continued, mendacious but determined, "and I will train at the Empyrean Academy, and because the pride of the Holy Host . . ."

Thoroughly nettled now, the Heraldic Voice said witheringly, "Your father may have been a soldier, but he was never one of the Holy Host. Nor can you be, Pilgrim Luzarius—even if the angels grant you citizenship. You were not born in Gelethel."

"Give me a sword," the boy returned implacably. "I will use it to defend the angels—and Gelethel. I will prove myself to the Host. I will—"

I lost the thread of his boast as I looked down at the girl again. Her eyes raptor-bright, her face furious, she had rearranged her body to mask her hands, which were working my penknife for all it was worth. She had lots of knots to deal with—the boy had been nothing if not thorough—but my penknife was a gift from the Seventh Angel himself, manifested for me on my thirty-seventh birthday; I was pretty sure it could cut through ropes or even chains like so many silken threads.

"—and then the angels will name me their captain, and follow me into battle!" the boy finished in a blaze of triumphal delusion.

The crowd laughed; the boy was amusing. But the Heraldic Voice was finished arguing. Adjusting a piece of parchment on their podium that did not need it, they asked merely, "And what is your sacrifice to be, pilgrim?"

Alizar Luzarius bent down, grabbed the trussed-up girl by her ropes, and hauled her to her feet. "I offer my half-sister, Betony Luzarius, as sacrifice to the angels!"

The angels reacted immediately, with pleasure and approval.

I knew it at once, but it took the Heraldic Voice a few seconds longer. I knew they had finally gotten the message when they gave an involuntary start and hiss. Their fingers twitched. They threw back their head, every tendon in their neck straining as they listened to thirteen voices singing their rapture and rhapsody and euphoric acceptance of the sacrifice. Probably to the Heraldic Voice it sounded like being on the receiving end of thirteen static shocks in close succession.

It was worse for me, being a saint. I could hear the angels with absolute clarity, at full volume, with all the bells and whistles layered in. But I'd been learning to control my expression for decades, and right now, I was doing a damned fine impression of a cow waiting placidly in a squeeze chute.

I'd never seen Dad look so sick with disappointment as he did the day he watched my face as I watched my first human sacrifice. When he saw no change whatever in it. But what could I do? It was either go cow-faced or do a tell-all. I couldn't risk letting go, not even a little. Surrendering, even for a moment, to the sensation of angels sucking up their death offerings, would have sent me into total transverberation. I'd've been lifted aloft by the sound of their singing: all those angels, all experiencing such orgiastic ecstasy. No, I couldn't let them see me crack, not even Dad. I had to be icy as the Gelthic serac. I'd promised Alizar. Like he'd promised me.

This being her first time, it was even worse for Betony.

Good for her that no one, human or angel, expected a full-grown woman— or older teenager, anyway—and a pilgrim from Cherubtown at that, to suddenly turn saint. Anybody looking at her might mistake her trembling for fear, perhaps devotion.

But I knew what those short, sharp convulsions meant. I saw her toes curl, her feet leave the floor—just half an inch, just for a few seconds. This was not the angels in full voice. No one, after all, had been sacrificed yet. Their singing was merely anticipatory.

But Betony heard it all. *And understood it perfectly.*

At the top of the Hundred Stair Tier, thirteen angels leaned eagerly forward in their thrones, urging the Heraldic Voice to move things along. I tried not to look at any one of them directly but kept my eyes vague, receptive at the periphery. Even so, even after all this time, they left a deep impression, like a bright scar on the brain.

There was Shuushaari of the Sea, crowned in kelp and bladderwrack, her body an ooze of radular ribbons, like a thousand starveling oysters without their shells; Tanzanu the Hawk-Headed, whose human-ish shape was just that—an assemblage of hawks' heads; Olthar of Excesses, also called the Angel of Iniquity, who was three big shining bellies, each piled on top of the other like giant pearls, each on the point of splitting open; Rathanana of Beasts, all matted fur and bloody fang, snarling maw, curving claw; Murra Who Whispers; Wurra Who Roars; Zerat Like the Lightning; Childlike Hirrahune, solemn and sad; Thathia Whose Arms Are Eels; Kalikani and Kirtirin, the Enemy Twins; Impossible Beriu and Imperishable Dinyatha, who had only one heart between them.

As they sang, more and more red mouth slits began to gape open on previously smooth expanses of angelic skin or hide or chiton. New, raw, wet lips, parting like cruel paper-cuts, appeared on shoulders, backs, arms, palms, throats, beaks, tentacles, tails.

All of the angels were singing, and all of them sang: "Yes!"

All of them but one.

Alizar the Eleven-Eyed, as usual, sat apart from the sacrifices, and sang nothing. He sat very still, looking anxious and troubled. Strange, to watch a creature
who was mostly eyes and incandescence cogitate so desperately.

He was coming to some momentous decision; I could tell by the way he
kept smoothing down the curling blue feathers on his arms, tugging and twining
the trailing plumes around his pinkie talons, then letting them spring back in
release. Thin coils of gold pushed out of his pores and wound up his limbs like
morning glories, occasionally lifting bell-like blooms as if following the path of
the sun. They all yearned toward the girl, Betony.

When it came, Alizar's resolve was absolute. He shook his head sharply, saying something to the other angels that pierced their song like a wire going right
through my right nostril. An emphatic, *No!*—angelically-speaking.

The Heraldic Voice shook their head, trying to interpret this new message.
At my feet, Betony went into micro-convulsions again, her left nostril beginning
to bleed.

Her half-brother noticed nothing of this, too busy watching the Heraldic
Voice's fraught face for any sign of the angelic approval.

"Well, Herald?" asked the boy eagerly. "Will they accept her? Am I to be a
citizen of Gelethel?"

"It is unclear," said the Heraldic Voice. " There is some . . . division. That is,
I think . . ."

Outraged at the Seventh Angel's interference, the others overrode his song,
upping their decibel level and drowning him out. I slowed my breathing as my
molars tried to dig their way deeper into my gums.

As this went on, the Heraldic Voice gradually lost their lost expression. The
angels were very explicit. They communicated the strength of their desire, their
wholehearted approval, and their eagerness to *get the hell on with it.*

"Yes, your sacrifice has been deemed acceptable by the angels of Gelethel,
Pilgrim Luzarius," the Heraldic Voice told the boy, almost kindly. "Leave it at
the bottom of the stairs. We will present you your citizenship papers when the
sacrifice is complete."

Radiant with gratitude, the boy complied. His grip tightened on his half-
sister's ropes, trying to drag her forward as the Heraldic Voice commanded.

But Betony abruptly jerked away from him, the ropes falling at her feet. Up
flashed her hand, slicing the gag from her mouth. Then she leapt forward and
jammed the point of her penknife—my penknife—beneath the boy's chin.

"Lizard-dick!" she bellowed. She had a deep voice, a smoker's voice. "Beetle-
licker! Should've left you in the desert. Let the Zilch eat you. You'd make better
barbecue than a brother. Just like your fucking dad."

"Don't you talk, don't you *dare* talk about my father!" The boy's monotone
cracked down the middle; he looked ready to burst into tears. "You—you're a
bad girl, Betony. A burden. A liar. Loose and wanton. You'll, you'll do anything
for scraps."

A stunned pause. Betony stared at him. Then her long mouth tightened, her bony fist whitened around the knife.

"Scraps I shared with *you*!"

"I would have rather starved," the boy retorted.

Throat-cutting words if I ever heard them. Betony stepped closer. A tiny thread of blood ran like a worm down the boy's throat.

"You are offal," Luzarius whispered, the frail sandpaper of his voice fraying. "Kill me, I die a martyr. But you are offal, and offal is for sacrifice."

At a gesture from the Heraldic Voice, two warriors of the Holy Host had marched off the Hundred Stair Tier to flank the girl. Bronze gauntlets clapped heavily on her bare shoulders, on the flesh above her elbows, but Betony ignored them, her gaze burning into her brother's face.

"You aren't my brother anymore!" she spat. But she didn't strike him down. She withdrew instead, slumping into the fists that gripped her as if suddenly spent.

Despite her skin-and-bone appearance, her dead weight must have made her unexpectedly heavy to the Hosts; their biceps bulged to keep her upright. The penknife, I noticed, was gone. Disappeared, between one blink and the next—I'd bet, up her sleeve. I hadn't seen sleight-of-hand like that since my bad Uncle Raz, "the Razman," pulled a contraband Super 8 camera out of his hat for my thirtieth birthday. The high-end, newfangled kind, that also recorded sound.

"Take her to the sacrificing pool," the Heraldic Voice commanded.

I followed where they dragged her. I, and her half-brother, and the other pilgrims, and everyone else in the Celestial Corridor who wanted a front-row view of her death.

The sacrificing pool was at the other end of the Hundred Stair Tier: a deep, round tank made of gold-tinted glass, redolent of warm brine and eucalyptus oil. It had been cleaned and refilled to brimming for petition day. Water sloshed over the sides onto the floor around it, which, unlike the rest of the corridor, was paved in red brick, not white. New flooring had to be put in a few years ago after surplus water from the pool damaged the original salt-based tiles beyond repair. A golden staircase with wide steps and delicate rails led to the top of the pool, where a shallow lip, like a gilded pout, allowed a Host to kneel as they held the sacrifice under.

At the sight of the sacrificing pool, Betony remained limp. Oddly limp, I thought, for a girl with a hidden knife and a strong grasp on reality. She didn't struggle (and at this point in the proceedings, most sacrifices usually did, even the very old or infirm), remaining completely flaccid when one of the two Holy Host slung Betony up over her massive shoulder and began carrying her up the golden stairs.

The other Host stood guard at the bottom, spear planted before him, the white shine of his eyes warning all of us who stood too closer to come no nearer.

The warriors of the Holy Host were called hosts because they were sworn receptacles. Sometimes they were called "chalices of the angels," sometimes "chariots to the angels."

My bad uncles said that the Hosts were more like "cheesecloths for the angels." They said that my good uncles, themselves all high-ranking warriors on the Hundred Stair Tier, spent so much time in the Celestial Corridor that they'd become practically porous. Ripe for possession. Ready garments for any passing angel to put on—or all of them at once.

The Host at the bottom of the sacrificing pool was but lightly possessed at the moment. No particular angelic attribute had manifested on his person, as it would have done if an angel were endowing a Host with their full attention. But if I squinted and looked sideways, I could see a sort of shimmering tether in the air, connecting the angel Beriu to the Host on guard.

The Host carrying Betony, however, was rapidly filling up with her share of angels.

All warriors of the Holy Host were strapping; it took a lot of muscle mass to host an angel, and then to recover from possession afterward. This warrior, already a tall woman, was growing taller with every step. Angelic influence flowed into her, augmented her.

The angels had to take turns on petition days, sharing the sacrifices between them. There were seven today, and thirteen angels to feed. But some of the sacrifices were on death's door, some so catatonic with despair and trauma that it was as if their animating spirits had already fled their bodies. To the angels, these lives, given up to them, would hardly seem a morsel.

Betony, however, they deemed a feast. Three of them had elected to feed on her, the most rapacious of the angels: Zerat, Rathanana, and Thathia.

Her soul, they'd decided, was large and lively enough to satisfy.

So eager were they for her oncoming death that they began engorging their Host too quickly. Not only was she swelling in size, but angelic attributes from all three angels began popping out all over her skin like boils—blue sparks, foul smoke, a slick of aspic, a roiling patch of fur. The rapid intensity of her transformation startled her, slowed her down as she mounted the steps, made her movements stiff and clumsy.

So when, at the top of the golden stairs, Betony blazed into action, the Host did not react quickly enough. She staggered, simultaneously flailing for balance and trying to pull the penknife out of her neck.

Freed from that sinewy grip, Betony went from limp to monkey-limbed in a shaved second. She twisted herself down from the Host's shoulder, dropping to the slippery lip of the sacrificing pool with the hardened agility of a trained street fighter. From there, she immediately barreled into the Host's knees, tripping her up.

The Host flew backwards. She landed hard, cracked her head on the side of the pool. And then she rolled off the edge, fell five feet to the floor, and hit the bricks with a moist thud.

Three angels screamed at once, fleeing that broken body like rats from a plague ship.

They could have healed her—she was one of their own!—but I hadn't seen the angels heal anyone for years now. Their excuse, according to Alizar, was that what with the fortnightly influx of pilgrims swelling the population of Gelethel, it was impractical to continue healing our sick or miraculously extending our lives the way they'd done since time immemorial, lest the citizens of the Angelic City bear fruit and multiply to the point where the serac could no longer contain them.

Still, we waited, breathless, expectant. All our eyes had tracked the Host as she fell. When she did not again stir—when the angels did not surprise us with mercy—we looked for the next moving object.

This should have been Betony, atop the sacrificing pool. Only she was no longer there. Or anywhere else to be seen.

I smiled to myself, hard and dry as the salt pan, a smile I'd learned from my bad uncles and was a hard habit to break.

Betony had done it—what no sacrifice had managed before. She'd killed a Host and escaped her fate. A true saint—and this, her first miracle. She was gone.

Not yet! Alizar groaned, and my hard smile melted, acid-splashed. *She hasn't made it to the doors!*

At that point, I heard a familiar deep boom call out: "Tiers one through five: activate!" and the Hosts stationed on the first five levels of the Hundred Stair Tier began to descend.

White eyes shining, in perfect lockstep, fifty warriors marched off their steps and into the crowd of pilgrims and Gelthic laity gathered in the Celestial Corridor. We heaved, adjusting. Alizar Luzarius, probationary citizen, reeled drunkenly, lurching into me as he tried to see what was going on. I automatically reached out to steady him. He didn't even know I was there. He was moaning:

"I gave her a chance. One last chance to do something good. To be righteous. But she is ruinous. She *always* corrupts *everything*."

My hand tightened on his elbow. "*You* brought her here," I growled. "What do you think they'll do to *you*?"

Bewildered at such venom from a total stranger, Luzarius glanced my way—first at my hand on his bony arm, then at my face. So close to him now, I saw that he was much younger than I'd thought—too young for peach fuzz, undersized for his age.

Withered child of a war-ripped desert, this boy had nothing—had *never* had anything—except his faith in the angels. I doubted he'd even have been able to overpower Betony and drag her this far had it not been for a stronger will puppeting him over the serac. Luzarius was the angel Nirwen's tool—and he didn't even know it.

Repelled, I released him like a noon-baked piece of scrap metal and stood on tiptoe, scanning the teeming corridor. I saw nothing but confusion, the Hosts on the floor conducting a systematic search, the citizens eager to help.

"Run, Betony," I breathed, so sub-vocally that only the Seventh Angel, eavesdropping on the inside of my throat, could hear me. "Run, Saint Betony. *Run.*"

And then, as if the angel Alizar were lending me his sight, I glimpsed her.

She'd made it to the far doors at the end of the Celestial Corridor. Each door was hewn from chunks of salmon-pink salt crystal as large as the Hundred Stair Tier was tall. Each was as wide as three banquet tables side by side, carved in reliefs of the original fifteen angels, along with their aspects and attributes.

The face of the Fifteenth Angel had long ago been gouged out. Because of that, Nirwen was the easiest angel to recognize at a glance. A featureless giantess with a tool in each hand, she was surrounded by a knot-work nimbus of Lesser Servants, the menagerie of hodgepodge creatures she had created in the laboratories of her district, and whom she had taken with her when she abandoned Gelethel.

Betony made it to the doors, but not past them.

I may have lost sight of her—and so had the rest of the laity—but the angels had not. Alizar knew it and despaired. Once the angels had marked her for sacrifice, she was theirs. The Seventh Angel's claim on her as his saint meant nothing to them; they had drowned out his protest before he could fully voice it. And now they would drown her, with even greater glee and giddiness and appetite than they'd ever exhibited before.

Because Betony had run.

And angels liked when sacrifices ran.

What is the sound of thirteen angels slavering as they sing? It is the sound of scalding solfatara and bitter saliva. Is the hard trill of a dentist drill going right down to the root. It is the sound of children throwing live frogs into their campfire, and then throwing back the ones who leapt out, but not before smashing them dead with a rock.

The angels reached out, and claimed what was theirs.

Today it was my good Uncle Razoleth, oldest of the Q'Aleth boys, who caught Betony.

I'd thought I'd heard his voice earlier, bellowing out the order to activate the five tiers. But I hadn't seen him, jostled as I was by the crowd.

Now there was no unseeing him. The angels Thathia, Zerat, and Rathanana, fleeing the dead Host at the foot of the sacrificing pool, had scarpered across the room to inhabit their most trusted and senior warrior: Razoleth, Captain of the Hundred Stair Tier.

All my uncles—good and bad alike—were tall. But Razoleth, oldest of Mom's younger brothers, was tallest. His bronze helmet sported a comb of fourteen spikes from forehead to nape, the first spike topped with a round nob proclaiming his rank. Captains of the Hundred Stair Tier always got the biggest nobs because, and here I quote my bad uncles, "they were the biggest nobs." Now, trebly swollen with angelic intent, Razoleth expanded as he walked, increasing in size until he was twice the height and girth of anyone in the room, massive and slab-like.

Unlike the dead Host, who was currently being cleared away from the corridor floor, Razoleth grew more graceful with each incursion of angels. He moved more easily, more swiftly; he wore his angels well—even when the attributes of the three angels, pouring into him at speed, began to warp him out of all recognition.

First, the kidney-pink leather of his breastplate glowed like flayed flesh. And then it *became* flayed flesh. The angel Rathanana of Beasts was draping him all about in freshly skinned animal hides, which were still tacky and membranous, still dripping blood.

My uncle did not have to roar like the angel Wurra to make room for his progress through the Celestial Corridor. Not with the angel Zerat inside him. No, pilgrims and citizens sparked away from him on contact—for he crackled with Zerat's lightning as he paced forward, his dark brown eyes swamped in blue electrical fire. The smell of singed hair filled the air like burning feathers.

Razoleth had become a mass of muscles, a rockslide tearing across the room towards Betony—all except for his arms. These were lengthening and slimming down to a filament-thinness. From his shoulders to his fingertips his dark skin was ghosting to gray-white, beginning to glisten with mucous. His elbows and forearms were fringed with delicate fins. Where his hands had been a moment ago were now two bulbous heads. His fingers fused into needle-fine jaws curving away from each other, lined in hooklike teeth.

Now he had the angel Thathia's arms. The angel Thathia's reach.

The angel Thathia reached, and the other angels reached with her—through my uncle's body—for Betony.

They snagged her snarled hair in Thathia's eel-mouths. The shock of Zerat's lightning bolt blew the rags off her feet, set her tatters afire. Rathanana's cloak of raw flesh peeled itself away from Razoleth's broad chest, flew off of him, and flung itself around Betony's bucking body, rolling her up like a carpet.

Caught.

Without a pause, Razoleth bent down, picked up the bundle and carried it back to the Hundred Stair Tier, to the sacrificing pool.

As my uncle passed me, he looked down and gave a short nod. My good uncles were not as loquacious as my bad ones, but they still held me dear: the only daughter of their only sister. I couldn't bear to meet his eyes, and he was too tall this way besides, so I dipped my head. Best, with the good uncles, to show a subordinate face.

By now, Betony had recovered enough to squirm an arm free of Rathanana's foul cloak. It was all I could see of her: one bare arm patterned in branching red ferns—a new red tree blooming out from the seed of her lightning strike—one desperate hand, fingers stretched as far as they could reach. Muffled by the stinking skins that wrapped her, she screamed, "Alizar! Alizar!"

Beside me, the half-brother who bore that name trembled. He shook his head, covered his ears. But it was not to him she cried out.

I glared up at Alizar—the other Alizar—he whom Betony had known and loved the instant she had beheld him. Alizar the Eleven-Eyed, to whom she had been sent, all unbeknownst to her, by the Fifteenth Angel—a gift from across the serac. Alizar, the Seventh Angel, who had made Betony his saint. His second saint. Something none of the other angels had.

"Do something!" I hissed at him aloud—though he could have read my thoughts just as well. No one else heard me; all attention in the Celestial Corridor was fastened on Razoleth, who, with Betony in his arms, was mounting the golden steps to the sacrificing pool.

High above us, the angel Alizar shifted on his throne, his inner glow increasing until it overspilled his skin in an agitated nimbus.

What can I do, Ish? Oh, Ish, what must I do?

During the New War, when the Koss Var Air Force tried to bomb Gelethel the way it had bombed our neighboring city-states Sanis Al and Rok Moris, the airborne ordinance would make a certain sound when it came within two hundred meters of the city. It was the sound of a glass mountain shattering. Not just shattering—atomizing. A smear of light would streak across our skies, and Gelethel would tremble within the cold blue diamond of its surrounding serac. The serac itself would whistle and tinkle, like wind chimes made of ice. And then the Angelic City would fall silent, unhurt and untouched.

That sound was just a memory. But it was what I heard when Uncle Razoleth dumped Betony unceremoniously into the sacrificing pool. It was the sound of Alizar's heart breaking. Or mine. Not much difference between us these days.

Inside the pool's deep glass bowl, raw animal skins unfurled from Betony's body like a ball of flowering tea. They drifted away from her, floating in clouds of their own blood, helped by Betony, who was thrashing herself free of the last of them. Bobbing to the surface, she splashed her way to the pool's edge, surprisingly nimble in the water for such a sand cat.

But Uncle Razoleth was kneeling on the lip of the pool, waiting for her. His hands-turned-jaws grabbed Betony by the hair and thrust her back down.

Betony gasped hugely and in vain before the water closed around her. I moved closer to the sacrificing pool, helpless, reaching out.

Her eyes met mine through the gold-glazed glass between us.

So did the large pale eyes of Thathia's eels, the eels that were now my uncle's arms. Were the angels suspicious? Was Thathia herself watching me, and through me, Alizar?

I couldn't be sure—and anyway, Uncle Razoleth was merely possessed of angels, not an angel himself. I was allowed to see him fully, just like everyone else, and if his fingers wanted to have a staring contest with me as they drowned this girl, well, there was nothing I could do about that. Better that than watching Betony refuse and refuse and and refuse and then, finally, take that fatal, watery breath.

I tasted brine all the way down my esophagus.

Thathia, Zerat, and Rathanana shrieked in three-part discord as they fed on her death. Their jubilation, their rapture, and the intense, disorienting bliss they communicated through song blacked out the rest of the Celestial Corridor to my sight, just for a moment—until the angel Alizar, high above me on the Hundred Stair Tier, flamed up hugely like a pillar of fire.

Then flickered out. Like a snuffed candle. Like the light in Betony's eyes.

I gasped, gut-punched.

Alizar's thirteen colleagues twisted in their seats to look for him. But he was no longer there. The Seventh Throne was as empty to their angelic senses as it was to the Gelthic laity. They stirred, uneasily. My molars started up the root-canal ache of their singing. They were calling for him, demanding he return. But they could not reach him, and it frightened them.

I swallowed a yelp as Alizar flashed into existence *right in front of me.*

Opposite Uncle Razoleth, who could not see him, he landed on the rim of the golden pool. On toes like golden claws he perched, clinging like a bird, glowing down into the pool intently, frowning with all his eyes.

And then a new voice sliced through the enamel-stripping song in my mouth. It flooded my tongue with copper and gentian, like biting down on a toothy bit of aloe vera.

Alizar the Eleven-Eyed was speaking from two red mouth slits that had appeared like slashes down either side of his face. He spoke softly, his words a prayer—a prayer not unknown to the other thirteen, who reacted variously: some crackling with rage, or cackling with terrified laughter, some sweating crystal clusters of resentful orpiment, others exuding miasmal perfumes of admiration.

It was the prayer of an angel declaring his saint for the first time in a generation.

Of course, no angel had claimed a dead person for their saint before; there wasn't a song for that. But now that the sacrifice was complete and Betony dead, Alizar could do with her as he pleased. Any salvage not recovered by the angelic collective was fair game to an individual angel; that was canon.

The angels watched him, fascinated. A few protested, others silenced them. The angels Zerat, Rathanana, and Thathia were practically formless with repletion, half-oblivious to the events. These were Alizar's greatest critics, the only ones who might have stopped him—but they could not be bothered to move.

The waters in the sacrificing pool began to boil. Uncle Razoleth snatched his hand from Betony's hair—it was a human hand again, bereft of angels. Blisters immediately formed on his skin. He was abruptly off-balance, half the size he'd been just a moment before, stripped of the armor that Rathanana had been turned into animal skins. Like all Hosts after a dispossession, he was urgently sapped from holding so much heat and light for so long. He swooned—and this time, his comrades of the Holy Host were there to catch him as he fell. They lifted him onto a stretcher, and bore him out of the Celestial Corridor—not without a few curious glances behind them at the foaming sacrificing pool, where Betony's body, released from Razoleth's drowning grip, was rising to the surface.

Oily brine boiled and foamed around her. After so many sacrifices, I knew that men mostly drowned facedown, and women face-up. This was not always true, but it was true today.

The angel Alizar made a quick, crooking gesture with his finger. No one saw this but myself and the angels. Everyone else simply tracked Betony's body as it skidded across the water toward him. Alizar flicked his finger again—one long golden talon entwined with trailing plumes and bell-like blossoms—and the body floated right out of the sacrificing pool.

It hovered above the surface, water sluicing from its hair and the torn remnants of its clothes onto the floor. A small wave ran over my toes, soaking my sandals. Corpse water. Martyr water. Dozens of pilgrims rushed in with kerchiefs and cloths to soak it up, to hoard as holy relics or to sell. Scavengers.

Other than me, only the dead girl's half-brother didn't fall to his knees and scrabble in the wet. He had raised his face blearily to the body buoyed up only by air, and I did not know what that expression was on his face—regret, perhaps, at a loathsome necessity. Not a little fear. Some relief. But mostly regret.

He stretched his hand toward the body, as if wanting to snatch it down from its levitation, eager perhaps to honor it in death. But his half-sister's body was too high for him to reach, and out of his purview besides. He couldn't stop whatever was happening now, any more than the angel Alizar or I could have stopped Betony from drowning in the first place.

The Seventh Angel made a complicated gesture with his talon. Betony's floating corpse spun around until it hung just before him, its face level with his. A third mouth slit appeared below the three green eyes on his chin, curving upward in a red bow, like a smile.

Live!

And then, aloud, for everyone in the Celestial Corridor to hear—and shining so brightly that everyone in the corridor could also *see*, just for a moment, the fire and feathers and flowers and eyes torqued into the shape of a man—the Seventh Angel sang:

"LIVE!"

A jet of water shot from Betony's mouth and nose, voiding her lungs.

For the second time that day, three of the fourteen angels screamed in outraged agony. Their sacrifice was coming unsacrificed, the feast falling away from them. Bliss blinked out; they were left sullen and starving as a saint was resurrected before their eyes—and there was nothing they could do to get her back.

At my side, the boy Luzarius groaned and bent double, as though felled by cramps. He groaned again when the Seventh Angel reached out his golden talon next and touched the un-drowned girl on her water-beaded brow.

All eleven of Alizar's eyes slid from their fixed marks on the lustrous parchment of his skin, and sank into him. This left his aspect weirdly naked: a collection of rainbow plumage, fronds, blooms, and green-gold flickers of light. A second later, those eleven eyeballs all popped up again upon Betony's brow, forming a perfect circle around it.

Everyone in the Celestial Corridor gasped. This, *this* they could see!

Not Alizar's eyes adorning her, but jewels—eleven jewels, set at perfect intervals into a braid of shining platinum. There were two star sapphires, a black pearl, three square-cut tourmalines, a chunk of polished tiger iron, three faceted red beryls, and a yellow diamond. The scorched shreds of Betony's clothes melted away into a shimmering, and the shimmering resolved into gleaming garments: silver satin, silver lace, thread of silver embroidery, and more twinkling silver sequins than had been worn by all the dancers put together who had ever appeared onstage at the Sexy Seraph Cabaret on robot burlesque night.

Turning to the Heraldic Voice, the angel Alizar said something in a stentorian tone.

The Heraldic Voice understood the order immediately. Cracks appeared in the lenses of Heraldic Voice's pince-nez. Two capillaries popped in their left eye. Their right nostril began to bleed. But they nodded at once, and gestured for a nearby warrior of the Holy Host who stepped forward and saluted.

"Take her to the Seventh Anchorhold," the Heraldic Voice told the Host. "Show her all reverence due a saint of Gelethel."

"Yes, Herald," the Host replied. She mounted the steps and approached the saint, arms held before her in worshipful salutation. "Come, my saint. I will bear you home."

The Seventh Angel smiled approvingly at her with all his eyes and mouth slits, but she could not see him. Nevertheless, he sent his saint wafting toward her with little puffs of the tiny insect wings that glittered and chittered all over him. Betony floated into the Host's waiting arms.

At this, the boy Luzarius squawked, "A saint!"

He slopped through the mess on the floor to fall at the feet of the Heraldic Voice. "Herald, my sis—Betony—she, she *cannot* be a saint. She is smirched. She doesn't even believe in, in the angels. She worships the false god of Cherubtown . . . she is *unworthy!*"

The Heraldic Voice paused, uncertain of procedure. The angels were reacting variously, some affronted at the very idea of a god so close as Cherubtown, some still howling with disappointment over the lost sacrifice, and many, many of them casting furtive, fearful glimpses at the Seventh Angel, Alizar—who had just done what none of them could do—who had *resurrected* a pilgrim girl to be his saint.

Resurrection was not an angelic talent. Resurrection was for the godhead, and the angels of Gelethel had eaten their god long ago.

The angel Alizar said quietly, for my ears only, *I am spent, Ish. I must conceal myself awhile and gather strength. I will come to you anon.*

"Don't let the others find you," I told him in the quietness of my mind.

I could only imagine what they would do to him, weakened as he was, and after such shocking behavior.

And how.

And he vanished, agitating the other angels all over again.

"You, young person," the Heraldic Voice was coldly informing the boy Luzarius, "are in a precarious situation. We must consult the Hagiological Archives for precedent. Meanwhile, your citizenship shall be held in abeyance until such time as this matter is resolved. Until then, you shall be kept prisoner in our saltcellars."

With that, they nodded toward the Hundred Stair Tier. A detachment of the Holy Host stepped down at once to drag the wailing boy away.

III.

ANGLE ON ONABROSZIA

"**H**i, Dad! You home?"

Opening the front door, I stuck my head into the faded yellow great room. Of course Dad was home. Where else would he be? Someone had to sit with Mom around the clock, and what with me running the Quick, my bad uncles working nights, and my good uncles working days, none of us were around to help much.

We each managed to take few shifts every fortnight to free Dad up for sleeping or shopping or tidying the house. If Dad allowed us to, we would've all bartered dune-loads of benzies for cleaning crews or nurses for hire, but it upset Mom no end to have strangers about. We tried it once, and she grew so agitated that Dad said it just wasn't worth it. That gentle tone of his—like the psi-ship *Vicissitude*, in the classic sav-nav film *Winds of Vicissitude:* that moment when, pirate-struck, looted, left listing in the waters, the ship decides to go down with dignity.

No answer from the house. I called out again, "Hello!?"

After a few seconds, I heard a muffled response from way in the back, so I headed deeper in. Not much to the place: after the great room, there was a hallway with three small bedrooms on the right, and a bathroom, linen closet, and kitchen to the left. At the back of the house was the master suite, maybe a handkerchief larger than the other bedrooms, with a sliding door that led to the back patio, and a half-bath big enough for an accordion to take a crap in—if the bellows were all the way compressed.

By the time Mom retired from Q'Aleth Hauling Industries—Gelethel's solid waste collection and management company, which she'd started herself at age eighteen—she could've afforded to live in a palace the size of the Celestial Corridor.

Instead, the "Garbage Queen of Gelethel" had kept the long, low, L-shaped rambler where she had grown up and raised her younger brothers. There, she had maintained her public facade as the devout only daughter of Umrir and Zaripha Q'Aleth, impoverished Gelthic layabouts who'd lived low and died young. Mom's modest choices only made her more respected throughout Gelethel as the angels-sanctified business woman who upheld her friends, terrified her foes, and ruled over her family like an idol of the outer serac.

Only her immediate family had known about her secret life. And none of us would ever tell. Especially not now.

There was no one in any of the small bedrooms. Dad slept in the tiniest one these days. Mom was in the master suite, also empty. But the sliding glass door stood open, the screen door letting in a bread-baking blast of heat.

"Hey!" I called out. " You two out back?"

"Yeah, Ishi! Back here!"

That sounded like an uncle. Dad would've just come inside to talk to me. He'd never raised his voice since I could remember.

I stepped out onto the back patio where Mom sat most days. Dad would drag her chair beneath a stand of verdy trees to take advantage of their shade, and had set up his own desk under an umbrella on the far end of the patio. There, on the typewriter he'd brought with him across the serac, Dad wrote his screenplays by the score.

The clackety-clack noises that old machine would make had so thrilled me as a child that I used to run around our backyard pretending I was starring in whatever movie Dad was writing. I was the "Moon Princess," leader of a smuggling operation between Gelethel and Cherubtown! I was a Zilch giant, riding my viperbike through the dunes of Bellisaar, terrorizing wayfarers! I was the old god of Gelethel, whom the angels ate! Dad was nothing if not prolific. A mechanic in his former life, he was also—thankfully—more than adept at improvising broken typewriter keys, re-inking ribbons, replacing rubber feet with wine corks, substituting shoelaces for carriage pull straps, and bending the typebars back into position whenever the alignment was off. His pile of movie manuscripts by this point was higher than my head.

"Movies," he'd say in his smiling, melancholy way, "that will never see production."

The whitelight of Gelthic noon dazzled me the moment I stepped out from under the awning's shade. In this part of the world, just south of the Bellisaar Waste, even our winters were twice as hot as anyone else's summers. And at the moment, we were far from winter. I stopped on the salt-brick porch, raising my arm to overhang my eyes.

I'd left the Celestial Corridor right after Betony's canonization. Her brother's was the first petition of the day, but I'd had enough—enough of starving fanatics, golden bathtubs, invisible angels, everything. I wanted my parents, even though I didn't plan on mentioning the sacrifice to either of them. Dad, because it made him sad and sick, and he was already both. Mom, because she no longer understood me. And even if she could, her relationship with the angels had always been so complicated, I probably would never have tried anyway.

Dad's desk was, unusually, cleared of all manuscripts. A single mug of cooling tea sat on the mosaic surface. His chair was empty. I squinted into the brightness towards the stand of verdy trees, and sure enough—there sat Mom, enthroned on her wheelchair She was draped in a lightly crocheted shawl of kidney-pink yarn shot through with bronze, the same colors as the armor worn by the Holy Host.

One of my mother's brothers sat on a chair near her. His face was turned away. I couldn't tell what kind of uncle he was today.

Then he saw me, and grinned.

A bad uncle then. My good uncles never grinned, only smiled. Always with their mouths closed. Always beatifically, as though through a veil.

"Ishi!"

Uncle Zulli leapt up, looking guiltily relieved to see me. A second later, I found out why.

"Watch your mom a sec while I take a piss, okay? Your dad had an appointment with the doc, so I'm a man short of a tag team. About to burp up my bladder. When you called out just now, I almost lost it. Nearly hosed down the back wall. Would've, too—but for Broszia here."

If Onabroszia Q'Aleth had still been herself, she'd have slapped Zulli till he peed out his nose for such vulgar talk. Mom wasn't the oldest of a horde of siblings for nothing. I folded my arms.

"Don't just stand there talking about it, Zulli. Go, go, go!"

"Don't say 'go,' Ishi," Uncle Zulli groaned. "You tryin' to bust me?"

Then, not hurrying at all, and so lightly he barely crushed the lovegrass beneath his feet, Uncle Zulli minced his way across the yard and went into the house. I took his place in the hard wooden chair beside Mom and covered her hand in mine. Her circulation was terrible. The texture of her skin was like torn tissue paper over hard rubber, and her arm was not only bruised in several places but punctured here and there with scabs. She kept hurting herself, often during one of her frantic bursts of energy—usually in the middle of the night, when Dad had finally dropped into a frail sleep. She'd forget where she was, and that she was barely mobile, and all too apt to fall into or out of things. Like doors. And beds.

"See, Mom, if you'd've given *me* a younger brother," I said, "I'd've made sure he was potty-trained before setting him loose on the world. Uncle Zulli forgets his bladder is the size of pea. He's always drinking gallons of tea—inevitably before visiting places that have no public facilities. Or places that have private ones that he can't get to for one reason or another."

I peered into her eyes. Cataracts clouded the irises, once dark and dagger-sharp. Now she was trapped behind those opal anchorholds. Mom stared at the backyard wall like it held visions. Dad interpreted that filmy far-off gaze as tranquility, but I wasn't so sure.

Still patting her hand, I blurted, "Alizar the Eleven-Eyed has a new saint."

Mom turned her head and, almost, looked at me. "I am a saint," she said serenely. "I was Kalikani's saint, before Kirtirin stole me."

Parts of my body tingled. Others went numb. It had been so long, so very long, since my mother had talked me.

"Right," I whispered, then cleared my throat. "Right, yes—I remember you saying that once. Tell me about that, Mom."

She continued with queenly graciousness, "Kalikani chose me when I was eight. I was wearing my green dress with the sparkles. I was so excited. It was my birthday and they took me to see the Heraldic Voice. They asked me if I saw the angels. I did. I saw them all and named them all, right away. The Heraldic Voice asked me to describe them. I said they were tall and beautiful, with flowing hair and flowing gowns. Kalikani wore a green dress, like mine. Green as, as this, this . . . ," she pointed to the trunk of a verdy tree, not knowing what to call it.

"Her hair was green, and her teeth were green, and her eyes had roots growing out of them. But Kirtirin, her twin, wanted me. He was green too, but like a lizard, with a lizard's tongue, and a long green lizard's tail. So he said, 'You cannot have her, sister; she is my saint.' And Kalikani smote him with her branches, and wrapped three branches around his throat and squeezed. And the Heraldic Voice told me that they were very sorry, but the angels would each have to choose their own saint, and for the sake of peace in the Celestial Cenoby, it could not be me. So they sent me on my way."

I nodded. "That must have hurt your feelings."

Mom nodded back, and to my surprise, started weeping. Great clear tears rolled from the clouds in her eyes.

I kept patting her hand, helplessly.

Her story about how the angels had rejected her changed every time she told it. The truth was, Mom had never been able to see angels, and everyone in Gelethel knew it.

From the time she was tiny, Mom was fixated on angels. She told stories about the Invisible Wonders to her friends, hosted backyard tea parties purporting to be graced by their attendance, and drew endless reams of pictures depicting—what she insisted were—angels. Her notions of their faces, forms, characters, temperaments, and relationships were as wild as her stories and as changeable. None of it matched existing canon. But that never made any difference to her. Mom just *knew* she was right about the angels—more right than any of the saints who ever recorded their observations down in the Hagiological Archives. Onabroszia Q'Aleth knew best.

At the age of eight, Mom stood in the Celestial Corridor, and publicly—*at her own insistence*—declared herself a saint. She spoke with such force and determination that the hundreds of Gelthic laity gathered there that day, the Heraldic Voice included, listened enraptured for the better part of an hour.

But in the end, none of it was true. Mom couldn't really see the angels of Gelethel. She was not a saint.

What *was* true was that the angels (particularly Kalikani and Kirtirin, the Enemy Twins) were so impressed with Mom's great faith in the Invisible Wonders (motley mix of grand delusion, self-importance, self-deception, and powerful imagination that the faith of a precocious eight-year-old was), that they offered her—filthy gamine daughter of no-account parents—a scholarship to one of Gelethel's best schools.

She quickly rose to the top of her class and went on rising, winning scholarships for the private schools usually reserved for the extended families of past and present saints (privileged among the laity), and then landed an angelic grant to start her business right out of school.

All that time, she was working enough odd jobs throughout the fourteen districts of the Angelic City that her barter-cache was stuffed with benzies—the benisons each angel manifested for its particular district. Soon, she had more than enough stock, both material and IOUs, to put her younger brothers through school as well. When they were old enough, she sent them on to the Empyrean Academy, where they learned to surrender their bodies to the angels. After that, Mom had eyes and ears in the Celestial Corridor: eyes and ears that were loyal to *her*.

Her brothers may have given their bodies over to the Invisible Wonders who ruled Gelethel, but when they were at home, they were ruled solely by their eldest sister. They were Broszia's boys, mind and soul.

And Onabroszia Q'Aleth had a bone to pick with the angels.

If Mom could not live as a saint in the Celestial Cenoby, then she would work as a devil within the Angelic City's walls. She would undercut the authority of the fourteen Invisible Wonders by bringing in benisons of her own from beyond the serac and distributing them to the Gelthic populace.

While by day, Mom and her brothers were blessed amongst all people of Gelethel, by night, they ran the Angelic City's underworld: a smuggling operation that spidered throughout the fourteen districts still extant within the Gelthic serac—and often, beyond. They knew that if they were caught, they'd suffer the same fate of all dissidents. If they were lucky, a period of penance in the saltcellars, while the angels worked them from within. If they were unlucky, a short walk and swift fall down the Hellhole in the Fifteenth District.

This was why Mom was the number one reason I could never tell anyone I was a saint. Even now, it just might kill her to learn it. If she didn't kill me first: I wouldn't put it past Onabroszia Q'Aleth, even in this state, to throttle me cold.

"Ishtu," Dad's light voice came from behind me. "I didn't think you'd come by today."

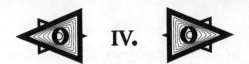

IV.

CLOSE UP ON MY FATHER'S FACE

Title Card: "Young Mechanic Goes Rogue!"

Dad starts out, fresh from trade school, as a mechanic for a film production company called Elixir Entertainment. Elixir is based in King's Capital, Koss Var, its studios converted out of old aeroplane hangars: huge concrete caves containing sound stages and construction bullpens, temporary offices, living quarters, community kitchen, laundry, and of course a huge shed out back for the costumes, all in different shades of pre-Pankinetichrome gray.

He works with Elixir a few years before the Koss Var Air Force re-requisitions the studios for hangars.

Dad smells the rats of war and is pissed right off. Not only is he out of a job he loves, but he's also an avowed pacifist.

But, surprise! The Empire of the Open Palm does what it does best; it intervenes. Mechanics being worth their weight in iron, when the KVAF "invites" Dad to stay on with them as a tactical aircraft design and maintenance specialist for their new fleet of bombers, it's an offer he can't refuse. Not if he wants to stay out of prison. Pay's okay, but that isn't the point.

By day, Dad's working for the KVAF. By night, he's a *filmmaker*. He's producing a stealth documentary—gathering intel, digging for gossip, following trails to undisclosed filling factories, interviewing similarly beleaguered colleagues under conditions of anonymity. Filming everything.

The night *Mystery Munitions and Hidden Hangars* releases, Koss Var's secret police come to Dad's apartment. But he's gone. He's just made it across the borders when the bounty on his head is blasted all over public radio and newsreels.

Too late—Dad's anti-war war documentary has blown the whistle on the Empire of the Open Palm's intentions for the Bellisaar Theatre. And while his film doesn't stop the New War from rumbling over the horizon, it sounds a fair warning.

And when the first KVAF bombers fly south to strafe the great city-states of the southern desert, Rok Moris and Sanis Alis aren't unprepared.

Title card: "Welcome to Gelethel!"

Tracking shot on Dad. His mustache is luxuriant. His brow is expansive, intelligent. His spectacles are crooked, and though he is a hunted man, his brown eyes twinkle.

He arrives at the Gelthic serac after crossing the desert in a rusted, half-wrecked jalopy. He has heard of that godless place southeast of the Bellisaar Waste called Gelethel—that mythical city that has never heard of motion pictures.

In the bed of his dilapidated deathtruck-mobile, Dad carries two projectors, as many cans of film as can be crammed, and a scrim. Those days Cherubtown is still just a shrine for actual pilgrims seeking congress with the angels, plus a little way-station selling food and drink and rental tents outside the western serac, where the Holy Host lowers Gelethel's bridge on petition days.

Dad stops at the shrine, asks some questions, gets his bearings.

Then, bold as a fighter pilot, as soon as the bridge is lowered, he drives straight up to the ramparts, over, and down the other side into Gelethel.

His and his jalopy follow the train of pilgrims all the way to the Celestial Corridor. He parks right outside, on a stretch of salt pan, and strides forward.

He will be the man who brings movies to the angels.

Title Card: "A Foreign Entrepreneur!"

Fourteen Invisible Wonders sit enthroned, watching Dad with perhaps more interest and curiosity than usual. Dad, a pilgrim petitioning for citizenship, tells them that he is a filmmaker, formerly of Koss Var. He says "filmmaker," not "mechanic," nor even "projectionist"—though he is both of those things too. He does not mention exile or criminal activity or the price on his head or the war he knows will come. Some instinct tells him the angels would not be interested.

But *films* interest them. The angels like stories. They demand an explanation.

Instead of explaining, Dad gestures to his rig: projectors, scrim, et cetera, that he has hauled in. He is ready and willing to give them a picture show.

The angels accede.

No, in fact, they *demand* a picture show: if he does not oblige them, he will eternally regret it.

Dad obliges. He needs an electrical source for the lamp; would the angels direct him to the nearest outlet?

Zerat Like the Lightning extends his hand in blessing over the rig. The Celestial Corridor is suddenly illuminated. The scrim begins to flicker: shadow, silver, shadow, silver, white, black, gray.

Miracle of miracles! It is just possible for the petitioners gathered in the Celestial Corridor that day to behold, in the flickering light, a rare sight for their naked eyes: fourteen eager outlines leaning forward in their thrones.

Mom is there too—Onabroszia Q'Aleth, Garbage Queen of Gelethel—twenty-four years old and the richest woman in the city. That day she sees what she has never seen before. She sees the angels. They are not as beautiful as she has imagined.

Title Card: "The Angels Are Pleased!"

The Invisible Wonders agree that this foreign filmmaker may stay in Gelethel. He will have a movie palace of his own, where he will proudly display his sacrifice: all the films he has brought with him to edify the angels and their worshippers.

But he must *never* leave Gelethel, they warn him. If he is caught trying to leave, the Holy Host will execute him. He is a citizen of Gelethel now: he must marry a Gelthic woman and produce a line of children who will protect and guard the magic of his movie palace.

Title Card: "Free Motion Picture Magic For All!"

When the Heraldic Voice, speaking for the angels, informs Dad of his new obligations, Dad protests. (He does not yet know better.) He tries to explain that silver nitrate degrades over time, that there is always danger of fire—it is not uncommon for entire archives of celluloid film to go up in flame and poisonous plumes and be lost forever—and that, most importantly, it will be *absolutely necessary* to provide new cinematic material for Gelthic cultural consumption on a regular basis.

The angels cut him short.

The fourteenth angel, Imperishable Dinyatha, breathes upon the cans of film, granting them the grace of her own longevity. As for the rest, the Heraldic Voice informs him, Dad need not import any new films into Gelethel; the angels believe that his films will enthrall audiences throughout the ages.

In their great benevolence, the angels evict—on the spot—the current tenants of the Gelthic Opera Hall. They bestow the building on Dad for use as his nickelodeon.

He is to show his films to the people of Gelethel (and any angels who happen to drop by) free of charge.

Title Card: "Foreigner Finds Love!"

Dad begins work. Since he isn't allowed to barter movie tickets for other benzies, he does the next best thing: decides to barter the Quick's concessions instead.

The citizens of Gelethel protest.

Citizens: Give us snacks! Angelic gifts should be free for all!

Dad: How is that? Every district is provided a variety of benisons by its ruling angel. Shuushaari fills the fountains in her district with fish the first day of every fortnight. On thirteenth day, the angel Beriu makes the flakes fall that, when gathered and set to soak, will rise into dough for baking. Zerat, on the eighth day, recharges all batteries, big and small, that fall within the lines of his district. None of these benisons manifest outside their zones—yet all of Gelethel eats fish, bakes bread and cake, and powers their houses with electricity. Every district trades their specific benisons with every other district. That's the basic economy of Gelethel. I'm doing nothing wrong.

Citizens: But before the angels gave you Quicksilver Cinema, we never needed movie concessions! Now that popcorn exists, it must be ours!

Dad: Then let the angel Olthar provide you popcorn outside Quicksilver Cinema.

Citizens: (resentful silence)

Dad: But he won't, will he? That's not how benisons work. My concessions are for the Quick alone. I prayed for them *specifically*, imploring the angel Olthar to add value for patrons of the movie palace. In return for his beneficence, Olthar receives more visitors to his district, is remembered fondly in their prayers, and, in this way, worship of his name increases. He gains power and favor among the angels. Meanwhile, I must live—and to live I must be able to barter. I *will* declare my concessions as benisons worthy of trade.

Citizens: What do you need benzies for anyway? The angels gave you a job, a movie palace to sleep in, all the food you can eat!

Dad: I cannot live on popcorn alone.

Citizens: How does a dirty pilgrim like you become such an expert in Gelthic economy?

Dad: (dryly) I'm a quick study.

After they are evicted, the dispossessed owners of what had been the Gelthic Opera Hall and is now Quicksilver Cinema, are forced to squat in Nirwen's Hell—the fifteenth district. The Holy Host goes only where the angels send them, and Hell, having no angelic oversight, is the least policed zone in Gelethel.

Now, they might very well have slept more comfortably in Alizar's Bower, where all the fruit and veg they could want might be freely plucked off vine and tree, or stayed with friends and family, or even huddled in the halls of the Celestial Corridor if it came to that.

But in their desire for revenge, the former managers of the Gelthic Opera Hall want no Host or angel to overhear their conspiracies.

What follows is no secret anywhere in Gelethel. Everyone knows who is vandalizing the Quick each night, but nothing is done about it.

At least, not outright.

(Later, much later, Dad learns all. How Onabroszia Q'Aleth reported the conspirators to the Holy Host; how the Host marched into Hell one night and rumbled those Hell-dwellers in their tents; how, when the Host left the fifteenth district again, they bore no prisoners with them, and nor was their purported quarry ever heard from again. In Gelethel, Dad learns, this can mean only one thing: that the bodies lay at the bottom of Hell yet, frozen forever in a particular, secret place where no one living can reach, nor any mourner recover them for burial. But that, as I said, is much, much later.)

Dad, still scorched by his near-miss with the Koss Var secret police, is leery about reporting to the authorities. He wants to maintain a low profile, behave like an ideal citizen, and keep the doors of his movie palace open, as prescribed to him by the angels. But no sooner does he see to one defacement but another window is smashed, another door kicked in, another imprecation smeared (with paint and other less benign materials) on the salt-white walls, slogans like:

GO BACK TO KOSS VAR, DOGMAN!

"Dogman," Dad learns, is a common slur for foreigners. It derives from "dogma," on the assumption that everyone outside the Gelthic serac are staunch theists who have unilaterally rejected a purely angelic rule.

Now, Dad has always been an atheist himself, but considers converting on the strength of spite alone.

At least no one dares steal or destroy the equipment inside the Quick. It is, after all, blessed by the angels. But the movie palace is not a safe place to visit— not even to see the strange new pictures Dad has brought in from outside the serac. Not even for the snacks.

But hark!

One afternoon, Mom—AKA Onabroszia Q'Aleth, radiant and blessed— surprises the entire Angelic City by attending a matinee with her younger brothers in tow.

The Q'Aleth family, everywhere watched and emulated, are observed strolling into Dad's empty movie palace at forty-five minutes before showtime. They are espied waiting in line at the concessions stand, where Dad, in a starched soda jerk cap and black-and-gold striped apron, stands eager to serve them.

The Q'Aleths pay for their movie snacks—mountains of them—in an array of barter: benzie slips—notarized IOUs from Tanzanu's district—of all kinds that Dad can trade in for meat, fabric, bread, fish, batteries, craft trade, municipal services, water lots, etc. All transactions completed to everyone's delight, they cart away their spoils into the theatre: buckets of popcorn, bags of peanuts, pretzels wrapped in cloth napkins, small paper cones stuffed with mint sticks and hard caramels and chocolate bullets scooped out of the large glass jars at the candy buffet, a frosty bottle of beer for Mom, ice cream sodas for the boys.

Emboldened by Mom's example, and salivating for the angelic concessions found nowhere else in Gelethel, citizens come flooding in.

By showtime, all seats are full: eight hundred seats in the orchestra, three hundred in the mezzanine. There is some double-stacking: parents with children, lovers cuddling. Standing room only. The concessions stand looks like no man's land between two enemy trenches. But that's fine; the angel Olthar's next Feast of Excess is in two days' time—when all stores in the OlDi will be automatically and lavishly replenished.

Dad, now with cap cast aside and sleeves rolled up, plays movies for his audience all day. He is tireless, elated, sweating spigots in the projection room. He doesn't notice when Mom comes in and sits quietly behind him, watching him work. He doesn't notice until after midnight, when everyone else has left the theatre, and he is shutting everything down, wrung out from nervous exhilaration. He turns around, and . . .

"Anyone ever tell you, Mister," says Mom, taking a long, lipstick-stained drag on her cigarette, "that you look just like an angel?"

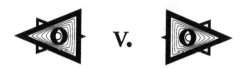

V.

DISSOLVE TO PRESENT

Mom stared at the backyard wall like it was a distant star. Behind me, Dad was waiting for an answer. I wiped my face quickly, smiled brightly at nothing, and then, still smiling, turned around.

"Hey, Dad. Of course I came. Why wouldn't I?"

I visited them almost every afternoon—never skipped without first flicking a benzie to some cheeky street g'lark as payment to run a message along to their house with my apologies and rescheduling plans.

"Well," Dad explained now with patience Dad-jokiness, "you know, it's fifteenth day, Ishtu."

Slowly—too slowly, he started crossing the sun-blasted yard.

"Yes," I prompted him, "and?"

"*And*," he went on, "we save fifteenth days for only our most loathsome chores. I thought you loved us more than that, Ishtu. You might have visited us on third day, the Feast of Excess, to show your excessive love. Or on thirteenth day, when we all strive to do impossible things with cheer and vigor. But you. Our only child. Beloved of her uncles. Heir to all our fortunes. You visit us on *fifteenth* day."

He shook his head sadly as he approached. But I could see the twinkle in his eye, and I knew him; Dad liked showing off his thorough knowledge of his adopted nation's traditions. And also to mock them.

Rolling my eyes, I stood up from the chair to hug him. "Nice to see you too, Dogman." Then, leaning close, I whispered in his ear, "Sorry I made her cry."

"Yes, she does that. It must be a very confusing state for her sometimes. But remember, Ish, she was talking too," Dad said, pleased. "I watched you both a while, from the back door. She'll still talk to me, sometimes, especially just after I sing to her. It only works with hymns, though. Well, and drinking songs. A complicated woman, our Broszia."

He took my seat, then. He endeavored to make it seem a hospitable gesture, as if he were merely settling in for a comfortable visit, but I saw it for what it was. A collapse. The gray exhaustion in his face, the blue cast to his lips.

His face had thinned down these last few years, but his mustache was luxuriant as ever, worn like a set of ivory tusks, well-maintained and lavishly drooping. I loved his bald head, his big ears, those faded brown eyes that watered as they gazed at me.

I sat at his feet in the dusty lovegrass, hugging my knees. My knees creaked. I wasn't the child my parents made me feel like anymore. I wasn't any kind of child at all.

"Dad, what did the doc sa—"

He beat me to it. "Heart disease."

He wore that little fatalistic smile that bespoke a lifetime of regret and resignation—and a mordant sense of humor about it all. I squeezed my knees hard, crushing them together.

Keep it together . . .

"If you asked the uncles, they—"

Again, Dad interrupted, "—could probably get me some S'Alian drugs, yes. At huge cost—even with the family discount. Worse, at considerable danger to themselves. But benzies and bad uncles aren't really the issue, Ishtu."

His smile grew at his slant rhyme. A man in love with words, my dad.

"The issue," he went on, "is a life in its eld. One of high stress, high fatigue, indifferent diet, no exercise, and constant internal moral strife. No drug imported from Sanis Al can cure that. I'm done for, I'm afraid. I could drop any minute."

"That," I said flatly, "is unacceptable."

Alizar! Alizar could cure him. He'd just resurrected Betony, after all—rose her right up from the drowned dead, and . . .

In front of the other angels, Alizar whispered.

If his voice had been an actual sound, he would have sounded as weary as Dad. As it was, it manifested as an ache in my bones, a trembling in my extremities, the hard burn of lactic acid in my muscles—as if I had climbed too high on the serac and now—exhausted, untethered—had only to fall.

Betony was already dead, the Seventh Angel went on. *I broke no laws to resurrect her. But I cannot give your father a new heart—or your mother a new mind. I could not keep such a miracle secret; the others would sense it; they would know. We all agreed, when the war began and the pilgrims came, that we would no more heal the people of Gelethel of their ills—lest they prove too fruitful, live too long, and burst the bounds of the serac to our destruction.*

"We" agreed, he'd said. But I remembered the day when all the angels sang up that issue. Alizar the Eleven-Eyed—with me silently backing him at every moment—had strongly disaccorded with the choir. But he was sung down, forced to abide. I'd never salted the wound by praying he would help Mom, even when she lost the ability to read and write, even when she stopped walking and talking—even when she forgot my name. But now, Dad . . .

"It is what it is," Dad said mildly, after too long a pause, too long a struggle for breath. He shrugged deeper into his stooped shoulders, lost his smile. Shaking his head from side to side, he began rubbing rhythmically at his knees, which always pained him as mine were starting to.

"The Quicksilver Cinema was *my* dream, Ishtu, not yours. It makes me sick—sick!—that you're stuck with it. It's like living inside a corpse, playing the same fourteen-damned movies over and over again . . ."

I interrupted him, "It's fine. I like running the Quick. I love all those old movies."

"Ishi." Dad leaned forward. He didn't touch me, didn't place his palms to either side of my face, or grip my shoulder like Mom would have done when she was driving home a point. Dad rarely instigated touch.

"Ishi—what you love, what you know—it's only a shadow of what is actually out there. Not even a complete silhouette—a scrap of shadow. Cinema alone . . . out past the serac, think where it's gone. Talkies, Pankinetichrome, and now, home movies. The world is moving on. And I want. . . I want *you* to move, to move on . . ."

His breath was coming in short, shallow, rapid. I took his hands in mine.

"Dad, Dad. It's okay." I laid my cheek against his cold knuckles. "It's better, isn't it, that I don't know what I'm missing?"

He sighed deeply, and after a time grew calm again. Sitting up, I tried coaxing a smile out of him, but his whole forehead had collapsed into a ravine that could not be remade smooth. There were parts of the serac like the look on his face.

"I should have walked out," he said. "When you were a baby. I should have walked out with you then, right over the ramparts on the fifteenth day, as the pilgrims were coming in. A capital punishment for a pilgrim made citizen, but who knows, in the crowd, I might have made it. If I were caught, they'd never have harmed you. And if I'd succeeded—you'd have had a chance then, at least. I understood Gelethel enough by the time you were born. I knew what it would mean to stay and raise you in this place, knew that no child, *no child*, should ever be so trammeled by her geography . . . But then, the war—and all the roads from here to Sanis Al or Rok Moris so salted with mines it was a death sentence either way, and . . ."

And, he did not say, *there was your mother.*

We both knew that Onabroszia Q'Aleth would have killed Dad the moment he tried to smuggle me out. But the war was a convenient scapegoat, so I shrugged, and stretched, and said, "Oh, well. Yet another reason Koss Var can go right off and fuck itself, eh?"

He grunted.

Slapping my thigh with exaggerated finality, I struggled to my feet. "Well, you two! Enough of this maudlin old nostalgia talk. I'm a working woman—and I have a cinema to run."

"Yes. Yes, of course." Dad nodded, rubbed his knee one last, troubled time, and smiled at me—or tried to.

Leaning down so I could drop a kiss on his sun-mottled pate, I looked into his eyes and said, "We're showing a double-feature tonight: *Godmother Lizard* and *Life on the Sun*. Want to come? I'll spring for a chariot and send it off for you two when it's time."

"No, thank you, Ishtu," Dad replied, awfully polite. "I'm just a little tired tonight. I think Broszia and I will stay in. I still have some of that vegetable soup you made us from Alizar's bumper crop benison in the Bower."

"What," I asked, only half-pretending to be aghast. "The one from *last year*? Dad! That was good soup! You should eat it!"

He managed to send one of his patented twinkles my way. "Well, you know, Ishtu, I've been saving it up for a rainy day."

"This is *Bellisaar*," I reminded him. "Even the angels can't make it rain. The best they can do is raise wells and divert rivers."

"Good for me, then, that angelic vegetables never go off. Now," he said, clearly doubling down on my farewell and dismissing me in turn, "I told your Uncle Zulli to take a break while we had our visit. I'll bet he's napping in the great room—working tonight, so he needs rest. Will you wake him for me as you leave, tell him I want to see him?"

"Sure thing, Dad."

I bent to kiss Mom, a double-tap on each cheek, Gelethel-style. "Bye, Saint Broszia," I said cheerfully. "Put in a good word for me with the Enemy Twins." I glanced at Dad. "See you both tomorrow?"

"How about the afternoon?" Dad placed his hand lightly over Mom's. "Broszia and I have been sleeping in till about ten or so. Sometimes it takes us a while to get going."

This, I knew, was code. Their nights, already horrific, were getting worse. Mom never slept for more than a few hours; she'd always been most active from eight in the evening to four in the morning, even when she was well.

"Of course. I'll bring lunch. *Not* soup." I grinned down at them both like a bad uncle, all cheeky swagger and one-sided dimple, one hand cocked on my hip. "Maybe a nice big salad!"

Dad's eyes bulged in mock alarm.

"Oh, no, Ishtu. Not another salad! If you love me . . ."

"Come on, Dad. Have to keep you strong, don't I? Your only daughter, beloved child, heir to all your fortunes, et cetera, et cetera. And just think of all those lovely, lovely leafy greens. So cool. So fresh. So good for you!"

Dad muttered something about "rabbit food." But I, as if he were the angel Alizar and I the other thirteen, blithely overrode his protests.

"By the time I'm done quacking you, Domi LuPyn, you'll live another hundred years under these angelic skies, hale and hearty as a Holy Host."

"God forbid," Dad muttered under his breath.

That was plenty blasphemous, even for him. There hadn't been a god in Gelethel since the fifteen angels ate Her—oh, millennia ago.

"On that note, Dogman," I said, "I'm off. Sleep well!"

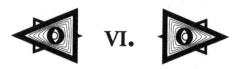

VI.

ZULLI'S TAKE

I dashed back into Dad and Mom's house so quickly that the dimness caught my eyes like a velvet hood. Swaying at the sudden blackness, I stopped, my dark mood plummeting to crush-depth, the tears I'd hidden from Dad returning.

Then, straightening my shoulders, I marched down the hall and into the great room, right up to that ratty old yellow sofa with the stains and spills of generations, and the stuffing and springs poking out of every cushion, and I shook the youngest of my uncles awake.

"Zulli! Uncle Zulli!"

His eyes popped open. "Wha—?"

"We need to get Dad and Mom out of Gelethel as soon as possible. It's urgent." I took him by both shoulders and shook him. "It's a matter of life and death."

The words came out of my mouth with such force that I almost didn't recognize my own voice. I meant what I said—every word. But I couldn't believe I'd actually said it. I was raised to obey: my mother first, then the angels, then my father and uncles, and then maybe my own conscience. The only secret I'd ever kept was the angel Alizar's, and that had made me quiet all my life, not confident.

Under my grip, Uncle Zulli's shoulders were relaxed as two cats. His expression became so serene , so implacable, that for a moment I thought he was Irazhul, my good uncle: warrior of the Holy Host, porous and shining with angels, ready to transmit a report of any misdeed committed within his hearing. Then he blew out his breath.

"Yeah," he said, sitting up and scratching behind his ear like a g'lark's gutter mutt. "Yeah, it's about time, isn't it? We been expectin' it for years, but the war, y'know?" He shrugged. "Disrupted all our big plans."

My knees and breath gave out. I squatted, inhaling deeply, and began to talk. "It has to happen soon, Zulli. Dad said, he said that, that he might . . . any minute."

I cleared my throat. "Look, I can take them to Sanis Al myself. But you and the Razman and the others have to arrange things for me. I . . ." I hesitated. "I remember where to go, from that one time. But . . ."

Zulli's face betrayed nothing, so I continued, "I just don't know *when* I need to be there, or what to do once I get there. And once I get us . . . out . . . I don't know *anything*! We'll need a guide, a . . . what do you call them?" I snapped memory into my fingers. "A possum! And I know Mom

50

used to trade goods for foreign currency, so I need to get my hands on that—except I don't know where she stashed it away."

I had a few ideas though, starting with the flour bin—which Dad, not being a baker, never touched. Uncle Zulli regarded me steadily, and then his neutral expression broke out into one of his rubber clown looks: black brows arched comically, eyes stretched wide, nostrils flared. He held up his hands to slow me down.

"Hey, Ishi, hey. Possum first. One thing at a time." He rubbed his chin sleepily, then tapped a fingers against his jaw. "We'll put word out right away we want a rendezvous with Nea. Great lady. Trustworthy. Knows Bellisaar like the crust up her crack. Has a viperbike the size of, like, if a camel fucked a tank—even has a nice cozy sidecar. Should fit you all with room to spare."

"Nea," I repeated. The name was not familiar, but then, Mom had never let me near this side of the business. "How long have you known her?"

Zulli shrugged. "Known her since the start—from back when Broszia started tappin' the serac for weak spots. Nea was already there, tappin' right back. She's an ace possum—piggyback you all the way to Sanis Al, hook you up with her contacts there. Hates Gelethel, loves helpin' people leave. We send out word we want her—you know, the way we have"—he waggled his eyebrows. Sometime things "fell" from the ramparts at certain spots when Zulli and the bad uncles were patrolling, or sometimes a pilgrim whose sacrifice had not been accepted agreed to act as mule—"And soon enough, she shows up. She'll send us a time and a password, we pass it to you. In the meantime, Ish—"

The next moment, he looked so intent, so preternaturally serious, that I drew back, once more expecting Irazhul to come shining through. He did not.

"—be on the beam," he finished. "You gotta be ready at a moment's notice to pick up and leave. That's the deal, or it's off."

"I'll be ready," I promised.

Zulli nodded, and then, throwing back his head, gave a mighty and insinuating yawn. Taking the hint, I stood up.

"Voice like an angel," I teased him.

Zulli stopped yawning long enough to award me that bad uncle grin of his that never failed to invoke its match in my face. "What d'you expect, you come prayin' to me for benisons?"

Reaching down, I scruffed the wooly brown curls of his head. "Thanks, Uncle Zulli. Sorry I came on so strong right off your nap. It's just—" I gestured toward the back of the house, the backyard.

Zulli nodded, his goofy, happy-go-lucky demeanor flickering off, then on, then off, then on again. By which I understood that he was as worried about my parents as I was.

"It's all killer-diller, lil dynamite. About danged time you up and blew this popsicle stand. If I weren't bound by circumstance," he gestured to his circumstance, his body, "I'd go haring all up and down the globe. Somewhere," he said dreamily, "*cold.*"

"I'll send you a snow globe. But," I added, leaning over to kiss him, "you'll have to smuggle it over the serac yourself."

"Right." Zulli looked wry. "Anyway. They say S'Alian medtech is outta this world. If anyone can give Broszia and Jen their right and comfortable twilight, it's the docs in Sanis Al. As for you . . ." He rose from the couch and looked at me fondly. "Me, Jen, Razman, Wuki, Eril—all we ever wanted was you out and over the serac since about forever. Even before Broszia stopped knowin' your name. We just thought *you* didn't."

My chest cracked open on the inside. Only my skin stopped all the panic and hope from pouring out over the floor. I shook my head, over and over. "I—I wasn't ready."

And the angel Alizar, I thought. He wasn't ready. Nirwen hadn't yet returned. She hadn't sent him a sing. His second saint. How could I have left him all alone, surrounded by enemy angels?

We will speak more of this anon, Ishtu, Alizar promised, his voice—for an angel's—very gentle.

"Well, you're more than ready now," Zulli was saying, though I hardly heard him for the singing in my bones. "I could tell right away. Never saw you look so much like Broszia than just now, stompin' in like one of 'em thunder monsters from days of yore. Loomin'. Makin' demands. Spittin' image. Terrifyin'."

His eyes a-flash with sudden tears, he set his forehead to mine and whispered, "You know we'd all walk through fire for her, right?"

And so you do, I thought. Every day. Every night.

"You may have to," I warned him. "You ever smuggle two seniors and a cinema-owner out of Gelethel before?"

He waved his hand. "Easy as seein' angels."

That was total Zulli. How every kid brother would have answered a dare.

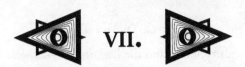

VII.

THREE VIGNETTES I WISH I HAD MADE
(with the Super 8 camera my uncles gave me)

Last year in Alizar's District—the day the miracle happened.
Nobody knew it, but it was my birthday—which fell, in this instance, on the seventh day of the fortnight. This was always Alizar's Feast Day, Bloom, and the bumper crop he manifested in his district for all of Gelethel that day was in fact his birthday present to me. Our own secret celebration.

Instead of being zoned for residence, the angel Alizar's district, Bower, was a butterfly-shaped patch of public parkland consisting of six hundred forty acres and situated in the center of Gelethel. Citizens from all over the Angelic City could stroll Bower's rock paths, climb its hillocks, explore its mosseries. There were many kinds of gardens to enjoy: fragrance gardens and herb gardens, orchards and berry brambles, stretches of vegetable gardens, swaths of grassland. A person might promenade the esplanades in high fashion, or sit quietly beside the bog pavilion, or bathe naked in one of the terraced pools, or sweat contentedly in the house of succulents.

On the Feast of Bloom, every citizen of Gelethel was invited to harvest whichever of Alizar's benisons they needed from Bower—fresh fruits, herbs, honey, and vegetables, mostly; the rest of the fortnight, the trees and bushes and hives and grasses all quietly cycled through their season.

But last year, on our double birthday/feast day, Alizar outdid himself.

All day long, every hour on the hour, all six hundred forty acres of Bower flowered and fruited, fruited and flowered. The trees bent double with their bounty; the hills were carpeted with plump drupes. Vegetables grew so large, they had to be carted away on chariots. The air was fragrant with wintergreen, white sage, thyme, lavender, lemon balm, rosemary, basil, chamomile, yarrow, marjoram, gentian, sandalwood, hops. The hives overflowed.

Everyone I'd ever met in Gelethel—in the Quick, the Celestial Corridor, out and about in the other districts—seemed to be in Bower that day, wandering around the Seventh Angel's dream: mouths sticky with sweet juice, hair yellow with pollen, eyes struck with a wonder I'd never yet seen in this city ruled by Invisible Wonders.

And the wind, smelling of wine and wildflowers.

And the light, supersaturated with kaleidoscope colors.

And the bumblebees, only just heavier than the breeze.

* * *

Our hike through Hell, me and the bad uncles—six, seven years ago?
They'd descended en masse on the Quick, storming up the mezzanine to my rooftop apartment and rattling me awake at an ungodly hour. They all had a rare day off together, they informed me—and they wanted to show me something.

Dark yet, as we ventured out onto the streets and hopped into Uncle Wuki's chariot.

Wuki and Eril both called out, "Steed!" at the same time, meaning that they both got to sit up front. This also meant that they were the ones operating the push-pedals, a chore I was glad to concede. Wuki took the wheel and handbrakes—since it was after all (as he was fond of pointing out) *his* chariot.

On the back bench, the Razman and I contented ourselves doing nothing. Zulli stood behind us on the tailboard, grasping the canopy poles and leaning far forward whenever the mood seized him, sticking his head between ours and making joyous whiplash sounds, crying, "Whoa, boy, whoa!" every time Wuki squeezed the handbrakes even a little.

I asked where we were going.

Uncle Raz glanced at me, smiled slightly (he only ever smiled slightly), and said, "Nirwen's district."

"We're going to Hell!" Zulli whisper-sang behind us.

Like his brothers, he seemed to have no desire to rouse the OlDi betimes, but there was a nervy mischief in his voice that made his words seem much noisier than they actually were. The Razman turned around and hissed him quiet.

Hell was Nirwen the Forsaker's district. Back when she was still Nirwen the Artificer, it had been called Lab. In diamond-shaped Gelethel, which was divided into fifteen equal allotments, Hell took up the southmost tip.

With no official angelic oversight and only sporadic patrolling by the Holy Host, it was an area let to run wild. All the old industrial parks and university satellites were still there, long since converted to unauthorized tenements where citizens new to Gelethel tended to squat till they got the lay of the land. But with no benisons incoming and a stigma attached to anyone who gave Hell as their forwarding address, few stayed long.

The roads changed the instant we rolled over the western borders of Mews—Tanzanu's District—into Hell. Here, the salt-pan was cracked. The weeds ran rampant. But it was greener than I'd expected. Green as if the angel Alizar himself, missing his friend, regularly wandered the streets, weeping seeds into the dirt from all eleven of his eyes. It was breathlessly, eerily quiet. Even the g'larks and others of the roofless preferred to rove elsewhere, camping each day in a different district to kipe benisons on the sly without having to trade for them. But here, the ditches and gutters and doorways were empty of sleeping bodies. Nothing rustled, nothing stirred.

Wuki and Eril pedaled us further and further in, heading south. The blue shadow of the serac loomed above us on both sides of the road, dovetailing into the southmost point of the city.

As at the other cardinal points of Gelethel, there would be a stair in the south leading from the street to the ramparts atop the serac, where Tyr Hozriss, the southern watchtower, stood. This stair would be much wider and more ornate than the access ladders and lifts that ran up serac at kilometer intervals all around the city. It would have carved railings and shining white steps made from the same compressed salt and starch bricks that most of Gelethel was built of.

But when we came to the place, I saw from the look of it that no one had used the southern stair for some time.

Wuki parked the chariot in no very neat way, then turned around on the bench to face me.

"You've never been here," he told me.

"No," I agreed with him, puzzled. I hadn't been. My uncles knew that. These days, I was pretty much confined to Olthar's District, the OlDi, where I lived and worked at the Quick, and the north side of Kir, where my parents lived. Those, and the Celestial Corridor—though not so much these days.

But Wuki didn't release me from his gaze. "You were never here today."

"Oh."

Now I understood what he meant.

"Yes, all right, uncle," I agreed, then at his expectant eyebrows, elaborated, "I slept in today. Till noon. Never stirred."

"We never showed you this."

"Of course not."

Satisfied, all my uncles spilled out of the chariot, me in their wake, and led me up to the steps.

Unlike the other cardinal staircases, the southern stair was gated off from the street. A ten-foot high cage braced the bottom of the steps, the iron stakes driven into the ground in a wide semi-circle that ended flush with the serac itself. There was no way up unless we climbed the fence, and even in my early thirties I wasn't what you'd call athletic.

At my imploring look, the Razman drew a key out of his pocket and put it to the lock.

"Captain's privileges?"

He frowned at me—"Do not say 'captain' here, Ishtu," he warned—and pushed open the gate.

Zulli wriggled past to bound up the steps. He was the youngest of my uncles, but still a good fifteen years older than I was, yet had the energy of a puppy. Eril followed, slightly hunched, as if a winter wind blew for him alone. It was coolest in Gelethel at this pre-dawn hour, and this close to the ice of the serac, probably just around freezing. But Eril's winter wind was not external.

Uncle Raz gestured that I go next. Wuki came to bear me company, offering me his arm, patting my hand reassuringly.

"Six hundred forty nine steps to the top, Ishi," he said. "You ready? Ready to burn some calories?"

I groaned. "Uncle, why do you torment me?"

"Because we love you."

Up and up and on and on we went—but not all the way to the top. The uncles stopped, finally, just about midway up the staircase, and for the first few moments, I didn't even know why, even care, because I was bent over my knees, catching my breath.

When I straightened again, I could see it. They had gone no further because we *could* go no further. Above us, the wide staircase had been sheared off, as if by some great sky hammer. Not only had the whole top half of the stair crumbled, but behind where it had been, exposed, the serac itself gaped open like a wound. The deep blue wall of ice that surrounded our city on all sides, two hundred meters high and fifty meters thick, showed here a dark fissure. Even in the brightening light, I couldn't see all the way to the bottom. There was just a cool blue drop into darkness.

But I knew what was down there. I'd heard the rumors all my life.

Bodies. Countless, frozen bodies. Those who had displeased the angels. Those who had fallen afoul of the Holy Host. Gelethel's criminals and apostates. The ones the angels could not bring to penance in the saltcellars. The irredeemable.

Their icy grave was at the bottom of a breach that extended almost all the way to the top of the serac. A few meters short of the ramparts, it thinned to a hairline crack, thence to a line like spider silk, thence to smooth blue ice once again. The salt-brick walkways built atop the wall ran uninterrupted into the arched doors of Tyr Hozriss.

I asked my uncles, "Does the breach run all the way . . . through?"

Staring down into that dark-blue drop, I thought, *Is that a doorway, Alizar? Is that our door?*

Is that our grave?

He didn't answer then. Neither did any of my uncles, who had brought me here to show me just this. So I repeated the question.

Uncle Eril turned to stare directly into my eyes. "What breach, Ishtu?"

I stared back, silent, until one by one, without another word, each of my uncles turned and headed back down the stairs.

The Razman was last. As he passed me, he took my hand and pressed it warmly, comfortingly. He did not meet my eyes. I stood still, waiting until all my uncles were far, far ahead of me.

And then, I opened my hand.

In it, the key to the gate.

* * *

O nabroszia—baking cake.

    It was not long after our chariot ride to Hell. Maybe a year? Anyway, more and more pilgrims were flooding into Cherubtown as things got worse in the Bellisaar Theatre. Badness came in waves, the periods of peace never lasting more than half a decade, and never enough to completely rebuild. This late in the war, the waves were only getting worse.

On petition days in the Celestial Corridor, human sacrifices had already started. At first the war had disrupted the smuggling side of Mom's business, but recently it had picked up again.

Cherubtown consisted of two types: pilgrims and cherubs. The former were desperate to get into Gelethel, the latter were just desperate for basic necessities that only Gelethel could provide: food, water, medicine, blankets, clothes. For those, they'd trade everything from family heirlooms to junk scavenged from the roadside that certain collectors in Gelethel wanted simply because it was not of Gelethel.

Legally, the Angelic City forbade commerce with any individual, corporate body, or government outside the serac. What the citizens of Gelethel needed, only the angels could provide—magnanimous in their benisons. Therefore Gelethel traded only in benzies, which no pilgrim could offer from the outside. In other words, if it weren't for the universal human desire for the exotic, illicit, and forbidden, the pilgrims would've been shit out of luck.

But humans were pretty much the same on both sides of the serac, and an infrastructure promoting the amiable flow of contraband—thanks to Onabroszia Q'Aleth—was already in place. In trading smuggled goods with pilgrims, Mom saw yet another chance to spite the angels, and took it. Gleefully.

Every fifth day—Whispers, sacred to the angel Murra—was trash day. Each dawn of Whispers, Q'Aleth Hauling Industries would send out their fleet of push-pedal chariots—the ones that required four pedalers, with the big beds in the back—into the districts to collect Gelethel's scraps and cast-offs. The carts would then haul their loads over to an area of Nursery, Hirrahune's district, that was built up along the southwestern wall of the serac. There, a gracious land grant from the Ninth Angel had allowed Mom to build a series of elevator platforms. QHI workers went in shifts, loading trash onto the platforms, hoisting it up to the ramparts, and dumping it off the side—into Cherubtown.

We hadn't chosen to dump our trash into Cherubtown. Cherubtown grew up around our dumpsite, because pilgrims were constantly scavenging the middens for anything useful to wear or eat or make things out of. But benisons from Gelethel quickly deliquesced outside the serac—and there was never enough to begin with.

Which brings us to the cake.

Mom's whole thing with the benison cake wasn't her idea originally. It was Zulli's husband's.

One day when we were all over at Mom's and Dad's for dinner, Mom had sidled up next to Zulli's beloved, his night sky, the cinnamon in his apple tea, and asked him idly, "Madriq, why are you throwing out a ton and a half of perfectly good bread every fortnight?"

When Mom got all idle and casual like that, it behooved the interrogatee to answer promptly and honestly. Madriq was no fool.

"I'm, um . . . Well, I was trying to feed the cherubs."

"Angelic benisons are for Gelthic citizens," Mom said piously. "Pilgrims and cherubs are not your concern."

He shrugged, looked sideways. "Zulli said he saw children down there. Looked down from the ramparts, saw a bunch of kids. No parents. No tents. Hardly a rag to their backs. Starving. So." He shrugged again, and while he didn't say, "Angels be damned," there was a tightness in his face that Mom could read like a scroll.

Madriq was a baker. As far as he was concerned, anyone who was hungry had a right to be fed, preferably by him. The fact that he was happiest stuffing pastries down Uncle Zulli's bottomless gullet was a cornerstone of their marriage.

"Carry on then," Mom said. "Q'Aleth Hauling Industries is happy to collect whatever waste you deem fit for the middens, regardless of content. Ishtu, my only begotten child," and her eyes glinted at me, "why don't you drop by tomorrow and I'll teach you how to make benison cake. My mother's special recipe. I saved it all these years to teach you."

Now, she knew, and I knew, and all the uncles knew, that Zaripha Q'Aleth had never baked a day in her life. But Mom was born with an ineffable talent to make herself and everyone else around her believe that every lie she told was true, and if she wanted to teach me how to bake our ancestral benison cake from a recipe that didn't yet exist, who was I, merely her daughter, to argue with her?

Mom's cakes were so dense with lard from Rathanana's Abattoir they were practically meat. She stuffed them with every conceivable kind of candied citrus, dried fruit or berry in Bower, and then dropped a coin in the middle—Mom was something of a numismatic, and enjoyed collecting currencies from outside the serac she'd never be able to spend—before slathering the top with honey and shaved almonds, then dumping them into the trash.

As for me, Mom's minion, I added only one thing: Alizar's blessing.

I prayed to the Seventh Angel that the cakes intended for the pilgrims and cherubs outside the serac would last longer than the other trash we dumped haphazardly into Cherubtown. I prayed that they would courier his benison rapidly and directly into their bodies.

Alizar was more than willing to try. He poured everything he had into the blessing. I felt it when the cupola-shaped cakes swelled with his intent. I heard them humming as they cooked, their slight singing hiss as they cooled. Even the sacks we loaded them into, which were to be hauled out by the QHI chariots, seemed plumper, shinier, and more sentient than sacks should be.

Alizar thrummed excitedly excitedly as the chariots drove away. He and I knew that a single bite of these benison cakes would bestow upon its gobbler a blast of necessary vitamins, minerals, and phosphates. They would cure scurvy, replenish deficiencies, boost the immune system, ease dehydration, whisk away nightmares, impart new vigor, and enhance reflexes with every bite. They were our small, beautiful rebellion, and one, moreover, that I had shared with my mother.

But.

It was Host Irazul Q'Aleth, who commanded the patrol atop the ramparts that day. He happened to be making his inspections near the QHI dump-lifts when the sacks with Madriq's bread and Mom's cakes went over. He stood, looking down into Cherubtown, and watched the pilgrims and cherubs stampede toward the food.

Later, stopping by Mom's after dinner, Host Irazhul reported to us that at least two children and an elderly person had been trampled in that desperate scramble. He stood at the head of the table, behind Mom's chair, his hands resting lightly on the carved back, and stared expressionlessly down at all of us. Mom alone could not see his face; she sat staring straight ahead. And so she did not see the wolf teeth and hawks' beaks studding the flesh of his face, submerging and surfacing in moving patterns, indicating the presence of at least least two angels.

"Furthermore," Host Irazhul went on, "there is only one baker in the Angelic City who produces loaves of such size and splendor that even I, from the heights of the rampart, could espy them and name with certainty their provenance. Madriq Urra," he said to his husband, "I am arresting you in the name of the fourteen. You are sentenced to an indefinite period of penance in the saltcellars, and when your penance has been deemed enough by the angels Tanzanu and Rathanana, we shall release you again into your family's custody."

"Zulli," Madriq whispered.

But Zulli wasn't ascendent that night. Nor would he be for all those long months that Madriq was imprisoned in the saltcellars, put to the question by the angels who dwelled in Host Irazhul. And even when Madriq finally walked free, Zulli wouldn't be at home in his own skin, or even his own home, for far longer than that. It was a long road of raging and baking, and walking, and talking, and a million small gestures of atonement and tenderness, before forgiveness became less an act than a practice.

All of that came later.

From that night on, however, a detachment of the Host watched the dump-lifts every Feast of Whispers, in case another deluded Gelthic sympathizer tried to pull a trick like that again. No one did, not so far as I know.

I do know that after her good brother Irazhul took Madriq away, Mom broke every dish in the house. And then she sat right back down at the head of the table, and seized snarled fistfuls of her own hair, and saw them off one by one with the bread knife at the table. Dad and I watched her and dared say nothing, lest Onabroszia Q'Aleth turn the knife on us.

It wasn't long after that that Mom's memory started to degrade. It happened rapidly. A whole year hadn't passed before she'd forgotten almost everything she'd ever known: her desire for vengeance, her business concerns, her baking recipes, her daughter's face, her own name.

All Onabroszia Q'Aleth could remember, and that only sporadically, were the angels. And how much—how very much—she loved them.

Fade to black.

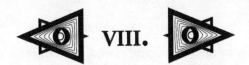

VIII.

AERIAL: QUICKSILVER CINEMA

D ad's movie palace—formerly the Gelthic Opera Hall—was three curvy tiers of compressed halite. A section of the first tier was topped with a glass dome—the roof of the lobby. The third and smallest tier, which sat well above the actual theatre, was my apartment, balcony and roof garden attached.

Opera had been around about a century before I was born, but it had never enjoyed more than a lukewarm reception in Gelethel. This was probably the reason the angels had conferred the building upon Dad. We Gelthic citizens had a sort of national aversion to singing. Maybe we thought that music always had to sound like angels, and, over the years, our operas began to reflect this. By the time Dad took over the GOH, operas had become three-hour shrieking events, full of discordant high-pitched whistles playing no melody whatever, huge glass objects shattering from great heights, flash explosions, stink bombs, and stroboscopes. Increasingly ambitious composers did their best to induce migraines in their audience, going their length to replicate the "music" of angelic voice raised in chorus.

Anyway, Gelethel decided it liked movies better.

On the inside, Quicksilver Cinema was what you might call shabby-deluxe. The lobby was lined with glass cases, only half of them sporting movie posters behind the panes. Dad had brought everything he had to Gelethel, but it wasn't much. Twenty-three feature-length films, four news reels, twelve cartoons, sixteen shorts, and his documentary—which he'd never shown anyone except family in private viewings. He'd owned just seven movie posters in all, and three of them weren't even for movies he'd brought with him. Over the years, he'd pasted drawings that the children of Gelethel (myself included) presented him based on movies he'd shown. The other vitrines he sometimes use as gallery space, to showcase any Gelthic artists who expressed interest.

But when Mom got sick, he didn't have the time or attention to sponsor artists. That's when he sold me the Quick.

Under my apathetic watch, the vitrines were getting dusty. So were the candy jars. And the chandeliers. I never vacuumed the deep red carpet. I often forgot to scoop out the old, stale popcorn from the bottom of the bins before Olthar topped it up with fluffy new stuff on his feast day.

I did still sweep the actual theatre after shows, and occasionally mopped up sticky spots, but my heart wasn't in it. I was afraid of washing the painted silk curtains that framed the big screen; they'd probably disintegrate into moths and despair. Or maybe I would.

Every time I passed under the grand marquee and through the murky double doors, it felt like cannonballing myself into quicksand. My lungs filled with suffocating mud. Darkness closed in on my skin, my eyes, my ears, deadening and pressurized. Even my clothes hung heavy and soggy on me in those moments, as if I wore the angel Rathanana's mantle of flayed flesh, no matter if I'd just come in from the hot dry afternoon air.

But we do what we have to do, we Gelthic citizens. No one could accuse us of shirking our duties. As we abided within the serac, so we obeyed angelic law, and angelic law stated that nobody and nothing must stop me from opening the Quick—for the glory of the Invisible Wonders who ruled Gelethel—tonight and *every* night.

Not even the body on my threshold.

T he boy Alizar Luzarius stirred. And moaned.
     Not dead, then.
"Hey," I said. "Hey, you. Kid. Get up."
Not astonishingly, Alizar Luzarius stayed where he was.
"What happened to him?" I asked the angel Alizar.
We proclaimed his official status "ghost" to the Heraldic Voice an hour ago. The Host released him from the saltcellars and left him for dead. He is neither citizen nor pilgrim. He has no rights in Gelethel. If he lives till next fifteenth day, he will be allowed to cross the bridge back into Cherubtown.

What he didn't say, what I already knew, was that most ghosts died in the gutter, left to desiccate for as long as the fortnight lasted, and then were taken out with the rest of the trash at the Feast of Whispers.

"But Alizar," I asked with trepidation, "why is a ghost—and a saint-killer—on *my* doorstep?"

The Celestial Cenoby was three districts over. The boy didn't look capable of dragging himself half that distance. Besides, how would he even know to come to the Quick—the one place he wasn't likely to be kicked into the curb, no questions asked? Even without a healthy Gelthic paranoia regarding the prevalence of angelic intervention in our daily lives (the Seventh Angel's in mine, in particular), this was too big a coincidence.

"*Alizar!*"

I started to turn, threatening to leave the boy where he lay, but the Seventh Angel stopped me with one of his patented see-sawing "Awwww, come on" sort of non-sounds, the angelic equivalent of twiddling his thumbs and toeing the dirt—which felt a bit like plate tectonics along one's cranial sutures.

You don't really want to leave him like this? Alizar asked gently/earthquake-ily. *Not your sister-saint's own brother?*

"The saint he intended to murder, you mean," I reminded him. "The one you had to resurrect. And speaking of which, I thought you'd still be recuperating your strength, not . . . meddling."

Actually, I feel fine! Alizar said brightly. *I just needed a nap.*

I bent my thoughts into a vulgar gesture and then, dismissing all eleven of his eyes to my back-most mind, took a step closer to the boy on the ground and lowered my voice still more

"Alizar?" I whispered. "Alizar Luzarius?" Then, after a moment, "Ghost?"

No answer. Kid was cooked. Literally—if he'd just dragged himself all the way here willy nilly on his hands and knees. I gingerly stepped over him, unlocked the Quick's doors, jogged over to the soda fountain, and filled a dusty pint glass with seltzer. After a moment, I scooped a few shovelfuls of nine-day-old popcorn into a bag, and brought both water and popcorn outside again. It wasn't Mom's benison cake—but then, what was?

I paused, put my hand over the popcorn, and said a prayer to the Seventh Angel. Mom's cake, after all, had only been the vehicle. And in Gelethel, anything could be a vehicle.

Outside, I stood and stared down at the boy, who still hadn't moved. He was like a cricket some kid had poured diatomite over. He was a murderer. A fanatic for the angels. Worse, a teenager. And now his sister was a saint of the Seventh Angel, which in Gelethel made her more *my* sister than his. And the Seventh Angel had given him into my care.

For what? For what?!?

No answer from the other Alizar, so I left the boy lying in front of my door. I also left the benzied-up popcorn and soda water. I had a business to run. I was showing a double feature in an hour and a half, and my projectors weren't going to load themselves.

An hour later, having done the least I could get away with in order to open the Quick tonight, I dragged myself back into the lobby and unlocked the doors for the evening show.

The boy was conscious again. Not only conscious, mobile. Vigorously. He was, in fact, polishing my glass doors with his sleeve, which he'd wet with the water left in his cup. My doors needed it. But maybe not like that.

He flinched when he saw me, his tar-colored eyes very wide. I nodded at him, handed him another pint of water, and a push broom from a closet just off the front doors.

"Drink that. Sweep that." I pointed to the vestibule. "And then I'll give you a hot dog for dinner."

He opened his mouth—probably to announce he was a breatharian, or solar scrupulist, or some other ascetic something—then shut it again, returned my curt nod, and took the broom.

I went back inside.

A few dozen patrons trickled in over the next twenty minutes. Everybody in Gelethel knew that the movies changed every fifteenth day, so I hadn't bothered to advertise my double feature. Everyone had already seen it before anyway. I'd only just changed the lettering (and a few of the lightbulbs) on the Quick's marquee this morning before petitions began. Till then, it was still advertising *Winds of Vicissitude* from last fortnight. We'd managed to fill half the house for that one—on the first day, at least. Our theatre sat eleven hundred at capacity. People still got excited about our "sav-nav" films, even after the whatever-hundredth time they played. Maybe because we lived in a desert, and movies about sentient psi-ships piloting themselves over impossible oceans on wild adventures seemed the furthest thing from reality, as unlikely as citadels on the moon.

When it was clear that no one else would be coming, I called the kid inside.

He crept into the lobby as if afraid his scab-cracked feet would disintegrate onto the carpet. But when the Quick's erstwhile splendor frayed his attention fourteen ways, he forgot all about his feet, and turned around and around, staring at everything with hungry eyes, ending by looking up at the domed ceiling, mouth agape. His arms hung at his sides, only his fingers pointing straight out. His eyes were lit by the thousand crystal pendants dangling from the chandelier.

"Is that," he gasped, "the angels?"

When I didn't answer, he dropped his head, smiled at me like a saint, and said shyly, "I always thought that was what the angels would look like. Beautiful. Like starlight and sunlight and snow. Just like that."

I shook my head, but he was no longer looking at me. The crystals had caught his eye again, and then the brass fixtures, the red carpet, the vitrines, the curving staircase to the mezzanine.

Instead of following him around the lobby like the owner of a naughty puppy, I walked behind the concessions counter and cleared my throat.

"Come here."

I used my Onabroszia From Before voice. The boy snapped to as if I were the High Commander of the Empyrean Academy.

"Hold out your hands. Here. Take these."

He obeyed, and I passed him a stack consisting of Dad's old uniform—a set of maroon livery with gold piping, tunic and trousers—a black and gold striped apron, and a black and gold cloth cap.

"Bathroom's that way," I said. "Wash up, put those on. They won't fit, but they're better than what you're wearing. Then come back here." I pointed to the precise spot where I was standing.

"Price directory is by the till—a list of things we accept as barter for concessions. No haggling. I'll start the first film at seven. You watch that clock," I indicated the handsome wind-up on the wall, "and every twelve minutes or so, I'll run a short promo while I change out the movie reels.

"Sometimes people will come to you for concessions. Barter away. Benzie slips only—they're kind of like our currency. Make sure they're notarized; it'll be an embossed sigil of a hawk's head for the angel Tanzanu. If we accepted straight trade, we'd be up to our hips in livestock and old boots.

"Now, we'll do a cartoon between features but skip the serial short. Before we run the cartoon, we'll have a longer intermission—about fifteen minutes. I'll come out and help during that one, but not during the promos. Once you've taken care of the line, wait a bit, then come on into the theatre—if you want."

I looked at him doubtfully. "You can stand at the back and watch the movies. Or . . . sit if there's a seat open."

There would be, I knew, and also that he might very well collapse if I kept him on his feet.

"But, mind you, leave a seat open between you and any paying customer. Oh, and," I added, "if I catch you with your hand in the till, you're done here. Apparently the angels have declared your status ghost, so I can't pay you with benzie slips even if I wanted you. If you're caught anywhere in Gelethel trying to trade them, it'll go bad for you. So. Anything you need, you come to me and we'll work it out. I'll see you don't starve, and have a place to sleep, and fulfill any reasonable request until we get the rest sorted."

I glared at him, because with every word, every order, the boy stood taller and brighter, looked more alive and eager and desperately attentive. The benison popcorn was still increasing its effect. Or maybe it was hope. Both.

But I remembered, every second we stood there, that he had walloped his sister and brought her over the serac to die. And she was my sister. Beloved of Nirwen. Beloved of Alizar. Our sign from beyond. And the only reason I'd be able to rescue my dying parents and take them to safety somewhere away from here.

"Any questions, ghost?"

"You can call me Alizar," said the boy breathlessly. He was not smiling. I didn't think he knew how. But his face was painful with gratitude.

"No," I said. "I really can't."

If crestfallen could have an identical twin, that twin's name would be Alizar Luzarius.

"No one in Gelethel calls their spawn after any of the fourteen," I heard myself explaining, and the comforting tone in my voice I neither recognized nor approved of. "It's bad luck. The angels might get jealous."

"Oh," said Luzarius, now even more crestfallen at this enlightenment. His own father, after all, had named him after an angel, and it was just possible that he was the unluckiest bastard on the planet. He shifted. He scratched behind his dirty ear. He yearned for something else, something beautiful, to look at in his shame. His gaze glazed over with chandelier crystals again, then focused on me, still glittering.

"What about Ali?" he asked. "Can you call me Ali? My sis—. . . I mean . . . some people call me Ali."

"Ali will do." I grasped him by the shoulder and spun him toward the bathroom. "If I can remember it. Now, go, ghost. I don't have all night."

When he was gone, I glanced up at the chandelier. The crystals were trembling slightly, stirred to rainbows by some invisible breeze. Some of the pendants opened and closed like shining white eyes. A few loosed a sharp, whistling chime, like wine glasses at a wedding toast.

"You and I," I told the angel Alizar, "are going to have a little chat. Later."

The chandelier sang back.

I was to meet him on the roof at midnight.

The double feature went over pretty well. There was even a smattering of applause at the end.

The first film I showed was *Godmother Lizard*, the epic tale of how a lowly orphan—former clerk of the Koss Var audiencia in Rok Moris—risked everything to join the oppressed Bird People in rebellion against the Empire of the Open Palm.

It was followed, of course, by *Life on the Sun*. Chronologically an immediate sequel, cinematically *Sun* had been made ten years later by an entirely different writer/director team. But it basically fell under the same broad histo-mythical war movie category, being a highly fictionalized account of the Old War: beginning with the first uprising in Rok Moris against Koss Var, and ending with the battle wherein Rok Moris—with the help of its neighboring nation Sanis Al—finally drove the occupying forces of Koss Var out of their cities and into the Bellisaar Waste.

Sun was made almost forty years ago, released to coincide with the actual, non-mythical Rok Moris celebrating its bicentennial: two hundred years of liberty from the Empire of the Open Palm. Halfway through that month-long celebration, the KVAF flew south and bombed the temples of Kantu and Ajdenia to smithereens. Thus, the New War began. And had been going ever since.

In recent years, a sort of smothered détente presided here in the Bellisaar Theatre. Koss Var had had global ambitions, too many of them, demoralizing and conquering the nations south of the Waste merely its opening gambit. But eventually, Koss Var had stretched itself too thin. Now the Empire of the Open Palm was crouched resentfully in the northlands, licking its wounds. I hoped it got sepsis from its own filthy tongue.

One long-running fantasy of mine, as I endlessly cranked the projector, was about a tiny studio apartment in Rok Moris where I'd someday live when I finally left Gelethel. I'd make bookshelves out of planks and cement blocks. I'd keep my clothes in baskets and sleep in my closet, cozy as a nest. I'd have a galley kitchen, a small refrigerator barely big enough for my daily needs. I'd paint the walls myself, all different colors.

I'd always wanted to move to Rok Moris. Dad thought I was crackers for that; he was all about Sanis Al. It was the largest nation south of the Waste, and, according to Dad, graceful in its plans, generous in its services, technologically and medically advanced, boasted incredible universities, and was just bursting over with the arts. Sanis Al was his favorite; I think he always regretted choosing Gelethel instead of heading further west.

But Rok Moris, smaller, scrappier, bombed-out, with her taped knuckles and broken nose and chipped teeth, was mine. She was *feisty*.

And soon, very soon, maybe I'd get a chance to see her: if the bad uncles could get this "Nea" of theirs word in time; if Nea could smuggle me and my parents out of Gelethel; if we could make it to Sanis Al alive—despite roads salted with mines, and Zilch roaming abroad, and all of us so naive about the world outside; if I could settle Dad and Mom somewhere, see them comfortable; if I could scrape up the wherewithal to do some traveling on my own—then, maybe, just maybe, that hole-in-the-wall studio apartment in scrappy Rok Moris would one day be mine.

That was a lot of "ifs."

D ad said that, outside Gelethel, in the days before talkies, movie palaces would hire full orchestras to play what he called "soundtracks." But like I might have mentioned, if you want to insult a Gelthic citizen, just call them a musician.

Music was angelic in nature. It meant possession, invasion, lack of consent. Silence was autonomy. We didn't mind title cards—they gave us structure: text, dialogue—because they were quiet, and because we could fill the flickering silences between them with our own stories.

Or we could, after the twentieth viewing, use that time of storied darkness to eat some concessions and take a very comfortable nap in the company of our friends.

That night, after the last of the moviegoers sauntered out, sleepy and replete from three hours of snacks and silver shadows, I met the kid—the ghost—Ali—in the lobby.

"That," he breathed, "that was, that was just . . ." He spread his trembling hands, held the silence of the movies between them.

"First film?" I remembered mine too. One of my earliest memories, from before I had speech.

"Well, no, I. . ." Ali frowned. "But it made me remember something. From maybe, when I was little? My sis—someone took me to see that one—the second movie you played—a long time ago. It was cold. The building had air conditioning, I think. Very dark, black, I couldn't see anything. And there was this monster, this huge bird, blotting out the sky."

He flung out his arms, demonstrating, the gawkiest young roc this desert had ever seen. "And she had a white jewel in her forehead that flashed with lighting, and horns, and when she screamed, there was thunder. And everywhere she flew, rain, rain beneath her wings. And people were dancing in the streets, because it had been so dry for so long. They played big drums to celebrate, but . . . it sounded too much like, like the explosions back home, and I began to cry and, and . . . and then someone took me outside again, and yelled at me for being a baby."

He was describing the final scene from *Life on the Sun*—but as a distant memory, not as the movie he'd just finished watching. I wondered if he'd fallen asleep and dreamed the memory as the reels played out.

"It does sound frightening," I said carefully, uncomfortably aware of how loud my voice had been earlier when I was issuing commands at him. It wasn't now.

Ali paused, looked down at his feet. Dad's were clown shoes on him. "Maybe she bought me an ice-cream later, though, to say sorry."

"That was . . . nice . . . of her."

Then, to my horror, the boy began to cry. Just folded up, completely and suddenly, and sobbed.

"Hey," I said. "Ghost. Ali. Stop. Stop it." I knelt beside him, put my hand on top of his head, a benison. "She's in a better place now. Your sister. You know that, right?"

It wasn't a lie. Just because I'd never wanted the silken sheets and salt-walled libraries of the Celestial Cenoby didn't mean it wasn't a million times better than Cherubtown. Or ten million times better than floating face-up in the Sacrificing Pool. But the kid was not to be comforted. A guilty conscience was like having a skull full of broken glass.

"Stay here," I muttered, and left him to sob himself out.

I had to find this boy a bed, and I didn't want him anywhere near my apartments tonight, where he might overhear me in conversation with my angel. The only place I could think of was the cry room. These days, I kept it locked, using it for storage and the Quick's lost and found. Back when Dad ran things, it had been fully equipped with everything a harassed parent needed when their kid had a meltdown in the middle of a movie. For my part, I thought parents could just quiet their babies in the lobby if they had to, or go to Nirwen's Hell, or home, or stay and make the other patrons suffer. I didn't care.

Betony might've appreciated a cry room though, back in the days she was taking young Ali to the movies. She must have wanted a place to escape, just for a moment, the terrible war outside. I wondered what it had cost her, those precious ninety minutes in the air-conditioned dark. I wondered what it had cost her to leave again, with an armful of screaming toddler in need of soothing and ice cream.

Inside the cry room was a padded bench. Not only that, but the lost and found box yielded a light jacket, a baby blanket still smelling softly of spoiled milk, and a broken parasol. The last I cast aside, then rolled up the jacket for a pillow, and laid the blanket on the bench.

There. The kennel was ready. Now to herd the puppy into it.

Ali didn't fight me; he was exhausted—despite the Seventh Angel's amped-up popcorn. I left a steel milkshake blender cup full of water, and a well-wrapped hot dog (fully blessed) nearby, in case Ali woke up hungry or thirsty in the night. I was no kind of saint for the Celestial Cenoby, but I was Alizar's own—and he fed all of Gelethel from his Bower and allowed no barter for it. And Madriq, my uncle's husband, had tried to do the same for the pilgrims and cherubs outside the serac. I could do no less for this ghost.

Then I was ready to go up to my roof garden and meet my angel. But it was not Alizar the Eleven-Eyed awaiting me there.

It was Betony.

IX.

JUMP-CUT TO THE SAINT

The Seventh Saint held my penknife loosely in her hand—for all the world as if her being discovered here by the Holy Host wouldn't get me buried up to my neck in salt, and her confined to the Celestial Cenoby. The other angels, already suspicious of Alizar, would question me closely as to my involvement with his saint. And his saint? She would be cloistered again, this time more thoroughly: bricked into her room, fed through a slot, and if they let her out at all, it would be on the tightest of leashes, under full guard.

But Betony looked rather cool about it all, perched on the edge of one my lounge chairs, waiting. Stripped of her outer robe, she was swaddled in a quilted silk vest the color of moonlight, its short slashed sleeves tied off above the elbows with silver cord, a white silk shirt billowing beneath that, with equally billowing trousers lashed to her legs below the knee. The braided platinum crown still haloed her brow, though her hair had been cut and styled since this morning. I could see all the old piercings in her ears, now ringed in silver hoops or filled in with jeweled studs. She was trimmed, plucked, coiffed, made up, salt-scrubbed-clean—like all saints, whom the laity only ever saw at a distance when they were paraded through Gelethel on extremely special occasions.

I stopped at the doorway, eyeing the penknife. "Returning my property?"

Betony slithered off my lounge chair and stood to face me. Losing some of her cool, she flipped my knife nervously in her hand. Nervously but, I noted, expertly.

"Not yet." Her voice was rougher and deeper than I remembered it. Perhaps a result of being drowned then resurrected. "Where is Alizar?"

"The angel?"

She snorted. "No, the treacherous little terg. Only got two eyes. Which I'm gonna carve out."

"Oh, you mean Ali," I said. "My new employee."

Betony looked at me with swift appraisal, surprise only sharpening her. "Yeah? You hire mugs on the regular this side of the ice?"

"I wouldn't say regular. Ali's a . . . mug . . . who merits special treatment. Brother of a saint and all." I pointed behind me. "He's downstairs. Probably still sniveling—if he didn't already cry himself to sleep."

Her gaze drifted to the distance beyond my shoulder, as if trying to pierce dark rooms, hallways, stairways, and several floors to see if her brother was weeping or soundly sleeping.

"Never stays down long," she murmured.

"Nightmares?"

Betony shook her head: not in denial, just returning to the room and the present. "Wets himself to this day. Used to call him Geyser."

"So much for my cry room," I replied. "But it's probably seen worse. Anyhow, I can show him where the cleaning supplies are in the morning."

She stepped forward, still gripping my knife. "He don't have till morning. Gonna eat his terg heart tonight. Swear to Nirwen, he'll wish those Zilch had got him that time."

I was a bit startled by her blasphemy—if it was that—remembering how her half-brother had accused her of following the false god of Cherubtown before the fourteen Invisible Wonders. Time enough to question her later, though. For now, I stepped through the doorway and to one side of it, gesturing for her to enter the building.

"These stairs lead down from the roof to the balcony just off my bedroom. Go through the apartment to the kitchen, where the door takes you to more stairs. Those'll get you to the mezzanine, whence you'll head down to the first floor lobby. Your brother's in a little room between two of the bathrooms. Door isn't locked."

Betony, glaring suspiciously, demanded, "Why you helpin' me?"

I grinned at her like a horned viper at a lizard hatchling, shoving my hands into the pockets of my coveralls.

"I am a citizen of Gelethel. We're very helpful. Or, at least," I added, "complicit."

She still didn't move.

"Go on," I urged her. "The angel Alizar gave you your life and my knife. He must've shown you how to sneak out of the Seventh Anchorhold, shepherded you all the way to the Quick. It can be no coincidence that he also led young Alizar Luzarius here earlier today. Practically gift-wrapped him for you, didn't he? How typical of angelic cruelty, to give the boy food and drink, a place to sleep, a promise of honest work, and then deliver upon him the wrath of a vengeful saint in the darkest hour of night. How utterly righteous it would be, to murder the boy who martyred you. Tomorrow, you can write an account of tonight's adventures, make it part of Gelthic canon; you'll be hailed as a hero. Go on. Do what you will. No one's stopping you. No one can. Saint Betony."

The tip of my penknife gleamed, and so—to my relief—did Betony's grin. "Big liar, ain't you?"

I relaxed as she went on in her voice like sharkskin, "Could be I might believe all that dungball 'bout any other angel. But Alizar Eleven-Eyes is a winsy little sugarbug. Wouldn't murder a kid—even a murderin' kid—even if you promised him big worship, blood-out, bone-in. And even if *he* would, birdie," she pointed my penknife at me, "I don't think *you'd* let him."

I didn't believe she was being truly aggressive towards me, but I considered removing the knife from her grasp nevertheless, just like Uncle Raz had taught me.

But maybe Betony would've fought me on instinct. Probably would've won too, despite lessons from both my bad and good uncles. So I just held out my hand instead, open-palmed. She relinquished the knife gracefully into it.

We stared at each other.

"You feedin' him?" she asked at last.

"Popcorn and hot dogs," I said, "along with Alizar's blessing—which is better than nut butter and enriched cream via feeding tube when it comes to malnutrition. The Seventh Angel is . . . is excellent at food."

"That's good." Betony sighed and sat again, heavily. Whereas before she had been spring-loaded and thorny, now she retracted, unwound, seemed to curl in. "Fucker's starved to death."

Dropping her head to her hands, she encountered the impediment of her crown, and cussed. I laughed softly; she reminded me of Mom. Or, not exactly Mom. Someone from my family. Some new family member I was just now meeting.

She glanced up, grinning wryly. "Still kinda wanna split his jug."

"Understandable."

"Why I came here."

"Not really, I think."

Taking off her crown, Betony tucked it into one of her inner jacket pockets and plunged her fingers into her thick black hair, rubbing her scalp vigorously. I flopped to the lounge chair next to hers.

"Nah. Not really," she confessed, bringing her legs up to hug her knees. "Actually—been dyin' to meet you. All day." That wry grin again. "I mean, dyin'-dyin'—not just lofty-talk. Saw you through that glass tub when they dunked me. Before that too, when you palmed me the shiv. Coulda sworn I met you before, or dreamed you . . ."

I tossed the penknife on the side table between us and stuck out my hand. "Name's Ish."

Immediately releasing her knees, Betony reached out and shook it. Her grip was firm and forthright, all callouses and confidence: the handshake of a woman out to prove at first touch that no scammer could scam her, no fraud defraud her, no marksman make her his mark. A lot of power in that grip. It seemed such a fragile defense against landmines and mortar shells, dysentery, starvation, angels.

"Just Ish?" she asked me. "That slang-bang for something? Your mama a fishmonger, you a squishy baby, what?"

I released myself of her thin and crushing fingers. "It's short for Ishtu Q'Aleth. I think 'Ishtu' means 'potato soup'—which my mother craved when she was pregnant with me. That was one of the stories I was told anyway, but there are hundreds just as plausible. My mother was, as you put it, a big liar. A storyteller."

"She dead?"

The words were curt and her expression didn't change, but Betony's clear eyes were flooded with sympathy, as if her own intense intimacy with death had opened her right up to the mourning of the world. Or maybe she'd always been like that, even before Gelethel.

"Not yet," I said, and received into my body her supernova of solace—just for a moment—before I had to turn the subject. "So that's me! Ish. Mistress of motion pictures and proprietor of Quicksilver Cinema: Gelethel's one and only movie palace now and forevermore."

Betony scrutinized me from under her eyebrows. They were formidable, thick and black. Already her skin was losing that iron oxide look, regaining a rosy-brown glow.

"Slurred a part, Q'Aleth," she said.

"Oh yeah?" I asked.

A frisson of excitement mingled with fear shot through me. Betony was giving me a look that I'd wished all my life to see on Onabroszia Q'Aleth's face.

"Yeah," she replied. "Slurred right over thirty-odd years you spent playin' crypto-saint to the Bug."

"Who?"

"Oh," she said, "uh, Alizar. The angel. Eleven-Eyes. I call him Bug, 'cause of all those little wings. He said it was okay. Wyrded me, callin' him by Alizar, you know?"

"I know," I said, remembering my earlier conversation with Alizar Luzarius, her brother. "So . . . have you two been chatting all day? Since . . . since this morning?"

Betony shrugged. "Gotta lotta bones to crunch, me and Bug. See, I blame him and Nirwen—if she's even real, which he says she is—for gettin' me killed. Now, Ali ain't clean of it by any means—but Zilch-balls, Q'Aleth!" she suddenly shouted, "Don't tell me that little hairshirt got all spunked up on his own, not when he could barely move for lack of vittles or cloud ale."

"Cloud ale?" I interrupted.

Betony gave me a look like I was half Ali's age and maybe just dumped in my pants. "You gethels'd call it water, I guess."

"Oh." I thought it best to stay quiet a moment. "And . . . have you decided to forgive him? Alizar, I mean. I mean," I amended, "the angel Alizar. Um . . . Bug."

She laughed suddenly. "Poor Bug! Keeps apologizin', makin' food appear, not to mention patchin' me up like a dollywyrd. I was so full of holes, Q'Aleth, even after he raised me—bruised like bad fruit. Hard to hate him when he's poppin' all my blisters like soap bubbles. Nothin' pangs now. Wasn't doin' so good, before."

Betony held out her arm to me, and I took it, tracing the branching red scorch mark from the angel Zerat's lightning strike. It took the shape of a tree incarnadined on the back of her hand, its roots disappearing under her sleeve.

"Only mark he didn't patch. No," she said, almost to herself, "not patch. What's his lofty-talk for it? Oh! 'Meliorate.' It was the only mark he didn't me-

liorate." Betony pronounced the word with evident satisfaction. "Said it was too risky—might draw attention from that staticky assface angel—you know, thunderbolt guy."

I wanted to kiss that bloody tree until it vanished from Betony's hand. But though we were sister saints, I did not yet know her well enough.

And besides, one could not lightly banish a birthmark of the angels.

"Zerat Like the Lightning," I supplied, even though she probably knew his name by now. "And, yes, meliorating this wound would be tricky."

"Why?" she challenged me.

Liberating her arm, I explained, "Zerat's scorch mark was a deliberate tagging of his territory. Removing it has repercussions. On the one hand, Zerat and the other three angels claimed you for their sacrifice. You were theirs; they drank your death. On the other hand, Alizar—Bug—in resurrecting you, sort of gave them a purgative. *You* get your life back; *they* get a hangover; and *he* gets a new saint—as well as his sign from beyond the serac that Nirwen stands ready to . . . to do whatever the two of them promised they'd do, a hundred years ago. But the mark remains."

Betony muttered something that sounded anatomically impossible—especially for angels, who didn't have anatomy.

"I know," I said. "It isn't fair. It's fabulous fucking Gelethel."

If I interpreted her next mutter correctly, Gelethel was doomed to get the same anatomical treatment as its angels. At length.

But presently, having cussed herself calm, Betony leaned back again in her lounge chair and asked, "Hey, Bug! Wanna weigh in? You been crypto this while. What're you and Faceless Nirwen hatchin' on the other side of the ice?"

We both awaited a reply from the Seventh Angel, who did not indulge us with one.

So by mutual consent, we waited some more.

When it became painfully clear to Alizar, eager eavesdropper that he was, that *we* wouldn't speak until *he* did, he deigned, reluctantly, to contribute to the conversation. Not in dialogue, no, but as a sort of shimmering, bewildering . . .

{shifty silence}

"Aaand . . . he's not saying," I interpreted out loud. "I swear, some days, you can't shut him up. Everything is bells and twinkling and chitinous wings. The rest of the time, it's like, if your name's not Nirwen, you don't even register with him."

"Maybe he's a shy bug," Betony mused. "Maybe Bug's got a secret so gloom-dig he can't trust us with it,"

"Is that true?" I asked Alizar.

{shiftier silence, slightly apologetic, a hint of maybe-yes?}

"Pike it," Betony shrugged. "Bug's keepin' his bones in the cup. As for me and my murder tree. . ." she rubbed the scorch mark with her fingertips. "Might be I get used to it. Or better," she brightened, "I'll find a tap-and-scratcher to ink me up a new tree right over it. Load it with fruits, flowers, climbin' ivy, like that dollopy great garden Bug keeps rappin' on about. Hey, Q'Aleth—you gethels have tattoo parlors in this city?"

"I . . . yes." I paused, imagining the ruckus in the streets if a saint from the Celestial Cenoby suddenly showed up one day in a tattoo parlor.

And then I began to smile.

"Why, yes," I repeated, "yes we do. Actually, there are several in this very district. There's one just down the street from the Quick. But," I warned, "you'll want to get it done in the OlDi if you're going to do it at all. Most of the real artists live here. Go anywhere else you'll end up with a hack job."

"Hack job," Betony cackled. "I get it." And she patted her emblazoned hand one last time, then pulled her sleeve down over the mark, done with it for the time being.

We relaxed into our respective lounge chairs, allowing a new but familiar silence to string itself between us, like an industrious spider dancing her trap between two trees. Gradually, but very naturally, we started breathing in sync. We realized it about the same time, caught each other's eye, and burst out laughing—in wonderment. But both of us kept quiet yet, hoping to spur the angel Alizar into volunteering actual speech.

He didn't, so I decided to help him along.

"I have to say, Saint Betony," I said with an idleness that Onabroszia's brothers would've recognized, "Alizar's been incredibly profligate with his healing powers today. I'm not talking about resurrection—which angels aren't supposed to be able to do at all. But fixing you up afterwards? That's a big no. Angels laid down the law a long time ago about healing the people of Gelethel. If the others found out that Alizar's broken that law, they'd tear him apart and scatter his pieces through the acres of Hell."

This—finally—provoked the Seventh Angel to reply: *We have special dispensations to heal our own saints!*

"As if you wouldn't do the same for, say, a ghost—via, say, a bucket of stale popcorn," I retorted. "It's not even your feast day! I never saw you act like this, out of turn—except that one time with Mom's benison cakes. How do you expect to get away with it?"

But it was Betony, not Alizar, who replied. "Already got away with it, didn't he? And that's just the start, right? Bug's showin' his grit."

"What grit?" I stretched my legs out and crossed them. "Alizar is not known for his . . . puissance, as it were."

"His what?" By this time, Betony was lying flat on her back, knees up, hands behind her head. I was on my side, facing her, chary of copying her gestures too closely even though my body kept wanting to imitate hers.

"His prodigious and unparalleled powers. No offense, Alizar," I put in quickly, "but everyone in Gelethel knows that among the angels, you're considered the weakest. They all bully you. They sing you down. They—"

Betony flung out a hand to stop me. "Wait up a cut. Bug's been showin' me how things work here. Gethel barter system and all. Your, whaddya call 'em . . . benzies?'""

"Benisons, yes," I said, "what about them?"

"So he told me how he, Alizar—" she shuddered, "*Bug*—doesn't let all you gethels chaffer your benzies for his stuff. Forbids it in his district. His, what do you call it, garden?"

"Bower."

"Told me he just gives it away."

"Yeah," I agreed, since I'd been saying the same thing anyway, "the angels call that weakness."

Betony scoffed. "That ain't weakness, Q'Aleth. Weakness is killin' someone for their bread. Strength is splittin' your last loaf with them. At least," she took a deep breath, "that's what I always told myself. And Bug's like that too. Big grit."

I stared at her, imagining her life thus far—twenty hard years of the New War, born into it—and said, "No wonder he loves you so."

Betony squirmed a little, and turned her face to the sky.

I thought of her brother, Alizar Luzarius, who had sacrificed Betony to the angels. I thought of the angels, accepting death as their due, sucking it up, whilst Alizar the Eleven-Eyed gave only life and kept giving it, without demanding anything in return. I reflected on how Alizar Luzarius would have been rewarded for his blood sacrifice: citizenship, a home, work, all the benisons of Gelethel that he could earn or trade. And then I recalled how Alizar the Eleven-Eyed was scoffed at, sung down, treated like a worm amongst dragons—when in fact all of Gelethel benefited from his blessings.

I thought it all through, for the first time, and assumptions that I'd held as gospel my whole life long began all at once to fracture.

"It's . . . true," I stumbled for the right words, "that angels amass power through . . . through the prayers of those who live in their districts. An influx of prayer—usually in response to a certain need, like electrical power or benison flakes or the silk thread that rains from the sky—results in a stronger angel. One who, ostensibly, is then better able to provide more and more lavishly to their worshippers. But—"

I scrubbed my face with both hands, my momentary glimpse of revelation eluding me. "But that's where Alizar cuts his own throat, right? Because he gives it all away before anyone can pray for it. No one even *lives* in his district, so how can he ever amass enough—"

"But everyone comes," Betony said, eager now that my attention was firmly fixed on something other than her. "Don't they? Not just on his feast day. Bug made his place a public park, right? Gethels go there just to nest out."

I blew out my breath. "Yes, right, but—"

And then I stopped, remembering my birthday last year. That look—the same look—on everybody's faces, from newborn babies to the bent and old, as Alizar the Eleven-Eyed gave and gave and gave unto them, until even *they* couldn't ignore the miracle of plenty anymore.

"Alizar," I asked the air suspiciously, willing him to manifest, "How many prayers of thanks do you get each Feast of Bloom?"

{*sheepish shrug*}

"Yes, but the number?"

The Seventh Angel intoned a number that I knew was roughly the same size as the entire population of Gelethel.

"Every *fortnight?*"

Every day, Alizar said, so quietly that he might have been Murra Who Whispers. I could barely hear him, and only if I listened all the way down to my feet.

I sprang to my feet. "*What?* Why, why didn't you tell me before? Why didn't I *know?*"

And what was wrong with me that I had never observed, never comprehended, the vastness of my own angel's strength? No other angel received that kind of prayer. They boasted of their numbers to each other in the Celestial Corridor every petition day, and mocked the Seventh Angel for keeping silent, singing that he had so few worshippers that he was ashamed to sing the number out. I'd listened so long to that rotten bilge that I absorbed it. I'd *believed* it.

It had to be secret, Ish. Until now.

Alizar's love and concern rushed over me like a beeswax breeze, and he manifested before me, his flickering gold-green figure bursting with flowers and tendrils, a thousand wings fluttering frantically, eleven jewel-like eyes beseeching me.

Do not be angry, my saint. I have longed to tell you your whole life long. But none of it mattered till this morning. Whatever powers I have amassed these years, I could not have used them to act. Not without Nirwen's signal. Not without my second saint, who has come among us now.

"But," I implored him, "what about the other angels? Aren't they more powerful yet? They've been taking sacrifices all these years while you've been abstaining. They're all . . . *engorged* with force and potency."

Betony broke in, in a very dry—almost Dad-like—way, "Tell me somethin', Q'Aleth. Does watchin' a bunch of invisible jackasses get high on dead refugees make you *more* or *less* likely to praise their names? Not talkin' 'bout out loud now. Talkin' 'bout in here," she tapped her breast bone, "in your hiddenmost."

"In my hiddenmost . . ."

Betony waited, listening. The breeze that was Alizar bent around me, listening.

"In my hiddenmost," I repeated, "I drowned all the angels of Gelethel in their Sacrificing Pool long ago. And then I burned the Celestial Corridor to the ground."

I smiled weakly, attenuated by my own audacity, and explained, "In my hiddenmost, salt can burn."

"Anything can burn," Betony said, "that hurt gets hot enough. I seen that." Lowering her voice—as if *that* would prevent Alizar from overhearing, she asked, "Does *he* know? How you feel about the other angels? Think he's scared you'll turn on him?"

She hadn't yet learned how to sense the Seventh Angel lurking in her own skin, her mind, in the words of her mouth. But she would, and swiftly.

"No," I said. "There's no turning. I'm his saint. Alizar knows my thoughts, even when I don't always know his. Whenever I speak, he's there in my mouth, sitting alongside the words." I added gently, "Your mouth too. Can't you hear him singing? It's clear to me," I said, "whenever you speak."

Betony gave another of those head shakes that didn't mean denial. We both, I thought, were operating on information overload and in dire need of refreshment, stat.

"Saint Betony," I asked, "do you want a beer?"

"Oh *fuck* yeah!" Betony blurted, and we both laughed.

And then we both got really drunk.

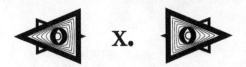

X.

ALIZAR'S DIEGESIS

"**S**o, Saint Betony . . ."

Betony lolled her head to the side. She was lying on her stomach on the lounge chair, the angel Alizar sort of hovering over her shoulders, giving her a massage with a few of his trumpet-like blossoms and golden tendrils and wing tips. Being massaged by flowers may not seem substantial, but I knew from experience that the Seventh Angel's attentions could penetrate the knottiest of muscle clusters.

"Mmnphlmph?"

I took a long slow sip of benison wine—or, as the laity liked to call it, beer. "Tell me, are the angels shitting themselves in the Celestial Cenoby over your resurrection?"

She flashed her half-lidded raptor eyes in my direction before lifting her head from her arms and nose-diving into her own tankard.

"Yup."

"And what does that look like?" I pressed.

Betony emerged, bearded with foam. "Looks like a buncha saints in fleeky trim rammin' up my door and demandin' answers for their angels." She snorted. "Mostly stuff like, what's he doin' with godhead powers anyway? And who the filthy fuck are you, cherub, that he pulled you from the deadwater?"

I was impressed. "Cloistered saints say fuck?"

"Not in so many words. But . . ." She took another drink. "Yup."

"Saints can be such little shits," I said.

Betony flopped over onto her back to stare up at the hovering wing-and-eyeball figure that was the angel Alizar.

"I'm *your* shit, bug," she told him solemnly. "And so is Q'Aleth."

The best two shits an angel without an anus could wish for, replied the Seventh Angel fondly.

I laughed so hard I almost rolled off my lounge chair. But as the empty cup I was holding had spontaneously begun to refill itself, I very carefully up sat straighter and held on to it with two hands. And I was amply rewarded for my care.

Alizar was all about the benison wine tonight. The drunker Betony and I got, the more gleeful he became, and his glee bubbled over as beer. Beer foamed and fountained out of our cups. It was perfect, crisp and tangy; it practically purred. Drinking it was like a drinking a cat made out of amber lager, and molten caramel, and ripe red cherries. I licked my lips.

"It ain't. . ." Betony hesitated, turning to me. "It ain't *bad*. Where I'm at. My new stake. Saints aside, it's thump swaggy. I don't mean to bellywhistle about it. I'm clean. New kit." She gestured to her clothes. "Servants. Food. The *food*, Q'Aleth—forget beer, I could get drunk on food alone. The Cleno . . . the Cnoby . . . that place they put me—"

"The Celestial Cenoby," I said grandly, not at all over-pronouncing all of my vowels and consonants. At all.

"Yeah, that." Her eyes became huge, luminous with wonder and not a little fear. "I'd live there forever, sure. Gladly. Part of me didn't even wanna leave to-night. Not even to meet *you*, bug-kin." She smiled at me, tiredly, as if knowing I would understand. "Know the last time I got a bed to myself—one I didn't pay ass over teeth for?"

I shook my head.

"Me neither. Part of me . . ."

Betony broke off, swinging her legs over the side of the lounge chair and heaving herself to a sitting position. Her shoulders crunched forward desolately.

I panged for her, then realized, a bit startled, that I'd sat up at the exact same time she had, in a mirror position.

"Part of me wants to thank that little hairshirt for whackin' my cap and drag-gin' me here to die. Because—without Ali and his sweetsmoke dream of," she slid a sideways glance at me, "fabulous fuckin' Gelethel, I . . ."

I leaned forward, breaking our symmetry to take her hands in mine and squeeze them. "Without him, you wouldn't be here."

"Yeah. That's it. Why?" Betony whispered. "Why am I here, Q'Aleth? Why me? Anybody else, they get drowned in a bathtub, they stay drowned. Why'd *I* get the regalia?"

The answer seemed obvious. "Nirwen chose you, didn't she? You're her holy sign. You're who Alizar's been waiting . . ."

"I'm no kind of holy. I'm not even religious!" Betony protested. "And if I were, I wouldn't worship *Nirwen*. Back in Cherubtown, there was all this talk about her bein' some kind of new god among us. You heard Ali mention it, yeah?"

I nodded.

"Well, I never saw a rag of her," Betony confessed. "Me and Scratch—my friend, my only friend: war vet, got her face burnt off in the fire bombin' of Sarro Ranch—we used to go 'round the tents, sort of takin' the pulse of Cherubtown, you know. Place is a powder keg. We were out last night, and . . . was it last night?"

She looked around, confused, as if freshly astonished that only a day had passed since then. I waited, wondering if this was what eternity felt like, and Ali-zar hovered nearer, patting Betony's head gently with various of his protrusions until she regained her bearings and continued:

"Last night, we came upon a tent meetin' of the new religious. Watched all the preachers preachin' and the converts praisin' Nirwen's name, and I turned to Scratch and said, 'Got no use for a god who walks around this trash-fire without takin' the trouble to fix it. I'd sooner worship the God-King of Koss Var, may his dick fall off.' And Scratch said, 'Hells, Bet, it's enough to make a gal a goddamn atheist.' And then we left early. That's all I can remember about . . . about last night. Guess Ali saw me leavin' that tent and took me for some angel-defilin' heathen. Then cracked me."

Realizing she was crying, a slow-seeping weep, Betony rolled contemptuous eyes at herself. I stroked her hands with my thumbs until she sniffed it all back in and wiped her face on her shoulder.

"Anyway. That's why I'm here. Didn't do nothin' special but raise a brother ready to murder me or martyr himself at a pin's pull. The other saints—they're right to look at me like I'm a sand-leech suckin' the dark side of their thongs. I don't belong here. But Q'Aleth," Betony leaned in, all the way in, "I'm *stayin'*. I'll eat their food, wear their clothes, stare at them fourteen fuckin' angels till somebody decides to toss my dead body off that ice wall. I ain't goin' back."

A faint thrum in the air, a coruscating disquiet, alerted me that Alizar was overwrought. All glee gone, all beer evaporated by his anger and anxiety, he shimmered and buzzed, busy with emotion.

He wanted to reassure her—badly. But he was stymied by his own secrets, by his and Nirwen's longstanding ambitions, by all the ineffable things mere mortals could not comprehend. So he said and did nothing to comfort Betony in her doubt.

Well, sometimes Alizar just needed to prodded a bit. Like the rest of us. I understood exactly what he needed, and what Betony needed, so I reflected the question back at her, and brought all my saintliness to bear, going down on my knees before her and squeezing her hands even more tightly.

"Why you?" I asked, my upturned gaze on her and her alone. "Why did Alizar the Eleven-Eyed, Seventh Angel of Gelethel, reeve of Bower whose feast is Bloom, defender of the Diamond of Bellisaar, choose *you*, Saint Betony? Answer me that."

She began to shake her head in that way she had, so I asked again—demanded—urgently, "*Why* did Alizar choose *you?*"

"Because I am not of Gelethel," Betony answered promptly—and I saw, shimmering on her lips, the fluttering of tiny, crystal-chip wings.

I glanced around, and smiled in satisfaction. Alizar had vanished from sight, only to have re-manifested in the mouth of his newest saint.

Betony had clapped a hand over her lips, but that didn't stop him. Alizar kept on talking through her mouth. He even used one of her hands to pluck the other from her lips and hold it in her lap, giving it the occasional avuncular pat.

"Because I've walked this world with my own two feet," Betony went on, faster and faster, speaking with the fervent tenderness her angel held for her. "Because I've seen the worst and broken for the better. Because I'm fast. And sly. And can lie quicker than thought. Because I'm good with a penknife. And . . . he, he likes my hair? Because I kept my shitty baby brother alive even when it cost me everything. Because I can infiltrate the . . .”

She stopped short, shook her head once, sharply, then blurted, “Because I can infiltrate the Celestial Cenoby!”

I sat back on my heels—my knees creaking—and loosened my grip on her hands. She did not pull away and I did not let go.

“And why,” I lowered my voice, “does the angel Alizar want you to do that?”

This time, I felt the fluttering of wings on my own lips, a flickering glow in my throat, and we both answered together:

“Because he is making his bid for godhead of Gelethel.”

“The angels are falling,” we said.

“They began to die the moment they ate their god,” we said.

“Alizar and the angel Nirwen knew this,” Alizar-in-Betony told us. “They could *see* it. They knew that if they did not act, this would be their fate too. That is why Nirwen the Artificer left Gelethel. A hundred years ago, she walked out into the world to learn how to become a god. Alizar promised to stay and do the same—for the good of all Gelethel. For the good of the angels, who are rotting like cankerous fruit on a once-thriving tree.”

“The angel Nirwen knew that once she left, she could never come back,” Alizar-in-me finished. “Once apostate, citizen no more. Once apostate, outsider. And no outsider whom the angels consider foe may breach the Gelthic serac. That is hieratic law; it is canon; it is written in the Hagiological Archives in the saints’ own hands. It was the last law of god before She was eaten, and it holds true for humans and angels alike. Nirwen left Gelethel. Her face was erased from all our graven images, her title revoked, her district left barren. She has no way back *in*.”

Betony and I gaped at each other, listening to ourselves speak with Alizar’s voice, our breath beery and warm. Strong golden fumes that I associated with the Seventh Angel—honey, pollen, warm berries, savory herbs, cherry blossoms— seeped from our skin, our mouths, mingling to form a mirage between our bodies: shimmering and vaporous, a gleaming bubble shaped of wings and eyes and twinkling lights.

“And *that* is why,” Betony and I said together, staring at our own faces reflecting off Alizar’s rainbow-slicked bubble, “there are *two.* ”

The Seventh Angel fell silent.

“Two?” Betony repeated, frowning at me. “Two what?”

“Two of *us*,” I whispered.

The soap bubble between us popped. Alizar vanished from the space he had occupied—to go back to wherever it was the angels went when they were not with us. Our cups disappeared too, and with them, the last of our drunkenness. We stared at each other with clear eyes, shivering in the aftershock of angelic possession.

A second later, Betony and I leapt from our chairs.

We stood back to back, facing out, listening. The hairs on our arms were bristlingly erect. Betony was about one hand-crank away from popping right out of her skin—and I'm sure I was as well.

"Somebody's coming," we both announced.

I shook my head to sever the connection between us, but it was like trying to disengage from a cat's cradle made of molasses. Betony thunked the heel of her left hand against her temple and looked at me ruefully.

"Can you climb?" I asked.

"Got up here, didn't I?" Betony returned.

"Then go over the balustrade, now—take the drain pipe to the streets."

She didn't argue. It wasn't like she couldn't listen in on my life whenever she wanted, or that I couldn't do the same with her. We were sitting inside each other's skulls now, right where Alizar the Eleven-Eyed had put us—two halves of the same saint.

"Be safe, my sister," I murmured to her. "Be swift and sly!"

Betony's grin was like a searchlight illuminating my worry as she slipped over the balcony. She nodded at my little penknife, now folded neatly on the side table.

"Blessed Q'Aleth," she whispered back, "thanks for the loan."

"Anytime, Saint Betony."

I pressed myself against the roof garden's railing, keeping my back to the door that led down to my bedroom balcony, masking her descent. Betony had only lowered herself a few feet when she beamed up at me.

"Always wanted a sister."

My heart belled within me; I became a cathedral. "Me too."

And then she was gone.

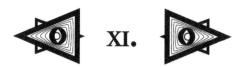

XI.

REVERSE ANGLE:

WUKI AND THE RAZMAN

"Hello, my uncles," I called out cheerily, my back still turned to the door. "Did you come singly or in battalions?"

"Little of this, little of that," replied Uncle Wuki's adenoidal tenor from just inside the stairwell. Uncle Wuki may have been puffy and brown and big like a bear, but he always sounded like a seven year old with a bad head cold.

Rotating until my back was to the railing, my elbows resting on the white brick, I nodded a casual greeting at him where he loomed in the doorway. His face was in shadow, but I could still feel him grinning at me—a dopey grin, big and childlike.

"Hey, Ishi," he said. "Zulli told us your latest plans. We came over to chat about 'em. He'd've come too, but . . ." He shrugged his broad shoulders.

"That's right," I recalled, "Uncle Zulli had to work tonight."

"Got called up for rampart watch. Drew the graveyard shift." Wuki giggled. "Poor slob. Always has the worst luck."

I nodded with mock sympathy. "Which you, his brothers, all exploit without ruth or mercy."

"Well, of course," Wuki replied guilelessly. "Zulli *is* the youngest."

Standing on tiptoe, I glanced to the silent shadow waiting behind him on the stairs. Not a bear—a colossus. The last time I'd seen him, three angels were riding him all the way to Betony's death. I softened my voice of its teasing edge.

"Hey, Razman. You had quite the morning at the Celestial Corridor. You sound?"

"For now."

Uncle Raz sounded unutterably tired. He gave Wuki a light push, then stepped out after him onto my roof garden. As he passed under the threshold, he reached up and removed a small box from a hidden cache in the lintel.

The box was stuffed with cigarettes. Raz took two, passed one to Wuki, and put the box away, sliding the door of the cache closed so that it was imperceptible to a casual observer, or good uncle.

Both of them simultaneously lit their cigarettes and held them loosely in their hands, letting the phantasmal plumes drift up into darkness.

None of Onabroszia Q'Aleth's brothers actually smoked; that had been Mom's sole domain. Cigarettes were her favorite vice long before she'd discovered a secondary use for them: tricking the angels in regards to her younger brothers.

Wheresoever one of the warriors of their Holy Host abided, there too might the angels dwell. In this sense, Hosts were barely more than receptacles to be engorged or engulfed by angelic attentions depending on a given angel's needs and moods.

And angels were capricious, self-concerned, often inattentive.

Fortnights could go by of my bad uncles going to work, dressing up in their Holy Host armor, and performing perfectly normal patrols. And then, without warning, I'd suddenly have to endure weeks, months—half a year!—of never seeing my bad uncles at all. The shadow side of Q'Aleth Hauling Industries would grind to a stop; nothing would come in through the serac or go out over it clandestinely, and certain citizens of Gelethel who had grown accustomed to their choice of non-angelic perks would get very uppity indeed. But I didn't care about that: I cared that Zulli, Eril, Wuki, and the Razman were vanished from my reach, and that the good uncles had taken their place: Host Irazhul, Host Hosseril, Host Wurrakai, and—of course—Host Razoleth, Captain of the Hundred-Stair Tier.

My good uncles were good uncles whenever they were wholly or in part possessed of angels. A trained eye could tell them apart at a glance—for all that they shared bodies with my bad uncles. But my good uncles were unmistakable—with their patient, gleaming faces, their bland, blancmange goodness, and their tendency, at any time, to manifest angelic attributes: a bloat of pearl, a hawk's head bursting from knuckles or neck, a child's tiny hands jutting from their shoulders like small, helpless horns.

It was easiest, of course, to recognize a good uncle when he was barbed with attributes. But the cigarettes were still my first and best clue.

They were Mom's idea. Warriors of the Holy Host did not pollute their bodies with depressants, stimulants, or anything considered a traditional offering to the gods who reigned outside the Gelthic serac. As tobacco fell under two of these three prohibitions, my bad uncles lit cigarettes as a signal to me that all was clear, that their bodies were their own. Of course, they couldn't keep cigarettes on their persons, lest the good uncles suspect rebellion, but we had hidey-holes all over the Quick, and at Mom and Dad's house too.

Raz came to stand with me at the railing. "Zulli says you want out. With Broszia and Jen LuPyn."

He always called Dad by his full name whenever he was himself—to make up, I thought, for all the times when he was a good uncle and never referred to Dad by name at all.

"I'm taking them both to Sanis Al," I announced. "There's no medical infrastructure here, Razman, and they're deteriorating fast. Dad came home after his doc's appointment this morning and he was . . . he just . . ."

I shook my head, remembering how Dad had seemed like a degraded film of himself, leached of color, just shades of quiet gray, flickering out.

Clearing my throat, I continued, "So . . . Uncle Zulli says he'll put the word out, and this Nea woman—your possum?—will make contact with us when she's back in the area?"

Wuki laughed. "Well, aren't you in luck, Ishi? Zulls dropped by the barracks to pass on what you told him—just as we were on our way to Broszia's to tell him *our* news. Because *we'd* got word just this afternoon that Nea's in Cherubtown. Some pilgrim passed on her message. Said she'd paid him to stick it under the brick."

He was talking about a certain loose brick near the gigantic pink salt-crystal doors of the Celestial Corridor—right beneath the faceless image of the Fifteenth Angel, Nirwen. It was how Mom used to slip word to her brothers, and vise versa, when they were working the tier. She'd piously attend every petition day, and piously walk away with a full roster of who among the Hosts was patrolling the ramparts the fortnight upcoming, how they would be distributed amongst the watchtowers, and when the changes of the guard were scheduled.

"Said she'd paid him in *benzies*," Uncle Wuki was going on. "No lie—he had slips for meat, cloth, water, ever a hotel voucher so he wouldn't have to squat in Hell. Notarized and everything. Wonder if Broszia smuggled a wad of 'em out, years ago. Ha! She'd've done it too, mark me!"

I though it much more likely that Faceless Nirwen herself was forging benzies in Cherubtown, sending them over the serac with the pilgrims every fifteenth day to help them survive their new home. In exchange for certain . . . favors, of course. Alizar might know what kind; I did not.

I made a little "go on" noise in my throat.

Wuki slung an arm around my shoulder. "We let the pilgrim keep his benzies in the end—after we threatened to take them away, of course. We'd caught him in the act, see—brick in hand. The Razman arrested him for vandalization. Man almost pissed himself. We squeezed him, got the buzz, then told him we'd let him go with a warning—this time. No more pulling bricks up in the Angelic City! Welcome to Gelethel, Citizen! May the fourteen bless and keep—"

Raz held up a hand, cutting Wuki off from his flow of speech like a guillotine. He turned to me.

"The note contained a password," he said, handing me a folded slip of paper. "Memorize it. Destroy it. This is how it works: yours is the call, Nea's the response. If she does not respond, retreat immediately. Tomorrow midnight is rendezvous. You know the place."

He could only mean one thing—the place that neither he nor the other uncles had ever mentioned again after taking me there in secret all those years ago. Nirwen's Hell.

That broken stair, fenced off from the streets. The key I'd never used. The crack in the serac.

"Ishtu," the Razman said clearly. I looked up at him. "Do you understand me? Do you have the *coordinates*?"

And he cleared his throat twice.

I nodded, understanding his meaning. The Razman did not lightly clear his throat—and never twice without good reason.

"I have the *coordinates*," I repeated, emphasizing the word as he did.

His shoulders relaxed—well, for the Razman, which wasn't much.

I glanced briefly at the paper in my hand. Four words. I committed them to memory, then took Uncle Raz's proffered cigarette and used the lit end to burn the paper with the password, before handing the cigarette back to him.

Wuki, who was taking surreptitious whiffs of his own cigarette, didn't see Raz's hand flash out and lightly slap the back of his ear. Resigned, he tapped a few ashes onto my railing, leaving little piles like bird droppings.

I enjoyed seeing them there. Small offerings to the new godhead. Both of them, maybe.

"Any news from the Celestial Corridor?" I asked. "Since this morning, I mean."

I wanted to know if word of Betony's extra-cenobian activities had gotten out. Saints rarely left their anchorholds, and never unaccompanied.

A sensation like a pair of ears pricking up on the insides of my ears startled me. Just my thinking about her had bound up our thoughts again. Betony wasn't anywhere near—she was, in fact, more than halfway across the city by now, loping boldly through the streets of Gelethel, made invisible by her own Invisible Wonder. My hands folded into fists, my thumbs stiffened and shot out: her way of giving me a thumbs up. Good thing my hands were in my pockets.

I flicked her off, then had to smother her smirk on my mouth.

"News?" Wuki replied. "Sure there is." He had started drawing random shapes in his ash piles. "The whole Celestial Corridor's been dancing the light shambolic all afternoon and evening. But that only happened *after* things got weird on the ramparts."

"The ramparts?" I stood up straighter. "Where? When?"

"Hirrahune's district. Southwest of Tyr Valeeki," said Raz. "Just after lunch."

"That's. . . QHI's dumpsite, isn't it?" Not just the dumpsite, either.

Wuki rubbed his chin, where there was always a shadow of a beard even if he'd just shaved five minutes ago, and intoned what I had feared: "There's unrest in Cherubtown."

I swallowed, nodding, trying to looking nothing more than interested. Ten percent curiosity, ninety percent pure Gelthic insouciance.

But . . . whatever was happening in Cherubtown, it of course had something to do with Nirwen and Alizar—therefore with Betony and me—and if so, why hadn't Alizar told us about it?

Here was a wonderful opportunity for the Seventh Angel to jump in, irritatingly meek and deflective, and say something like, *Well, Ishtu, there's been rather a lot happening at once . . .*

But he didn't.

So I laughed a little, and asked Wuki, who was dying to tell me, "Unrest? What kind? I didn't think Cherubtown had the calories for unrest."

Then again, I thought at Betony, *if they're all like you, I'm surprised the cherubs haven't laid siege to the serac.*

We yakked about it, Scratch and me, Betony replied. *But we didn't have the ladders and stuff. You need a lotta ladder to climb that ice.*

She was approaching the walls of the Celestial Cenoby now, contemplating her ascent. She thought briefly about asking Alizar for a boost, then decided it was more fun to jam her bare hands and feet into the nooks and crannies available to her.

Oh, to be nineteen again.

I withdrew my attention, not wanting to distract her, and focused on the Razman. He was standing to my right as Wuki was to my left, his hands folded together on the railing—all but the fore- and middle finger of his right hand, which pinched the steadily shrinking stub of cigarette between them.

"The cherubs were throwing a festival," he murmured, so softly it might have been a prayer. "There were fireworks. The angels were . . . distressed."

"I'll say!" Wuki put in. "I was on duty at the ramparts when it went down. We of course sent word about the festival—the long way, with a runner," he explained, "since none of us were activated as Hosts at the time. Apparently, when our message reached them at the Celestial Corridor, the angels starting issuing so many contradictory commands that the Heraldic Voice fainted dead away from interpretive stress. They took to their bed with a migraine—haven't emerged since. So, lacking an instrument, the angels themselves joined us at the western serac."

"What, all of them?" I asked. "Joined . . . all of you . . . Hosts?"

Wuki nodded, momentarily grim. I reached out, grasped his hand, and silently squeezed it. If he'd been angel-ridden today, it meant he was probably feeling just as sore and used as Raz. No wonder he was chattering so: Wuki always got maniacally cheerful whenever he was in pain. Uncle Eril sunk into melancholy; Zulli tended towards dramatics, overeating, and long naps; Raz got quieter; but Wuki. . .

He was practically dancing. He spread his arms. Smoke swirled around him.

"Now you might ask, Ishi: where did those cherubs get all their fireworks from? They don't have bread, water, or medicine, but they're setting off sparklers like it's the Feast of Zerat? Big ones too—thunderbirds, flowering trees, mushroom clouds, the lot. And the answer is: who knows? Miracles, they say! The new god of Cherubtown provides, they say! And not just *fireworks*, Ishi, but a *feast*! Dancing! Bonfires! *Bonfires burning on bare sand*—no fuel to feed them. The multitudes sated. Wine and cake. And even the scrappiest beggar wore ribbons in their hair!"

"What . . ." I cleared my throat, "what was the occasion for the festival? Did the angels ever find out?"

"Our newest saint," Raz said.

This, of course, was no surprise. But it still felt like surprise. Right in the center of my chest. I couldn't speak, only stare.

Wuki gesticulated another wild rollercoaster of smoke. "Think about it, Ishi! First: Saint Betony isn't a Gelthic citizen but a *pilgrim*. From Cherubtown! Second: she's no child, like all our saints when first they're plucked. She's a woman grown. Third: she was *dead*—a sacrifice. And she was brought back to life!"

"*Reputedly* dead," Raz corrected him.

I frowned at the warning note in his voice, watched his hands open and close, clench into fists. Betony had died by those hands, which the angel Thathia had turned into eels. He knew it, and he knew that I had witnessed it. The murder of a saint.

His gaze met mine but cut away too quickly. Wuki waved off his brother's qualifier.

"The *cherubs* think she was dead," he said. "And if dead, then raised. They're taking her resurrection as a sign that the sacrifices must stop. No more pilgrims, they say. No more petitions! No more angel fodder!"

"So, you see, Ishtu," Raz concluded, in his deep way, "the angels have some reason to be upset."

"And did they . . . how did the angels respond?"

Wuki couldn't contain himself; he practically howled, "We trumpeted their answer down from the ramparts! We shouted it from the skies! We spoke in angel voices and were heard!" He was shuddering, his lips trembling, his brown face gray behind his stubble, but at the last his outburst seemed to calm him.

Steadying himself with a deep breath, he said, "The cherubs want an end to petitions, sacrifices? Very well, the angels proclaimed: the serac is henceforth closed; the bridge shall ne'er again be lowered on fifteenth day. More than this: the angels shall double—nay, treble—their patrols on the ramparts; they themselves shall ride the Holy Host day and night, making certain no illicit commerce, communication, or pilgrims can creep through. Gelethel is at capacity; it has all it wants of the outside world. Let Cherubtown choke on itself."

I exchanged a glance with the Razman. We were both thinking the same thing: that Nea's timing that afternoon was extraordinary. Providential, even.

I crossed my arms over my chest to keep my hard-beating heart trapped in its ribcage. "It sounds like . . . if I don't get Mom and Dad out tomorrow, I might not get another chance."

"Well, yeah, that's why we. . ." But there Wuki stopped. He began to cough uncomfortably, as if the smoke were irritating his throat. I reached out to pat his back, but he jerked away from contact, still coughing, holding out his hands to stop me from coming to his aid again. The cigarette fell from his fingers as he made the sign of the angels: 1 and 4.

Raz moved forward quickly, taking Wuki by the shoulders and whispering something in his ear. Wuki's eyes slowly unfocused as Raz's words did their work.

I couldn't catch the actual phrase this time; I was too busy kicking Wuki's cigarette through the open space between two white railings. It fell like a tiny meteorite, blinking out somewhere between the roof and the sidewalk three floors down. Raz's cigarette followed it, sailing over the ledge. We both hastily brushed piles of ash off the railing before turning around. Wuki's coughing had stopped.

I knelt immediately, and kissed my uncle's instep. "Hail to thee, Host Wurrakai. And to the angel enthroned in thy flesh."

The angel was Childlike Hirrahune. I knew it by the baby-faced tumescence bursting from the side of my uncle's neck.

"Niece," said Host Wurrakai mellifluously, helping me to my feet. His high, nasal voice was now sweet and flutelike, pure as a boy soprano singing anthems in the acoustic perfection of the Celestial Corridor. "We have been listening on the night winds for talk of saints and angels. Now. What is being spoken of here tonight, O Brother?"

He peered, bright-eyed, white-eyed, from me to the Razman. No sign of Wuki remained; he was completely subsumed.

Raz stepped up to my side. "We came to take record from a witness," he reported. His voice and face were relaxed, but I felt the bunched muscles of his arm tense against my shoulder.

"This afternoon, while at prayer," he continued, "I recalled that our niece Ishtu was present this morning for the events in the Celestial Corridor. Wishing to secure her statement, but reluctant to interfere with her cinematic vocation, I betook myself and you, Host Wurrakai—then, unactivated—to the Quick once her work was done. The sworn oath of a Q'Aleth—one who is among the most respected business owners in Olthar's district—will go far in quelling the rumors of the new saint's supposed demise and resurrection. It would not do, after all, to have our citizens believe that gossip from Cherubtown."

Childlike Hirrahune's round-eyed likeness blinked agitatedly at me from Host Wurrakai's throat.

I blinked back. The protuberance was about as like the actual angel Hirrahune as a plaster cast was of its model. But it was an extension of the Ninth Angel nevertheless, a sign of her engaged presence, and she would think it odd if I did not stare. Any devout citizen so privileged as to witness even the smallest physical manifestation of an Invisible Wonder would drink in the sight and dash off to tell all their friends at first opportunity.

"Ah!" Host Wurrakai nodded, the attribute in his throat bobbling like a bit of stuck pudding. "An inspired notion, Host Razoleth! Should diamonds and pearls fall from her lips, Domenna Q'Aleth could not speak better value than to swear by what she saw today."

Raz glanced at me, adjuring me with his eyes to agree with his every word. "Our niece was closer to today's events than we two are standing now, Host Wurrakai. She saw the young saint sink into the Sacrificing Pool. She saw her sink to the bottom of it—*but not drown.*"

I had seen it all.

How Betony fought. How she struggled and reached and cried out to her angel. How Host Razoleth held her down with his arms that were eels. How the light in her luminous eyes blew out.

I thought about screaming.

If I opened my mouth right now, I'd have no choice but to scream.

But behind my eyelids, eleven other eyes opened inwardly. A soft feeling petaled apart in my skull, as if I stood in the very heart of Bower, in Alizar's Moon Garden, with jessamine and albatross and angel trumpets loosening all around me, and nectar-sipping night moths fluttering to feed in the falling night.

This deception can harm neither me nor your sister-saint. No lie they make you tell can abrogate the miracle. No lie can undo the resurrection. Nothing can.

Betony chimed in: *And it's totally fine by me if you lie to these fuckin' angels, Q'Aleth. Might even be fun.*

And so, with their permission and blessing, I perjured myself in a voice that was strong and clear.

"True, the girl did lose consciousness briefly." I cupped my hands together at my breastbone in prayer. "But all saints must undergo some trial before canonization; that is tradition. We are gentler, of course, with our own Gelthic children, but surely this feral cherub required some sterner induction? After all, what kind of saint runs *away* from the Sacrificing Pool? Rather than staging such a coy escape, should she not have rather dove into it willingly?"

I shrugged. "But what can you expect from a saint of the Seventh Angel—known to be the weakest, the meekest, the most disregarded of the Invisible Wonders who rule Gelethel? Surely, Host Wurrakai, such matters are beyond my mortal ken."

Host Wurrakai leaned closer. "And you will swear by this, Domenna Q'Aleth? You will swear that the saint was not dead when the Seventh Angel plucked her from the water?"

"It was clear to me," I continued importantly, "that when the saint was lifted and levitated before us all, she needed only a minor resuscitation, not a resurrection. Any child would know the difference."

Host Wurrakai paused, gazing down at me with radiant fondness. "You are a good child, Niece."

I did not remind him that I was but two years shy of forty. My uncles were all in their sixties—still buoyant and youthful, in the prime of their manhood. The warriors of the Holy Host, so often infused with angelic essence, enjoyed what used to be the privilege of all Gelthic citizens before the New War: a decelerated aging process, immunity to disease, the assurance of attaining supercentenarian status, and an easy death at the end of it all, dignity intact.

Mom, who was only seven years Uncle Raz's senior, looked like she could be his grandmother. In appearance, I looked to be around Uncle Zulli's age, or slightly younger, more like a little sister than a niece. Alizar, upon my request, was allowing me to age naturally. But he balked at the idea of me dying any time before I reached twice eleven times seven—which was old even for a Gelthic citizen. I was working on bringing him around, not keen on spending the last fifty years of my life being mistaken for a cricket.

"Thank you, Host Wurrakai." I beamed at him but leaned ever so slightly against Uncle Raz for support.

Against my shoulder, his s arm grew tense, then tenser.

No—not just tenser. Bulkier. Stonier. His muscles were growing muscles. His skin began to crackle and shine.

So.

Zerat Like The Lightning, again.

Of all the damned angels, the bully Zerat! That strutting, arrogant scourge of helical discharge. No other angel disdained Alizar the Eleven-Eyed the way Zerat Like the Lightning did. The other self-styled "strongest" angels followed his voltaic lead—even Rathanana. Even Thathia.

But there was no time to glare at my uncle's charioteer like he was some kind of coiled viper of ionized plasma I'd happily crush under my heel—no time to speak the word Uncle Raz had given me earlier—for I was dropping to my knees and kissing my uncle's instep.

My voice caught in my throat when I tried to greet him. My poor Raz! To have been possessed of multiple angels already that day—and then to be seized *again*, in the black hours before dawn, before he'd had a chance to sleep! Brutal.

"Hail to thee, Host Razoleth."

The eldest and most honored of my good uncles, Captain of the Hundred-Stair Tier, placed a beneficent hand upon my head.

"Niece. Greetings. We thank you for bearing witness to the truth about this morning's proceedings. Now we must ask you once again to knock upon the door of your heart, and speak the truth that opens there."

I stared at him with all the vacuous adoration I could summon. Host Razoleth's pupils were spirals, sparking with Zerat's high-current charge.

"Now, Niece. Were the circumstances surrounding Saint Betony's resurrection *all* that we three—" he gestured to himself and Host Wurrakai—"were speaking of here tonight? For as I cast my mind back, aided by the Invisible Wonder within me, I recollect—as but through a lens dimly—some talk of . . . Cherubtown. And . . . gods."

Fulgurating fuckhead.

I bowed my head and said, "Yes, Host Razoleth, you recall correctly," all the while furiously thinking how to thread the word that the Razman had given me earlier into the conversation—and do it in such a way that neither my good uncles nor their angelic parasites would suspect it.

Host Razoleth expression was one of such supreme complacence that I bitterly wished to rip the angels from his flesh. To let my uncle slumber peacefully—just once!—without fear of occupation or metamorphosis.

"Remind me. What was it?" His eyes searched mine, white and radiant as Host Wurrakai's, but shot through with veins of snapping blue. "Something about . . . *tomorrow*."

There were always a few moments of muzzy shift as a bad uncle became a good uncle. A few moments to redirect the mind of a good uncle down a path predetermined by the bad one—a path that avoided certain pitfalls of memory that would expose a good uncle to his own worse nature.

Raz had used Wuki's shift to whisper the keyword at him that diverted his attention down their agreed-upon narrative: the one wherein they two had come to question me about Saint Betony's resurrection—and *not* to give me Nea's co-ordinates for tomorrow.

But though Uncle Raz had given me his own keyword earlier, and made sure I'd understood it, I hadn't been quick enough to speak it. The trap that Raz had set for himself during his daily "prayers," deep meditations in which he con-structed mazes for his better nature to wander around in, remained unsprung.

Gooseflesh ripped through my skin, but I kept my face upturned and eager. "We were speaking of the serac," I prompted him helpfully. "You told me of the unexpected festival in Cherubtown. Some nonsense about the saint who didn't drown. And you mentioned . . . *coordinates?*"

"Coordinates?"

Wrong. Something was wrong. His was an awful excitement: the Eighth Angel's electric elation.

"I'm sorry," I corrected myself quickly, "I misspoke. You were explaining to me how perhaps the festival was an early sign of Cherubtown's intention to coordin*ate* an attack against the serac."

Whenever a given keyword did not work, or had the opposite-than-intended effect of clarifying instead of obscuring near memories, a close variation to the keyword might re-ignite the misdirection. My mind skidded forward giddily, ready to split "coordinates" into its parts and roots, explore its conjugations, perhaps spout a slant rhyme . . .

But the infinitive form, in this case, tripped the trap.

The excitement—and the dangerous blue spark—faded from Host Razo-leth's eyes. His shoulders slumped silkily—the only time I ever saw Uncle Raz slump like that was when he wasn't Uncle Raz. I could see his memories begin to re-write themselves, keeping the angel Zerat busy examining and analyzing them.

And then Host Razoleth did that thing I hated. He cupped my face in his massive hands. I tried not to flinch from the static shock. Failed. He smiled.

"Do not trouble yourself about the serac, Niece—neither in the west where the cherubs plot in its shadow, nor wheresoever else within our ice-blue diamond of Bellisaar. Tomorrow, perhaps the day after, we the Holy Host shall ourselves be coordinating a strike on Cherubtown. The Invisible Wonders desire that we rain down fire and salt from atop the ramparts. We are to punish those ungrateful trash-eaters and false pilgrims—and show the agitators among them the extent of our power."

Everything in me shuddered except for my body. I turned my head and kissed one of his rough palms, receiving another bright shock for my devotion.

"Obliterate them, Host Razoleth," I said softly, "for the glory of Gelethel."

"We shall do so. And so, to that end, I must ask you, Niece, to stay away from the serac for the time being." His voice very deep, very terrible and tender. "We suspect the cherubs have allied themselves to a new benefactor—whom they call god—one who has been building secret siege engines for them, seducing them with provisions and weapons, inciting them with promises of paradise to swarm the Angelic City. Perhaps they think to slaughter us. Perhaps they merely mean to scatter throughout the fourteen districts and hide in the crevices like the cockroaches they are. We will not allow neither, nor any other act against Gelethel.

"For the next fortnight at least," he continued, "the ramparts and watchtowers of the Gelthic serac shall be safe for no one but the Holy Host—as we smash the infernal engines of Cherubtown, and their Dogmanic architects, to dust."

"The ramparts and watchtowers hold no interest for me, Uncle," I promised faithfully— lying like a feral cherub, like my beloved angel, like I'd been lying every day of my life for thirty years. "I will turn my face from the outward ice and direct my contemplations inward to the Celestial Corridor: as all the devout of Gelethel should do."

Host Wurrakai laughed. Not his own silly little giggle, but sharper, higher, a child's piccolo yip, a sound that might have been a cry of pleasure or pain.

"Very wise, Niece!" he praised me. "For we shall smite their verminous heads with fire, and salt the bloody furrows of their wounds, and cover their tents in smoke and sorrow."

"Yes, Brother," agreed Host Razoleth. "We will show them the righteousness of the fourteen."

At last my good uncle released my face from his shocking hands.

"Farewell, Niece. Give my fond regards to your mother my sister, and my enduring hopes for her health. And," he grimaced slightly, "greetings to the immigrant her husband."

"Yes, Host Razoleth, I'll see them tomorrow."

He stopped, cocking his head slightly, as if "tomorrow" had sent him reaching for another memory. Tomorrow had brought him here in the first place. *Tomorrow.* The possum Nea, her password, my apostasy. *Tomorrow*, a bell ringing faint but sure. *Tomorrow*, midnight, in the very heart of Hell. . .

But the Razman's keyword had done its dirty work. The more Host Razoleth sought for that elusive *tomorrow*, the more it retreated. Other memories crowded in to sew dust and discord across the pathways to revelation, and instead of lingering to pursue them further, Host Razoleth just nodded at me again, advising me once more to:

"Stay away from the serac."

Then he walked across the roof to the stairwell that would lead him down to my bedroom balcony, Host Wurrakai in his wake.

They passed under my lintel, one after the other, but they never looked up at the cache of cigarettes hidden there.

XII.

LONG SHOT: THE SERAC

On our maps, Gelethel was the center of the world, a white diamond enclosed by a blue diamond labeled the Gelthic serac. This was the wall enclosing the Angelic City on all sides, two hundred meters high at the jagged tips of its peaks, fifty meters thick at the base, all of it pure compressed ice.

From its foundation, Gelethel, rhombic in shape, was fifteen kilometers long on each of its sides, with a total area of two hundred twenty five square kilometers. Most citizens assumed it was the shape that earned Gelethel its nickname, the "Diamond of Bellisaar," but the saints, who studied such things, all knew that the origins went back much further than that. In ancient times, what later became our city was an inland lake fed by the Anisaaht River: Lake Amoula was its name, sometimes called, for its glimmering, the Diamond of Bellisaar.

Angelic revelations came piecemeal to the saints, but over the centuries, a picture of Gelethel's pre-history began to emerge. The saints recorded their findings slowly and painstakingly in the Hagiological Archives, but only a privileged few of the laity were ever permitted to study there, and so the story was not well known.

I knew it, of course, because Alizar the Eleven-Eyed had told me.

Lake Amoula had once been a shining, shallow, saltwater plane. Only brine shrimp and brine flies lived there; most living things found the waters undrinkable and for this reason, humans never lingered long in its vicinity. And because gods did not go where their worshippers could not, it was a godless lake, content to be so.

But millennia of quiet contentment was shattered when one day, from out of the burning depths of Bellisaar, a god did indeed flee to Lake Amoula, pursued by an army of demons.

With her fifteen angelic companions she ran, from who knew what war-ravaged realm beyond Bellisaar, from what army of conquerors or converters who upended her reign, from which sorcerer-priests of stronger gods who had unleashed the demon horrors seeking to devour her. Harried through the wastes, the god bolted at all speed, until she came to the edge of that deathly, glittering basin, Lake Amoula.

And, springing from the salt-rock shores, the god dove into the very heart of the shallows.

She made such a splash that the lake waters flew up in all directions, like a startled flock of birds, like a rainstorm in reverse.

Then, from the epicenter of her own quake, the god reached out in all directions and wrenched the waters rising around all her—billions of tons of brine, a vasty saline ring of waves—into the shape of her desire: a rhombus.

Which is to say, a diamond.

A diamond, after all, could pierce in four directions at once—whichever way her her foes came at her. Within the four walls of her diamond, she and her fifteen angels would be safe.

And so, into this shape the god froze the waves of Lake Amoula, enormous fortifications of compacted ice. These she set as palisades of protection for herself and her angels. As long as her precious ones remained within the prescribed boundaries—her unmeltable, unevaporable, impenetrable ice walls, smooth as volcanic glass, hard as adamant—then, the god promised, the walls would protect them. Nothing that crawled, flew, limped, or slithered out of the desert could harm them. Not even demons. Not even other gods.

With the very last of her strength, she pulled a palace out of the drying salt pan that had been the floor of Lake Amoula. (Salt, the philosophers say, is a substance especially dear to the gods, being as it was, anathema to demons.) The god's new palace was dazzlingly white, a kilometer-long corridor crowned in colossal domes, its walls and halls of compressed halite, its honeycombed chambers shaped like shells of all different varieties, and all its doorways arches.

But now the god had spent herself, spilling out almost unto self-emptying. She was everywhere in the pristine ice of the serac, and she was at its salt-white center too, and being everywhere, was also diminished.

More tired than any god had ever been tired, she beseeched her angels to make a home of her palace.

It was theirs now, she said, to guard and be guarded by while she rested.

So declaring, she stretched out on an altar of sparkling rock salt: not white like the rest of the palace, but glowing like the gigantic doors of the main corridor, pink and damp as the flesh of the inner lip, and finally—*finally!*—on this crystal bed she slept.

And while she slept in tender form, the angels descended upon her, and devoured her.

Thus perished the god Gelethel.

And thus was born Gelethel, the Angelic City.

*A*ngels, I'd told Alizar when I was eight and freshly appalled to discover I was his saint, *have always been assholes.*

You have no idea, said Alizar, and proceeded to tell me how the fourteen angels had, of their own free will, accidentally cracked the serac.

A hundred years ago, right after the Fifteenth Angel Nirwen forsook Gelethel, the remaining angels attempted to shrink the city.

They hated that its dimensions honored a false number. The angels were not fifteen anymore, but *fourteen.* Should not, therefore, the area of the Angelic City be squeezed down to a more divine one hundred ninety six square kilometers?

Yes! And could not this feat be accomplished by reducing the serac by a mere kilometer on each of its sides? Yes again!

However, not being gods—no matter how they styled themselves—the angels could not quite manage it. A great trembling rolled throughout the Angelic City. Fissures opened in the salt-paved streets. Worst of all, a crack began to appear almost at once in the immaculate blue ice—starting just beneath Tyr Hozriss, the south-point watchtower.

The angels left off their attempts. The city remained—in shape and in scope—as the god had originally intended it: except godless, and a little worse for wear. The serac still stood strong, but part of the southern wall had been compromised. This was an easy deficiency to conceal from the people of Gelethel, as it had occurred in the district of Hell, formally Lab, abandoned when Nirwen took her Lesser Servants and departed the city.

The broken stair that no longer led up to Tyr Hozriss was caged off and locked away. Long-term squatting in the fifteenth district was strongly discouraged. Nothing more was officially said about the crack in the serac—or the dark drop into an icy death awaiting anyone curious or stupid enough to trespass into this most disgraced and forbidden corner of Gelethel.

I didn't know how the Razman had come into possession of the key he gave me. I'd bet Mom had passed it along to him when she started getting sick. Or he'd taken it from her, recognizing when she was no longer able to do so.

I *did* know that throughout her shadowy career, Onabroszia Q'Aleth had, in fact, smuggled dozens of apostates—former citizens of Gelethel—*out* of Gelethel. I didn't know the number exactly, but from what little Uncle Zulli had told me, Mom's association with the possum Nea had begun years ago.

Mom would get word—she always got word—of someone wanting out of the Angelic City. She would arrange the exodus—clandestinely—with Nea, and then anonymously alert the apostate to time, place, and password. She would make sure the gate was unlocked when they arrived. The apostate would rendezvous as directed, never knowing it was Doma Q'Aleth who so gleefully guided their path astray from the angels.

And then Nea would just . . . spirit them away. I didn't know *how* she did it.

The problem was the ice. The Gelthic serac was divine in nature; it resisted hook or axe, crampon or screw. Even the angels could not build *into* it, just atop it—the watchtowers, and the ramparts that ran between them—from bricks of compressed salt and starch. Even these chemically anathema structures could not melt the unmeltable ice.

My bad uncles told me that from time to time others—apostates and pilgrims alike—had tried to navigate the Hellhole, either from above or beneath, in order to sneak out of or into Gelethel. But they did not have Onabroszia Q'Aleth's blessing—or her resources—and because of their folly, the bottom of the Hellhole was littered with corpses, preserved forever on ice.

Nea was the lynchpin of this mystery. Her, and only her. No one knew how she navigated the ice. Anyone she'd ever taken outside the serac never returned to say, and my bad uncles kept themselves as ignorant as possible. They'd contented themselves partaking of all the smaller smuggling operations, usually using pilgrims as mules, or the Q'Aleth Hauling Industries dump-lifts. Certainly none of them had ever been present at an exodus. They would never risk exposing their sister's greatest secret to the good uncles—and to the angels who rode them.

Not even Alizar, it seemed, knew how an exodus was accomplished. Or if he did, he never told me.

So when I arrived in Hell on the appointed midnight, with my wheelchair-bound Mom and my heart-weakened Dad, I had no idea how the possum Nea was going to tote them up the better part of six hundred forty-nine uncertain steps, down a hundred-meter crevice of impenetrable ice, through the glacial labyrinth of the southern wall, and into the Bellisaar Waste.

Dad was done asking questions, and Mom—as usual—said nothing as we disgorged ourselves from the covered chariot that I had pedaled for the three of us and all our luggage across the several districts composing southeastern Gelethel.

Despite my doubts, despite the stubborn silence my angel had maintained on this matter, assuring me merely that all was arranged to his satisfaction, I approached the gate caging off the southern stair and called out the password Uncle Raz had given me.

"*Mother Scratch.*"

Beyond the cage, from the deep shadow of the stair came the response, so low it was practically seismic.

"*Father Bloom.*"

And Nea rose out of the darkness, where she had been crouched and waiting.

The moment I saw her, rising up and up, all my doubts and questions and theories crashed away in a fresh avalanche of panic.

Nea was Zilch.

"**Y**ou're Zilch!"

Dad, who'd been trundling Mom's wheelchair close behind, lurched into me. I was carrying everything. All he had to do was push Mom. Even that, I feared, was taking its toll on his blue-beating heart. But he'd assured me that he'd be peppy as prickly pear jelly: so long as we didn't go too fast.

Fast be damned, I thought. The shock of seeing the giantess before us just might kill him.

Then Mom yelled gleefully, "Angel-sucker! Fucking Zilch! Baby-eater!"

For a woman who, for the past twelve hours, had been doing the best imitation of moribund I'd seen outside a morgue, Mom's decibels were alarming. Her voice echoed off ice and darkness, salt and stone. All of abandoned Hell seemed to hear her.

I cringed beneath the weight of our packs.

Nea looked down—way, way down—through the cage that separated us. "We don't use Waste-cant for ourselves," she said thoughtfully. Her voice was quiet, very deep, like the Razman's—only with more vitality, a green vein of youth and hope.

"'Zilch' is, anyway, inaccurate," she went on. "Not that a Gelthic shut-in could conceive the difference at first glance, in the dark, with no other frame of reference."

Nea moved out of the shadows, coming closer to us, until her hands wrapped the bars of the cage. Her hugeness loomed. She clinked softly; from the intricate full-body harness she wore swung all kinds of straps, clips, grips, and other tools I didn't know the names for. They glinted in the darkness, but they did not look like any kind of metal I could name. Several coils of slim, black rope dangled from loops on her belt. Her hair was covered with a dark helmet, her hands with dark gloves.

"I see we have offended you," said Dad with weary sweetness.

"Please—I'm sorry," I said quickly before he could apologize further. "I was very rude."

I moved forward and jammed the key Uncle Raz had given me into the padlock securing the cage. It popped reluctantly, but as the gate swung open, the tension in the air seemed to slacken.

"You *were* rude," Nea agreed dispassionately. "But then, you have lived in Gelethel all your life. The technical term for what we are," she added, standing aside to let us in, "is 'nephilim.'"

Dad turned to her, startled. "Half-angel?"

"After all," Nea said, seeming surprised at his surprise, "it was the angel Nirwen who created us. We are half her own material, half the material of mortals."

"Where do the Zilch come in?" I couldn't help asking, which set Mom off on another happy howling diatribe against the Zilch.

But Nea's voice, so deep and cool, so instantly soothing, hushed Mom's tirade like a lullaby. "'Zilch' is a philosophy of despair resulting from an occasional mutation in our code. It is not a species. Many genetic outliers live quite happily amongst the nephilim majority, and do not subscribe to the Zilch credo. Take me, for example. I will not live a tenth as long as most of my community. I may not live out the year. But I do not, I assure you, go around barbecuing babies."

I saw the outline of her hand move to her shoulder and tap something there. Suddenly, a small light flicked on, radiating from a tiny button on her lapel. The intense pinprick bathed her face in eerie blue twilight, like the heart of a star or a glacier.

That button was S'Alian spell-tech; it often featured in cloak-and-dagger type movies set in Sanis Al. But no film I'd ever seen told the story of what Nirwen the Forsaker, former angel of Gelethel, had got up to once she'd left the serac behind her. No news reels spoke of Nirwen's get, the nephilim—her greatest experiment. All I'd ever heard—mostly from traumatized former pilgrims—centered around the Zilch: gangs of bandit giants terrorizing the wasteland interior on their viper bikes.

I never knew they were *Nirwen's*.

Nea went to one knee in front of Mom. Kneeling, she was almost three meters tall. That was bigger than Uncle Razoleth, even when swollen by angels. Her large, long face glowing like the aegis of an ancient knight's shield, she engulfed Mom's hand in hers.

"Onabroszia Q'Aleth. Greetings. Do you remember me? We met when I was a child. Nirwen sent me to test the serac, looking for cracks. You were doing the same on your side, searching for a better way to move contraband through the ice. You'd had some success—but you hadn't yet managed to smuggle *people*. But you'd discovered the Hellhole, and sent secret messages out into Cherubtown letting it be known you wanted a way to climb the ice, to explore a possible egress. Night after night you came to this place, waiting for answer. And one night, I climbed out of the dark, and we spoke."

Mom stared, her brow wrinkled.

"Nea," she said.

"Nea, yes." The giantess smiled soothingly. "We are old friends. Now," she became suddenly very businesslike, "I need your attention, everyone. This is the plan."

Her gaze encompassed mine, making sure I was with her, was hearing and comprehending everything. I nodded. She did the same with Dad, who also nodded. She turned back to Mom, radiating complete attention.

Mom watched her like a moth watches a lamp, transfixed.

"Doma Q'Aleth," she began, "I am going to lift you from your chair and strap you into a cradle harness, so that I may carry you up the steps with my hands free. It will perhaps make you feel like a child, but there is no other way."

Nea unsnapped a small bag clipped to her belt and unfolded it into what looked like a piece of re-enforced canvas dangling a snake pit's worth of straps. Squatting before Mom's chair, she began working the canvas under and around Mom, weaving her limbs into the chaos of straps, adjusting here, tightening there, making certain her neck was supported by the canvas, until she was bundled like a babe.

When she was finished, she said simply, "Now I will lift you and secure your harness to mine."

Mom sat, placid, as Nea hoisted her up, clipped the cradle to a loop on her chest, and adjusted a few more straps so that she could carry Mom freely and easily. Nea was not even breathless. She appeared even more enormous now, with Mom, doll-like, cradled against her. Mom stared up into her face, suddenly bewildered.

"We will climb the steps together, you and I," Nea told her. "You will be very safe, Doma, I assure you. For all my size, I walk quite lightly. When we reach the Hellhole, we will take a few minutes as I harness up Domi LuPyn."

She gestured to Dad, her hand just brushing his elbow. "When he is secure, I will lower him down first to the bottom of the serac. Then it will be your turn again, Doma. Your husband will have your tag line. He will use it to help you slide over the edge, and also keep you well away from the cliff wall. I hope it will be as pleasant as being rocked to sleep. When you reach the bottom, your husband will unclip you from the rope, and tie the second rope—the tag-line—to the first, so I can gather both ropes back up. Then I will harness your daughter, Domenna Q'Aleth, and lower her down. All of this will take less than twenty minutes. After that," she concluded, breaking eye contact with Mom to check in with Dad and me again, "I myself will rappel down the serac using the naked anchors I have left in the ice. I will hitch Doma Q'Aleth onto my back again, and we will all depart the serac the way I came in, beneath the ice—and leave Gelethel to its angels."

She said the last with a great tranquility, but I had the sense that beneath that calm, she hated this place. She couldn't wait to crawl under the labyrinthine serac and escape out into the open blast of Bellisaar again, trailing three refugees like trophies from an enemy encampment she had successfully infiltrated.

Which, I suppose, was exactly what she would be doing.

I closed my mouth, which had fallen open. My heart was skidding triple-time. "How did you get in at all?"

"I told you. I climbed," Nea replied, surprised. She drew from her belt two axes. The heads were long, thin, curved, serrated like the skulls of pterodactyls. I also saw that what I'd at first mistaken for a strange metal was not metal at all. It was ice.

"You *climbed?*

"Yes. You know—kick, pick-pick?" she explained, as though it were a rhyme every child should already know.

My throat swelled with disbelief. I forced a breath to hush my voice, which otherwise would have bellowed out. "But how did you leave your anchors in the serac? No tool can pierce the ice!"

Nea beamed with pleasure. Now it was she who looked like a child. A very large, very intimidating child.

"A hundred years ago," she began, almost in a sing-song, "when fourteen angry angels cracked the serac, shards of ice splintered off, and fell to the far side of the southern point. Nirwen the Artificer was lurking outside the city, in the long shadow of Tyr Hozriss—at last beyond the range of the other angels' senses. She gathered up the pieces of ice and took them with her into the Waste. From them, she made these. And these. And those."

Sliding the ice axes back into her holsters, she pointed to an array of what looked like long, hollow screws of various sizes dangling from her belt: all translucent as crystal, all a deep vivid blue.

"Ice screws," she explained. "They make holes in the ice—I thread my ropes through to make my anchors."

She directed my attention to the toes of her leather boots, from which two profound spikes of blue stuck out like teeth. She opened her mouth to expound further, but Dad beat her to it.

"Crampons!"

He'd been watching everything keenly; he'd never been one to interrupt or speak out of turn. But now he glanced at me. "Do you see, Ishi?"

"Nothing pierces ice from the Gelthic serac," I said slowly, "except ice from the Gelthic serac."

Nea slid a hand over her belt lovingly. "Nirwen made these tools long ago. When I discovered that I. . . that I had the mutation, rare for my people, I went to her. I confessed I felt the despair that might drive me to the Zilch. She told me I needed to give my life meaning, and to that end lent me these tools to wield."

Turning abruptly, she pointed to Mom's wheelchair. "Does that fold up?"

"Uh, no," I said, trying to keep apace.

"We must leave it then. You will have to get her another in Sanis Al. The chairs are all spell-tech there. They fold up on command, go where you direct them, are durable but paper-light. Some of them fly. S'Alians have such sorcerers, such physicians! Perhaps trying to make up for years of child sacrifice."

She dismissed my startled expression and the wheelchair together. "Don't worry; they don't do that anymore. Unlike the angels of Gelethel, the Fas of Sanis Al evolved. But until we get you settled in that city for good, never fear: I will carry her. And so, are you ready, Doma Q'Aleth?"

Mom mumbled something from her canvas cradle. Her expression was quickly melting from bewildered to tearful.

Dad reached up and patted her ankle. "It's all right, Moon Princess. It's a throne worthy of you."

Mom smiled tremulously, and Nea smiled down at Dad with approval. Without another word, she began hiking up the white brick steps to Tyr Hozriss.

Dad and I stared after her a few moments, stricken with something like awe. He cleared his throat, but I was the one who spoke first.

"You go on. I'll stow the chair and chariot and be right up."

Dad nodded and started slowly up after Nea and Mom. I first wheeled Mom's chair, then pedaled the chariot, into the deep shadow beneath the southern stair. When they were hidden, I hurried to re-lock the gate that caged off the steps to Tyr Hozriss. These tasks done, I ran up after Dad. It did not take me long to reach his side.

When I offered him my arm to lean on, he looked at me, raising his wire-bush eyebrows. "I shall have to buy a special cane in Sanis Al, I see." He sighed, his stooped shoulders heaving with exaggerated melancholy. "So that my daughter may walk unburdened again."

"Yeah, what a burden," I teased him. "It's not like I owe you my existence, my cultural education, and whatever vestige of a moral compass that remains to me or anything."

I could barely see his face, now that Nea's blue button was far ahead of us and masked by her bulk. But Dad's smirk had always had an unmistakable air.

"A moral compass can get you lost in Gelethel," he noted.

"It's getting us out now."

Well, a moral compass, a new saint, and the help of a rebel angel.

Dad shrugged a little. "We're not out yet, Ishtu."

When I'd come to Dad this afternoon and told him my plan—basically, that I was taking him and Mom to Sanis Al tonight, willingly or *un*—he hadn't argued. He'd looked, briefly, astonished.

After that, a fierce focus possessed him. Dad turned from me and right away began packing, slimly for himself, bulkily for Mom.

I left him at home so I could wrap things up at the Quick, where I spent the afternoon giving Ali a crash course on the projectors and changeover system, teaching him the cues to look for, how to unload and reload the feed and take-up spindles, and telling him that he'd be in charge, because I'd be busy the rest of the night. Our last exchange went thusly:

"You're to look after the place for me, Mister Ali. You're my manager, okay?"

The glow on his face. The radiance. How he'd basked in the honorific, in the blessed respite of a new title.

"Yes, ma'am. Yes, Doma Q'Aleth. Thank you."

I wasn't a Doma; I'd never married. But to him, I probably seemed too old to be called Domenna. Instead of arguing, I simply gave him my keys, saying, "Eat whatever you want from the concessions; the angel Olthar replenishes the snack counter biweekly—on third day—the Feast of Excess. That's day after tomorrow. Make sure you clean out all the old stuff before he does—we don't want bugs."

I was mindful that I never bothered with any of these chores anymore—but, really, why should Ali be idle? He came more alive with every demand I made of him.

"What else?" He clasped thin, imploring hands before him. "I found your carpet sweeper. Shall I vacuum?"

I strove to sound authoritative, not guilty. "Of course! Once or twice a fortnight should do nicely, unless there's a spill."

He looked at me with a hint of disapproval, a little lift of the chin. I had a feeling that Mister Ali was going to be sweeping the Quick's carpets nightly, and possibly daily too. And why should he not?

I cleared my throat, which seemed, suddenly, full of briny toads. "QH Industries picks up trash every fifth day before dawn. Oh, you'll want to know: that's the day after Feast of Meat, when Rathanana manifests megabovids in his district for slaughter. You take your benzies over to Abattoir, and they'll trade you for your portion."

"I don't have any benzies," Ali reminded me politely.

That froze my stream of nervous disquisition at the source. I snapped myself out of it. "Never mind. After this, I'll show you the safe. Tell them you're trading for the Q'Aleths at the Quick. You'd be surprised how much bovid you can get for a few buckets of popcorn."

He nodded, his eyes wide and solemn. "Yes, Doma Q'Aleth."

"Fifth day," I continued, "—trash day—is Murra's day. We call it the Feast of Whispers, or just Whispers. Everyone in the city must speak quietly on that day, Ali, so bear that in mind. People would look at you askance if you yelled. The noisiest thing around will be the QHI chariots pedaling the city's trash to the dump-lifts."

Something flashed across Ali's face that reminded me strongly of Betony, his skeletal features suffusing with something far older and sadder than his years.

"That's when we ate." He looked down, knuckled the corner of his mouth, his whole body crying out though his voice was very quiet. "We didn't call it Whispers. We called it Vittles—in, in . . . Cherubtown. No one whispered then. There were fights over what came over the ice—I mean, the serac. We'd all be waiting at the dumpsite, lined up since dawn, looking up. And when the dumping started . . .it was like bombs dropping."

He passed a hand over his eyes. "I'm glad. I'm glad to know its real name. Murra's Day. The Feast of Whispers. It's . . . right."

This boy, this murderous boy. Living off the rot of Gelethel and still in love with the angels.

I took his chin in my hand almost helplessly, but then I didn't know what to do with his face. He waited. Utterly trusting. Utterly faithful. He wanted only more chores, every task an anchor in his new life, making him less a ghost.

"Come on," I said. "I'll show you the safe. Put all the benzie slips from the till inside it every night after the show."

He trotted after me, absorbing everything I said like a cactus in a once-a-year rain. "Also, you know, Mister Ali, the Quick is dark all day. We don't open till after sundown. So in the morning and afternoon, you're free to do whatever. I recommend going to the library. It's called the Shush—in Shuushaari's District. We missed it today—but in a fortnight on the Feast of Fish, take some benzies over to Shuushaari's fountain square, and fill a bucket with whatever the First Angel has manifested. Swordfish is my favorite, but cod and tilapia are great too. If you think ahead, you can go to Bower and harvest a bunch of lemons from Alizar's orchards. Lemon and fish are great together. Shuushaari's salmon is good and fatty—sometimes it arrives pre-smoked! Oh," I added, "my library card is in my sock drawer. Use it."

"Your s-sock drawer?" Ali stammered.

"There's nothing dirty about my socks, gh—Mister Ali. I promise. Good Gelthic socks. Borrow a pair if your feet get cold. And use the library. Books are good for you. All Q'Aleths are educated, so you have to be too."

He started glowing as soon as I said this, and stopped asking questions, which was why I'd said it. I was worried about him, but I knew I shouldn't be. He was getting everyone once I was gone. He'd have the Quick . . .

But I thought I'd drop by Uncle Zulli's, last thing before I left for Mom and Dad's again. I'd ask him and Madriq to keep an eye on the boy. They'd know what to do.

"All right," I said. "I'm off. Think you can handle things tonight, Mister Ali, while I go on my hot date?"

"Yes, ma'am! I mean, yes, Doma!"

"Maybe I'd better start calling your Domi Ali, eh?" I teased him. "You're just that important."

He beamed, and his mouth was missing too many teeth from too many years of deprivation and malnutrition and who knew what other abuses? I wanted to embrace him. But this was all the goodbye the kid was getting. One misspoken word, and I'd wager half my heart he'd go straight to the angels. And why shouldn't he? Loyalty to me would mean him losing everything all over again.

When I returned later to my parents' house, I found Dad ready and waiting. Mom was napping on the couch, and Dad was reading an old textbook about Gelthic architecture called *Salt and Starch: the Stuff of Angels*. He'd left his stack of finished screenplays in a teetering heap by the trash pile, and never said a word about them, so I didn't either.

But I lingered on the back porch those last few hours to mourn them. His screenplays! I reread a few of my most beloved favorites. I even read one I'd never seen before—and it wasn't my favorite, but it was still so good, so very good, so *Dad*.

The urge to empty my backpack and stuff it full of his scripts leapt like flame in me. It itched in my fingers, my palms, the soles of my feet. So rash, so ludicrous was this obnoxious urgency that I almost thought it was the angel Alizar trying to tell me something. But it was only grief. And I didn't have time for grief. I had time to do the last of Dad's dishes, and that was all.

Then, when the bells rang midnight in, I loaded my parents up into the chariot I'd chartered for the purpose, and we set off for Hell.

"**Y**ou say something, Ishtu?" Dad asked me.

"Nah. Just my knees creaking. How about you. You good?"

"Never better."

But he sounded winded, tired. And no wonder. We'd been climbing the beard of Grandpa Forever and hadn't even reached his chin yet. I didn't remember it seeming this long when the uncles took me up. But then, I'd been six and a half years younger, and had my ageless uncles to buoy me along. Now, worry for Dad, and our frequent stops to catch our breath had me constantly checking the night sky for signs of dawn.

Not that I'd let on for a single second.

"When we get to Sanis Al," I told Dad in a conspiratorial whisper, "if you ask very nicely, I'll take you to see a *talkie*."

In the dark, Dad's deep-eyed smile deepened. "Pankinetichrome, even?"

"All the colors of the rainbow." I flared my hands and shook them like a burlesque dancer. "Full orchestra!"

"Don't think they do those anymore. But now that you mention it," he mused, "I might fancy a musical after so many years of Gelthic drought."

I groaned. "Music! Okay, Dogman. If we must."

"A musical," Dad continued, "with dancing. *Tap*-dancing, Ishtu."

"Oh, bells. What about . . . tap-dancing and sword fights?" Dad didn't like fighting movies, but I loved them.

"Mmn," he countered, "tap-dancing and sav-nav?"

I loved sword-fighting, but I *adored* sentient ships with an agenda. "Very well," I agreed. "A musical might just be about bearable if singing psi-ships are involved."

Dad leaned sideways into my arm, heavy with affection. "Then we'd better get a move on."

We didn't. We continued at our tortoise pace, and the night burnt on and on, until—at last—the stair ended abruptly in its deadly shear, and there were no more steps to climb.

The giantess Nea awaited us, still holding Mom, who was trussed up like a baby and singing quietly to herself.

The song was crass and folksy, *very* Onabroszia Q'Aleth: a drinking song about Nirwen the Forsaker. How she'd wandered into Bellisaar and got herself fucked by every cactus, coyote, snake, vulture, scorpion, and wild dog of the desert. And at long last, limping but still horny, the Fifteenth Angel slept with the moon herself—who gave her ten children in quick succession, all giants. Nine were perfect beings—heroic colossi: gorgeous, honorable, intelligent. One was a villain, and Nirwen loved that one best.

"Yes," Nea hushed her quietly, her low voice drifting back to us. "I know that one. Gently now, Doma—we're approaching the Hellhole. The crevice is full of echoes, and it's only a hundred meters from here to the rampart. We don't want to be overhead."

Nephilim, I presumed, were masters of understatement. They had to be; everything else about them was so over the top.

I stretched my neck back to gaze above us at the silent tower of Tyr Hozriss, which overwatched the whorled dunes of southern Bellisaar. A bitter black wind blew down over the serac and whipped my short hair straight up from my head. It smelled of mesquite and creosote, of sage and of sand. Not a hint of petrichor this time of year; the rains came later, if at all.

I looked up because I did not want to look ahead, and down—to the place where the salt steps crumbled away into ice, and the fissure opened up like a scream.

So close to the Hellhole, the ice was no longer smooth and blue but chipped and mottled, cobweb-white. Another black breath blew up from the depths below, this one smelling only of ice, ten thousand years of ice. I listened and it sighed again, as if something inside the serac slept uneasily. The wind chilled the sweat on my brow—which made me realize I was sweating.

Nea was unclipping a coil of rope from her jangling belt. "You are here. Very good. Your turn then, Domi Jen," she said to Dad, approaching him. "Time to harness up. Quickly now."

She glanced at the ramparts, and I could read the tension in the dim silhouette she cast against the sky. But the southern watchtower and its environs remained dark and quiet. Most of the patrols were concentrated between Tyr Valeeki, the west-point watchtower, and the area around QHI's dump-lifts in Hirrahune's district, halfway down the southwestern serac. Cherubtown.

Tyr Hozriss was no more than perfunctorily patrolled. Bellisaar was at the bottom of the continent; not much lay to south of us but more Waste and, eventually—so our contraband maps informed me—the sea.

Dad stood ready to follow Nea's instructions as she knelt to weave her ropes around him, explaining everything in her under-hush. When she fell silent, she sat all the way down on the ground so that he could peer in at Mom. To all of our surprises, she was sleeping.

"Broszia must feel safe," Dad remarked.

"And do *you* feel safe, Domi Jen?"

Nea actually seemed to want to know—as if it mattered to her, as if she would stop at any time, and carry both him and Mom back down the steps, and leave Gelethel without us if he asked her to. He didn't.

"How about just Jen?" Dad's wheezing laugh was jovial, if thin. He white-knuckled the straps of his harness under each armpit. "And safe is never the way to feel on an adventure. I'll be fine."

"All right, then—Jen." Nea smiled down at him. "I promise you, you'll soon have your fill of ice. Henceforth, you will take all your whisky neat."

"You bet." His face mostly in shadow, Dad glanced over and waved a pinkie finger at me. "See you on the other side, Ishtu."

Nea took me by the elbow and backed us both up as far as we could get from the Hellhole without falling off the stair. There, setting her stance like a tree taking root, she planted her left foot forward, her left hand holding the rope knotted to Dad. The rest of the rope was wrapped almost all the way across her waist, gripped by her right hand. On her command, Dad plonked himself down on the sloping steps, scooted forward on his buttocks to where the salt met the white-cracked ice, and dangled his legs over the edge of the Hellhole.

I stood beside Nea, watching her pay out the line of rope as Dad slid closer and closer to nothing but space.

And then, he went over.

Nea blew her breath out slowly. She fed out the rope even more slowly. The only sound in the world were the fibers of the rope scraping against her gloved hand as she controlled the friction. Controlled his descent.

I realized I wasn't breathing. Hadn't breathed since I don't know when. My thoughts were so cold they had begun to to crystalize. They ran down Nea's patient line like fire along a fuse, racing toward my father, following him down and down and . . .

Without looking at me, Nea said, "The ice is not infinite. It only feels that way."

I turned away from the Hellhole before I blacked out and scrabbled down five, six, seven steps until my shaking grew so convulsive I couldn't move another inch. My arms and legs were numb. I put my face between my knees. Everything was pressing in, squeezing in. Was this how Betony felt as the angels had drowned her? My heart. . .

"There, Doma Q'Aleth." Nea's whisper carried down to me. She was talking to Mom, but I knew it was for my benefit. "He's made it down. See? That's his signal, that tug. Easy, no? Your turn now."

Which meant I had to return, to drag myself back up the steps and watch as Nea carried Mom right to the edge of the Hellhole and laid her there in her canvas cradle, laid her where the salt sloped into the dropping dark.

She was kneeling beside Mom, feeding two ropes through the clip on the cradle harness. When she was done, Nea placed a hand on Mom's white hair, like an angel blessing benison wine.

Watching this nephilim was exactly as strange as encountering with my saint's eyes a new Invisible Wonder. Even describing her to myself felt like raving with sun-sickness. Talons and teeth of ice, the spell-tech button on her collar glowing like a single blue eye—she was an enormous armored silence in this cold-crackling night, a shadow burgeoning with ropey tentacles.

Standing swiftly, Nea tossed the second rope—the tag-line—into the Hellhole, and then leaned out over it.

I shut my eyes, shut out the sight of her, but heard her call something into the darkness. Her voice echoed; I couldn't hear the words, or the answer that came back to her. If one did.

But when I opened my eyes again, she was nodding to herself, and turning and walking away from the Hellhole, satisfied.

"Jen has the line. I must stand back farther now and be Doma Q'Aleth's anchor. Come with me, Domenna," she commanded me.

Dizzily, I came to my feet, my mouth full of bad water.

This time, though, I didn't watch the rope, or Nea's face, or my mother—Onabroszia Q'Aleth, the once-great, now ruined, Garbage Queen of Gelethel—sliding into the Hellhole. I craned my head to the sky instead, and prayed.

Alizar the Eleven-Eyed was waiting there to welcome me.

He was there, in the firmament, in the clusters of star-like eyes and the spaces between them. He was also all around me, sitting in my bones: jewel-flame flower bells, feathering ferns, the fluttering of membranous wings, a warm and golden thing, like a lamp filled with fireflies.

Pure poetry, Q'Aleth, Betony told me admiringly, from the inside of my mind. *You know, you gonna be a poet, you gotta get yourself some ink. In the real world, real poets are head-to-toe tattoos. 'War flowers,' we used to call 'em, in Rok Moris.*

"You're here!" I was so delighted to hear her voice again, I almost looked around for her.

In the Seventh Anchorhold, actually. But I'm rootin' for you. Or—yeah, yeah, Bug—prayin'.

I closed my eyes to see her more clearly. Against the white walls of her anchorhold, Betony's heavy hair was loose, black at the roots, red at the tips. She was sitting cross-legged on her bed of pink rock salt, which was covered in silks and furs. Her dark face was pinched with concern and concentration. Her eyes were like lamps filled with fireflies.

My panicked breathing slowed. My lungs were not my own; my friends were breathing for me, angel and saint together. I inhaled, and drew in not the shallow gasps that brought only a be-graying numbness, but deep, easy breaths. My racing heart calmed. The roaring in my ears settled. All was quiet.

Nea's own breathing was tranquil somewhere behind me.

"And . . . Doma Q'Aleth is down," the nephilim whispered.

"Thank you," I said and sighed, and opened my eyes.

"Your turn ne—"

A noise interrupted her.

We both froze and glanced toward it—not at the ramparts above, but at the gate below—far below, at the bottom of the steps. The cage rattled. Someone was testing the lock. Voices. Sonorous, confident. A bark of command. A ready assent.

It could be no one but the Holy Host.

Nea's eyes were very, very wide. "Into your harness," she said, whipping me toward her. "Now."

"No. Take this."

I shucked off our packs, shoved them at her. She clipped them all on so quickly to various loops on her webbing that her hands blurred.

"Are you ready to rappel down right now?"

"Domenna—"

"I can't get my parents to Sanis Al alone. You can. You *must*," I hissed. "Nea, please. Don't leave them down there with the ghosts."

She did not argue—there was no time—just placed an enormous hand on top of my head. Even through her gloves, I could feel her body heat, like a wildfire.

"I will see them safe," she swore.

The cage rattled again. This time, I heard the scrape as the gate was pushed open, chafing against broken paving stones and salt pan. Nea was moving swiftly to the edge of the Hellhole. She plucked one of the ice axes from her belt, dropped to her belly, and slid over the edge backward, feet first. I crept as close as I dared to watch her, but had to drop to my hands and knees to get even as far as two meters from the hole.

There was her anchor, just below the rotten white ice. Two clean holes, drilled into the perfect, deep blue. She climbed right down to it—*kick, pick-pick, kick, pick-pick*—and grasped the two ropes she had placed before she met us. One rope ran through the top hole of the anchor and was threaded through the bottom. A second rope was tied to the bottom of the first. Nea grasped both ropes together, let them fall between her legs, wrapped them up and around her right hip, over her stomach and chest, and over her left shoulder. She grasped them, leaned back, her legs perpendicular to the wall, appearing almost as if she were sitting, and gave me a little nod. Then she moved her chin toward the lapel of her jacket, tapping the blue button there—and the ghostly little light winked out.

Slowly, trembling again, I backed away from the Hellhole. My palms were cut in a dozen small places, stinging with salt. My fingers were shaking, freezing cold. My knees, scraped up from such rough usage, bled through the rips in my coveralls. Back, I scrambled. Back and down. Down the steps, hugging them, head down, eyes on the solid bricks beneath me.

Safely back, safely down.

Down a few more steps. Away from that drop. Away from that icy emptiness. Away from escape, from my parents, from. . .

I backed into something hard. Into hands that reached down and plucked me into the air. For a moment, my spine connected with a scaled surface. The smell of leather and bronze enveloped me, the smell of ozone and fresh-welling blood and dirty feathers. Hard hands turned me around in the air, set me on my feet again, held me until I could stand on my own, and then released me.

"Niece," said Hosseril of the Holy Host, second in command to the Captain of the Hundred-Stair Tier. "What are you doing here?"

I stared up at him. Several angels stared back from my good uncle's face. Turgid galls shaped like pouting baby faces pushed out from his forehead. White enfouldred foam frothed at the corners of his mouth. A hawk's head jutted from his left ear. A spray of long fingers and even longer fingernails spiked up from his shoulder.

The angels were there—four of the fourteen. Watching me. They would know if I lied. Zerat Like the Lightning himself had been there inside Host Razoleth when he commanded me to stay away from the serac. *Me*, specifically. Just yesterday.

Other warriors from Host Hosseril's cohort were spreading out behind him on the steps, rank on rank, heads upturned, eyes shining white. The Holy Host, as the angels had promised, were trebling their guard, as on the ramparts above, so below on the streets.

Talking to them would not help. Weaseling and waffling and negotiating were useless. All the tricks my bad uncles had taught me in the back alleys of Gelethel would not avail me now.

I had one goal: to lure Host Hosseril and the squad he commanded away from the Hellhole. I must give them no excuse to put ears to the ground or torches to the dark. No spears or arrows must fly from the lip of cracked serac into the icy black below, where my father and mother and the nephilim who rescued them might even now be waiting at the bottom like trapped fish.

And then, clarity.

I didn't have to outwit them. All I had to do was lead them *away*. All I had to do was get the Holy Host to chase me down the steps.

Thankfully, angels liked it when people ran.

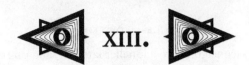

XIII

DEEP FOCUS: TO SIT BELOW THE SALT

B eneath the desert, beneath the salt pan, beneath the domes of the Celestial Corridor and the shell-like anchorholds of the Celestial Cenoby, there was darkness.

And in this darkness, the angels kept their prisoners.

Not for long. It was only a matter of time before they sang themselves to a consensus regarding the details of a properly histrionic finale. And what was time to the angels?

I could hear them even now, thrumming at me from Host Hosseril. Mouth slits opening all over my good uncle's skin.

Count the angels covering him like paper cuts, like seeping sores:

Zerat Like the Lightning. Wurra Who Roars. Tanzanu the Hawk-Headed. Rathanana of Beasts. Kirtirin: Right Hand of the Enemy Twins. Impossible Beriu. Childlike Hirrahune. Thathia Whose Arms Are Eels.

Count the angels absent from the Host:

Shuushaari of the Sea. Olthar of Excesses. Murra Who Whispers. Kalikani: Left Hand of the Enemy Twins. Imperishable Dinyatha.

And, of course, Alizar the Eleven-Eyed.

Absent were all the weaker angels: those who, while not friendly to Alizar, and while falling in line with Zerat and his ilk, had not actively attacked or harassed the Seventh Angel since Nirwen's departure. Did they fear him now that he had paraded the powers of the godhead before the Celestial Corridor? Were they hiding behind their saints, watching to see how his power play would play out? Or were they busy on the ramparts, raining fire and salt onto the cherubs?

Wherever they were, they were not here in the saltcellars, crowding Host Hosseril's fleshly chariot, jeering him on, chittering in seven-part harmony, seven separate red-hot knitting needles going right through my eyeballs.

What to do? How to handle her? How to punish the apostate?

Being caught with a key I ought not to have had, on the southern steps where I ought not to have been, close by the only egress from Gelethel—and that, a secret kept by the angels and the Holy Host—meant my execution, of course.

The question was . . . how?

Drown me in the Sacrificing Pool? But that would not be very satisfying, would it? The pool was for pilgrims, after all—to cleanse their filth, make their deaths fit for the angels—and I was a Q'Aleth, a citizen of Gelethel!

Dash me down into Cherubtown? Fitting, since I apparently wanted to flee fabulous Gelethel to live there in squalor. Why not drop me right at the dumpsite—where a fine fat Gelthic body might feed a fortnight of desperate pilgrims?

Or, better yet—consign me to a lonelier fate still, and one of no use to those god-rotted scavengers. Walk me right into the Hellhole where they had found me. Yes! Toss me unceremoniously into the lonesomeness of that perpetual night, with none to see me, none to mourn my name.

Or . . . well . . . it had been such a while since the last auto-da-fé! How grand they were, a sight to behold! The angels stopped the practice some while back—a few of the early saints had lamented the stink. But what were the plaints of saints in the face of angelic desires? And did I not, after all, merit punishment suited to my crime?

For—and this could not be denied—I was a special occasion. I, Ishtu Q'Aleth, only child of a favored family. An apostate. A forsaker. A follower of the Fifteenth Angel. A traitor.

Where is your father? sang all the angels, and before me in the saltcellars Host Hosseril demanded, "Where is the immigrant your father?"

I was hanging from my feet. I was bound to a wheel. I was pinned to the wall. I was tied to a chair. I flung backward into a water barrel. I was, I was . . .

"Gone, good uncle," I said, again and again—but sometimes only in my mind.

Gone, screamed the angels, like a migraine aura. *Gone?* And Host Hosseril's flesh crawled and rippled with their revulsion as they sang their hymn of displeasure, like guts wrenched fresh from a carcass, stretched into strings.

How could he be gone? And where could he go? Why did he dare? What was he when he came to them? A dirty hunted Dogman of Koss Var! What had they made him? Their chosen one. Chosen! By the fourteen! To be a citizen of the Angelic City! This pilgrim, this *criminal*, this Jen LuPyn—how did he dare? He was asked to do one thing and one thing only: to run his movie palace for the glory of the angels. He was treated like a prince, like a very native babe of Gelethel—he even married the beautiful Onabroszia. They gave him *everything*! And he was *gone?*

"Gone?" roared Wurra, through Host Hosseril's too-stretched mouth.

"Gone, good uncle."

They knew I spoke truth. The angels could not sense Dad anywhere within the serac. They! Who could, if they so chose, extend their radiant essences from ice wall to ice wall, overlapping the diamond and invading everything and everyone within it—like a city-wide stench, like music howling from the paving stones—they! *They* could not sense him. Jen LuPyn was outside their purview.

Gone, or dead.

Dead! the angels sang. *Heart-withered, blue-stuck, frost-limned.*

Deciding this, they dismissed my father, and turned their attention to Onabroszia Q'Aleth.

Where is your mother? they howled. And Host Hosseril leaned over me, pulled seven ways, metastasized by angels, and demanded, "Where is my sister your mother?"

"Gone, good uncle."

So he asked me again.

And asked me, and asked. Again, and again.

Never did his eyes lose their white shine. Never did his tone vary from amiable curiosity. This was not my bad Uncle Eril, who still wept at all the old movies we played at the Quick, even the corny ones. Not our beloved Eril—who would have followed his sister, the Moon Princess, the Garbage Queen of Gelethel, into fire.

Uncle Eril knew exactly where my mother was, and he wasn't telling Host Hosseril. And neither was I.

He understood—we both did—that Onabroszia Q'Aleth had gone long ago, to a place neither her brothers nor her daughter could follow. She had wandered into her own inward desert, vaster than Bellisaar, and from those wastes where she had strayed no one could retrieve her.

No one but the angels, who might at any time have cured her. *Now* they regretted her? *Now* they keened?

O Onabroszia! wailed the angels. *Fairest daughter of our city! She whom we sponsored from a child! The highest we have ever raised any Gelthic maid short of sainthood! Where has she gone and why did she go?*

They asked this through Hosseril their Host—through his fists, his whip, through the angelic attributes that burst from his appendages. But no matter how many times they asked, I gave them the same answer.

I told them "gone" until they took my tongue.

Was it pliers? A knife? Nothing so mundane. It was Tanzanu's curving beak. It was Zerat's cauterizing flash.

And then I too was gone.

Like my mother, I wandered all the way inside myself, into the very flame at my heart's core, there embraced by Alizar the Eleven-Eyed and Betony, my sister-saint.

I felt nothing but their breathing all around me. Heard nothing but the faint flutter of wings, and Betony whispering:

"That angel Wurra's a real wink in the tusher, ain't he? I'd like to pike him where he pisses."

Or:

"You know which angel I could live without? All of 'em. No, not you, Bug. You're not an *angel* anymore, remember? Gotta think like a *godhead* now. Oh, Bug, on that note, got a query: are the hells real? Which one's worst? Gonna send my bratty brother there. Ha—just kiddin', Q'Aleth. Know you got a soft spot for the kid. And he worships you. Gave him a sweeper of his own, didn't you? Never knew a kid could love vacuum cleaners so much—but swear to Bug, it's all he ever asked for his last five birthdays. Not that I could swing it, war and all. Glad you worked that out for him. Really gets to you, don't he? Shitty little hairshirt."

But she said the last almost fondly.

Or:

"Hey, Q'Aleth. Ishtu Q'Aleth. Ish, my beloved. All done now. Your uncle—is he really two people? Whenever you think of him, my vision goes all prism-y—anyway, he's gone. Him and all his creepy angel augs. Saltcellar's clear of the Holy Host. I'm comin' down. Wake up."

Wake up.

I opened my eyes, which where already open—which were peeled open, pinned open, stapled to themselves, staring.

Betony was grinning down at me where I lay on the floor of the saltcellar, and her grin was a thin mirage over her horror. But I felt it in her gentleness, how she spoke so gruff and glib, how her tears fell on my opened ribcage.

"Got you good, didn't they?" she commented. "Bug says the angels flashed mad when they couldn't enter you. Like to work a body from the *inside*, he says. But they couldn't get inside *you*. 'Cause you're his saint. But they don't know that. Drove them waxy."

Her grin went grimace. Just for a second. Then it curled back in place. She was a natural bad uncle, cheeky in the face of terror. I'd have to tell her that, once my tongue grew back.

"You be jammy now, spar. Jam cake. Jelly roll. Sweet 'n' easy. Bug's workin' on puttin' you back together—from the inside, Q'Aleth. New parts, new heart. Growin' you just like a garden."

This body, which no other angel could invade, was altogether occupied by my angel. My godhead. I was more Alizar than myself, so much of me had Host Hosseril stripped away.

But Alizar was changing all of that.

My bones receded back into my flesh like shipwrecks into the wave. My blood-blooms furled down to bud again, smoothed themselves to unmarked skin. New fingernails pushed right out from the snipped, burnt, stumped bits left, and new toenails, too. And new teeth. A new tongue.

And then I screamed.

Betony was right there, plopped next to me on the floor. She was sitting against the wall, braced, so that when I slumped out of my rigid levitation, she could catch me and lower me down. She held me, as my leaking blood dried up and blew away like dust, as my scalp re-sutured itself, as my hair came unmatted and stuck up in all directions, as my skin-flaps folded back in and rejoined the rest of me. And when I could manage it, I turned the unexposed part of my jaw to her, and I showed her that I could still, after everything, smile.

"Want some water?"

"Please."

The word wheezed out like air through a broken bellows. Apparently Alizar was still rebuilding one of my lungs. He blew it up like a balloon; I could feel it glowing in my breast like a tribute to the dead before it was sent into the sky. I tried to wet my lips—I had lips again—and found that I was too parched to succeed.

Betony opened her hands.

"Bug?" she said, and her palms filled up and spilled over with pure sweet water. I bent my head and drank, and drank. And when there was water enough in my body again, I wept. I leaned against her shoulder, and wept.

That was how Ali found us.

"Bet!" he yelped, and we both snapped upright.

Alizar Luzarius was staring at us from beyond the bars of my prison cell. Betony let out a noise that was mostly growl.

"Come to gawp, lizard dick?"

"What are you doing here?" her half-brother demanded, haughty and offended.

"Tendin' the sick and dyin'," she told him. "That's arrant saintly of me, ain't it?" Her chin jerked up, and I saw all too well where Ali had learned his death-before-shame face. "What're *you* doin' here? And," she added more curiously, "what the hells you wearin'?"

Ali's skinny shoulders straightened under Dad's old black and gold Quicksilver Cinema livery. "My uniform," he said, very stiff and grand, but now with more pride than arrogance.

"He's my manager," I whispered. The wheeze was less but my voice was still not strong.

Ali's gaze flew to my face. I must not have looked too bad by this point because his pinched features relaxed in relief.

"They said, they said . . ." he stumbled to repeat what "they" had said, words which had obviously sent him scurrying to find me. "The Holy Host came to the movie palace. They wanted to search the place everywhere. They took some of your things," he added. "I couldn't stop them. I—I'm sorry. I, I hid your library card. But . . . but he said you'd be here, in the saltcellars, and that I could find you if I was brave enough to come."

"Who said?" I croaked. Croaking was good. An improvement.

"Um," Ali's large brow screwed up in concentration. "Host Irazhul Q'Aleth," he pronounced. "He came with the others. There were so many of them, and—" he scowled—"and they turned the Quick upside-down. But they didn't harm anything. Said Quicksilver Cinema was blessed by the angels. And Host Irazhul, he said that you were his sister's daughter. . ."

He glanced at me reproachfully, as if hurt that I'd never mentioned once in the whole two days we'd been acquainted that I had relatives in the Holy Host.

" . . . and that you were going to be executed for a traitor. And he asked me what I was doing at the movie palace."

"What did you tell him?" I was now well enough to sit up against the wall, with Betony's help.

"I told him you'd hired me to be your manager." At that flash of pride, that shoulder-wiggle, that straightening of his spine, I could not help but smile.

I felt Betony struggling with her own response: smile, scowl, smile, scowl—a series of micro-expressions skittering by on the inside of my mind. None of it showed on her face. She did, however, loose a snort so soft that if Ali hadn't flared his nostrils at her, I wouldn't have known she'd made an actual noise. I cleared my throat, nudged her to quiescence.

"And what else did Host Irazhul say to that?"

The real question was, I thought, was it *Irazhul* at the Quick today—or was it Uncle Zulli *pretending* to be Irazhul? I'd been to see him and Madriq just before going to Mom and Dad's house . . . how long ago was that now?

Ali cleared his throat importantly. "He told me that it was very well, me being the manager, and to carry on. He called me 'Mister Ali'! He said I was doing the Angelic City a great service by keeping the doors of the Quick open. He said, to reward a job well-done, he would return later with papers, and claim me as a foundling for the Q'Aleths. He can do that," Ali informed me eagerly, "because ghosts are unwanted scraps, and therefore fall under the province of the garbage industry. But if Q'Aleth Hauling Industries claim me as salvage, he said, I won't be a ghost anymore!"

Oh, Zulli! I thought, reaching out across time and space to fling my arms around him one last time. *You big softy.*

Ali went on, "He also said that, with you . . . out of the way . . . I'd soon be owner of Quicksilver Cinema. Me! But then, I—I thought . . . I didn't want that. You, out of the way. So I came here, to ask the angels to maybe, maybe spare you."

Betony stiffened. "What did you offer them? They don't just give out favors, sebum. Angels always want somethin'—just like everyone else, everywhere else we been."

Ali turned to her, his tar-colored eyes glowing with the death-fires of martyrs. "I offered myself as sacrifice."

Betony's mouth swung open. "You little—"

I felt it then, yawning inside her like that icy black rift at the bottom of Hell: her despair. That she, Betony, who would have given her life to spare his (and had!)—must forever be consigned to be watching her brother offer it up to every passionate cause, to everyone but her—who'd given everything she had to keep him alive.

Ali interrupted, "—they refused!" His voice broke. "The angels refused me, Bet. They said I don't count—because *you* are a saint. You are a saint, so *I* don't count!" he repeated, his eyes flooding with such aggressive tears that she had to turn her face away from him.

After some quick, shallow breathing, Ali wiped his face and turned to me. "So I wanted, Doma Q'Aleth, I don't know, I wanted . . ."

But he couldn't seem to say what he wanted. It was, I thought, "goodbye."

Wearily, I patted Betony on the arm, crawled over to the bars of my cell, and beckoned him down to my level. Immediately, Ali sank to a crouch, his expression earnest, his eyes still pooling with tears.

"Isn't there anything I can do for you, Doma?"

I had my reply ready, and hoped he'd listen. "You do whatever Host Ira-zhul asks you to do. And you go to the library, like I told you. Read books. Every book that interests you. When you've read enough books to understand yourself a little better, ask your sister for forgiveness. Watch movies. Eat what-ever the angel Olthar puts in front of you, and trade for better. Be kind to pil-grims: don't forget where you come from. For the rest," I shrugged, "live. Live a long life in Gelethel, and for the godhead's sake—" Ali flinched; he already had the Gelthic god-flinch down pat—"be *happy*. You bought your happiness dearly enough."

I slipped my hand through the bars to set it on his shoulder like Mom used to do. "Now—go. With my blessing."

Ali, ever obedient, rose to leave.

At which point, his namesake, Alizar the Eleven-Eyed, decided to make his appearance.

He was feeling more than a mite mischievous after all the miracles he had wrought in me, his saint. He was, apparently, feeling quite zoomy.

He splashed out from the tips of my fingers in an arc of green-gold fireflies. Seven times seven this swirling flame zipped around Ali's head, before hurtling back into my cell, and then out again—darting and weaving between the prison bars until the Seventh Angel—the godhead—was all tangled up in them like a quick-growing vine.

He swelled, he greened, he ramified: each twining tendril of him growing and lengthening, sweating sap, until, like a forest reclaiming lost desert, Alizar prized those iron bars apart.

Of course, this was not showy enough for him; Alizar was, at heart, a clown. He wanted a rumble, a rooting, a verdurous upheaval. He wanted to turn all the ruins into flowers.

So he did.

Alizar pulled Bower from the stones, and made it bloom.

Chunks of compressed halite and iron and stone fell. Falling, they turned into the glowing bell-like flowers that Alizar favored for his personal appear-ance—blowzy, drowsy angel trumpets the size of chalices—which clumped at Ali's feet like he was the statue at their chosen shrine.

I knew that Ali could not see angels. He never could and never would—though, like Mom, the longing for Invisible Wonders had all but bent him inhu-man. And so I had no idea, at first, how he was tracking all of the angel Alizar's activities so closely.

"Not an angel." Betony took my hand in hers and squeezed it. "Bug's a god now, spar. Anyone can see gods. Or," and she examined Alizar with a critical eye as he disported himself about the saltcellars, "godheads-in-trainin' anyway."

In any case, it was clear that Alizar the Eleven-Eyed was sufficiently godhead enough to reveal himself to the laity.

Each of his attributes danced before Ali's astounded vision—arcs of fiery light, green-staining vines, enormous flowers—until, overwhelmed, Ali crashed to his knees. He pulled his attention from Alizar and gazed up at me with an expression that I'd never seen on any face turned to mine before.

"You're a saint!" he whispered.

He was weeping from the miracle. He had gathered up as many of Alizar's flowers as he could hold to his thin chest and was busy burying his whole face in them. Betony shook her head and sighed, but said nothing.

"You're a *saint!*"

"Shh," I said, letting my sister-saint help me to my feet. "Don't tell anyone."

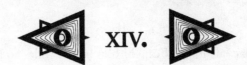

XIV.

EXTREME LONG SHOT: FLOODWATERS

I n the end, it was auto-da-fé after all. But don't let that stop you from watching.

F irst, we sent Ali home. *His* home now: the Quick.

"You'll be all right," I reassured him. "Lock the doors till evening. Stay inside—*stay away from the ramparts*. Open tonight as usual—that's your job now." I wasn't at all sure it would still be his job come nightfall, or if Gelethel as we knew it would even still be standing, but it would give him something to think about.

"Yes, Saint Ish! At once!" Ali beamed at me, his arms spilling over with flowers, and he ran—ran!—where yesterday, he could only crawl.

Betony stared after him.

"He'll be all right," I said again, trying to convince both of us.

"Yeah, I dunno." Betony shook herself from the head down. "He's such a fuck. He's such a little kid."

Alizar breezed between us, chiming crystalline wings and urgent eyeballs, spurring us on, through this corridor and that, the rat-paths of the saltcellars, and on and on, and into a small hall with some stairs, leading up.

To the barracks, as it turned out. Which were emptied of the Holy Host.

Or—almost.

Uncle Eril was hanging by the neck from one of the light fixtures in ceiling: a monstrous thing, with its brass coils and long glass tubes blown into the spirals associated with Zerat Like The Lightning.

He was not dead; he'd been a Host too long to die so easily. It might take him hours. Perhaps he'd thought he had hours, with the other warriors of the Holy Host away at the ramparts, and the angels occupied with Cherubtown. But since he was obviously not activated by angels at the moment, he would indeed die, and soon, if we did not pull him down.

"Alizar!" I cried out, just as Betony bawled, "Bug!" at the top of her lungs.

But Alizar was one step ahead of us. My feet were already lifting right up off the ground, and I flew to the ceiling as if launched—too fast, too fast! I grabbed one of those gleaming brass coils to stop myself, swinging around to face my uncle. His tongue was protruding from his mouth; his face was flecked with strange spots. I forced myself not to look too closely—for fear it would freeze me—and grasped the rope my Uncle Eril hung by right at its seventh knot.

The knot frayed apart at my touch, and then each successive knot exploded, until the choking loop itself burst from my uncle's neck as if repelled by his flesh. He would have fallen, but I caught him by the collar and lifted him away from that abominable light.

He had shed his kidney-pink armor, his helm and gauntlets, was dressed in a simple shift, like a penitent, or a child who has readied himself for bed.

I began to lower us. It was as if we were floating in water—in one of Shuush-aari's public fountains, where Uncle Eril had taught me how to swim—only now it was he who was lying on his back, trusting the hands beneath his shoulders to keep him afloat, and locked together like this, in trust, we drifted lightly to the ground.

He was not conscious. His face was riddled with scarlet petechiae. The bottom of his clean-shaven neck was branded with an inverted V from the rope.

I stroked the side of his cheek.

My gentlest of uncles. My beloved Uncle Eril, whose favorite movie was *Balais of Entayle*: a swoony courtly romance, full of outlaw ladies lying in ambush on the God-King's Highway, ready to pluck rubies from off the brows of pretty young noblewomen, and rebel poets locked away in towers needing rescue, and the God-King of Koss Var: a shadowy menace at the center of it all. He was always talked of, never seen—or, at most, a hint of profile as he bent to whisper in the ear of one of his advisers. Even his throne was always shot from behind. He was terrifying, like the angels of Gelethel. Of course, the poets and the outlaws won against him in the end. That's what they did, in movies. Maybe the only place they ever did.

And that's why we need movies, Uncle Eril had once told me. *That's why it was such a great good thing—the day your father came to Gelethel.*

Betony knelt on Eril's other side, resting a gentle hand upon his chest. "Which way?" she asked, and I knew what she meant: which way did I want us to push him?

A terrible choice.

Uncle Eril had always been sorrowful—persistently, unceasingly sad—for as long as I knew him. This was his chance to escape all of that, to go back to the salt, and I could help him. The three of us, together, could help him.

But it was I who had pushed him to this, today—I, and the angels—for they had ridden him hard and forced his hand against me, his niece, whom he had left for dead in the saltcellars. And then they had abandoned his flesh, left him sick and sore and wild with regret, all of his memories still cruelly in tact, as they themselves flocked to the ramparts to teach Cherubtown the lesson of the ages. They would be occupied now, the other angels, and would not turn their attention back to the Host they had used up for some while.

"We call him back," I decided. "Alizar, Betony—we have to breathe for him. Like you breathed for me, remember? At Tyr Hozriss? And also . . . below."

Betony nodded. Alizar was already sinking tendril-first into the V-shaped mark on Eril's throat. He did it so gently, so delicately, and with such woebegone diligence that Uncle Eril's chest began to move almost at once. Betony kept her hand on his heart, I kept mine on Eril's head. The entire time, Alizar was pouring images into us, translating Eril's afflictions from the inside, sharing them out so we might experience them all.

A chalice pierced through with holes, leaking wine.

A chariot upturned in combat, crushed under the wheels of other war machines.

A dead tree, strangled by vines.

This last one startled me, for I associated vines and green growing things with Alizar—and this was a vision of Alizar as parasite, Eril as host.

The image burnt to ash as I opened my eyes. Alizar was angry—as much with himself as with the other thirteen angels—but he just as delicately lifted himself back out of Eril and returned to his place hovering above us.

Regrets and remonstrations continued to course out of him, into us:

He should have acted sooner, done better, been braver; he should have gone for the godhead without waiting a hundred years for Nirwen to rescue him. He should have. . . .

Uncle Eril moaned.

I recognized that parched sound. I had just been there myself, down in the saltcellars. Imitating Betony, I cupped my hands to his lips. Water spilled out of my palms before I'd even prayed for it: more than water—benison water—shining like moonlight and alive with healing.

Uncle Eril sipped, semi-conscious, until he was awake enough to spit it out again, horrified. He opened red-speckled eyes and stared desolately around. He would have screamed, I thought—as I had screamed—except his throat was still too damaged.

"No, no, no," he rasped. "Why. . .why didn't you leave me?"

I leaned over him, stroking his heavy hair back from his brow. "O my uncle! I could not. You would not have asked me to. Nor would you have done so, had you been in my shoes. Please forgive me. Please understand."

Finally, he saw me. His eyes focused. His mouth formed my name, but he couldn't speak it. He thought I was a ghost, perhaps, or that he had joined me in death.

"I'm here," I said. "I'm alive. You didn't . . . Host Hosseril didn't kill me, Uncle Eril."

And he started to sob.

That was what one did, I supposed, when one was pulled back from the dead.

"I can't go back, I can't," he said later, when Betony and I had helped him to clean up and dress. "I can't be taken again, Ish, I can't. I should have waited. I have my quarantine word, now—I should have waited to take one of them with me. We all agreed to it, now that Broszia's gone. And you—you were supposed to be gone too. We were never supposed to find you; I don't know how they heard about your assignation at Tyr Hozriss, but I . . ."

"It's all right, it's all right, Uncle Eril," I tried to soothe him. "I'm whole, see? It's as if they never touched me."

He pinched a bit of my torn and bloody coveralls between his fingers. I covered his hand with mine.

"I will tell you everything, Uncle Eril, if—if there is time." I glanced at Betony, who nodded. "If there isn't, come see Saint Betony here, any time day or night, and will be able to explain it all. But for now, Uncle Eril—before we make any more decisions—I have to ask you," I inhaled deeply, and dipped my head, trying to catch his eye, "what did you mean by 'quarantine word?' What did you all agree to?"

Eril seemed to stop breathing. He touched his throat, where the V-shaped mark now glittered golden-green. The small flecks on his face and in his eyes were no longer red but shining like chips of mica. Alizar's mark was still upon him, but he did not yet know it. Uncle Eril hated mirrors.

"We're done," Eril said flatly. "My brothers and I decided, as soon as you and Jen and Broszia were safely out of here, that we were through. You can't resign from the Holy Host—you can only die in service. But we can't wait another sixty years for that relief. So Razoleth led us in our meditations, and assigned us a quarantine word: one word to speak to ourselves, or to each other, the next time we feel the angels taking hold. It will allow us—for a short time—to seal off our minds from angelic incursion. Though the angels posses our bodies, our brains should, briefly, remain our own. We thought that if we . . ." he glanced uneasily between Betony and me, "if we took our own lives while the angels were still inside us, we might kill them too. Or at least, damage them."

"Is that canon?" Betony asked me in an undertone.

"I . . ." I appealed to Alizar. I'd never been to the Hagiological Archives; I didn't know all the teachings of the saints but what the Seventh Angel—the godhead—had told me.

It is . . . unprecedented. Risky, he admitted. *It might work?*

Eril was starting to stutter, "But I . . . after . . . after the saltcellars, I couldn't wait. . . couldn't bear the thought of them, of them entering me a-again." He was shredding at the edges, his words boiling off into the threat of unstoppable sobbing.

"No, no, of course not, of course not, it's all right," I said, crowding in to hug him. "You did the only thing you could, Uncle. I would have done the same thing."

He began to grow calmer, even as I despaired. Poor Uncle Eril! Raz! Poor Wuki! Poor Zulli—what would Madriq do without him? What would young Ali do? And how could I go on—wherever I went in this world—knowing that back in Gelethel, my uncles were nothing but bones in the salt?

Alizar chimed and whistled, winked and tinkled. All I had to do was reach up to him; he would give me anything I asked for. Anything.

I let my head fall.

"I can protect you from the angels," I told Uncle Eril swiftly. "You won't ever have to use your quarantine word, because the angels will never enter you again. I promise. Uncle Eril, you don't have to leave this world until you are ready—not a second sooner."

He brought the heels of his hands from his eyes, and his face was wet, amazed as a babe woken from a bad dream.

"You can't, Ishi," he said. "No one can."

"Uncle." I took his hand. "Haven't you guessed by now? My secret? You may as well know it—now that Mom's gone."

Now that all of Gelethel might be gone before the day is out, I thought but did not say.

Eril was silent, his eyes downcast, gaze fixed on the blood-stained hem of my trouser leg. He looked exhausted, dejected. Everything in me, like it always did, longed to comfort him. Alizar was a-whir with the same desire, and beside me, Betony looked so frighteningly, fiercely ready to slay whole demon armies for him—and she didn't even know him, except that he was mine. But we all stayed very still, waiting.

"You," and Eril looked up at me, smiling with just the corners of his eyes, "you are the daughter of Onabroszia's desire. You are the truest saint of Gelethel. The saint who walks free."

But then his smile flickered. Misery flooded him again. His dark hair fell into his eyes as he began shaking his head.

"But all the angels have saints, Ishi! You cannot fight them, not with only Alizar to protect you. They will rip you apart—and him as well! You cannot keep me safe. And I would die, I would *die*, to keep *you* safe. To prevent myself from, from . . ."

"Uncle Eril!" I joggled his arm until he focused all his wild fear into this present moment. "I *used* to be a saint of the Seventh Angel. I'm not anymore." I leaned my forward against his and whispered, "Eril Q'Aleth, there is no Seventh Angel. There is only Alizar, the new god of Gelethel. And we," here I stood, pulling him with me, "will make it so that no angel ever, *ever* possesses you again. Saint Betony?"

Betony rose up behind him, and we locked our wrists together, enclosing Eril in the circle of our arms. Looking up at the scintillant sphere of godhead as he threatened to go nova, she asked, "Hey, Bug. How's this goin' down?"

Alizar was too excited for translatable words. He was shedding feathers and petals and image after flashing image in a rainstorm of revelation.

"With honey and beeswax, we seal him," I interpreted for Eril's sake. "With pollen and drupe—"

"—with rich loam and cool stone, we seal him," Betony and I said together. "By the bounty of Bower, Eril Q'Aleth, we seal your sovereign soul against all angels."

Heavy golden light dripped down.

* * *

Afterwards, while Eril rested, Betony and I stood a little aside, and argued.

"He can't stay here," I glared up at the spiral light above us with revulsion, "and he shouldn't be alone. He's still very fragile. I have to get to the ramparts before my uncles trigger their quarantine words and do what cannot be undone. They have to know that there's another way—that I can seal them off from the angels—that they don't have to die to be free."

"Well, yeah, and I'll trot along and help," Betony insisted. "Got two legs and a godhead, don't I? Could fly the fuck up those stairs as good as any other saint—right at your side. Where," she added vehemently, "I *belong*."

She did belong with me, always, cradled in my skull, hand in hand, back to back, saint with saint. I hated to leave her behind in this city, with people who did not love her as I did.

"Yes," I said. "You could. But I'm asking you to take Eril to Bower. He needs you more than I do."

Betony folded her arms tightly across her chest, and I could see her wishing, just for a second, that I was her brother Ali's size, so she could sit on me and subdue me until my temper tantrum passed.

"Q'Aleth," she said through gritted teeth. "I met three of your family now, yeah? One killed me. One killed you. Now you're off to get yourself killed savin' three more of 'em. What's with the death wish? I don't get it!"

She stepped close to me, right under my chin. I was of average height for a Gelthic citizen. Though Mom's people were tall, my Dad wasn't, really. Betony, I realized, was tiny. And she was also immense. "I seen enough death!" she spat. "I ain't sendin' you to yours without backup, spar. Got me?"

"Betony—!"

But then I had a better idea than arguing with her. Just as she had smiled with my lips, and flashed her thumbs up with my hands, now Betony opened her mouth and said exactly what I was thinking, word for word, in my cadence and with my Gelthic patterns, so different from her own:

"You know what is going to happen up there! Alizar and Nirwen are ascending to the godhead. They have spent a hundred years amassing power enough to overthrow the angels and rule Gelethel—Nirwen, by perfecting her nephilim in some secret lair in the heart of Bellisaar; Alizar, here, lying low and making Bower bloom. They need both of us. One to remain. One to cross over. You and I are at the heart of their plans."

Before I could make her say anything more, Betony clenched her teeth and ground her jaw, so I continued with my own mouth.

"I have to go. I have to go alone."

"To the ramparts," she hissed resentfully, involuntarily.

"To the top of the serac," we said together, and clasped hands.

But Betony was alsop shaking her head. "I don't care. I should be there. I *will* be there."

O my saint, Alizar the Eleven-Eyed told her mournfully. *I need you here with me—in Bower—and everywhere else in Gelethel, come the time.*

"But Q'Aleth. . ."

Betony's lambent eyes sparked with the prophecies that the godhead was pouring into us both. Fire and salt. Ice and floodwater.

"I can take it," she said, almost gray with terror. "You know I can. I . . . I already did it once. You saw me. Ain't right you should bear that too, nobody should have to.. . ."

"No one should have to go through that *twice*, Betony," I corrected her gently. "It's my turn now."

*Y*ou scared? my sister-saint asked from me across the city, from the heart of Bower, where she sat cross-legged beside my sleeping Uncle Eril, where he lay in the soft green tiles of the mossery, in the shade of a flowering chilopsis.

"Nah," I said aloud. "I've seen this movie. Remember—*Life on the Sun?*"

Spar, that film was old when I was sperm. I grew up with talkies.

"It's so great. No, really," I insisted when she chuckled tiredly.

The sinking sun was of course right in my eyes—still high enough that the serac did not block it, but low enough to be obnoxious, and to tell me that the summer hour was growing late. Strange to think that in King's Capital, Koss Var, where Dad was from, it was the middle of winter. I shaded my face, and jabbered on—out loud, since it served the double purpose of reassuring me and scaring everyone away from the blood-stained, ragged woman talking to herself.

"So, the movie's all about how Sanis Al got its current god, Kantu. Well, that's what its about *philosophically* anyway. It's a war movie at heart. But there's all this set up: years of drought, famine, civil unrest, dissent at the Shiprock. Things got so bad, someone had to come along and become their god and take back control. Bring the rain. Someone had to self-sacrifice. That's how it worked in Sanis Al."

Don't see how all of 'em angel sacrifices hereabouts yielded you gethels any great godsdamned result, Betony mumbled.

"Well, first of all, ritual sacrifice isn't the same as self-sacrifice. And second of all, we got you out of it, didn't we?"

Dungballs, Q'Aleth. You gotta do better than that. But Betony sounded flattered.

The northwest and southwest walls of the serac were narrowing on either side of me as they shot toward the bottleneck of Tyr Valeeki. It grew colder as I approached the dark blue ice, and soon, I was walking out of the sunlight and into the west-pointing shadow.

Tyr Valeeki, fang-like, rose above me.

So, you ain't scared. But . . . are you ready?

I looked up. The white steps zigzagging their way to the ramparts as well as the ramparts themselves—from Tyr Valeeki at the west point all the way to the dumpsite ten kilometers to the south—were packed with warriors of the Holy Host. All of them were radiant with angels: their attention, for the moment, directed outward.

"Shit," I breathed.

We have you, Betony told me sternly. *We're holdin' you between us.*

We will not let you go, my saint, said Alizar.

"Nevertheless," I swallowed at the sight of all those stairs, "I'm going. But, um . . . Bug?"

Betony laughed in surprise at my use of the nickname. Somewhere inside me, the god Alizar grew a plumy, sparkly, rainbow-and-rose-petal tail, and began wagging it like an overgrown dragon-pup at his first sight of doughty maiden fair.

Yes, my saint? Yes? What can I do for you?

"Can you . . . give me a boost?"

It was quite something, not having to take the stairs.

I found Uncle Zulli first, partly because he was stationed right there at Tyr Valeeki, and partly because Alizar dropped me right smack on top of him. I didn't even wait to catch my breath before I looked straight into his cold white eyes, and spoke the quarantine words:

"Bad uncle."

The angel rays vanished from his eyes as though snuffed. The half of his face encrusted in Shuushaari's barnacles began to shimmer. I watched as the First Angel reared up and rose out of him, frightened as an oyster who has suddenly found herself shucked of a shell. I stared at her next, though she thought herself now invisible to me, and let her know that she was seen.

"The godheads are coming," I told her. "I wouldn't stay anywhere near this serac if I were you."

Shuushaari whipped herself into nothingness—but I could not tell where she decided to go, or who she had decided to warn before she went.

I bent down to the astonished Zulli and hauled him to his feet.

"Ish—*what?*"

"By honey and beeswax, I seal you," I began, and didn't end until he was safe from all angels.

Zulli began patting himself down almost immediately, as if searching for some stowaway angelic attribute in his back pocket: an eel, a pearl, the head of a hawk.

There was nothing.

"Uncle Zulli," I said urgently, "Zulli, listen to me. I need to find Wuki and Raz."

"They aren't . . . ."

He looked around, gathered me up under his arm and drew me into a sheltered doorway where the other warriors of the Holy Host—and their angels—would have trouble seeing us.

He whispered, "I mean, they're *Hosts* right now, Ishi—not for fakes, but—" he glanced at me, and then threw up helpless hands at whatever expression he encountered there. "What are you even doin' here, girl? I thought we got you safe out of this rot!"

"I'm not a girl, I'm a saint—and even if I weren't, I'm thirty-eight years old! Now," I said briskly, before he had a chance to recover, "I have just retired you from the Holy Host, Zulli Q'Aleth. Congratulations. Go home to your husband. There's a boy at the Quick right now who's going to grow up to be a good man even if it means him eating half your share of Madriq's cakes, and you telling him all your worst jokes. Right now you're the only Q'Aleth in Gelethel who knows his name. Can I trust you to leave now—get Madriq, get Ali, gather whoever else will listen to you, and bring them to Bower—or as close to the center of the city as you can get."

Uncle Zulli peeled the bronze helmet from his head. He contemplated it for a moment, then turned, wound back, and hurled it over the crenellated parapet. It arced, glinting, into the burning desert beyond.

Released, his hair porcupined straight up, just like mine, and he ruffled a bemused hand through it.

"I don't know what in Nirwen's Hell is going on," he said. "But you're givin' me that Broszia look, so I know my answer. I'm outta here. And, Ishi. . ."

He touched his face again, where the angel Shuushaari no longer rode his flesh like her chariot. "Thanks. My niece. My saint."

W uki was harder to find, not least because the angels had diverted part of their Holy Host to apprehend me.

Those white-eyed warriors, however, weren't much more than a distraction—no matter how many attributes they bristled, or what mighty swords they brandished. Alizar was only too happy to lob me high into the air and out of their reach. Between us, Betony and I made a game of foiling the spears and arrows that came flying at me, transforming them into increasingly harmless and ridiculous things, things to make our god giggle: balloons, confetti, silly string, paper flowers, real flowers, stuffed toys, and once, when two Hosts launched a small rocket my way, a circus tent—the big top—which dropped down like a mushroom cap over a considerable length of the ramparts, bringing red-and-white-striped darkness and confusion to the warriors milling beneath it.

A circus! cried Alizar. *There has never been a circus in Gelethel! Tell me of the circuses you have seen, my saint!*

Later, Bug, Betony promised. *Bedtime stories all around.*

When I came to a section of the ramparts empty of the Holy Host, Alizar eased me lightly onto the parapet. I leapt from merlon to merlon, balancing like a dancer, my knees the knees of a twelve year old . . .

My knees?

"Alizar!"

Oh, Ishtu, just this once? he wheedled.

"Oh—!"

. . . and because I knew that this was probably going to be the last gift my Alizar would ever give me, and because I knew that the end, my end, was rushing toward me like a blood-rain cyclone from the east . . .

"—I accept," I said. And then added, "Thanks."

You're welcome! Alizar shouted joyously, and all the youthful elasticity and buoyant energy and dazzling speed that he could put at my command pounded into my body. I ran across the crenellations like they were god's own teeth—south, toward my Uncle Wuki.

Confetti and big tops were, well, wonderful, but I wished I could expel the angels from the bodies of all the Holy Host. Warriors who were not my uncles, however, hadn't trained their minds to the trick. They had no quarantine word to separate out one spare bit of themselves, keep it sacred, keep it for their sovereign own. Most of them had worked all of their lives to be seats of the angels. It was their vocation. They consented, enthusiastically, to be so used, and it was in this consent that the angels had truly taken root, branching out from that utter faithfulness like hyphal networks and spreading through their Host's entire foundation, body and soul. There was no space left to dig out the angels without scooping out most of the Host along with them.

So I spared the warriors my exorcisms. But as I ran along, I tried to make Alizar promise that one day, all of Gelethel would be safe from infestation by angels—or by gods.

Gods? Even me? But, Ish. What about . . .us?

I didn't answer. I didn't think that I'd be a part of any "us" before too long.

Betony took the debate away from me with a firm, *We'll talk later, Bug.*

And so my sister-saint assured me that she would carry on this conversation after I was gone. I let it go for now.

"Where is he?" I wondered aloud, and my words were whisked away by the high wind. "Where's Wuki?"

Further south.

Further south, it turned out, was where a greasy black smoke had started rising from Cherubtown.

The Holy Host had apparently been busy earlier this afternoon, setting fire to the Gelthic dumpsite. From there, the fires had spread through the whole of the dried-up shantytown—and the way-station—and the ancient little shrine that had stood outside the serac for almost as long as Gelethel had been the Angelic City.

Cherubtown was in flames.

But—and this was odd—it was a Cherubtown curiously empty of cherubs. I stopped running to take it all in. Barefoot and balancing on the parapets, I turned to scan the desert for any sign of life.

My eyesight sharpened (Alizar again, ever eager to help), and all at once I could focus in on them clearly, as if staring through a telescope: several kilometers out, a hasty smudge of refugees stretched quite a ways across the dunes.

Surrounding them was a semi-circle of giants, all of whom were straddling enormous, gleaming viperbikes. Some sat casually, some were upright and alert, as if awaiting a signal.

"Zilch?" I whispered, and then was ashamed for forgetting the first lesson Nea had taught me. "Sorry," I corrected myself. "Nephilim?"

Nirwen sent them, Alizar explained. *They'll be protecting her cherubs—possibly from those of their siblings gone to the Zilch. And other terrors of the desert.*

Demon armies, right, Bug?

Betony was, I thought, referring to the mythical origin of Gelethel as Alizar had related it to both of us. But Alizar shuddered, her words conjuring for him the slinkycold/quickburrowing/twicetongued/insideout/mildewsmogwithteeth that had pursued the god Gelethel and her angels across Bellisaar.

His memory of that time was so visceral, so venomous, that I almost puked it out right there. But Betony, half a city away from me, flung out a hand—and so, then, did I—and I caught myself before I belly-flopped right over the serac.

That was close, Q'Aleth.

Too close.

I huddled down, clinging to the merlon beneath me with both arms, and turned my head to spit the taste of mold out of my mouth.

Sorry, Ishtu, Alizar said penitently. But any remonstrations I might have returned to him were cut off at tongue's root as I perceived, from my new vantage, what I had originally missed:

Not all cherubs were hanging back in the Bellisaar dunes as the fires of the Holy Host consumed the last hope of home they had.

Some were swarming the serac.

Forgetting my nausea, I scooted sideways and leaned as far over the parapet as I could, peering at that section of serac that ran along the dumpsite to the smoky south. A line of furious, determined, possibly demented refugees from Cherubtown seemed to be climbing the ice with their bare hands.

The leaders were already more than halfway up the wall. More followed. Not many—a few dozen, maybe, all told. No match for the numbers of the Holy Host above.

But no matter what the Host flung down at them (chunks of salt, torches, rocks, spears, other saboteurs) some invisible force—dome-shaped, like a gigantic parasol—deflected the missiles and scattered them harmlessly into the smoldering middens below.

She may have allowed Cherubtown to be consigned to flame, but Nirwen the Forsaker was brooking no harm to befall a single lock of hair on one of her cherubs' heads. Not now that her powers were ascendant. Not anymore.

"But *how* are they scaling it?" I muttered, flattening my body until it was practically vertical, and leaning almost all the way through one of the crenels, trying to make it out.

Alizar obligingly augmented my eyesight. Again.

I saw, and shared what I saw with my sister-saint, that what had appeared at first glance to be bare blue serac that the cherubs were shinning up was in fact a long ladder. It was wide enough for five people at least to climb abreast, and carved out of the ice itself.

Only the god of Cherubtown could have made such a thing. Only she had the tools to carve the serac like that.

Nirwen the Artificer.

This wasn't part of the plan, Alizar murmured. *They were all supposed to be well back—safe! In the dunes, with the others! The ladder wasn't for* them.

"I think," I surmised slowly, backing myself up, palms flat, belly down, and slipping off the parapets to walk the solid salt-bricks of the ramparts once more, "that when they saw that ice ladder, some of the cherubs disregarded any instructions Nirwen left them and started climbing. I think they're . . . angry."

Anger ain't the word, Q'Aleth, Betony said, in a tone of voice I hoped to never to hear again.

"Whatever they are, they're moving really fast."

Nirwen must have spiked the food and drink at Cherubtown's surprise Feast of Saint Betony yesterday. I'd wager she had stuffed her chosen people with more benisons in a few hours than all fourteen Invisible Wonders ever managed to manifest in any given fortnight. The cherubs on the ice ladder were moving so rapidly that even I—I, who'd learned how to fly that day, how to prance across the parapets like some kind of teenaged gazelle-girl—was astonished. Though their bodies were small and lean, they all looked strong, not stunted and skeletal like the other pilgrims I'd seen on petition days. After years of paucity, the god of Cherubtown had not stinted on the gifts she bestowed.

I was so busy looking ahead that I did not see what was before me: Host Wurrakai, charging forward, a war axe in his hands.

"Bad Uncle!" I shouted, but Host Wurrakai did not stop, could not hear me.

Flaps of flayed flesh had grown up over his ears. Clusters of baby faces sprouted from his forehead and cheeks to sing to him in shrieking voices. Wurra Who Roars had opened a second maw on the underside of his jaw, and was howling along.

I froze, watching the axe fall. I looked up at its edge, my eyes crossing as they focused on my own razor-thin reflection bearing down.

The blade cut the first layer of skin on the bridge of my nose.

It cut no further.

Alizar, terrified and enraged, knocked the axe ajar, sending it flying. And then he scooped me up in a hook of serac-cold air and flung me up high over Host Wurrakai's head. Alizar tumbled me through space like a pilot operating his toy aeroplane remotely, with radio transmitter and joystick—such as Dad used to play with when he was young. He landed me squarely on my good uncle's back, jarring my everything. Host Wurrakia stumbled but he did not fall, and I was too dizzy to do anything other than cling to him with all my shaking limbs, and remember, remember, in fast-flickering monochrome, how Uncle Wuki used to take me up on his shoulders when I was a child, and run around Mom and Dad's backyard pretending he was my Zilch giant whom I'd tamed to my hand, and calling me "Moon Princess, Queen of Smugglers," as we enjoyed a thousand adventures together.

And then, and then, I was taking the gory flaps of flesh over Host Wurrakai's ears, Rathanana's attributes, in my fists, though the blood of them slicked my fingers, and I ripped them off his scalp, leaving bald bleeding patches where his hair would never grow again, and I stuffed the torn flesh rags between the doughy little lips of Hirrahune's attributes, snuffing their meeps and squeaks. And then I shoved my whole fist down Wurra's gaping mouth, and silenced his roaring.

"Bad Uncle!" I screamed again into Host Wurrakai's open, bleeding ears.

And Wuki's shoulders stiffened beneath my hands.

"Ishi?" he asked, his voice as high and fearful as a child's.

This time, instead of fleeing like Shuushaari had fled Zulli, the angels in Uncle Wuki fought me. They rippled through his body, multiplying their attributes. Rathanana tried to unseat me by pushing great swollen lumps of matter—bulbous proto-beasts without limb or face—right out of Wuki's back.

But this time, Wuki was also fighting them. Once the quarantine word was coursing through him, his mind was his own again, even though his body was invaded. And when the angel Wurra's roaring mouths opened up all along both of Wuki's arms—every one of those mouths ringed with rows of barracuda teeth,—and when the angel Wurra would have used my uncle's arms to tear me off of his shoulders, and then simply to tear me, Wuki clenched his great fists, and grunting with the effort, folded himself down to a fetal position, crushing his arms between his knees and his chest.

Wurra's muffled shrieks of protest, and the small, vicious, chewing sounds that followed frenzied me with worry. I seized one of Hirrahune's vapid little baby faces where it bloated the back of Wuki's occiput, and squeezed its chubby cheeks between my fingers, growling, "I will rip you out of him, Ninth Angel, and give you to Alizar to eat! How do you think turnabout will taste—god-eater?"

The angel Hirrahune's attribute whimpered, blinked cowardly wet eyes at me—once, twice—and then fled, vanishing from between my fingers.

Sensing the desertion of his fellow angel, Rathanana's great bestial lumps, until that moment writhing and rising beneath my knees, suddenly stilled. I turned all my attention to them.

"Rathanana," I said in my silkiest voice, laying both hands deliberately over one of the trembling lumps. "You were with Saint Betony in the Sacrificing Pool.

You devoured her death. I should lay you at her feet for a present. What would an angel like you look like, mounted on the wall of the Seventh Anchorhold?"

The lumps on Wuki's back deflated so abruptly that I slid off of him and tumbled down to the brick walkway in a way that would have wrenched my old knees—had Alizar not recently given me new ones.

"Uncle Wuki," I said, crawling over to him, "let me see your arms."

"No, Ishi—I—"

"Please. Please, I have no time."

His arms were fountaining blood from shoulders to wrists, still trying to devour themselves. So I did the only thing I could think of: I started sealing off Uncle Wuki from the angels—with Wurra Who Roars *still inside*.

"With honey and beeswax, I seal you—

With pollen and drupe—"

How the Sixth Angel clamored and yelled, how dozens more mouths opened on Wuki's face, on his chest, his legs, his back, how the very bricks beneath us began to shatter at the sound of Wurra's celestial rage. . .

"With rich loam and cool stone, I seal you—"

How he gnashed his ten million tiny teeth, and grew ten million more, teeth within teeth within teeth. . .

"By the bounty of Bower, Wuki Q'Aleth—"

But all the angel mouths in the world could not stop Alizar the Eleven-Eyed, godhead of Gelethel, from un-Hosting this Host. . .

"I seal your sovereign soul against all—"

The angel Wurra fled.

H ost Razoleth, Captain of the Hundred-Stair Tier, straddled the parapets, legs wide, each foot planted on a separate merlon. He was staring down at what was left of Cherubtown. He held in his left hand a spear that was no spear at all, but a dazzling arc of never-ending lightning, emanating from the palm of his hand.

He awaited the arrival of the first cherubs who dared climb the serac. When they did, he would drive Zerat's lightning right down through their skulls, piercing their throats, their lungs, their viscera, their loins, purifying them with heavenly fire from the inside out.

In his right hand, Host Razoleth held nothing, for he had no right hand anymore, and no arm either. His shoulder simply extruded a writhe of moray eels, bright green against the salmon-flesh sky, oral jaws and pharyngeal jaws agape, waiting for their first taste of pilgrim flesh.

I slowly approached the eldest and strongest of my good uncles, keeping to the ramparts below. Above me, boosted by the parapets as by a pair of great stone shoes, he towered taller than I had ever seen him. He seemed another Tyr Valeeki, this one built of flesh of angels. I advanced, and was allowed to advance. Host Razoleth had issued orders that he be the one to deal with me.

And the closer I came to him, I saw why.

One by one, the greatest and most powerful of the Invisible Wonders who ruled Gelethel were sucking back their angelic presences from the Holy Host at large, and flocking instead to Host Razoleth, engorging him, engulfing him, reenforcing their seats in his body. This was to be my punishment, then, or the start of it: to witness my uncle crammed beyond all endurance with angels. To watch them as they corkscrewed, not just a single thread of themselves, but the whole entirety of their magnificent manifestations, down into his flesh. Making him eight thrones in one.

Yes, eight I counted. Eight I named. The same eight who'd been present in Host Hosseril in the saltcellars—only more so. Zerat. Thathia. Wurra, whose wide mouth had again taken up residence, as it had in Wurrakai, just beneath Razoleth's chin. Tanzanu, whose black talons and sharply curving beaks jutted out from my uncle's vertebrae, like the spikes and spines of the prehistoric monsters who once roamed Bellisaar. Rathanana, who had transformed my uncle's right leg into a wolf, his left into a bear. Kirtirin: Right Hand of the Enemy Twins, whose elegant twelve-fingered hand was pushing itself out from Razoleth's stomach, while from its palm, another twelve-fingered hand was already growing. Impossible Beriu, who was a color I could not describe, a sound I should not have been able to hear, a taste in my mouth that did not match the odor in my nose—and all of it poisonous, poisonous. And lastly, Childlike Hirrahune, who vied for her place somewhere on Host Razoleth's body and found it at last: covering his face with a half dozen faces of her own.

My good uncle had no face left. His eyes were two Hirrahunes. His nose was Hirrahune. Each of his ears and his mouth were a Hirrahune. All of those tiny, bow-lipped, defiant, flaccid faces, watching me as I approached.

Approached, and counted all the angels absent from this Host:

Shuushaari, who'd fled Uncle Zulli at Tyr Valeeki. Olthar of Excesses, whom I wished well and far from here, pouring himself into popcorn and beer at the Quick. Murra Who Whispers, who made Gelethel a place of cleanliness and quiet contemplation once a fortnight. Kalikani: Left Hand of the Enemy Twins, who probably considered me a friend, since her brother was my foe. Imperishable Dinyatha, who loved the movies.

And, of course, Alizar the Eleven-Eyed, who flamed in me.

And, of course, Nirwen.

Host Razoleth—and the angels who all dwelled inside of him—turned to regard me as I paced toward him.

And because they were turned toward me, they did not see the first pilgrim, the one who had been leading the charge up the serac. They did not see her make it to the top.

She was tall—as tall as a nephilim—and clothed in the tatters of a refugee. Her face was burnt away, whether by acid or fire, I did not know, and her eyes were the cold, deep blue of the serac itself. No pupil or sclera. Just endless blue.

Two of Alizar's eyes were that very color. I now recognized that he must have manifested them in her honor.

Her hands shooting through the crenels to grasp the inner edge of the parapets, she heaved herself onto the ramparts behind Host Razoleth. And then she removed from the webbing she wore beneath her dirty outer robe two spikes of pure blue ice—which she plunged into the faces of Childlike Hirrahune where my uncle used to have ears.

The rest of those faces shrieked.

Staring over his shoulder at me, she gave me one, shockingly short, nod.

Hey! It's Scratch! Betony said, surprised, when she saw her with my eyes. *She with the rebel cherubs?*

She is their mother, Alizar replied, satisfied.

Mother Scratch. Father Bloom. Nea's passwords flashed through my mind. But there was no time to sink into saintly revelations, for Nirwen was turning away from Host Razoleth as if he were of no consequence. As she bent over the parapets to help another cherub over the ramparts, I leapt at my uncle. Rathanana's bear swiped a swatch of flesh from my flank, his wolf snapped at my thigh. I swung up Kirtirin's forest of branching hands, and twelve times twelve times twelve times twelve fingers grasped at me, seeking to pull me apart. Thathia's eels darted at my face, tangled all around me, sent their aspic to slicken my path. And Zerat, Zerat, in his form of a blue-white spear of fire, burned so bright it was like climbing into the heart of a star who wanted to kill me.

But I reached my good uncle's shoulders, at last, balancing disparate parts of him like a monkey on a treacherous tree. I felt I had scaled the serac itself. The ramparts were far below me, and the ground was much further away than that. Letting me cling, he spun on eight paws, so that he faced the serac, and my back was to the empty air.

I looked into his eyes that were not eyes, and I grabbed on to the two icicle spikes jutting from the angel-swolle sides of his head, and I yanked them out.

"Bad Uncle!"

I could not see my uncle smile, for the angel Hirrahune was his mouth. My uncle could not embrace me one last time, for his arms were not his own. His legs would not move in the direction he bade them; there were too many legs, and the angel in them was too strong. Nothing of him was his own except his mind.

And the Razman had always been so very, very strong-minded.

The quarantine word—the one he'd invented, and planted in each of my uncles, and in himself—took hold, took root, and he wasted no time.

He swung Zerat's lightning bolt at me, and blasted me off his body. Not, however, off the serac, but back onto the ramparts. Two hundred million volts passed through my body at one third the speed of light, and if I were not a saint with a god in me at every single moment, I would have remembered nothing from that moment to the next, but I was, and he was, and I saw everything. I remembered everything.

I saw how Uncle Raz threw himself backward, over the serac, and fell two hundred meters to the bottom, his fall unbroken even by single smoldering midden heap. I saw him take all eight angels with him, and watched them, as from a bird's eye view, as they tried to flee his body in those six point three nine seconds between his fall and the impact. I saw Scratch—Nirwen—the scar-faced giant—leap to take his place on the parapet, robes billowing, and call out in a tongue I did not know. But though I did not know the words themselves, I knew their meaning.

Alizar was not the only god who could seal off a sovereign body. I had used his incantation to keep the angels out of my uncles. Nirwen used hers to keep them in.

I remember screaming.

I screamed and I screamed, and I tore down from my bird's eye view back into my body, and lifted myself right off the ground as if I myself was a second lightning bolt passing through me. I tried to follow Uncle Raz down—to fly down to him as Alizar had taught me. I hoped to swoop beneath him, break his fall, snatch him in my arms, lift him up—just as I'd lifted Uncle Eril earlier, just like that—breathing for him, *bringing him back!*

But Nirwen caught me before I went over. She pulled me back. Held me close. Her arms were pilgrim arms, wiry prisons, and I hung between them, enervated, my throat scraped raw.

He's gone, the god of Cherubtown whispered, *and he took eight angels with him. It's done. And now you have one last thing to do, Saint Ishtu.*

All around us, more cherubs were swarming over the serac. They launched themselves from the top rung of the ice ladder onto the parapets, and then down to the ramparts, and then at any of the Holy Host who still stood by.

But many of the Hosts, finding themselves now deactivated of angels, had started fleeing towards Tyr Valeeki, or leaping onto the dump-lifts, or taking the nearest emergency ladders back down into Gelethel. Wild-faced cherubs followed them close behind, some screaming for blood, others just bent on finally—finally!—entering the Angelic City, the paradise so long denied to them.

End this, Saint Ishtu, Nirwen told me. *You must end this . . .*

Alizar—heretofore a voice, an icy and invisible wind over the ramparts—manifested fully before us. He unfolded wings upon wings—some of feathers, some of delicate chitin, some of thin but tough patagium—and I fell into them, and was enfolded.

"Raz!" I cried to him. "Raz is gone—he's gone—he went over."

I know. I know. He was so brave, so ready. He knew what he had to do.

And so did I.

I wanted to ask if it would hurt.

I wanted to ask if it would be slow or fast. Slower than six point three nine seconds. Faster than a lightning strike. Would it hurt like Host Hosseril had hurt me, so profoundly that I felt nothing until I began to heal? Or would it hurt like it hurt now—much, much worse than anything I'd endured in the saltcellars, or anything before or since. This all-over grief that was like drowning in air.

Well. There was one way to put an end to that, anyway.

Untucking myself from his wings, I let Alizar lead me to the place where I should stand: the exact center of the ramparts, at the halfway point between the edge of the serac closest to Cherubtown, and the edge of the serac closest to Gelethel, with a god standing behind me and before me.

Before me, the godhead Nirwen reached her arm over her head, and drew from a sheath at her back a great spear of ice. Raising this high above her head, she drove down into the ramparts between her body and mine. It pierced the salt brick and cracked the serac beneath it, splitting the ice deeply, and sliding in until it was wedged solid. A slender blue pillar.

My pyre.

I stepped forward and wrapped myself around it, a twining vine trained to grow up a trellis. A flower about to bloom. I leaned my sweating forehead against the freezing ice, and allowed myself to fuse with the material. No separating us now.

Behind me, the godhead Alizar gathered himself into a hurricane of wings. I felt the wind of him at my back. I felt the heat. The light. I smelt him, green with growing things.

And then I felt him everywhere, and he was no longer separate from me, for he was blowing himself right through me: a solar wind, a stellar nursery. I was his fatwood, his tap root, his heart knot, and Alizar released into me all those billion billion billion pinpoints of gold-green light that he contained within his lantern self, and each one of those points was the seed of a star.

Every molecule of me burst into flame.

Wing. Light. Wind. Ice. The heart of a star. The heart of a saint.

And I am become kindling.

And I am become bonfire.

And I am become detonation.

The heat that melts the serac.

The floodwaters rising up.

The river that flows in four directions, and drowns me.

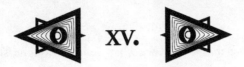

XV.

ELLIPSIS

The first thing I saw after I died was the facelessness of god.

All the pictures and carvings and statues I'd ever seen of Nirwen the Forsaker depicted her with her face gashed out. And that was how she appeared to me now, after the end of everything: a giantess as big as the sky, with an empty black oval where her face should be.

At the bottom of that black—maybe—stars.

Her rags had fallen away. She wore coveralls, like me. Sensible boots. Her wide belt bristled with all kinds of tools, devices, automata, other things for which I had no name. Her hands were massive, gentle, ridged with callouses. When I saw them, their shape, I thought at once of the nephilim Nea. Nea, I now realized, had her mother's hands.

I rolled over on my side, and vomited up what felt like a whole saltwater river.

"Saint Ishtu," said the erstwhile god of Cherubtown.

Erstwhile, because there wasn't any Cherubtown, was there? Not any longer. I didn't think there was even still a Gelethel. Not like the Gelethel I'd known, anyway. That was what we had wanted, wasn't it? And yet, and yet . . . had anything of the Angelic City survived? Or of the six angels who had refused, at the last, to stand against Alizar?

I tried to see beyond Nirwen, but she was everything, everywhere. Nirwen, whose face was the night sky.

But then she tilted her head, and the night shifted. I could see beyond her, further off from that faceless face. There was another sky, this one of dawn, and it haloed her in its frame.

It was a desert dawn: parched white with a hint of peach, remorseless, cloudless, perfect, without scrub or shadow.

"The serac has fallen," Nirwen told me softly, sinking down in the sand beside me.

Too softly: my ears were still logy with water. Water leaked out of me, out of my hair, my nose, my my clothes, my crevices. All of it was immediately absorbed into the thirsty sand that I was lying and she was squatting upon. My whole head felt grainy. My mouth tasted like a hundred years of salt.

"Do you wish to see?"

I must have moved my head in a way that indicated willingness. Or perhaps Nirwen merely decided that it was time I stopped lolling about the dunes of Bellisaar. Either way, she lifted me up high in both her arms and, cradling me, turned me around so that I could see what we had wrought, she and Alizar and Betony and I.

We were standing on a tall dune a kilometer or so outside of Gelethel. I'd never seen my city from this vantage—nor ever could have imagined it. The serac, with its uncanny cliffs of glittering blue ice, must always have impeded my view. But now the serac was gone. And I saw—for here the sand ran high, much higher than the Angelic City, which sat below sea level—the white domes of Gelethel, the white arches and white streets, all gleaming out across a shining expanse of river.

"The river surrounds the city on all four sides," Nirwen told me, satisfied. "The diamond of Bellisaar, running as meltwater. It flows in four directions at once, has no source and no mouth, and the brine of it has been purified by the death of a martyr. It is a hallowed wet. Once unpotable, now it flows clean and clear, sweeter than any water in the world. Anyone may drink from it. The sick shall come to it and be cured, the weary find rest, and gardens shall spring forth from its banks—from *both* sides of its riverbanks. Trees will grow there, vines and shrubs, sedges and grasses and mosses. My people will settle near its floodplains, and more will come. They will dig canals to water their crops, and wells and reservoirs for their families and their flocks, and all the Lands of Nir surrounding these four rivers will grow fertile and be farmed, and all the people in it, prosperous and favored."

She told this to herself like a story she already knew. I wondered if the god Gelethel had told herself such a story, as she pulled her palace out of the salt. The palace she had died in. It was the story of a beginning--but not even Nirwen could know how it would end. Not even Alizar.

Still.

It was a good story.

"The Land of Nir." I worked my brine-dried lips around the words. My mouth worked, but it wasn't emitting much in the way of sound yet.

Nirwen set me gently down. I was unsteady but found I could at least stand. My coveralls were mostly dry now, damp at the crotch and under the armpits. What I could have used was a long drink of real water and an even longer piss.

And possibly some time alone, out from under the all-seeing eye of a god. So that I could process some of what had just happened.

So I could think about what it meant to turn into a supernova and melt the serac, yet still remain enough of myself to drown in its meltwaters, and then be resurrected again.

So I could think about Alizar and Betony, on the other side of those waters where I could no longer dwell, and my uncles—if they lived—who remained there. And my parents, somewhere beyond these dunes, in the company of a nephilim whose mother had just saved my life. Or given me a new one.

So I could think about Raz.

My eyes stung with tears, and it was as if that triggered a wellspring inside me—for my mouth filled with cool water. It flowed over my tongue as if I had just drunk from a fountain, and washed down my throat, sluicing the salt away. I was refreshed throughout my body, and distracted from my grief. I tried to speak again, and found my voice was stronger now.

"Nirwen," I said to the god, "will you build a bridge from the Land of Nir across the waters to Gelethel?"

"We will build a hundred," Nirwen replied, "Alizar and I."

I smiled. Or tried to. I really had to pee.

"Then I wish you both luck, Artificer. And a host of saintly architects."

And some privacy, I silently added.

But of course, there was no such thing as privacy among gods. Nirwen touched the back of her huge hand to my cheek. She smiled down at me with such a slant to her scarred lips and a glint in her all-blue eyes that I understood she knew perfectly well the reason I was hopping from foot to foot, waiting for her to leave me alone so I could dash behind the nearest sand dune.

"To you, Saint Ishtu, I wish luck, and good health, and adventure—" Nirwen gestured to the dawn horizon, "and that the roads to the world will open before you in welcome."

I began to nod. "Thanks. Sure thing. So lo—"

"And," Nirwen added, "if you would: please bear my love to my daughter when next you meet her in Sanis Al. You saved her life on the serac—when she would have sent you through the Hellhole before her. You let yourself be taken in her place. Nea would not have survived the angels or their tortures; she is nephilim, not saint."

"No problem."

I didn't know if Nirwen knew for certain that I would meet Nea in Sanis Al, or if she was merely prognosticating a likelihood, god-like. But I found the thought encouraging. The world as I'd always known it had ended. But it was an end I'd worked towards; it was what I wanted. And now I had another task. I knew my next destination. I knew who I had to find. All three of them.

I. Just. Needed. To. Make. A. Pitstop. First.

"Oh, all right, Ish," said Nirwen the Artificer, Nirwen of the Land of Nir, Mother Scratch, god of Cherubtown, formerly the Fifteenth Angel. "Enjoy your piss in peace."

And she was gone.

I immediately dropped my pants and loosed a river to rival the one surrounding Gelethel. And when I was done, I stood up and buttoned up.

The horizon unfastened before me: sand and sky—infinite fathoms of each—both in this odd morning's gloaming of the same peculiar sea-foam shimmering. I stretched out my arms as far as they could go, opening myself to it, and let out a yawn that nearly cracked my jaw. Then pulled back from all that vastness, and looked to the place where Nirwen had just been standing.

Parked on the sand in that very spot was a brand new viperbike. Not a Zilch-sized one either. A me-sized one. Chrome and leather, with a sizable tailpack strapped to the pillion behind the rider's seat and stuffed full of something I hoped was clothes and food.

I went to it, my hands flying out before me eagerly—as if possessed of angels—to unzip the top of the pack. A few sheets of paper spilled out, each one drifting in a different direction.

I picked one up at random and read aloud, "*The Moon Princess*. A screenplay by J.L.P., dedicated to my daughter, Ishtu."

It was a screenplay. Dad's screenplay. *The tailpack was stuffed with Dad's screenplays!* No food or water or fuel or supplies or anything practical—and all I could think to do was jump up and down and dance. I couldn't care less what I lacked. I had Dad's *screenplays!*

Falling to my knees, I scrambled around, picking up every single one of the fallen papers before they could blow away.

And then, still kneeling, clutching the papers close, I spun to face east. To face Gelethel. Fabulous fucking Gelethel.

"Alizar!" I called to him, and oh, the city seemed so far away—and its new god and his good Saint Betony with it.

But that was a lamentation for later. For now, I had only one thing to say. "Thank you."

No answer. Just the wind, stirring the top layer of sand around my feet.

"All right," I said aloud. "No point hanging around here any longer. Guess I'll have to try this baby viperbike out. At least, I presume it's mine. If it isn't, well . . ." I shrugged, and put on my best Onabroszia voice for exactly nobody but myself. "Well, then, Q'Aleth Hauling Industries is within its rights to claim it as salvage."

I started looking around the viperbike for compartments, saddlebags, rings, attachments. But though I found plenty of detchable pieces and secret storage, I did not find any keys. Neither was there an ignition to put them in. (In the movies, there was always an ignition.) Even the dashboard was blank: no fuel gauge, no odometer or thermometer.

Disappointment, and something like panic, and along with that, the deep grief I was fighting to keep at bay for now, seized me. I sank onto the seat, and leaned forward onto the handlebars, resting my head on my forearms.

"Maybe it's Nirwen's idea of a joke," I murmured. "Or a toy. I mean, who abandons a viperbike in the middle of the desert?"

On the center of the dashboard, right below my face hung between the two handlebars, a great golden eye, large and lashless, opened up against the blank readout screen. It glowed. It flashed. It stared soulfully right into my face, and then—slowly—it winked. Or blinked. Whatever it is a single eye can do.

I bolted upright. "Alizar?"

The eye rolled to the left, glanced back at me, and rolled to the left again.

Taking the hint, I grabbed the helmet that was hanging from the left side of the handlebars, and jammed it onto my head.

Surprise! shouted Alizar. His voice rang clearly through my skull, as though amplified by the helmet.

Happy Feast Day, Saint Ish! Betony added. *Fuck, wow, that bike is* hot! *Hear it purrin' all the way over here. Nirwen says it's powered by your touch and thought. Practically unstealable, she said. 'Course, in my experience, some people like a challenge . . .*

She sounded wistful.

"Don't touch my viperbike, Saint Betony."

Ain't very saint-like of you, Betony sniffed. *Shouldn't you be palmin' it over for free without me askin'?*

"Nah," I said, teasing her, then immediately felt guilty about it. "Why? Do you really want it? I could see if I could get one of the cherubs—former cherubs—to ship it across the river to you. Once they get some boats. Or something…"

Nah, I'm stable, spar. Rode enough bikes in my life. Rode enough everything. Glad to walk a spell. Besides, you need it—journey you'll be goin' on. Eh?

"I'm going to Sanis Al," I said—and really believed it, for the first time since announcing my plans to Uncle Zulli in Mom and Dad's great room all those lifetimes ago.

Of course you are, Ish! said Alizar, as if there had never been any doubt—which, I knew, there was. *And we will be checking in as often as you want us. We discovered immediately that it will be harder for us to communicate across the rivers, and our connection will become much more tenuous the further you roam from Gelethel—but Nirwen said that wearing her helmet should help you to hear us.*

Betony added, *So, learn to sleep with it on, Q'Aleth. Hope that thing's got comf, 'cause you and it are gonna be real boon from now on. From now until . . . when was it you finally gonna let let us die, Bug? Twice seven times eleven, you said? And*—Betony was starting to sound very smug and saint-like indeed—*Bug says he's startin' the countdown from* now, *not from when we was born, so you and I can ascend together.*

That sounded very much like Alizar was cheating on his word to me, that he would let me age naturally and die at the end of a normal human span.

But maybe a long life wouldn't be so bad. Now that I had better knees, and a viperbike, and Dad's screenplays, and Betony, and could—when the occasion merited it, and with Alizar's remote help—maybe fly a little.

Maybe it would not be so bad now that I was living for two—for Uncle Raz, who had taken eight angels with him in his fall, and who would never look out over the dunes of Bellisaar from the other side of a melted wall.

"I miss you so much already," I said—to the Razman. And to Betony. And to my own dear godhead, who'd loved me as his own for most of my life. "But I have more than I'd ever hoped for . . . and I am so grateful."

Alizar made a hum of disappointment that was like radio static playing directly in both of my ears.

But, Ishtu, your gratitude comes betimes . . . you have not found your other present yet!

Bug! Betony yelled. *We pacted on this, recall? You were s'pposed to let her come happenstance to it!*

Oh, bells.

On the dashboard, the god of Gelethel's golden owl's eye pouted. But only for a moment. The next moment, it had grown a thicket of lashes three centimeters long—which it batted with unbearable wistfulness up at me.

Won't you have a little look-see around, my Ish?

I reached out a finger and stroked those curly lashes until his eyeball began to purr.

"You're too good to me, Bug. I promise I'll do a nose dive into those packs of yours in a bit—before I take off the helmet. But first tell me—how's the city?"

Betony answered for him: *Fuckin' busy, spar! We made a hale mess. Your Uncle Wuki's in charge of the burials. Zulli and Madriq set up outdoor kitchens in Bower, feedin' everyone. Everything's upheavin'. Half the angels dead, the other half hidin' in the Celestial Corridor. No one knows when, or if, the next benisons'll come. So they're all lookin' to Alizar—who's workin' his garden overtime. Eril's there too. Set up a hospital tent with the help of a few pilgrims who know what's what, herb- and plant-wise. Lotta people hurt when the serac came down. Some gethels washed to the far shore. Some pilgrims washed in—some of 'em climbed in—no tellin' who's who, so everyone's keen to accept whoever as an accident of the gods. The saints have all come outta the Anchorholds. They're mostly pretty okay. I think. No stew, spar. It'll all be—*

"Jammy?" I guessed.

Betony cackled, and so did I, and it was good—so, so good!—not to be alone.

"I wish I could be there," I told them both, leaning even more forward to lay my head against the dashboard, right next to Alizar's eyeball. "I wish I could help too."

You are helping, my saint, Alizar assured me. *You are outside the loci of my genius, traveling abroad to give me wider notions of the world. If I ever knew its many ways and wonders, I have forgotten them these ten thousand years in Gelethel. It is not good, Ishtu—it is never good—for gods or angels or human-kin to forget the world beyond their walls. I need you, my saint—my first and most secret saint—to move through this world for me, and teach me all you learn.*

I swallowed, and nodded, and wiped away my tears before they splashed onto Alizar's eyeball. "I can do that," I whispered. "I can do that for you, Alizar."

There's a whole lotta sand to explore out there, Betony observed. *And it's a war-torn world, Q'Aleth—landmines and all. What's a saint do?*

Kicking up my legs, I swung around on the seat until I was facing the back, and the large pack on the pillion.

"This saint," I told them, "is going west to find her Mom and Dad. I need to know Mom's settled, and help with that if I can. Also, I owe my dad a tap-dancing psi-ship movie musical at the best nickelodeon in the Red Crescent. And *also*," I added, bending over to check out the back of the viperbike: fender, tail lights, rear paddle tire and all, "I have a message for a nephilim—from the god, her mother. Can't neglect that. And after *that*. . ."

I trailed off, seeing for the first time, a second bag, much smaller than the first, lashed securely to the tailpack by thick velcro straps.

This bag I recognized. The last time I saw it—going down into the Hellhole clipped to a loop on Nea's webbing—it had contained a gift that my bad uncles had smuggled into Gelethel on my thirtieth birthday. The Razman, whose rarely flaunted hobby had been stage prestidigitation, had pulled the gift—bag and all—out of his hat at my surprise party in Mom and Dad's backyard.

Alizar and Betony said nothing as I unzipped the bag. But the silence inside my helmet buzzed with their bated breath.

Inside the bag was my Super 8 camera.

The kind made for home movies. The kind that recorded sound.

The one I'd never yet used.

My heart broke like the serac, and the floodwaters poured through me once again.

Oh, my uncles! My worst of all possible, best, most beloved uncles!

Oh, Razman, who'd kept all his secrets so close for so many years, and then doled them out to me one by one until he had none left.

Oh, Onabroszia, who had destroyed her own brothers to spite the angels—and whose brothers had, in the end—helped us defeat those very angels.

Oh, Dad—who'd given up everything to come to Gelethel, and then given up everything again to leave it.

But I would make it up to him, starting now. I would learn to use my uncles' gift; I would move through the world as they could not. And I would record it all, what I experienced and what I remembered, so that the memory would live on, long after my mind, like Mom's, failed me.

"After *that*," I whispered to those in Gelethel who could still hear me, "I think I'll make a movie."

AN UNKINDNESS

JESSICA P. WICK

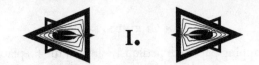

I.

IN WHICH I RECEIVE AN
(UNWELCOME!) GIFT

The only person who has never pointed out how ridiculous my dread of ravens—and by that reckoning, how ha ha amusing—is my older brother, Aliver. Even friends are ghoulishly eager to explain that not only is it impossible for a 'mere bird' to do me injury, but that one lives in my name. This is the last thing I wish to be told, excepting perhaps *'here is a raven to keep as a pet, look he likes you.'* The words 'mere bird' are spoken by those who have never gone hawking or seen crows mob a larger predator or spent any time observing nature at all, and I have received far more raven-themed gifts than anyone, whether their name is Ravenna or not, should be forced to put up with.

If pushed to give a cause for my fear beyond 'ravens are scary,' I might mention a terrifying unkindness—was ever a collective noun so apt?—of raven puppets I was given when I was still a child. Each raven was meant to represent a different kind of person I might become in the future, outfitted according to their prophetic narrative. Those puppets lurked in a dark clot above my wardrobe until the nightmares grew so sharp my nurse removed them.

One day a gift came for me care of the ambassador from Carawdin. The ambassador requested an audience with me especially and placed a small box into my own two hands. She didn't do as much for Aliver, who had letters from Carawthian acquaintance of his own. Those were left on the table, sealed and bound, and he took them up himself. The box was wrapped innocuously in old broadsheets and tied tight with a string. Usually gifts especially for me care of an ambassador are wrapped in fine cloth or gilt paper.

I was pleased to see the package was from my pen pal Erdyth. Such an unusual gift, I thought, meant she had either uncovered another interesting bit of Carawthian mountain lore (Carawdin is named for the Carawthian mountains and they are tall with story) or (and this was my fervent hope) was to able to escape her duties and visit. Finally, we would have the decadent coffee house tour of my kingdom we'd been planning since we were children.

I tore into the gift as if it was cardamom-honey cake. I decimated the wrapping, distributing it with careless liberality across the floor.

Aliver watched me. He had claimed the whole sofa for himself but I was perched in my favourite window seat. It has fine sea-green curtains that can be pulled closed so nobody can see me but I can see the gardens all the way to the labyrinth. Aliver was going through his own correspondence at a more reasonable pace.

A sheet of wrapping paper fell perilously close to the fireplace. Aliver, who is always curious, paused to pick it up.

"Ravenna, this is interesting! I think this is one of those illegal border ballads." His voice went all light and intent. Probably his eyes went light and intent too, like a day that promises rain but is too full of indeterminate light to fulfill that promise, but I was too busy opening the box to look at him. "Is Erdyth coming to visit? Save the rest of these!" He asked. "I'd like to meet her and talk about the—"

By then, the gift was unleashed.

It was a pen holder in the shape of an extremely sinister white raven, onyx chips for its soulless eyes. The expression on its face, beak half-open, was malicious; as if it wanted to drink my pens dry and break my words mid-letter. I felt my breath unsettle, and my bones too.

"*No*," I said, really despairing because although I'd never said anything to her about my dislike, I thought Erdyth would just naturally know.

Aliver immediately set aside the border ballad and his own papers. He plucked the pen holder from my hand. I was only too happy to let him.

"It's nicely crafted. And this is heartstane oak. I'll get rid of it for you." The penholder disappeared up his sleeve.

"Please," I said, my jaw tight. "You're fortunate nobody is inspired to give you themed gifts."

Aliver is named after The Wolf, Queen Alivera, our conquering ancestress. He did once receive a belt embroidered with a bloody battle: spears, pennants, horses with rolling eyes, men falling beneath hooves and hacking at each other with swords. It is a masterpiece. He has never worn it.

"Perhaps," he said. "But look, I think the real gift is in the wrapping. If you don't mind, I'll take it."

"Trust you not to be satisfied with your own letters—you really want to take my trash?" I was still sharp from disappointment.

But Aliver is good-natured and only laughed at me, in a way that made me ashamed of being sharp, but not feel any worse for being so. "'Never satisfied, always curious,'" he said. "Father hasn't yet agreed to officially change our family motto, but as far as I'm concerned, call the artists and change our crest."

Here was one of Aliver's pet subjects: art, and work, and what was owed, and what was owed curiosity. Occasionally, I liked to hear him speak on it. Father almost never did. Aliver really has tried to get father to change our family motto, which is the tedious and rather surprising (given our rather bloody history) *Loyalty Is True*.

"This is their home, too. It should defend them and be a shield as well as a hearth; wouldn't the King say *work* is the best shield? He'd say so to me." He smoothed the page out on the table. "Let's try and put the ballads to music. Maybe we can uncover the border bandits code. Erdyth probably knew you'd like the puzzle of it. Perhaps there's even an important message in it."

We spent hours working on the ballads although we are both only just musically proficient.

It was such fun. It was history and invention and math and music.

Not long after that, Aliver became a stranger.

He became one so slowly I almost didn't notice. Do *you* keep track of the sun as it courses across the bowl of heaven? The dark came and I was surprised. I am still surprised. He would inflict these little wounds with his behavior, but I kept putting it down to a mood or he wasn't feeling well or it just wasn't a good time. Of course Aliver couldn't keep our weekly tradition of Friday brunch; he was busy. Of course Aliver had nothing to say after I was honored by the museum and Archivist for my paper on flowers poisonous to shapeshifters and their frequent appearance in embroidery of the medieval period; the museum honors our family with very little effort on our part, since we're practically living relics. Of course he didn't appear when he was supposed to be my partner in the game of Swallows and Larks, and so I didn't get a chance at the lark ball even though I could have won the match on my own because Finula and Ambray—blast their eyelashes and toenails—said the rules didn't allow for two against one. He had other things to do then play sporting games, even if he'd previously said he would and I particularly dislike losing at Swallows and Larks. It wasn't his responsibility to save the newspaper for others to read; of course he threw them away when he was done. It wasn't sinister that he didn't save the last bone for the dogs, or never invited his friends for drinks in his chambers, or ignored the cats and rarely went out of the city and never into the woods and gave away his horses.

But then on Green Moon, his friend mentioned that Aliver wasn't going to visit the wishing well. Green Moon is when you can write letters to the dead and feel better about not forgetting them, and Aliver never missed a Green Moon revel.

I realized how long it had been since I'd seen Aliver do any of his usual activities. How long since we had spent time together. He was always disappearing. I watched him closely, but trying to figure him out was like trying to read the middle of a closed book without opening it; willpower will only take you so far. The cover only tells you so much.

II

IN WHICH I AM
(WITH GREAT EFFORT EXPENDED)
GOOD AT SNEAKING

D eciding to follow Aliver was easy. Successfully following him was more difficult. Unfortunately, he caught me immediately where I was loitering and asked whether I needed him to give me something to do.

"Brother!" I exclaimed, perhaps just a shade too like a character in a play. "I am encouraged by the warmth in your voice. Are we going to see a concert in the park? Let me get my cape—it is chilly for Flowermoon, isn't it?"

"You are going to your rooms," he said, and walked me there. His hand on my shoulder was just a shade too hard. "And I am going to mine."

His tone was the most discouraging thing, but I decided to take heart because he wished to quell my investigative spirit.

It seemed to me Aliver discovered my plan because I hadn't heard him leave his room, giving him opportunity to go around the long way and surprise me, so one morning—when I knew he was at council—I secretly removed the pin from his bedchamber door's middle-most hinge, soaked it in vinegar, dented it with a hammer, and replaced it. His door squeaked very pleasingly after that.

The squeak was meant to warn me if I was lying in wait by the stairs, but my rooms aren't far from his and I began to hear the hinge regularly at night. Each time my gaze jumped to the clock on my fireplace mantle, the one in fairy glass with the golden clockwork tree my Aunt Una brought back from a quest and which is no trouble to read in the dark. Each time I read half-past one. Judging by sound, Aliver opened his door and stood at its threshold for a good three minutes before closing it, slowly, behind him.

Seven nights of this and I went to confront him.

The hall was long and dark and moonlight falling from the great windows cut pale squares into the general shadowiness, but there was no sign of Aliver. I was on high alert. My brother means well but isn't necessarily to be trusted. Grandmother used to say Aliver has a player king's soul, when she wasn't calling him a fool and encouraging father to have another spare.

His door was open, a dense block of impassable dark. I threw a ring across the hall to see whether he was hiding just out-of-sight, but only attracted the attention of one of the Keep's cats. It poked its head around the corner, the triangles of its ears pricked high. It stared; I stared. It whisked, quick-soft, belly low, toward Aliver's room, but stopped before reaching it, arcing its back and spitting. It leapt sideways, batting at the darkness, then streaked away.

I decided Aliver's room was empty of Aliver, so I crept to the Big Stair. As I peered cautiously downward, I heard the hinge.

I turned.

Aliver's door was closing. I grew very still and looked very hard for a cause: the small compact shadow of one of the dogs or even another cat rubbing against the door's edge, causing the hinge to quaver like that. Maybe I did see a low shadow flickering away, or maybe I had dust in my eye and was blinking rapidly because shadows are not supposed to skitter in that way. I know the Keep is supposed to have ghosts, but I've never interacted with any. They usually stick to tourists and the more impressionable distant relations.

"I am not impressionable," I whispered, and then the probable-figment-of-my-imagination slithered quickly in my direction. I had just seen an animal in the low light; I knew what one was supposed to look like. This was something else.

The thing-I-was-probably-imagining was as dense a shadow as the darkness in Aliver's room; when it came toward me, it seemed purposeful. I fled to my room, my nerves thoroughly in tatters. The darkness nipped at my heels and I had an unpleasant swarmy slimy oozy woozy feeling up my shin and I slammed my door and turned on all the lights. I thought I saw light moving underneath my door and spent a terrified, sleepless night.

I felt ready to let the mystery go. The next morning, my leg throbbed, and I had things to do besides worry about Aliver all the time. We were both adults. He could take care of himself, certainly. It shames me to admit how rattled I was.

Aliver must have complained about the hinge because it stopped squeaking, but I knew he was leaving his room at the same hour every night. I'd gotten into the habit of listening for his footfalls. I couldn't sleep until I'd heard them go by, and then the door close—and then some Thing whispering by the crack between my door and floor, a Darkness pressing against it which I always took as the beginning of an unsettling dream.

Do you ever just need to know? Need, not want. The need drives you forward and you can't seem to rein yourself in? I never could stop myself from asking questions, and even though I was frightened away for a few nights, I couldn't leave the mystery. Not when Aliver refused his favorite dishes and was careless with everybody's feelings.

So came the night I stationed myself beside a wall hanging, the one depicting a bridal quest in a silver and gold wood. Behind the hanging was a bit of dust and a lot of cold stone. I couldn't stop imagining little shivers of movement in the dark and my shoulder went numb. They say that people's eyes adjust to the absence of light, but what about their hearts, if their hearts are cowardly like mine?

That's the sort of thought I was having when Aliver finally opened his door. A finger of light unfurled across the hall, only to be swallowed by his shadow. His hand on the light-switch finished the light off. I barely got behind the hanging in time.

His footsteps came nearer and, without pausing at my hiding place, turned leftward.

This is the point where I restrain my tour guide inclinations, but only a little. Left is the Big Stair, which spills toward the Twin Little Stairs and the Hidden Stair. The Hidden Stair is on the second level of the Left Twin behind a short archway and a walnut door. Its iron handle is shaped like a swan with wings outstretched—as if it were beating back an enemy, about to take flight, or (most likely in my experience) attacking a child at a picnic.

Aliver went down the Big Stair and I crept after. I was very conscious of his open door but refused to look at it. Tonight I would not be frightened away.

I missed my brother.

He was waiting for me where the Big Stair ends and the Twins begin, arms folded over his chest and mouth a paper-cut line. That portion of the stair is always lit electrically and there is nothing but glass overhead, so I could clearly see the sarcastic way he had an eyebrow raised—like a thorn on a flower stem you've just circled your fingers around, the one that cuts you.

"Aliver. You're awake?" I tried for a tone of convincing surprise.

He raised the other eyebrow. The flower had two thorns. "No. I'm sleeping as we speak. Can you guess what I'm dreaming?"

"Um, no."

"Good." His tone was even more discouraging than it had been before. "Because it's none of your business what I'm dreaming, any more than it's your business where I'm going. Why are you following me, Ravenna?"

"Don't be vain, Aliver," I said, sounding really very scornful. "I'm not following you, I'm—"

"You shouldn't lie." He measured out each syllable. "If you must lie, do it with your shoulders back and your back straight."

I thought the best course of action was to brazen through. My eyes went all bright and hopeful.

"Can't sleep? I can't either. Where are you going, since you mentioned it?"

He didn't immediately answer and I began to think he wasn't going to, until he huffed with impatience, just like a cat that has had enough of your human inattention.

"For a breath of fresh air. Alone." He frowned. "Why are you looking at me like that?"

"I'm trying to see if your shoulders are back and your back is straight."

He would have laughed before. This Aliver shook his head and said something that cut me to the bone. "I'm beginning to believe it prudent to revisit your marriage tasks. They could be too difficult for any suitor and that wouldn't be fair. Even grandmother's tasks could be overcome."

There is a law that our suitors must complete three marriage tasks, which are set by the family head, and we cannot refuse the first to complete all three. It is an archaic tradition, but in such traditions we are bordered by every day of our lives. Some Law-minded flower in the family tree had discovered that there was nothing that said the tasks couldn't be changed after they were set, as long as no one was in the middle of attempting to complete one, and so we get by. My tasks were presently very difficult, daresay impossible, because I have no wish to ever marry.

Never mind that he sounded weary under the sharp edge. Such a suggestion was meant to wound, and it wounded. Aliver might have said more, he might even have apologized, but I couldn't rally my attention until he turned to go.

"Don't follow me," he said, instead of goodnight.

"I wasn't. You are not that interesting. But I very likely could. What if we made a bet about it? And as a special favor, I will ignore your bad joke."

He never refused a bet. Not once in the nineteen years I've known him. He might have in the three years before I was born, but I suspect his nanny got him to eat peas by betting him he wouldn't. Aliver once bet his best friend he could walk backwards for three days without bumping into anything. The bet was over quickly, but that's only because the dogs didn't know Aliver was betting.

The president of our National Bank bet Aliver he couldn't find fault in their records or flaw in their security. The president didn't mean to bet Aliver, he was practicing his word play, unctuous in his assertion that the National Bank was like a fine jeweler, cutting away imperfections, presenting a flawless work of art. Five months later, Aliver returned with a smile, ledgers of research, and a suggestion for an improvement. He'd found a crack. Even the president had to admit so.

After the first lady Aliver kissed decided she didn't like him, Aliver moped until his best friend bet he couldn't charm this fierce little fox which had somehow become lost in the Keep and was attacking cushions and boots and driving the dogs mad. I remember him with the fox tucked away in his shirt, the smug hook of his smile. How he let the fox go, and let me come with him to watch it go free under the stars.

After reading the journals of our great great grandmother, Aliver's namesake, I bet Aliver he couldn't eat a raw wolf heart and wash it down with three bottles of nettle wine. Alivera had done that on her first night as Queen, right before she went on to conquer five kingdoms and give our nation's name to the whole peninsula. Aliver thought that too easy; he bet himself he could devour three raw wolf hearts and drink seven bottles of nettle wine.

He was so sick we thought he was dying, but he didn't die, and he venged himself on me by pretending for the next week to be turning into a wolf.

He licked and smacked his lips whenever our eyes met. When he saw the moon he howled and cocked his head like an animal. He gazed upward with fixed and glassy eyes, ignoring everything until he'd suddenly shake himself and re-engage in conversation as if nothing strange happened. He even changed the way he walked to be more wolfish, slinkstery, loping. At dinner, he panted and bared his teeth at the servers. He asked for his meat bloody. He ate it, looking at people meaningfully.

I was terrified.

Unfortunately for Aliver, and indeed for us all, this was the same week a diplomatic delegation from Forestwine visited, which really was having lycan-thrope problems. Lord Gervase wanted to burn Aliver alive, or at least brand his palm with a silver pentagram and rub salt on his tongue to see whether he was infected. When Aliver kissed Lord Gervase's daughter's hand and happened to graze her skin with his teeth, Lord Gervase called for a musket and pulled a silver knife from his boot.

It was very awkward, not least because we were half-afraid Aliver really was turning into a wolf and weren't certain we should be defending him. There have been rumors about great great grandmother. I fled the scene and made a fort out of my books to cry in, which I was far too old to do, and Aliver came to apolo-gize.

He gave me a wolf carved out of ice and said we could melt it down together if I was still frightened. Aliver had carved the ice-wolf himself. He is good at carving things, whether out of bone or wood or ice or stone or apples. He liked to say that he'd rather carve a fox out of ice than a victory out of flesh. It drove grandmother mad; she was the one who convinced our parents to name Aliver after Alivera.

When Aliver's best friend was killed by an arrow it was sad for everybody, but Aliver didn't cry. He bet himself a new circlet he could walk barefoot on the snow from one end of the city to the other. He almost lost a toe and I never saw him wear that circlet. If he had lost a toe the law would have kept him from becoming king. Our parents were furious and so was the Cabinet of Lords and Ladies but what I remember most is how pale he looked. As if winter were using him up, as if he were the wolf carved out of ice and set in a hot bath.

He was that sort of pale now as he stared at me.

I tried to sound enticing, but it was not my best work. "I bet you that I can—"

"No. I wasn't joking." He fiddled with a button on his wrist. He was dressed nicely; I hadn't noticed that before, but the rust coat was velvet and his trou-sers fine gray with black stitchery, a silver pin depicting corn at his collar and a feather curling out from underneath it. "Good night, Ravenna," he said.

"Aliver, you can't—"

He waved me away with his left hand, apologized curtly for being poor com-pany (Aliver always thinks he is excellent company, even when he is not), and continued down the Left Twin.

So did I. It would have proved I was following him if I turned around just because he caught me. I had nowhere to go but once I reached the ground lev-el—he was waiting for me, ready with a sardonic bow and a faint smile—I swept him an equally sardonic bow and headed for the door. Then I paused as if re-membering something very important. I turned back to the stairs (he was still standing at the bottom) and sailed back up as la dee da as possible.

I thought that was it for the night, I'd have to try again another, but in the hall I couldn't avoid looking at my brother's door.

Closed. A seam of darkness under the door, darker than the one under mine. My calf burned in memory.

My skin crawled, and I whipped around, running back downstairs. I tried to guess which way he might have taken. I chose the Hidden Stair because he was dressed so finely and I knew there was nothing going on in the castle that night; the Hidden Stair let out into the gardens, near the labyrinth.

There was no Aliver, but the new green glass gate hung open at its hinges.

The gardeners are very protective of the green glass gate, for it is a treasure that shines like a sea-jewel when the morning light falls on it. And besides, they'd lost the last gate, which had been of good (if slightly rusty) iron and had creaked admission to the Labyrinth of the Three Fairy Ladies for over a century. Aliver said that the new gate made a sound when he touched it like a silver bell chiming in a drowned city and I have never seen the Head Gardener so pleased.

"Would that we could go there, eh, Gardener?"

Aliver had smiled, but this was after the Arrow Incident, so it was a sad smile. The Head Gardener had been much moved and said, "To make a study of such gardens would be a dream."

The Three Fairy Ladies were rumored to have been seen by Alivera's husband at the spring in the labyrinth's center. The spring is old old old and the Archivist says it predates our family's existence. He knows it because every now and then, during flood season, the spring will cough up an old artifact, and that old artifact will be taken to the museum. It was on the instruction of the Fairy Ladies that Alivera's husband built the labyrinth, the better to beautify our grounds or bring tourists to the nation. Alivera was a conqueress, but her husband was a mad artist and he died while writing the schematics for an invention (on his lover's back!) that went on to become the modern piano. We make the best pianos in the world. My mother's marriage task was to tune the piano built by Alivera's son, great grandfather King Ludvec. Many are said to have died attempting to do so, and it is the originator of at least one ghost.

At first glance, the Labyrinth of the Three Fairy Ladies looks like a hedge maze. It has high walls, leaf and stone, root and wood, thorn and blossom all coaxed into a contemplative line and no way to see it unless one was in the Keep and in one of the upper-floors. Quite a number of tourists are thoroughly disappointed to discover there is only one possible path to follow. They come hoping to get romantically lost. If Aliver did go into the labyrinth to meet someone, the labyrinth's path would take him to the spring at its heart. Knowing there was only one path to follow did not, alas, preserve me from bumping into corners and being brought up suddenly by statues, and I was quite scratched up by the time I reached the center, which is where I did catch up with Aliver.

The spring was rich with a surfeit of starlight and the whole clearing bathed in a milky glow. The dark seemed darker and the light brighter. Night had taken away color, but there was a beauty in silvered dark. I was the drabbest thing in that clearing, with my moth-colored sneaking clothes, chosen for their ambivalent occupation—I might wear them in a coffee house, at the opera, or at council, and go unremarked. I might wear them for tromping, and it would only be a little strange.

Aliver walked into the spring without even taking off his boots.

He kept walking until his shoulders were submerged. The water eddied around him; it was bright, as if he had a star cupped in his hand, and I thought maybe he had a light. There seemed to be a mist coming off the water as if it were warm enough for clouds of steam to roll back.

I watched his head disappear beneath the eerily bright water.

I watched as he didn't come back up for air.

I waited. He must resurface now, I thought, and then with more fervor, *now*.

I hurried to the edge of the spring and plunged my hands into the water. It was not warm; it was cold enough to send an ache up my arms, make me grit my teeth in an unladylike fashion. I flailed about hoping to connect with Aliver's coat or his shoulder, but all I felt was water, so I adjusted my grip on the edge and reached deeper. I knew the spring was quite deep, numerous nannies and elderly relatives had made a particular point of telling me so, and it had a strong hidden current which could have swept Aliver away—could even now be taking him somewhere far, somewhere we'd never find. It felt as though there wasn't much time but I kept a cool head. I shimmied out of my sneaking coat, tied the end of it to my ankle and one of its arms to a stone. The precaution turned out to be unnecessary, but I think it is important that you know what a care I took—that if Aliver were swept away by the current, I wasn't so panicked that it would take me too without a fight.

I sucked in a deep breath and stuck my whole head underwater. There I opened my eyes, expecting murk and an Aliver with a foot stuck under a stone.

What I saw was a steep stair the same granite as the spring's lip and a white road. All illumined, all twilight-bright through a green haze. I saw an apple grove and a stable. I pulled my head from the water, gasping. Obviously, a road and a stable and so on beneath the spring was an impossibility, but when I again stuck my head and opened my eyes beneath the water nothing had changed.

I checked twenty times or so before I decided to copy Aliver. After all, I knew people who had gone into other worlds before and come back dandy as a feather. I untethered myself, and—pulling on my coat to give myself something less ridiculous to focus on—walked straight into the spring.

La dee da.

After the first five steps or so, it was like walking down any old stairway in any old building. I confess that I flinched at each step, prepared to suddenly find myself drowning. I marveled that I never did. Halfway down a handrail appeared, green glass and smooth. I gripped it hard but didn't really need it. My clothes billowed around me, and my hair, but both ceased moving when I reached the apple grove.

There I took the shallowest sip of air and found I could breathe.

The apple grove was in blossom. The blossoms were the color of dawn-light, all rosy and sweet, and I yearned to make a crown of them. Before my yearning could distract me too much, I turned away from the stair then whirled around and went "*Ha!*" As if I would catch the stair gingerly lifting itself up, abandoning me to the world under the Fairy Ladies' spring. It did no such thing, but from the apple grove the view up was so strange: a stair leading up into a watery fog, a green haze.

The stable door opened and out came the stable master. He was dressed plainly in kitchen-pot blue and had the body of a cook but the head of a rat, which is cute in proper proportion but human-sized was grotesque and frightening. It wasn't a mask; his whiskers twitched at me, and his nose, and he seemed taken aback by my presence.

"I will take a horse," I told the rat-headed man, loftily. He held his hands up and shook his head.

I repeated myself, although not as confidently. "I will take a horse? Never fear, Master of the Stables. I will bring it back. But I wish to go riding. Now."

I didn't believe he could speak, or at least if he could it wasn't in a language I would understand. Now that I know more, I think he could speak, but chose not to. He just shook his rat head, whiskers bristled out and teeth a little bared, and gestured toward the stable as if showing me something I was too, too stupid to see. I began to cry.

"Listen, Sir Stable-rat," I said, around copious amounts of snot and tears. "If you have some other mode of transportation I will take that, but I need to take something, because I need to find my brother. He came this way. He had to have. Did you see him pass? He came down the stairs too. He has very black hair and—"

The rat-headed man spat on the ground. When he turned his back on me, I saw he did not possess a tail. He slammed the door of the stable's office, took a pipe from his coat, and proceeded to smoke it furiously. When he saw me staring through the window, he turned his back again.

III.

IN WHICH I AM TOO BRAVE
(AND THERE ARE CONSEQUENCES)

I took one of the horses, a pretty little mare with a splash of gold on her fore-head and again on her flank. She was already saddled and ready, as were all the horses in that stable. Evidently, a great company was expected, but I am a princess and would pay later for the inconvenience. The mare balked at being lead out without her match, a stallion entirely gold except for a white stip-pling along his neck. The stallion stamped his hooves as she was lead away and pressed his chest against the stable door. The door rattled in its frame. Once I was astride, the mare calmed enough that I could guide her to the road. It went in one direction if one did not count the stairs up into the spring and I hoped Aliver hadn't too great a head start on me.

Trees in blossom turned to trees in fruit, apples red as a gory remainder. I was not tempted by them as I'd been by the flowers; they had a carrion smell and a sticky look. The weather was temperate and the mare sweet enough to keep a steady pace while I used both hands to wring out my hair. My clothes were, somehow, merely damp.

The road left the orchard for a forest. The air smelled of heath and musk and spice and cinnamon and rot. The light was ruddy as torchlight but no fire to be felt or seen, only imagined in how a-blaze the foliage was. Leaves fell there in scattered bursts of ember-spray, but drifted so slow it was as if they would never quite reach the ground. I was disconcerted and caught a leaf between my palms, careful 'lest it actually singe me. But in my hands it was what any leaf might be in autumn—dry as a rattle, ready to crumble. When I dropped it, it fluttered as it should always have done, winking pale gold and dark honey round and round until it met its friends on the side of the road.

It clinked. The mare's hooves chimed on the leaf carpet. We sounded as if we were rifling a cutlery drawer. I dismounted—I was so curious—and picked up the same leaf. It was turned to true gold, the kind of leaf that monks would press into a god's portrait. I tucked the leaf into my pocket and rode on.

The road left the autumn forest for a silver-white wood where every tree was in bloom and there was a smell of brine and metal. There the flowers were pearly with life and wore the inviting black of tarnish where they weren't iridescent in purples and greens. In stark contrast the branches of those trees were moon-white or bone-silver, as pale as frost and almost luminous. Nothing fell. I had the feeling nothing ever fell and not one petal ever lost its luster.

I gaped like a fool in the silver wood, but I kept my hands to myself. It felt hungry there, and the stillness too attentive.

The road split at a crossroads and I let the mare have her head and choose our way. We passed a gallows. I'd only seen gallows in nasty pictures before; they weren't allowed in my nation on account of history. This one was constructed from driftwood and bone—human bones, I was guessing, as I stared in repulsion and fascination both. I tried to ignore the figure hanging from the pole after I'd ascertained it did not have hair as black as pitch and a rust doublet and, anyway, was much too tattered and weathered and picked clean of anything resembling life to be Aliver.

A shadow solidified into a raven, which caawed my name as we passed. My bladder made its presence known with a sharp squirt of treachery. The raven leered on the gallows' pole like an executioner in a ballad, the kind who makes unseemly deals regarding virtue lost.

"Did you speak?" I said, drawing the mare up short. "Did you say my name?"

It picked at a knot of rope tied there, then caawed again.

It *was* my name.

I straightened my back and shoulders and urged the mare to greater speed. The raven followed for a short while.

We reached a vast lake. There the air was the deep blue of late evening after the sun has gone but before the world has forgotten it. The lake reflected the evening and the palace floating at its center as lightly as one of those long-legged insects which walk on water. The mare stopped when the road stopped and I wondered how to get to the palace.

The mare wouldn't walk into the lake so I presumed I probably shouldn't either.

People who claim to encounter ghosts in the Keep generally begin by describing a scraped-thin and verge-of-tearing sensation in the air. Some claim they know things they couldn't or feel emotions that aren't theirs. Looking at the lake was like that. I was glad it was evening here. A lake so perfectly still would be clear down to its bottom in daylight and I didn't want to see what might be beneath its surface. I felt certain I knew the lake was fashioned by a fairy silversmith; that the silversmith had been killed so no other lake would ever be so perfectly clear and smooth; that the fairy silvermith had had masterpieces yet to create; that the weight of their absence haunted the lake. I could imagine it inspiring envy and passion and the spilling of blood. I could taste blood in my mouth.

That is when the silence began to really bother me. It wasn't right—there should have been a clamor about. I felt as if I'd just been hearing it, noise of some great company camped all around, but instead there was nobody and nothing. It was the same unexpected discomfort as trying to speak naturally in the morning, but there's still a frog in your throat so your voice doesn't come out at all. Twice I felt as if someone was about to grab me and I turned.

I think I could have sat there on the mare for a long time, but I thought of Aliver, and forced my attention across the lake.

The Fairy Palace on the water was dark, but glittered attractively against the evening.

Behind the Fairy Palace was the largest and most improbable waterfall I have ever seen. I don't know how the lake's surface took no notice of it when the Fairy Palace itself was drenched by the white froth. Towers and domes, flying buttresses and circular windows, all disappeared into that soft mist. Glowing lamps shone forth fragmenting into green rainbows. Perhaps the waterfall was actually quite distant and my sense of perspective flattened everything, but mist from it obscured the far lakeshore. Under the dull basso profundo roar of the falls, I thought I heard music. It seemed lively.

I reminded myself I'd met a person with a rat's head keeping a stable under the spring in our labyrinth and shouldn't expect things here to conform to my expectations.

I waited. Have you noticed things don't happen when you wait for them?

Eventually, I urged the mare as close to the water as she would get, intending what I did not know. As we approached the water's edge, it parted as if it were silk sheared open by a pair of sewing scissors. Through the part rose a narrow and most untrustworthy-in-appearance bridge. It was narrow and slippery and sleek and uneven. A narrow little house was built into the bridge's first arch and a man and woman opened its green door and came to greet me. Each had the head and elongated neck of a swan.

They did not turn their backs on me as the rat-headed man did, but tried to take the mare's reins. With a pang, I gave them up and dismounted. The man helped me. His hand was human, but along the bone ridge of his forearm I saw a line of feathers. There might have been more under his shirt.

"Before I go in, oh I know this is too too silly," I said, in what I hoped was a confiding manner. "But please say you can remind me how to pronounce my host's family name?"

I think the swan-headed couple was confused. I have never seen a swan's head look anything but vapidly menacing, but their body language was hesitant.

"No matter," I said, when they said nothing at all.

As I crossed the bridge, I was plagued by imagining it plunging suddenly and how, if that happened, I might not die but be kept forever, the lake a perfect fairy-smithed curio cabinet door. But the bridge did not suddenly plunge down, and servants with bushes—branch and leaf, topiary tightly managed—for heads opened the palace's doors and let me into a ball.

All balls have certain similarities. There's always someone who looks as if they'd rather be anywhere else than with the person who has them cornered. There's always someone who has lost a glove or a wallet or a ring or a dance card. There's always someone laughing too loud, either from nervousness or too much drink or because they will be damned if somebody else flirts with more aplomb than they.

The fairy ball had these, although I took note of other differences. A wet, coppery smell; a table in the center of the room with nothing set on it and the dancers avoiding it; how the water from the mist condensed into dew droplets shining crystal snail-trails of verdigris greening down pillars and over statues and balconies, foliate, everything foliate. I touched a wall and my palm came away wet. I've never seen such architecture outside a storybook's illustrations. The ceilings were taller than a streak of lightning. A third of the guests were inhuman—or part-human part-animal or part-plant; another third went about with their eyes closed, as if blind or sleepwalking. The final third seemed to be human, but human in a *tugging* sort of way. They weren't necessarily beautiful, but they were difficult not to look at.

I was feeling out of my depth and wishing I hadn't been so hasty in following Aliver into the fountain. That I'd at least gone and woken Aunt Una, whose depth this very much seemed to be. Una might even have known the name of this underworld. She might have visited it herself.

A woman swooped down on me as I edged along the wall; I never heard her coming. She wore a black justacorps sewn with pearls, tiny translucent snail shells, and little mushrooms—actual, living mushrooms!—along the pocket edges. She asked me something, but I didn't hear. I couldn't stop staring at her face. It never moved when she spoke, as if it were dead—but oh, it looked so alive! I could touch it and it would give! I was fascinated.

And then it whisked down, and I realized that the woman's human face with its pretty bow lips was a mask on a stick, and the woman's true face was an owl's.

She repeated, "Have you seen my glove? I was sitting here," and gestured to a cushioned bench I'd been about to stumble over.

"Um, I have not," I said, with what I'm afraid is my typical level of cleverness when taken very off guard at a ball. "What does it look like?"

"It has four tubes for my fingers and one tube for my thumb. Like this." The woman held up her still-gloved hand.

"I will keep an eye out for it," I said, sympathetically, but also in a firm conversation-ending way.

Instead of moving on, she tilted her head and moved the short hook of her beak back and forth. Having come to a decision, she leaned closer. I was at eye-level to the little bone broach pinned in the lace at her throat. The bones were mice: sleepy mice encircling another rodent skull, its eyes rubies. I moved back away from her and found myself sitting abruptly on the bench. She continued to lean over me.

"You're not a sleeper. Who is your patron?"

"He has dark hair to about here," I said, vaguely, "and a coat. Longish. Very much the mode. Shoes. With good soles. For dancing. He dances. This is a ball where we dance."

"I wish that you will dance with me," the woman said, after considering my description. She whisked the human-woman mask over her owl-face again, but

I could see the glow of her golden eyes through the eyeholes. She held out her ungloved hand.

"I—I can't," I said, rather desperately.

"It is a ball. Where we dance." The human-woman mask stared at me.

I scooted along the bench and stood, brushing off my trousers. The bench I kept between us, but she turned her head to follow my movement.

"It is a ball, buuut . . . I swore an oath," I said, because Aunt Una had told me that fairy creatures were creatures of law, even more so than the Cabinet of Lords and Ladies, and they loved oaths and would abide by them even when it wasn't in their interest to do so. "I cannot dance yet; ask me no more, or I will be forsworn."

"If you bleed, you bleed like prey," she then said to me. She had eased back after I mentioned an oath; her tone of voice was observational rather than menacing. Even so, I felt a keen desire to distract her with something—anything—else.

"Is that your glove over there? With those gentlemen?"

'Those gentlemen' were a pair of bush-headed people dressed in the manner of a mid-rank soldier, albeit from fifty years ago. Their necks erupted into towering, improbable snarls of goldenrod. There were bees nosing around some of the flowers, and it was lovely, if one did not look too hard for a face inside the botanical. One was smacking his palm with a glove.

The woman abandoned me immediately, bearing through the crowd with singular purpose.

I hastily removed myself to another location, almost knocking into a vaguely familiar woman, plain but with sharp eyes, who stared after me. I willed myself to find my brother quickly.

And then, there he was.

I almost didn't recognize him. He was smiling at someone, eyes gone mellow in a way I'd nearly forgotten. His forehead was smooth instead of marked by irritation. His companion was wearing something that glittered and was one of the most tugging to look at. I took an awkward little step towards them but she grabbed his hand and swept him into the dance. He never looked in my direction.

The last thing I wanted to do was dance, especially in case the owl-woman saw and asked how my oath had been concluded so quickly, and so I lurked. I am quite good at lurking at balls. The key is to be in constant motion, always on the periphery. I found a refreshment table and lurked there, but touched none of the food. I found a table with a game of cards and lurked there until the players made noises as if I should join them. The cards they used looked nothing like any deck I have ever seen. I lurked beside a little silver bear who I mistook for a statue at first, until she asked me for the name of a color.

"You have forgotten the word?" I said, cautiously.

"I came here to get the name of a color. I want the name of the color of your hair; you will give it to me, then I will have it," she replied, frowning.

"Will I forget the word?" I tried to keep my voice light, but think perhaps a wee bit of how unsettled I felt crept through. The silver bear seemed to loom.

"I cannot remember the name; *give it to me.*"

There was a rumbly kind of imperative in the request and a darkness to her eyes. My calf throbbed. The darkness in her eyes became fibrous, matched by darkness leaking from her mouth.

"I couldn't say," I told her, and moved on.

The dancers never rested. The music grew wilder and lovelier and more like a sparkling display of mysterious objects translated to sound and given a heart. Candles burned down and were replaced. Musicians with their eyes shut tightly were replaced, their bloody fingers painted in salve and wrapped carefully in fabric.

And Aliver whirled with the glittering woman. He didn't seem to grow tired any more than the other guests did. If I hadn't been in such a panic I would have been very bored.

To keep my mind alert and my attention on course, I began to plan what I would do next. Some people become overwhelmed by the future, I know, but I am the opposite. My penpal Erdyth has said she thinks my mode of planning for the future is a steadying influence on me, perhaps my interest in history. Ever since a tutor drew the idea to my attention, it has seemed to me that one has time to plan the accomplishment of even the most elaborate goals when one considers the scope of history.

I like lists. They make me feel calm and in control.

First, I would follow Aliver home. At breakfast, I would tell him just because he spent all his nights dancing in a secret fairyland, that was no reason to behave as he was behaving. He would say, 'Ravenna, I don't know what you mean,' and I would say, 'Aliver, you really must give me more credit. I know we didn't bet but if we had I would be the winner, even father couldn't contest that, because I followed you and if that creepsome shivery enchanting world makes you happy, I am happy for you. Because, Imaginary Breakfast Aliver, I miss you. I miss you so much and so does everyone else. Surely, we can work out a schedule where-in you follow your heart without taking your lack of sleep out on those who here-to-fore had adored and supported you.'

The imaginary conversation dissolved when the scream began. The scream crawled under my skin and scratched at my bones and went on and on. I sometimes think I still hear the echo of it. The dancers barely slowed, but the other guests began to chatter in that hushed expectant way of a crowd that already knows what manner of surprise is for it.

There came a hand hard on my elbow and a voice like a chip of light on black glass in my ear.

"Careful, now."

I batted at the hand and turned toward the voice.

It belonged to a young man, black hair oiled in antiquated waves, wearing the face of a raven. Beneath the raven's long beak was a pillowy mouth and an anticipatory smile. Had he taken the face from a man with a raven's head, like the swan-headed gatekeepers, and placed it atop his own? Was that blood cooling between the feathers, crusting at the edges of his skin?

"Do you like my mask?" he said, cheerfully. "My sister has its match. You wouldn't believe the trouble they took to get. The previous owner did not want to give them up. This is your first ball thrown by Princess Kiss-While-the-Melancholy-Evening-Silvers, isn't it? You must choose a more judicious vantage point. And if you return, don't forget your own mask. Do you not own one yet? Have you considered weasel or ermine—something in its winter coat?"

Without waiting for response, he steered me forcibly toward a pillar.

The scream took on a shredded quality, but the edges still cut. My throat was raw listening to it.

He looked at me so expectantly I stopped looking wildly about and gathered up my dignity.

"Your mask is atrocious; I suspect it suits you very well," I said. Then, more pleading than I'd like to remember, "Let go my arm and tell me what is that sound?"

He did release my arm, placing a finger against the tip of his beak. Then he pointed.

I saw the unicorn.

At least, I think it was a unicorn. It was as small as a doe, bright as light on water, and wounded. Sometimes as it fled through the crowd it stumbled and seemed to have the shape of a man. Mostly it ran on four hooves. Wherever it went, the unicorn left behind silver liquid, viscous as honey. Its belly was open and ropes of something hung toward the ground. The something seemed very much as if it shouldn't hang like that. The guests applauded when it fell against somebody's legs, tangled its horn in a sword hanging from a belt or in a cluster of ribbons dripping from a wrist, whenever it seemed to look for help. They laughed politely, as if this were a common game, and sometimes with real delight.

Coming up on the unicorn's trail were six men, each handsome, all repugnant. Two held bows ready, arrows notched. I looked to see my brother's expression but could only find the back of his head. His hands were raised and still, mid-clap. The other four had clubs and silver-bloody hands. One wore a crown of candles burning, tallow in rivulets down his earlobes, his earrings, his jaw and his neat-trimmed beard; another, a stag's crown, antlers thrusting from his forehead, moss dripping like lace from the tines. Another had an eagle on a leash, which seized one guest's wig and dropped it on another's head, to general amusement.

The guests pressed close but from my vantage I saw it all.

How the unicorn collapsed at last and did not move except to breathe and roll its head. How one guest threw up her skirts and pretended to ride the horn. How an old man with a sketchpad came forward to do a hurried sketch, dipping his charcoal into the silvery blood after. I saw him kiss it and lick his lips.

The hunters with their bows, their notched arrows, approached it from two sides. I waited for Aliver to say something; he was right there. There was silver on his shoes. They shot the unicorn. Its sides had not stopped heaving when their knives flashed and they began to carve steaks from its flanks. The glittering woman raised a hand and closed her fingers into a fist. Her fist conjured silence – all ceased chattering, squawking, growling, tumbling, clapping. I would have spoken but I didn't so it doesn't matter saying so. I knew if I opened my mouth I would vomit.

Then, in the perfect silence, which was a perfect stage, the glittering woman fed Aliver a sliver of unicorn meat with her own fingers.

I threw up on Ravenmask's shoes. They were fine shoes before I vomited on them: blue velvet with silver tassels shaped like foxgloves and fastened in place by bird talons. The vomit's yellow did not set them off. Ravenmask was moved to say, "Ugh!" But he held my hair back.

"Does he think it is cake?" I whispered. "Like thinking leaves are gold?"

"Unlikely," Ravenmask whispered back. "Unless you hunt cakes in the world above. Who invited you here, darling? You're so springy."

The glittering woman called for a cup. An appreciative murmur went through the room. Peals of laughter, scattered bursts of applause.

"I'll pay for your shoes. When does this end?" I asked.

"After the Dead Lord in Waiting toasts the dance. You couldn't afford my shoes. My sister – "

I stopped listening because the hunters were hauling the unicorn onto a table—it shrieked, desperately; it was still alive—and one was pressing a cup into the glittering woman's hand. The cup was green glass like the garden's gate and it caught light from her. Aliver grinned. The last time I saw Aliver grin like that was at the turn of the year, before his best friend died, before he'd gone cold and secretive and stopped liking us.

He took off his shirt. There was a scar on his chest. The woman stroked it and I – did I start forward? I want to think I did. I need to think I did. I believe Ravenmask held me back but I'm not sure. I am a coward. I am a coward. Nobody so much as glanced towards me except a plain woman with sharp eyes, the one I almost knocked over earlier who seemed so familiar. Everybody else was intent and happy, licking their chops like cats at feeding time, except perhaps the hunters, who stood blank as a cracked bone.

They opened my brother's chest and cut out a piece of his heart. He did not, contrary to my expectations, die. Instead, he dropped the meat into the green glass cup and it was bloody and disgusting. He toasted the company and they all drank from the same cup. It never ran dry.

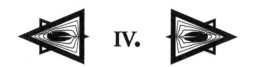

IV.

IN WHICH I MAKE A DEAL

The green glass cup was coming my way. I was determined to avoid it and I flattened myself behind a pillar. There was an abundance of pillars. Spitefully (and unfairly), I thought it was so the whole preening malice of fairy creatures could pose for one another. Ravenmask stayed beside me, though he followed the cup with his eyes. I think he wanted it badly but was, for reasons of his own, unwilling to take it while I was there. I was grateful for that.

"He's enchanted," I said. I saw the cup again, and moved along the periphery. The guests who'd already taken of the cup were entangled with one another if they were not gazing upward, a hand pressed over their hearts or touching delicately their lips, beaks, teeth, masks, flowers.

"He knows what he does." Ravenmask scratched his jawbone beneath the feathers and a long flake of dried blood came off under his nail. He ate it. "Did you come by the fountain or the fen?"

"Pardon me?" I said. There were less people between myself and Aliver, but he still did not look in my direction.

"The seed-pearl way or the gull's, pet? I shouldn't go by the green glass way were I a springy lass. The green glass way will make you rue your day." He sounded as if he was trying to give me a hint and snorted, pleased with himself. "But I've become a Rhymer! My playwright will be jealous."

"Your playwright?" I startled. The plain woman with the sharp eyes—she *was* somebody I knew! Or rather, somebody I had seen at the Yearturn Festival when she won a prize, best new playwright or maybe best new tragedy. "Evelisse Demorgen?"

"Mine insofar as I am her captive, her patron, and her friend when none other title applies. She could lure the moon down to hear her work. I know, for she has. And see, you know her name."

He'd been a good sport about the shoes but I didn't have time for a poetic digression. He reminded me of Aliver when he is being very Aliver, charming and sincere and full of poetry, and thinking about Aliver was hard to bear without looking at him, his chest still undone.

"Did she send you over to me?"

But while we had been distracted, the cup came to us, courtesy of the owl-faced woman in the black justacorps. She handed it to Ravenmask, nodding with solemn courtesy to us both. I suspect that she thought he was my patron. There were globs of silver unicorn blood on the side of her coat and she'd re-claimed a glove. It wasn't the one the two goldenrod gentlemen had been play-ing with nor was it the match of the one she'd shown me first.

He toasted her, and sipped, then handed the cup to a man with closed eyes, who toasted Ravenmask and sipped, then handed me the cup. I stared at the liquid, the shadow at the bottom of the cup, and then held it out. Somebody took it away from me.

"How do I help Aliver?"

"You don't," Ravenmask said. He was trying not to lick his lips.

"I don't now, but I will. Soon as we are home."

The glittering woman closed Aliver's chest with a finger and put it to her lips, and that seemed to signal an end to the ball. Clumps of guests unraveled, threading toward the doors. I stayed by the pillar. Ravenmask stayed by me. The hunters had hauled the unicorn onto the table in the middle of the ballroom. One hunter was carving up the unicorn, handing slivers of meat to those who paused to ask for it. The cup came back to Aliver and he held it up. It caught the light like a star.

"He helps himself," Ravenmask said. "Listen, don't try to leave again by the green glass way—that's the way you came in, pet. And if you return, bring a mask!"

He took my hand and pressed it close to his chest. Through his fine velvets he was as clammy as a rainy day. When he released my hand the crowd swept him immediately out of sight into a troop of well-heeled, well-coiffed guests.

My stomach was still wavery and so was I, but I refused to accept 'you don't' or 'he helps himself.'

I would save Aliver. He was doing a poor job of helping himself judging by tonight's antics. I would talk to him back home at breakfast. I knew he came home. I would find Evelisse Demorgen and make her tell me everything about this underworld. Aunt Una would help, or the Archivist who'd catalogued so many objects from the spring. Perhaps I would jam Aliver's door shut until I figured out a better way to keep him from returning here. I would go to the library and suggest to father the spring be paved over and a very heavy iron obelisk be erected in its place in honor of somebody. There's always somebody who deserves an honor.

The glittering woman and Aliver were no longer standing where my eyes had left them, but I found the starlight gleam of her by a door. A brace of footmen handed coats and cloaks to departing guests. Near the starlight gleam was Aliver's rust doublet and his black hair. And the owl-headed woman, looking around in the poised way that predatory birds have, where you just know they are ready to drop on whatever they see. I hoped it was not me and was not ready to confront Aliver yet so I hid in a convenient alcove. It was framed by two ornamental statues and beside a narrow window with a view of the bridge. From that vantage, I watched the guests leave two by two on steed or, eschewing the bridge altogether, in pearl-crested boats trailing water lilies and covered in blue lichen. These left no wake on the water. Occasionally, I allowed myself to be distracted by the statues; they were outside my realm of experience, one depicting a satyr disporting himself by himself, the other an almost too ornate statue of a woman with a rose for a head fondling a very protuberant flower.

Once I guessed most of the guests had gone, I descended with a most convincing yawn. Ravenmask told me not to leave by the green glass way, but I had no idea what he meant by that. I yawned all the way to the door, rubbing my eyes and behaving like somebody who had shoe polish for brains or too many drinks. At the door, I waited haughtily (and for quite a long while) until a youngish man with a hound's head bounded over, panting in distress.

"My horse, please. I am tired and anxious to be on my way."

The hound-man's eyes were dolorous in that way some dogs have, as if the whole of them is tangled in the good they want to do you and they fear they have failed and there will never be another kind word. I was tempted to pet him and assure him that really, it was all right, he was a good boy.

Fabric rustled like leaf-fall.

"But why so swift away when you took such pains to come without invitation?"

The glittering woman did not menace from the shadows. Menacing was clearly beneath her. She regarded me with unblinking eyes and a smile like a scratch-poison needle, something delicate and lethal. A wasp's stinger. I thought her a monster. I wanted nothing to do with her, but somehow I wanted her to like me at least as much as I wanted to slap her. I didn't dare slap her.

"It was a singular event," I said, which sounds polite but actually means nothing. Her smile grew not in size but in concentration of poison. I tasted bile and swallowed. Were they bringing my little mare? The twinkling lights at the back of the last escaping boat vanished into the changeless blue of the fairy evening. "You are familiar with my brother."

"Yes. Walk with me, Ravenna."

Up close, she didn't glitter like stars. She glittered like dew on a spider's web or a veil of raindrops on a wave of hair or a fall of wool. She took my arm companionably and drew me away from the Fairy Palace and onto a little meandering cliff-side path that circled it. She felt human.

I'm afraid I gave the hound-headed man a dolorous look of my own.

"You know you should not have come," she said. "You have not the right."

I suppose it sounds as if I was lead, quite docile, by this woman. I am meek sometimes, and also a coward, and anyone like her was clearly deserving of my terror. Generally, I find it good policy to give people their just desserts, and I was terrified. However, I chose to ignore terror in favor of fury. The glittering woman lead me onward and I walked without protest at her side (since, after all, I'd been rather thoroughly caught, and what else was I to do?). While I burned with anger and tried to come up with something to say that would be so cruel and cutting she would be devastated, it was easier to be lead and not worry where I was going to put my feet.

It was easier not to wonder what waited at the end of the cliff-side path. Whether it was worse for me that we were alone, away from her huntsmen, her retainers with flowering foxglove stalks and hound's heads instead of human faces, all giddy on unicorn flesh. Whether Aliver would wonder about me.

"Why do you call my brother the Dead Lord in Waiting?"

"I do not call him that," she replied, gently.

"But he *is* called that. I overheard."

The glittering woman looked upward; I think if she actually had been more human, she would have sighed.

"Do you not all wait to die, you people from above? That is what I have always seen."

We must have been approaching the waterfall I'd seen from the lakeshore for the sound of water, drumming, became loud, unless that was the blood in my ears. Mist made everything clammy and cold and green but there were pale silver rainbows dancing around the glittering woman, half-submerged and subdued radiances attending a queen.

"We d—Who told you so? You are very wrong. We do not all wait to die." My fury was in my voice. I felt my words were stones; I wanted them to blind her. "We live, most of us, and wait to live again the next day. Or we wait for something good to . . . For *something* to happen. My brother *Aliver* is not waiting to die."

"You are young," the glittering woman said. I am always being told I am young, especially after expressing a conviction; it was almost a relief to be treated the same way by this frightening creature. "You are also not Aliver. What do you know of what he wants? Have you asked him?"

"I will ask him at our home," I said, with dignity, my head held high. "As I will be on my way there, um, shortly. And so will he. I trust."

A part in the falling mist, an easing as of tight laces undone, and there was the lake again—perfect and silver and flawless, and the waterfall somewhere—somehow—behind us now. The cliff walk turned another corner of the Fairy Palace and began to climb upward.

The glittering woman stroked my arm and I felt the lake pull at me as it had when I first looked upon it. How it had been created so flawlessly by that unknown fairy silversmith, how that flawlessness had demanded secrecy, had demanded blood; still demanded it.

The taste of metal-tarnish was once again in the back of my throat and I was glad the mist still rolled by the Fairy Palace's isle and obscured our reflections.

Still. I *felt* how our reflections were there and was oppressed by the feeling, as if they could be summoned by my thought. By my thought, they would crawl out of the lake and pour through the cliff's shadow and into my own; then the taste of blood in my throat would be more than just a taste.

"A reflection or shadow summoned with a thought has no allegiance to what cast it," the glittering woman said. "Sometimes quite the opposite."

"What did you say?" I said, sharply. I turned my head quickly and thought I saw my shadow settling back into my shape.

She smiled at me. There was something pleased and heartless and mocking behind her expression; a secret joke, of which I was clearly the object, I'm not sure she meant me to see, although perhaps she didn't care that I saw it.

"There is no need to wait so long," she said, giving my arm a gentle squeeze.

And I saw Aliver on the cliff walk. He was gazing out across the lake with his hands clasped behind his back, his knee bent and one foot resting on a stone. His hair was damp in the mist and curling. My brother is not to be trusted and this place was certainly not to be trusted and the glittering woman, whatever she'd just done, was perhaps the most not to be trusted, but this was the first time, leaving aside the smiling I'd seen at the horrible ball, that I recognized in Aliver the inimitable *himness* that is Aliver at his most Aliver—a perfectly sincere player-king.

"My Wolf heart," the glittering woman said.

Aliver turned. Recognition shivered through his expression like light on glass when he set his eyes on me, then blotted out as if somebody had overturned an inkpot.

"Yes, Kiss?"

"Your Princess Ravenna wishes to ask you a question."

He looked at me expectantly. His expression was forbidding, something about the eyebrows and the flare of his nostrils. This was my brother as he has been for the past three or so months, wasn't it? All aloof and cold and impatient? I felt hope the sight of the old Aliver had kindled in me gutter out, replaced by fear.

Which expression was the real one and what did I want to say to him?

"Are . . . " I clasped my hands together. The physical pressure of finger against finger unknotted my tongue. All my nervous energy and effort went into the clasping. "Are you waiting to die? Is that what this whole thing is?"

He blinked. Once. Then he looked at the glittering woman with apology. My face went red.

"In a way, we all are waiting," Aliver said.

My brother, who would not wear the belt with the battle on it, who apologized so extravagantly to Forestwine that Lord Gervase commissioned a song about Aliver the Wolf Who Wasn't A Wolf and it became a smash and Aliver replied by writing a proposal for the safe study of lycanthropy and agitating to fund that study. My brother, who liked to attend the hatching of kestrels, who made our niece giggle so hard she peed herself, who argued with father over the foundation of the Council of Patrons so there would always be money for Arts, who everybody loved because he was so full of living. My brother, who broke every arrow in the castle after his best friend died, except the one. The one he hung over his bed, in memory. My brother, who wouldn't wait for anything except the perfect moment to spring a surprise. Who wasn't to be trusted, but whose heart was always where it should be.

"You don't really want to keep coming here, do you?" My voice dropped, shamefully. I was going to cry again. I wanted badly not to cry. "They opened your chest and took out your heart. It's sorcery. It's bad. You don't really want this, do you?"

"I told you not to concern yourself with my dreams, Ravenna." Aliver sounded exasperated. "Ask no more questions. I am satisfied. I am where I want to be."

"You're lying." I turned to the glittering woman. She was watching Aliver. "He's lying. Aliver would never say that, not ever. He's never satisfied. He always wants to be somewhere else."

"I am where I want to be," Aliver repeated, but I ignored him.

"'Always curious, never satisfied.' Even when he's happy, he's not. He's not waiting. You're both lying. He'd never tell me to stop asking questions. Never."

The glittering woman's eyes glittered, but she turned to Aliver.

"It looks, my lord, as if you have not given satisfaction."

"Leave us alone, Kiss."

Kiss—a ridiculous name!—did not want to leave us. Her face was very cold and her glittering very pronounced, but she said, "Not too long, my heart," and went back down the cliff walk, holding her skirts up. I felt my heart stutter, and my hand made a fist, and my mouth went dry; how dare she call him that, so sweetly? A chain of jewels around her dainty ankle flashed in the evening. I will never see fireflies in the distance again without wondering.

Aliver turned to me. He looked and looked but I'd just accused him of lying so it was his turn to speak.

"I am partnering with this realm for the good of our own," he finally said.

"Twaddle!" I was indignant. "They were eating your heart."

"Yet I stand before you."

"Because they're magic. This whole place is magic. You can't put me off, Aliver. They were eating your heart and you ate that unicorn alive." I had to swallow bile again. "You ate it when . . . And they used arrows, Aliver. Arrows. You swore you'd never hunt again or participate in a hunt. But they used arrows just like—"

"I want you out of this." It was as if his flesh remembered it was a living thing, not stone, so transformed was he by the passion in his voice. "I know. I know I'm changing, Rav, at home. I know it, I know I am different, and I need you to keep your nose out of it. Just leave me alone. I am bound by certain constraints. They exist. There is nothing I can do about them."

"But you're the heir—"

"I have made a bargain. I come and take part in their sports, I am their Corn King—"

"Aliver!" I shrieked. "Corn Kings die. Don't you ever read a history book?"

"I know that," he said, quietly. He did, too. I saw in his eyes how he knew it. How perhaps the glittering woman wasn't absolutely wrong. I hated her more than anything in that moment, except, perhaps, Aliver. In that moment. "While I am their Corn King they give me . . . resources I need to . . . create on a certain level. Rav, remember the mad king's library, wonder of the world? How we all went there, you and me and . . . " He ran his hands over his chest, as if brushing something away. "And we were so moved, all of us?"

He waited until I said, grudgingly, "Yes."

"That kind of genius doesn't come without cost. I am paying the cost. I'm building a house by the sea and it will be a marvel."

"I don't see what cost you need to pay these peopl— creatures— people for your own ideas," I said.

Aliver ignored me. "Perhaps it will be a school or a home for the arts, but I can see it now so clearly—" He stared off into the middle distance, and so full of longing. "It will last, Rav. It will last and be a ward against violence. It will be a torch."

"A torch is no good without a light," I said, through gritted teeth, but he did not seem to hear me.

He was wistful. "How good would it be for something we made to last? Years from now people will remember and drink it in and—" His tone changed. "More importantly, by making this deal I keep another from being taken in my stead. They've been taking our best artists for years."

I wanted to scream. This was just like Aliver, grand gesture and all. I could imagine how he'd found this otherworld—well, no I couldn't, but I could imagine just after he'd found this otherworld! How he'd met with the glittering woman and decided it was dangerous and he should offer himself up on a table instead of telling anyone.

"Don't you see, this is the best I can do?" he said.

"We don't need a marvel of the world. We already have interesting things and historical battlefields and a very nice shoreline and just about the loveliest fall anywhere. Besides, artists have created without feeding their hearts to a primpish parade of well-dressed monsters and murdering a unicorn for I dare say centuries! Just say you've changed your mind and stop coming here."

He sighed at me. He dared to sigh at me!

I yelled at him. "We do need you! Who found those flaws in the bank's security and put that man in his place? Who created the Council of Patrons? Who made friends of Forestwine? That wasn't father or mother or anybody else! You're good for so much more than—"

"It's not that simple."

"I didn't say it was simple."

"Nothing lasts, Rav."

"So? Say you've changed your mind, Aliver."

"I couldn't if I wanted to." I thought maybe he did want to. He was no longer looking at me but gazing down the cliff walk. "If I've learned one thing about them, it's that our aunt is right. A promise here is far more immovable a bond than anything back home. Even the marriage tasks. They won't refuse a bargain and will abide by it no matter the consequences. They live by contract and the letter of the law. There's no escaping a deal, Rav. But that doesn't need to be all an ill thing. I've been sad a long time about promises I can't keep. Promises I'll never get to keep."

He still would not look at me, though I saw his eyes shift as if he were going to.

"I want one good thing to come of it. This way I feel."

"*Selfish*," I said. That's when the glittering woman returned, while I was glaring at Aliver and more scared than I'd ever been.

But I was going to save him. I was going to win; not her. I wasn't going to allow Aliver to erase himself in service of history when there was still so much for him to do. I stamped my foot before she could speak.

"Pardon me! Madame. Aliver has explained about the bargain he made with you. I accept your challenge to a duel for Aliver's life and heart."

"I challenged you, did I?" The glittering woman placed a hand on Aliver's shoulder. I would have liked to snap her fingers off.

"Yes. By—well. You have challenged me by, um, being challenging and engaging my own blood in what is a conflicting office to the office of Heir Apparent. So I am going to choose the time and location of our duel according to the laws of my people. Which should really have precedence even if we are in your nation, because Aliver is the heir so his body is actually a piece of our nation according to the law—he's the soil, you know. You do know, I can tell. So."

She did not argue with me. "So?" she prompted.

Aliver covered his eyes with his hand. I thoroughly ignored him. I was surprised enough to find I was getting my way with this haphazard challenge and didn't want to take my eyes off the glittering woman, 'lest she try another trick like whatever she'd done earlier just before Aliver came into view.

"Yes. So. The time will be tomorrow at noon. The location will be at the spring in the Labyrinth of the Three Fairy Ladies. Were you one of those ladies? No, I'm sorry, I don't care. Do you object?"

"I will be there," the glittering woman promised. I'd hoped to have earned at least a frown or have her say something I could be vicious about. Instead, she seemed pleased, which was quite lowering to my already sewer-dismal spirits. "Traditionally, our duels have two contests of strength. We will have one contest with weapons from your nation and one with weapons from mine. Is that acceptable, little raven?"

"Ravenna is my name; you will call me by it," I said. "And yes."

"Until our duel is concluded, I will forgive your trespass without passport into my lands. Now go."

On which ominous note, our audience was apparently over.

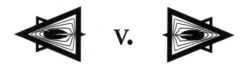

V.

IN WHICH I REGRETFULLY
PREPARE FOR A DUEL

I don't fully remember how I got home. I think I can recall Aliver escorting me back to my bed. The knap of his velvet, soft against my cheek. I think I leaned on him. I almost recall him looking down at me, face stiff as an ancient copper grave-mask and little shadows skittering at his heels and his eyes gone to darkness. The same darkness I'd seen come at me from under his door. I think he asked me to leave it. To let it pass.

I woke in my own bed with a pounding headache. According to the fairy glass clock, I had six hours to prepare for the duel. I made a list. Lists have never failed me, however little information I actually possess.

1. Find Aliver and question him about the glittering woman's weaknesses, etc. Do not lose temper! You might die later!!

2. Ask Aunt how to duel fairies. Maybe she knows useful books? Maybe fairies all swore an oath to never touch cheese so cheese would be perfect weapon?

(I prefer strongly not to look at my cheese joke as hysteria; especially as I really did wonder whether such a weakness existed.)

3. Acquire perfect weapon.

4. Win duel.

(My hand was shaking just a little as I reached this point in the list, but I thought it best to get the shakes out before I had to duel.)

5. Humbly accept Aliver's gratitude.

6. Forget entire ordeal.

(I pressed very hard when writing 6 and 6a.)

6a. Except when we discuss paving over the spring and what to do about the fairy nation beneath our home which is, and has been for some time, apparently kidnapping our artists and making them attend sinister/boring balls. Tell father & council? Gardeners definitely need to know. Replace green glass gate with new iron gate?

7. Write another list about what to do.

Numbers four through seven weren't immediately helpful, but I put them down to motivate myself.

I found Aunt Una sharpening her collection of knives in her parlor. She had what I have always thought of as her quest bag open beside her, half-packed. Aunt Una can be an intimidating person if you know any of her accomplishments; otherwise, she does not look particularly like someone who is a repository of high adventure. She looks like anybody you'd see on the street at twilight. Her hair is auburn, streaked in white and silver, and it is her habit to wear it in a loose braid; her eyes are keen, but her default expression if she is paying you attention is a gentle and whole-hearted intentness.

But then sometimes she is herself in such a manner as grabs your attention, and you wonder, who is this woman?

"Just missed Aliver," she said.

"He was here?" I repeated, like a fool.

"Mmhm." She wasn't paying me attention.

"Did he, um, what did he want to talk about?"

She made a noncommittal sound, which I took to mean that they had discussed nothing of great import. There was something soothing about the scrape of her knife against her sharpening stone that set my teeth on edge but also comforted me.

I lingered to ask what the date was (just in case) and whether or not she'd ever dueled a fairy lady. Of course she had. Twice.

"What does one use for that kind of duel?" I said. "Salt? I think I remember reading about salt. Can it be table salt?"

I tried for nonchalance but think I failed. She gave me a cool look up from under her eyebrows.

"Your wits, my dear," she said.

"But besides wits or cleverness what does one use? What did you use? Do they have any useful allergy or weakness? Like Forestwine's moon thing? Though I suppose that's less a weakne—but I'm wandering. I mean is there any weapon that they might fumble if forced to use?"

"Time. But meh." Aunt Una set down her knife and clasped her hands over one knee. She lifted her chin and looked directly. "Time or iron, both if you can get it. The passage of time confuses them. The need to care about the passage of time confuses them. That's why bells can summon or banish them. Bells can make time's thresholds manifest and push them out again."

"Time's thresholds. Very well. And iron. Not salt?"

"Salt might keep you safe at Yearturn if you make a circle . . . but it might not. Salt circles are easy to break. Are you planning on dueling any fairy ladies?"

She so clearly thought I had no such duel on my daily agenda.

I thought again about telling her what I'd discovered, what was happening to Aliver, just dropping the whole mess into her lap.

But then I thought twice. Sometimes in this sort of affair trying to bring in another party is the sin of breaking bread and then murdering one's host at the dinner table. In which case bringing, say, a contingent of guardsmen or one's extremely canny adventuress aunt would only make the contest forfeit and be a declaration of war and anyone watching the opera based on the following bloody tragical events would shake their heads and say 'if only honor had held true. Ravenna had the opportunity to do right; why didn't she hold?'

There are always consequences. I do know that.

"I just want to know," I said.

"Aliver would be a good one to ask about fairy duels," she said. I sharpened right up like one of her knives. "He wanders around as if he's on his way to one."

"Do you mean this morning?" I said. "Did he say anything?"

"No," she replied. "But of late. There's a certain look you get to recognize." She paused. "Are you up to something, Ravenna?"

"I'm writing my memoirs and, uh, I want to talk about the tradition of fairy ladies in our nation's oral folk history."

The lie was a perfect one even by my standards. Who wants to hear about a young person writing their memoirs, especially when one is an adventuress constantly besieged with requests from the publishing companies to write her own? She let it pass.

"Mm." Her knife scraped across the stone again. She flipped it over, whetting the other side. She tested it gently against her thumb. "Time and iron," she said, dismissively. "Salt is for Yearturn circles, and table salt will do. Remember, there are the Brine-Courts, so it follows that salt is chancy."

"Thanks, Aunt," I said. "If you see Aliver again, tell him I'm looking for him."

Next, I found father seated alone in the breakfast room. He was in a chair by the window, reading a broad sheet in Sylvanian script and sipping from a small porcelain cup chased with silver. The scent of roast coffee warmed the air; my mouth watered. I became aware I'd had nothing to drink yet this morning and my head was throbbing.

"Aliver just stepped out," he said when I asked.

I drifted toward the coffee. It was served on a grand buffet—plenty of interesting oral folk history about that buffet, at least among the courtiers. By the buffet one of the servants was sweeping up a mess on the ground. I recognized the bright blues and whites, the patterned claw belonging to a dragon. They were pieces of Aliver's especial favourite cup, the one I'd given him a few years ago.

"What happened?" I said, really and truly upset. I do not strictly believe in omens, but I do not strictly disbelieve in them either.

Father didn't want to tell me. He's not a king used to getting his own way in everything but he has no patience delivering news which might cause an emotional reaction. He is very good at being silent in the face of 'frivolous expression.' But the clock on the mantle showed me I was already losing time, so I was not to be put off.

Eventually, he gave in. Aliver had smashed the cup in a fit of temper.

"Why was he in a temper? Who put him in one?" I said.

Father sipped his coffee, a stitch between his eyebrows. "He has a bee under his skin about some project requiring a deal of money. The bee will make honey or sting him to death, but he'll settle. He always does. In the meantime, he'll be forced into resourcefulness. That young man could use a lesson in practical resourcefulness."

"What if he doesn't settle?" I wanted to know.

"Then he will be unhappy," father said, as if it were the simplest thing in the world. As if it did not touch him in the slightest.

Outside the breakfast room I heard Aliver's name. I swallowed what I wished to say—it was spiteful—and abandoned father to his morning. Three members of the court—Ambray, Claris, and Finula—clustered by a suit of armor in what looked a very intense gossip session. They were a splash of bright summer fabrics, dyed colors with names like Wasp Heart Yellow, Blushing Sunflower, Oil Puddle, and Fog's Wound. Two large golden candelabra flanked the entrance to the breakfast room and I lurked behind one and listened in. A small kitten hissed at my shoes and batted at their ribbon (dyed Fog's Wound), but was easy to ignore though it set its needle teeth and claws into my shoe's toe.

They were discussing bell clappers, of all things. Some prankster had taken them from the cathedral bells and disguised them as lewd candles on the altar. Mistress Dardru was apocalyptically furious, ruin and wrath.

"My handmaiden saw Aliver loitering by the bell tower this morning," Claris said, smoothing down her elegant smock in a meaningful way. She glanced idly around the hallway to see whether anybody was paying attention to them, and I held my breath. Holding your breath does not render you invisible, but I find it steadying when I am trying to lurk.

I think she must have noticed the kitten's tail waving about because she made a tsk tsk sound and the kitten abruptly sat up, poking its head around the candelabra. I willed it to leave my shoe, or to find Aliver, or both.

Ambray accepted immediately that Aliver was to blame, and I did not blame him. Aliver has played many tricks on Ambray. Ambray has participated in many of Aliver's schemes.

But Finula said, in a voice that held a shadow, "I saw something odd this morning. Ravens clustered around the bell tower when I went for my ride. I've never seen so many in one place. The roof was black. I thought somebody had painted the copper at first but they flew back and forth. I wonder your handmaiden didn't mention them."

I felt my blood chill.

"Surely you cannot imagine a flock of birds is responsible for stealing the tongues from our bells," Claris said, with a superior little smile.

"They were very large," Finula replied.

Ambray suddenly clapped his hands. "Ha! Oh! This! Here, listen! This is very good! Earlier there was a commotion outside the cathedral!"

"I said as much," Finula replied. She sounded understandably annoyed.

"Yes, well . . . " Ambray was too pleased with himself to sound sheepish. "Now I am confirming it. I'd utterly forgotten. I didn't see a cluster of ravens,

Finny, but an altar girl chasing a bird! I thought it very good clown! She tripped over her cassock."

I cleared my throat, and was somewhat gratified to see Claris start.

"Were the ravens . . . Did they . . . Were they of unusual size?"

"They were as big as dogs." Finula adjusted her hat and looked at me sidelong.

Ambray shook his head and laughed. "Aliver's been so serious, Ravenna. You will need to take up the slack for him. And it sounds as if your namesakes already have, doesn't it? Did you send them, Ravenna?"

They snickered. I excused myself hastily. I should like to say I was in the beginning of a panic, but really I was firmly in the middle of one.

All the talk of ravens reminded me of Ravenmask, the blood at the edge of his mask, the mask taken I imagine without consent from some unusually large raven. And then I remembered about the Yearturn Festival playwright—yes, I know I should have remembered earlier, but I hadn't any coffee—and sent a messenger to find and bring her to me. "An emergency," I said. "If you find her dying, bring her still."

Our three captains of the guard were little help when it came to iron weapons. Did we have any in our armory? No. Perhaps in the museum, Princess? Did you look at the museum, Princess? Did you ask the Archivist? The Archivist will show you an ax from the iron age before your ancestors controlled the peninsula.

Aliver's jacket was in the Archivist's office. Need I say that he was not? The Archivist was also absent.

I went into the museum myself and took what I needed. Who could stop me? (Many people would have been eager to stop me had any of them happened to be around, but the museum wasn't open to the public that day and security didn't keep an eye on me.)

I took an iron ring belonging to the kinswoman of a queen of olden times and a handful of iron nails from an exhibition on industry, and then became flustered in the clock room. Usually the clock room is a flurry of ticks and tocks, but today only one clock made a sound. The others had lost their tongues, which were lined neatly on the floor.

As I passed through the courtyard I made especial note of sounds coming from the cathedral's bell tower. I asked one of our guards, the ones who do nothing but stand around prohibitively, if she knew what was going on.

"Some animal. They're having a difficulty in fixing the bells, Lady Ravenna."

Inside my room I checked the time. My lungs were having a difficulty, too, and my head: Unfortunately my eyes could see all too clearly that I had less than an hour until noon. I gave up on Aliver and Evelisse Demorgen and set out the iron ring and the iron nails. They did not look particularly intimidating, and I had neither a hammer nor confidence that flinging the nails in the glittering woman's face would do more than annoy her.

Some years ago an uncle had given me a pair of dueling pistols. They were very pretty, pearl-handled with ivy and roses etched onto the body and a hammer like a—sigh—raven's head. There was no expectation that I would ever need use them for any purpose not ceremonial or theatrical but I had been taught to use them. I set the pistol box beside the nails and ring then I brought the golden clock with the fairy glass down from the mantle.

I checked its bells. They still had their tongues. My aunt had said iron and time.

While filing the iron nails so shavings dusted my pistols I suddenly became certain someone was at my door and about to knock. When I looked at the door I saw shadow welling at its edge. I stared for a tense moment, then got to my feet and flung open the door.

The hall was full of brightness but empty otherwise. I closed the door carefully, staring at the gap between floor and door.

No shadow there but mine now.

"I will not be intimidated," I said. "And it is not fair."

At a quarter 'til noon, prepared as I would ever be, I passed through the green glass gate and into the Labyrinth of Three Fairy Ladies.

By day the labyrinth is short pleached trees and stone walls, pleasant sun-dappled corners with gracious benches. It is meant to be meandered and contemplated. It is not a very long labyrinth at all. It takes no time at all for a determined walker to reach the center.

My attention was so much on the nearness of the duel—or my doom, or my brother's doom—that I didn't notice my messenger until I tripped over his feet. He had the playwright in his shadow. They were both out of breath and his expression was verging on wild. I dismissed him and looked Evelisse Demorgen over.

Dark circles were around her eyes, but there are often dark circles around the eyes of artists. They do not get much sleep on account of their creative devils. Of course, Evelisse Demorgen had other more treacherous reasons to have dark circles around her eyes.

"Carry this. I need a second," I said, although I wasn't entirely sure I did. "If you don't know why, your—friend—isn't keeping you well-enough informed."

I shoved my picnic basket into her hands. The basket had belonged to my mother when she was young and it was the fashion to have a picnic at a moment's notice. She told me it was unheard of to go anywhere without a dram of flower wine or a square of blue cheese tucked away in a handkerchief. A miniaturist had painted the basket's weavery with flowers and berries, and if you know where to look there is a hidden swan. Aliver says there is a satyr, too, beckoning, but I have never found him. It was the only thing I had large enough to carry the clock and the pistol box without occasioning some sort of remark. Old picnic baskets are on the verge of becoming very much the mode, which amuses mother very much. Even father has cracked a smile at it.

"As you wish," Evelisse said.

"I don't wish," I said, viciously. It felt good to be vicious after being in a panic all morning. I am not proud of myself. "I don't wish to duel at all but since

I am, you'll do. What I wish is for Aliver to be well and un-enchanted and not name himself a Corn King."

I set a brisk pace toward the fountain, worried my cowardice would tempt me to delay and forfeit and later I would say oh but I was distracted.

"Your Ravenmask . . . person. He said he was yours and a lot of other nonsense. Why?"

Evelisse smiled briefly, but not as if she noticed she smiled. Most of her seemed grim and rather drawn, as poised as a cup set on a precarious edge. The cup is settled, but you know it is dangerous to have there and disaster looms.

"I sent him to keep you from enchantment. I've been watching the prince."

"Tell me about that place. You know more than I do." My voice cracked. I hated to think she'd see me cry. I do not ever like to be seen to cry, but I especially did not like the idea that I would cry mere moments before my death or transformation into a bush. "This is a command. If you don't, I'll have your head lopped off. Why didn't you say anything?"

I wouldn't really have had her head lopped off, but I was so angry; it felt good to finally be vicious to someone. She was probably rueing that her fate was in the hands of an imperious brat.

"I couldn't." Her tone did not invite further inquiry but I am a princess and she is my subject and I do not need to wait for an invitation.

"Why not? Do remember the head lopping."

"I couldn't because I cannot, your highness." Evelisse flexed one ink-stained hand. There was a smear of blue on her wrist like a wave, darkened to indigo at the creases. It stained the pad of her thumb, even the metal of her thumb ring. "If I try—I cannot."

"Try," I said.

Evelisse opened her mouth and began speaking about the properties of barley water, sacred and medicinal, and different vessels used to carry it. "There is a famous cup belonging to the Chevalier of Carolignas—"

I cut her off. "No. Stop. The place your Ravenmask fellow is from. Tell me about that place."

Evelisse adjusted the basket on her arm and gave me a look I still find difficult to read, though I have thought about it rather more often than I ever expected to think about a look. This time she began to speak about the sort of tree one grows from a golden thimble and whether ravens make better judges than owls and why gold is a judgment color but owls will not eat mice with golden tails and what birds live in a tree grown from a golden thimble. Her words began to come faster. She seized her own throat, face red. Spittle hit the ground.

I asked her to please stop, and she did. And so we weren't in the middle of conversation when we came to the last corner before the center of the labyrinth and the spring. Before I could turn it, Evelisse touched my elbow. I squinted at her hand.

"Don't let go anything you hold onto," she said. "That's how they win; using their strength of vision to break ours. She is playing with you and the prince."

I did not find this at all encouraging, but the adrenaline surge gave me the wherewithal to hold my head high.

The glittering woman was seated at the edge of the spring, her arms looped around her knees and her feet in the water. I'd half-hoped that full daylight would be sufficient to ruin her; she seemed such a creature of the evening. It was not. Noon's glare did do its best to cover her, as if light was a spill of chalk or hair powder or flour, but its very best fell short. She still glittered like dew gone to diamonds under a silver dawn.

"So," I said. I regretted not asking the playwright for an opening line. A trickle of sweat itched under my left breast and I was certain my face was as red as if you'd held me down and smashed raspberries all over.

The glittering woman stood to greet me, green rills of water gone to lace at her bare ankles and calves. Though she smiled at me, she swept Evelisse a freezing glance. A bush I'd never seen before was very conspicuously situated beside the spring and I took it for her second. Her second's branches were gold and its berries were white and it, when Evelisse nodded to it, rattled its branches.

"Your weapons?" she said.

I snapped my fingers. Evelisse set the picnic basket down and opened it for me before stepping back with a flourish.

I drew out the golden clock and opened its back.

The glittering woman said, sharply, "What are you doing?"

"I'm setting the time," I said, with a great deal of malice. "Ten minutes from now a bell will ring. We will shoot at one another. Do you, um, know how to duel with pistols? We'll stand on opposite sides of, um, either side of the spring. The bell rings the time. We aim and shoot."

The glittering woman said nothing. I closed the clock. Evelisse opened the box of dueling pistols and brought them first to the glittering woman, who examined them closely before pointing to the left. The last time I took one from its box was a costume party in Firstleaf. One of my cousins crammed roses into the barrel and tried to shoot them at our uncle, who was extremely unamused. Evelisse loaded the pistols with brisk efficiency, which was a relief for in that moment I'd forgotten how, and anyway did not wish to take my gaze from my enemy.

The glittering woman flinched when she took her pistol up and seemed to have difficulty holding it. She met my eyes and said, without humor, "It would appear that your curved stick with its wasp heart has taken iron for a lover."

We went to our respective marks. The glittering woman stepped delicately upon the ground and the grass did not bend under her heel. I tromped, trying not to hyperventilate. As an amateur historian, it would be useful to pay careful attention to the scene at hand, but my palms were sweaty and once I had my breathing under control there was a squeeziness in my chest to contend with. The clock ticked. Evelisse chose to stand far back from the engagement, shielded by a statue of a dolphin with curling goat horns and a foliate tail.

The glittering woman copied my stance, but hers somehow came out better. I wondered where Aliver was. If he'd name a room in his stupid House by the Sea after me. If his descendants or our cousins' descendants would decorate it with raven-themed items. If he'd miss me. If he'd finish his House before they harvested their Corn King. If there was anything I could have done to stop him from feeling so sad.

Idiot, idiot.

And the bell rang.

Don't close your eyes, I thought, fiercely. You watch what happens.

The glittering woman's perfect brow was perfectly furrowed in an expression of perfect perplexment. She shook her head as if to clear it and didn't shoot. You'll notice I have said nothing about my own shot; I hadn't taken it yet. I reminded myself she had carved up a unicorn while it still lived and fed the meat to Aliver. She had preyed on Aliver, too.

I fired my pistol. Sneezed.

She swayed as if struck, and then she fired too. I dropped into a half-crouch with my hands over my head. I hoped the gardeners weren't near. What if someone was shot through my carelessness? I hadn't thought to tell them to do work elsewhere. I hadn't expected they would be my very first thought upon being shot at for the very first time. I had expected to think something defiant, or more wishful about my own life.

The glittering woman's bullet passed through the clock, shattering the fairy glass, scattering golden leaves and pieces I rather thought essential to the clock's ability to function as a clock. But still it ticked, and I was not bleeding.

The glittering woman set the pistol down. I felt a swell of fury at the thought that perhaps I had failed to hit her. My blood-thirst shocked me. I am more competitive than Aliver when it comes to sports (excepting dares, of course), but I've never wished to kill anyone before. She tried to keep her hand from my sight but I saw it was as raw as meat. Movement: as molten glass at her thigh, bright blood flowing. A hit! I'd won!

I thought I won for one bright second, forgetting there was more to come.

"My brother—"

"Such haste," she said. She limped back into the spring and the water fountained up and over, bubbling white as bone and pearl, higher until it covered her. When it collapsed, a spray of water slapped me across the face, and she was gone.

I coughed and wiped my eyes. "Did I win? I won!"

"You didn't lose," Evelisse said, slowly.

"She ran! Did you see that? Ha!" I said, though this is when I began to feel trepidation. "I should have asked her where Aliver is. Will there be no second contest? Am I supposed to follow her?" Would the water whip out and grab me if I didn't?

Behind me, Aliver said my name.

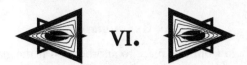

VI.

IN WHICH WE COME TO IT

I wanted to see Aliver more than I've ever wanted to see anyone. I took in his familiar shape, hair as black as burnt paper, eyes as clear as water in a silver cup, and I flung myself on him. I wanted assurance he was not a bush pretending to be Aliver or an illusion shaped from glittering and water. I wanted to feel his oven-warmth and knotty shoulders and tell him that I would fight any duel for him, so he certainly owed me first pick of dessert but he was welcome to anything he wanted if only it would make him happy.

Aliver didn't want to be hugged. His face is angular to begin with but it somehow becomes even pointier when he doesn't want to do something. I hugged him anyway.

"I looked for you all day but you were always just gone. You—"

He interrupted. "How could you do this to me?"

The last time I heard Aliver so raw, as if his throat were unraveling into a tangle of strings, was when he hung the one arrow he didn't break over his bed and swore never to use a bow again.

"You mean save you? Not easily."

If Aliver had stepped back I would have let him go. He stood as stiff as a corpse or a chair in the circle of my arms and scoffed in his throat. I felt when his shoulders tensed; his bicep jumped. I flinched. My brother had never looked at me as if he wanted to hit me before.

"Smug idiot. Have you ever thought of anyone other than yourself?" When I did not reply, he said, "You're not the only one capable of making well-informed decisions. You are not always right."

I hugged him more tightly as if I could remind him that he liked me through sheer strength.

"I know," I said, wretchedly. "But they're—"

He cut me off again. "Did you know I paid people to put up with you? I paid them not to mock you when you cried. I paid them to put up with your incessant questions, which you think make you sound interesting and intelligent, but instead make you sound so desperate to be liked. You know you sound as if you don't know what you're talking about but want people to think you do? I protected you—I protected you constantly, and this is how you're repaying me? I have a chance at happiness. Are you interfering out of spite? Because you don't understand it? Because I dared, once, do something without you?"

My reply is not worth repeating; it adds nothing to the story, so I shall leave it.

"I hate you," Aliver said. He said it so easily. As easily as a stone thrown through a pane of glass will break it. The glass doesn't concern the stone. The stone just wants to go from one place to another and if the glass were strong it would stop the stone and not break. But glass isn't strong.

"Aliver," I said, into his shoulder. At least I couldn't see his face.

"Now let me go," he said.

Over his shoulder, Evelisse stared at the ground with her jaw set and her arms folded across her waist. She looked as lonely as I felt.

"No," I replied. Sobbed, maybe. "You're staying. I want to help. I'm helping you. Let me help."

He transformed into a lion with a black mane and quartz gray eyes. I hiccoughed in terror. He set his teeth into my shoulder hard enough to draw blood but not to savage me. At the moment, I was not terribly interested in the difference and I screamed. The Aliver-lion snarled like a true monster and the sound of it reverberated through my chest. I held on, though it hurt, and snapped, "No," just as if the Aliver-lion was one of the dogs with father's slipper.

The lion dissolved into light and shadow. Briefly, I felt Aliver again, but I couldn't keep him in his shape. He became a wave on the water. No water beneath us and the spring a few feet away but the Aliver-wave was a movement, all salt-brine and iron. The iron came from me. I bit my cheek when the wave flexed and boxed me in the eye.

How do you hold a wave? I kept my arms in a circle and braced myself against the ground. I clung to the water, though I couldn't get purchase, and I couldn't get a breath.

And then the wave transformed into a pillar of flame. I think the glittering woman was showing off, going from water to fire like that. One moment I was drowning, the next I was burning. The fire twisted up like thread being pulled from roving, spinning high; it roared more loudly than the lion. I could feel my eyebrows scorch and my cheeks blister. My hair crackled as the air filled with burnt-hair stench and in my eyes was an unbearable brightness, so I shut them. I felt my skin split and crack before it became a scream.

Still, I clung to Aliver.

"You're just a piece to them, 'ver, you're just a game. But you're important to us and we love you and you can do great things without them. You don't need them. That's the game," I said, or tried to say. My throat was was clogged with heat and came out a whisper. How I spoke at all, I did not know.

The fire quieted. I radiated heat like a coal; I was in agony. The skin of my face still screamed, and my throat, and my arms, and my chest, and the dissonance between knowing I should be cracked like a cinder and knowing I wasn't was almost worse than the fire.

The quiet became something Aliver-shaped and Aliver-sized, but not quite right. I couldn't figure out what I was holding.

So I opened one eye and peered through my eyelashes, after all unburnt. I still felt the heat but think it was only the memory of heat, like walking through a spider web and still feeling the web against your face after it's gone.

I saw darkness. I opened the other eye, so cautiously! But caution could not keep me from seeing.

The Aliver-shaped thing was all over glossy and the color of a shadow or Aliver's hair.

It had a face.

I found myself staring at it, trying to make sense of its smile. There was a suggestion of mouth with a glint of teeth, but teeth covered in black pearl-dust or stained by ink. Under its eyebrows, which were also only suggestions of contour, its eyes were beady bright and small. I stared at that pinprick of brightness until the brightness peeled away from the Aliver-shaped thing's face: The raven the eye belonged to had turned its head to point its beak at my eye. It cocked its head. The point quivered a scant quarter inch away from my pupil.

It was an unkindness of ravens, latched together in the shape of a man, talon by talon, feather by feather.

"Ravenna," it said. It would have been easier if it had the hoarse voice of the gallow's raven, but it sounded like Aliver.

I made no sound. I couldn't. One by one the ravens turned their heads. The Aliver-shaped thing became jagged. They opened their wicked scissor beaks and flexed their talons and stirred against me. One croaked. Another clicked. I understood the rattle in it to be my death rattle. These had taken the tongues from the bells and if I moved they would engulf me.

I held on.

My brother deserves a hero who is not a coward and can love him enough that they forget to be afraid but I didn't forget to be afraid. I am ashamed. I held on to the Aliver-unkindness but I think I held on out of fear. I don't know. I don't know.

Fortunately, before I had wit enough to flee, the unkindness burst—like an old egg, like an overripe fruit. It burst into feather, bone and blood, bloody shrapnel, nuggets of feather, some ravens winging away, others torn to pieces, snatching at my hair, scratching at my face. This doesn't sound fortunate, but it was, I swear, for no longer did they stare at me and press their hard bodies into me and what was left afterward was Aliver.

An Aliver who looked like Aliver: Human-shaped, wearing what Aliver usually wears, rumpled but solid-flesh. He was breathing hard, as if he'd just run hard down the long bridge to the moon palace. He stood as still as if he took a care not to startle me. Instead, he looked steadily at me until some tension eased from my muscles.

"Ravenna," he said, coaxing, gentle. "I'm sorry."

"You are?" I said.

"I am." He sounded sorry, but how could I trust it? I listened. My own breathing came hard, too, from wanting to run. He said, "I'll carve you a bookshelf with a secret back like our aunt's. I'll go out and find a first-person account of Alivera's visit to the Isle of Moonwest. I'll do it by Firstleaf. I'll do it shoeless.

I'll," his voice cracked. "I am so sorry. I love you. I've been a selfish fool. You are in the right. I don't know what I was doing."

I could tell it cost this Aliver something to say I was right though Aliver has never before balked at admitting a wrongdoing. He looked sorry, the sorriest I'd ever seen him. The way I sometimes imagined him being sorry when we fought.

"I love you, too," I said.

"Let's go inside," he replied. He shifted in my grasp but didn't pull away. He waited for me to let him go. When I didn't let my arms drop, he said, "Ravenna. Let me go."

"No," I said. "Stay. Please."

We looked at one another. I think he saw me more than he ever had before, which is strange to say, only I felt so thoroughly looked at.

"Where is she?" I said. "This contest is over."

The spring bubbled, green shadow and a sharp green scent, and the glittering woman rose out of the water. The only unglittering thing about her was her eyes. There was a quick movement on the other side of the spring, Evelisse hiding again behind the statue, careful to stay out of the glittering woman's sight. The playwright hid her head against the satyr statue.

"Well, my Wolf?" the glittering woman said.

Aliver lifted his eyes from mine to hers. She continued to ignore me.

He might have been a puppet with the strings cut such was the drama of his shoulders going slack. I didn't release him but tried to put myself between them. I didn't like my back to her, but I'd rather my back than Aliver's front. And I felt it when Aliver steeled himself and slid an arm around me. He hugged me! I made an awkward goose-honk noise and my brother's arms—both of them—came up around me and tightened.

The glittering woman finally looked at me.

I'd been glaring at her, awkwardly and over my shoulder, with what I like to think was so vicious a glare, so daunting, that it was simply easier for her to ignore me until that moment. It was difficult to look down my nose at her, considering her height and my terror, but I tried. She was not noticeably ruffled.

"The field is yours," she said.

I meant to be dignified and stoic and so cut her with my surprising detachment, but I smiled hard enough my cheeks hurt.

The glittering woman returned my smile with a warning.

"Do not come again without invitation to my nation. If you do I will turn your heart to stone and skin your thighs for dancing shoes."

"I won't do any of that," I said. "But you stay in your nation, too, or else. No more taking our artists or our heirs. They're ours."

"I wonder if they are," she replied. Then she walked into the spring, trailing little stars. They drifted from her like sparks from a bonfire. The spring closed over her head, this time without theatrical water displays, and the golden bush left too, and as the sparkle of its leaves going down the green glass way was treasure.

Aliver pulled my arms from around him. I resisted but he continued to put pressure until my grip eased. I waited for something terrible to happen when I was no longer holding him and wondered what I would do if he rushed me to get to the spring. And I wanted badly to go to the spring's edge myself and poke around with a stick to assure myself the stairs were gone.

But Aliver gripped my shoulder with his left hand and squeezed. I put my hand over his and squeezed back.

It felt like another moment of really seeing and looking. I saw how really very sad Aliver was, and I think there was some constraint on him still. I realized I didn't know what effect on his heart the balls he'd already attended, the cups already drunk, whether a disenchanted Aliver would still be detached and irritable.

He didn't look detached as he looked away from me to look at the spring, though I don't know whether I have a name for his expression—or want to have a name for it. He said, "You're more stubborn than I am."

"Untrue," I replied, and then all in one breath, "*Thank-you-for-staying-I-am-glad-you-are-here.*" I clutched his hands and held them to my forehead because I didn't want to hold him again but I wanted to feel him connected to me and I wept.

Then I cried, repeating again and again how glad I was to have him here. How I wanted him to stay, and be happy.

He didn't reply to that by sprinting for the spring, or by saying very much at all. He hadn't looked away from me while I wept; he'd only looked vaguely hurt and very weary. He turned the attention away from himself by turning to the playwright.

"Did I see you there, Demorgen? With your eyes open?"

I thought about the look she'd given me before demonstrating that she could not speak of her time there. She did not look at me. She regarded the pool, thoughtfully, then spoke in a voice as thoughtful as her regard. "You have eyes as sharp as mine, my lord. You see things most others don't."

AN EPILOGUE

What I think was Aliver's true response to my concerns came weeks after the duel. I'd fallen asleep in front of his door. Since the duel, I'd taken to sneaking out of my own rooms and standing guard, the better to make certain that when he went to bed he truly went to bed and stayed there. I'd taken to being snappish about his plans, overbearing even to myself, but I couldn't keep myself from it. He and Evelisse Demorgen began to spend a lot of time together, and I wasn't sure whether to make relief or concern my standard policy for that friendship, but the truth was I felt easier when I knew they had been together.

Aliver tripped over me on his way to breakfast. He looked well-rested. I grouched awake and got an eyeful of sunlight from the open windows. My ribs throbbed. I swatted his ankle.

Before-All-This-Happened-Aliver would have laughed. Now-Aliver's eyes creased with resignation, any humor just a hint, like Spring-grass under ice.

"Thank you. Thank you for watching so carefully over me," he said. He said it just gravely enough to seem a character in a play. He was good at being solemn and sincere, Aliver, always one for the grand gesture.

"*Somebody* needs to do it, and I suppose that's me," I said, and my voice broke. I wish it hadn't. We both pretended it hadn't.

Aliver hesitated. "I have something for you," he said, finally. "Josev"—the second gardener—"found it by the fountain. I was going to keep it."

Behind Aliver, his room was well-lit, all the curtains thrown back; everything looked safe and bright and gleaming. He looked safe and bright and gleaming.

"What is it?"

He went into his room, leaving the door open. I hovered uncertainly in the hall until he returned, holding in his palm the white raven penholder with the soulless onyx chip eyes. Only the onyx chips had been scraped from their sockets, scratches on the wood to show it had been done with deliberation and inexpertise; a crack on its breast, as if it had been dropped, or someone had struck it very hard and found a flaw.

"Josev found this and gave it to you?" I said, hardly knowing when I'd reached out to take it from Aliver. "By *the* Fountain?"

"So he said," Aliver replied. "I threw it into the spring after you asked me to get rid of it, but," and he shrugged eloquently. "The fountain decided to spit it back. We should throw it in the sea, together, unless you want to keep it."

We, he said, and *together*, and I love Aliver. I think he meant his thank yous and his we shoulds in that moment, but Aliver isn't necessarily to be trusted. He's impulsive.

"I think I'll keep it," I said. "For remembrance."

VIRIDIAN

AMANDA J. McGEE

E than stands in the foyer of Evergreen, looking out the ripple of the window to the lake beyond. It is a bright day, the last molten edge of summer hardening on the chill of fall to come. Summers are always so brief in Vermont. He built this house in defiance of that fleeting light, surrounded it with conifers that do not shed their leaves beneath the scythe of winter. Named it for the nature of his love.

"Ethan," Nora says impatiently behind him, "focus." The rebuke is mild, for Nora. He pulls his gaze away from the sunlight on the marble floor, turning back to the door before him. The lock of the door is bright brass, the face of it a deep blue. He twists the key in the lock and opens it. Descends. The descent is always hard, but it is hardest when he has been away so long. Nora ventures here more often than he does. She follows with no hesitation, crowding him down.

The door swings shut behind them.

There is another door at the bottom of the staircase, thick and plain. Ethan opens it. The room revealed is windowless. To one side stretches an apartment. The bed is hung with brocaded curtains in dark blue, the rugs intricate and thick, but underneath everything is tile. There are bookshelves on the walls, though. She gets bored otherwise.

Down the center of the room runs a groove, an inset in the floor matching one above, space for the bars to drop when they have to use them. To the left of the groove, the tile is bare and exposed. The walls hold locked cabinets, and two metal tables take up the floor, gleaming and clean. He does not see the room's occupant.

"Nora," he says, but he hears a rustling moan from behind the brocaded canopy and he knows, then, why he has been called.

"How long?" His voice is weak. Ethan firms his chin, turns to face her.

"Since last week," Nora says. There is an icy disapproval on her pinched face. Ethan narrows his eyes. The moan comes from the bed again. He doesn't shudder.

"I've been looking," he says. He has. He knows what he has to do.

"Look harder," Nora says. There's a flash of grief on her face. Ethan notes it, but says nothing.

Nora turns, and leaves without another word. Leaves him alone with the sound coming from the bed. Ethan crosses the room. He opens the curtain, looks inside.

A monster peers out at him, through the darkness. Moans his name.

"Soon, my love," he whispers.

Then he turns and leaves, closing the door behind him. He tells himself that he is not running.

1

A car slips down the black road of a highway in Vermont, and in it sits a woman. Her hair is shoulder-length and curly brown, her face is lined with the tiny wrinkles that begin to etch themselves into the skin when a woman hits thirty. Her few possessions are piled haphazardly in trash bags and cardboard boxes in the back of the small Toyota, obscuring the rearview windshield. Beside her, belted into the passenger seat, is an urn. It is shiny with newness. This grief has not gathered dust.

The woman's name is Lorelei Adams, and she is running away.

Lori Adams is, or was, a real estate agent. She had sold houses and condominiums in San Antonio, a sprawling city with highways stretched seven lanes wide, whose skyline was mostly uninterrupted by such pesky things as mountains. Lori had loved her brown, flat city, loves it still. But some wounds make familiarity into salt rubbed over something raw and bleeding. The sting cannot be borne. And so Lori is driving to Burlington. She passes trees and windmills and more trees, and not a single thing she sees reminds her of the life she left behind. Not a single thing.

Burlington is small, and traffic is light. She drops into the tiny downtown with surprising ease. Parks on the street, walks inside a cafe called the Smiling Fox. She has an hour before she is supposed to meet the landlord to get the keys to her apartment. Lori hasn't been hungry since Annie died. She is not hungry now. The sign on the door says this place is hiring.

The woman behind the counter looks up when she walks in. She has a streak of gray in her hair. Despite Lori's best efforts, she can't bring herself to meet the woman's eyes. Lori asks for an application, receives that and a coffee that can't quite warm her insides. She tips well, though she can't afford it. Writes her name and the new address and her experience in the boxes on the paper with a pen from her purse. She can't sell houses up here. The market is too small, and besides, selling houses was what she was doing when Annie—

Lori puts down the pen with a click. She exhales. Inhales again.

When she hands in the application, the woman with the graying hair introduces herself as Christine. Lori makes herself smile, makes herself act as if she isn't missing something so integral even breathing feels hard. She's been doing it for months. What's one more day?

"If you come in tomorrow morning," Christine says, eyeing her as if she can see through the mask of her smile, "you can start on a probationary basis."

Lori thanks her. As she leaves, she feels a momentary sensation of satisfaction, of purpose. She can do this. She can make a new life, find footing caring for herself, not just for her sister.

The urn is waiting for her in the front seat.

* * *

T he apartment is not what she hoped for.

It's situated above a Chinese restaurant only a few blocks from the coffee shop. The stale odor of fried food and old cigarette smoke chokes the halls, even with the sun shining outside and fresh air moving in behind her as she climbs the stairs, Annie's urn in hand. The landlord met her below, handed her the key, and left. He didn't even stay for a walk through.

The carpet in the hallway is gray with age. Lori turns the key in the knob, swings the door open. The space beyond is small, empty, and clean enough. The smell of cigarettes is faint, but still present. Burlington is a college town, and, if small compared to San Antonio, it's nonetheless the largest city for miles. Finding something decent within her budget was difficult. There's a little bit of life insurance money, but not much. The funeral expenses were covered by what was left in Annie's bank account, with enough left over to get her here. This place will do. It's not forever. She's just not sure what happens next.

It takes her the rest of the day to clean, to move in her things. That night Lori lies on an air mattress and dreams that her sister is walking through the halls of their home in Texas, the scars from the autopsy she never had black against her breastbone.

 2

Lori first meets Ethan Locke on the ferry which crosses Lake Champlain. The ferry brings commuters and some tourists from shore to shore each day. Lori supposes she is the latter, since she rides the ferry for something like the scenery. It is the stillness that attracts her, the peculiar weightlessness of public transportation. She has felt its like on buses, when she has taken them, and on planes. There is nowhere to go except where you are being taken. You must trust the pilot or the driver, or in this case, the captain. Their competence can be your only truth. She recognizes that many people find this the opposite of restful. They want to control their own fates.

Lori has given up on control. She is burnt out on decision making. She used the last of her fire to make it here. In the mornings, she goes to work at the coffee shop. Christine sells tacos delicious even to Lori's Texan tastebuds and doesn't talk about anything important unless Lori brings it up. The cafe closes by four, and she takes the ferry to Port Kent at five thirty. The ride lasts an hour. On clear days, the mountains seem to cradle the lake, and Lori can breathe. She stays on the boat as it makes its long way back, and over another endless hour the peacefulness recedes in grating inches. She feels the waiting turn into something like expectation.

It is at this time, with the pall of another day's ending settling on her like a film, that she meets Ethan.

He's older than Lori, square shouldered and confident, his hair going to gray. He looks like a publicity photo of a corporate executive. Only his eyes are surprising, a sharp blue that unsettles her. He is wearing an expensive gray suit, the jacket unbuttoned, and standing at the prow of the ferry, such as it is, just before the orange webbing. Lori pauses between the gunwale and the nearest car, a polished black SUV, her eyes caught by his.

"I'm sorry," she says after an awkward moment. "I didn't see you there. I can leave."

"I hardly have a monopoly on the boat," he says, gesturing widely. "You're welcome to join me."

It's habit, not interest, that starts her walking again, to the opposite corner of the orange barrier. This is where she comes more often than not while the boat makes its final churning march to the dock. The cool air over the water, the bright colors of the sunset already nearing a close this late in the summer, these things aren't enough to distract from the deep and awful loneliness she feels as another day passes without Annie. Still, the sound of other people chattering makes her want to scream. The water and engines drown it out down here. She can't stand the thought of listening to other people once she gets like this, though she knows it's not their fault they are bright and alive. Annie is gone, and Lori is a ghost still wearing human skin, a monster meant for storybooks. The same kind of shapeless, powerless monster all women get to be eventually, the keening banshee in the dark.

Lori hangs her arms over the tall wall of the ferry's side. She splays her hands, then tightens them again, watching the water pass as if through her fingers, another thing she can't hold on to. For a while, she forgets that the stranger is there. He's feet away, obscured by darkness. Ahead of them both, the lights of Burlington glimmer along the shore.

"What are you running from?"

The question shocks her to standing. Dusk has settled in, and she cannot see the man's face, though he has come close, his approach hidden by the thrum of the engines.

"Who says I'm running from anything?" Lori asks, but her throat nearly closes on the words. There is no answer. She's not even sure he's heard her, but then he shrugs, a disturbance in his outline. It's a casual gesture for such a clean-cut man.

"Like calls to like," he says.

They stand in silence, Lori grasping for words. She's not sure what she'll say, if it will be angry or if she'll do something horrible like cry on a stranger in the dark, so desperate for human connection that an unlooked-for intimacy can shatter her.

The engines under their feet kick on before she can find out, the ferry juddering to slowness. She staggers. The man catches her and sets her aright.

"My name is Ethan," he says.

"I'm Lori," she replies, and the words seem to come from someone else, shouted over the engines' roaring.

3

A few nights later, Lori finds herself getting ready for dinner.

Going on a date is an absolutely foreign activity. She is sure that she is going along with this plan just to spite herself. To thumb her nose at the dreadful despondency in her chest. Two months she has lived in Burlington. Three and a half since her sister died. Their biological mother had flown in from Boston for the funeral, the only clear image in a blurring carousel of faces wishing her "sorry," saying "she died so young."

Their biological mother is named Hannah, and they have spoken only rarely. Lori only knows Hannah because Annie insisted on looking their parents up when she turned seventeen. No father, but they found their mother, nested in with a new family in a quaint suburban house that must have cost a fortune given metropolitan Boston's housing prices. Hannah had been excited to meet them, at least at first. But when it became clear that luck had not followed her daughters into fosterage, things had grown strained. She had two boys with her husband, babies then. As an adult, with the weight of being a caretaker for another fresh in her mind, with the tears of her sister's loss drying on her face, Lori found her resentment towards the woman dulled to cinders. There was no energy left to feed the fire.

The viewing room was crowded already when Hannah had entered. The years had been kind to her. Her face was plump and pleasant, though lined with grief. Lori even imagined that grief was real.

"I didn't even know she was sick," Hannah said, laying her hand on the body's black-clothed arm. Lori looked at the neat makeup, the glued shut eyes. Annie wasn't in there, but if she had been she would have shaken off that hand.

The thought of touching her sister's corpse had never crossed her mind, but she thinks about that moment now as she pins back her hair, so like Annie's. The black dress she is wearing wouldn't look out of place in a casket, though her arms are bare. She shudders.

This is why she has said yes to Ethan. Even coming to Burlington, a thousand or more miles away, to this ratty apartment and this strange half-life, even that has not stanched the seeping wound of grief. Perhaps nothing will.

They meet at the restaurant, a place with seasonal menus and artisanal cocktails unimaginatively called The Farmhouse. It's a venue for a special occasion. Lori straightens her dress before she enters, running her hands along the lines of it nervously. The host sees her and rushes to open the door. She smiles at the man wanly as he welcomes her.

"Are you looking for someone?" he asks. So young this man looks, with wide shoulders unbowed by any burden. Lori almost walks out. She glances around the restaurant instead. The ferry is her only pleasure, and she doesn't dislike Ethan. He will no doubt be waiting for her. She is late enough to be bordering on rude.

And there he is, waving at her from the table towards the back. She thanks the host and moves towards Ethan with firm strides.

He stands as she reaches him, gesturing welcome. Lori smiles despite herself. She cannot tell if the response is ingrained or genuine.

"Lorelei," he says. "I thought you weren't going to make it."

"Ethan," Lori says back, and lets him seat her, pushing the chair in like a gentleman.

Dinner is excellent. Lori orders fish, though she does not usually like fish, because she has decided tonight is for trying new things. She is astonished by the simple preparation, by the flavors of salt and citrus. When she closes her eyes, she can almost smell the blossoming trees of California, where she and Annie lived in their teens, after Lori was old enough to claim Annie as hers. For once, the memory doesn't cut.

She does not take him home that night. She does not even kiss him, though the wine renders grief distant and the lights of the streets sparkle. Lori has never been the kind to sleep with someone casually, though she likes sex well enough. She couldn't afford to bring someone home who could hurt Annie. She doesn't have to worry about that now, but the habits of a lifetime are ingrained. So it takes another date and a few more quiet conversations on the ferry before she feels comfortable enough to invite him back to her place. After that, the sex seems inevitable.

She wants to enjoy it, but all she can think about are her sister's ashes. They rest, in that smooth marble urn, on a table in the living room. If Annie were alive in this small, terrible apartment, she would hear them. It makes Lori feel wooden, distant. Not the recipe for enjoying anything. She should stop this, but they are in her bed, their clothes are on the floor, his mouth is on hers. She rides it out instead. Tries to feel something besides cold.

When it's over, when she is lying naked in her new, small bed with his warm body stretched beside hers, Ethan asks her if she is okay.

"What?" Lori asks. She touches her face. She has been crying.

It's a surprise. Lori has not shed a tear since the painful, bone-wracking sobs she shed over her sister's newly abandoned corpse, but this is not the same. It is a quiet weeping like blood seeping from a wound. She wipes at her eyes in confusion.

"I'm sorry," she says, feeling something like relief. Surely now he will make his excuses, leave, take a different ferry, disappear.

"Don't be," he says. "I know what it's like to grieve."

She looks at him. He hasn't yet told her what he is running from, but his piercing gaze says he will now, if she asks. She feels naked in a way that has nothing to do with clothes or sheets.

"Most men would run screaming," she says.

He shrugs. "I'm not most men."

His arm goes around her then, sliding under her pillow and shoulders. She is forced to nestle into his chest. He smells of male and some pleasant, expensive cologne. She finds she does not mind the change. Below her ear, she can hear his heartbeat.

"Who was it for you?" she says, giving in at last.

"My wife." She did not expect that answer. "It was sudden. We were young, thought we had our whole lives ahead of us. Then she was just gone."

Lori says nothing. She cannot think of what to say. That all death is sudden? Something about the finality of it, she thinks, the irrevocability. You cannot escape death. Every ending seems too soon.

Ethan steps into her silence, prying it open.

"Who was it for you?"

Lori hesitates. She fears speaking, lest her grief crack open further. The words lodge in her throat like a thistle's green leaves, long and speckled with spines. She has told no one here of her loss.

She shudders. Ethan squeezes her close.

"You don't have to tell me if you don't want to," he says.

Lori shakes her head, the motion strange against his chest.

"No," she says, her voice cracking. She clears her throat, tries again.

"She was my baby sister."

They fall asleep like that, in the cramped apartment that smells of cigarettes and the air freshener which Lori uses to keep the odor at bay. In the morning, Ethan makes breakfast. She awakens to the tang of bacon and the sounds of him alive in her kitchen.

He says nothing about Annie's urn.

4

Lori does not see Ethan again for two weeks. It is a surprise to find herself pining.

She texts, and he texts back, but the replies are perfunctory. Lori lies in the bed where she told him her secrets and stares at the words on her screen and tries not to feel the restlessness they evoke. She cannot make herself call. She cannot be so vulnerable again.

So instead, Lori binds up her stinging heart. She goes to work at the cafe, listening to the college kids she works with gossip about boys and bands and exams. For the first time, she feels like joining in. She wants to tell someone how it feels, to suddenly want something. How she finds herself checking her phone in hope, just like them, and exhaling deeply when the screen is still, inevitably, blank.

When Lori moved, she cut all ties. She left Texas nearly overnight. No forwarding address, no word to her and Annie's friends. The contacts are still in her old phone, dead in a drawer, but would they even want to hear from her after everything?

She could call her birth mother. What an alien idea, to call Hannah, but Lori sits with it for a moment before rejecting it at last.

When Lori leaves work that Thursday, four days into Ethan's absence, she fetches her sister's urn with its polished marble face and takes off in her Toyota.

The car is small, which was an advantage in San Antonio where parking was sometimes a hazard and the highways were several lanes wide. In Vermont the interstate is nearly empty. The road noise is Lori's only company, that and her memories. Annie helped her pick this car out. Her sister had a broken-down secondhand Nissan that rattled when it started and had red, chipped paint, but Annie refused to get anything newer while it still ran. Lori was the more practical one, as always. She insisted they had one decent car between them, and this dark blue four door was the result.

They take a roadtrip once a year, or they did, usually around Annie's birthday. It is not Annie's birthday now. That passed in the last months of her illness. There had been cake and ice cream, balloons and card games. The friends Lori has worked so hard to leave behind had crammed into their small house in San Antonio with paper flowers and liquor and food—tamales in their rippled corn husks, salsa in bright reds and greens, macaroni and cheese, chicken tikka masala with its aromatic bite, a fruit tray arrayed like a sunburst, long stalks of grilled asparagus—all of Annie's favorite things. Together they had feasted until they groaned, screamed with laughter and stories, and Annie presided over it all in a paper crown sitting on her newly grown curls. A few weeks before, the doctors had officially ceased her chemo treatments. It was her twenty-sixth birthday. She had told none of her friends that she had only six months at best. The cancer took her in two.

Lori remembers that night like a foreign country. Annie's birthday was in January, and the darkness clung to everything, making the lights of the party fever-bright and glittering. Lori laughed with the rest of them, of course. It is possible to laugh and grieve all at once. But it felt as if it were all happening to someone else. A stranger sat in her chair and used her face. A stranger sliced the cake with waxen hands and served the slices of decadent chocolate wrapped in bone-white icing to each unsuspecting mouth.

Later, alone in her room, she stared dry-eyed at the dark ceiling. She imagined the end that was coming. But of course, Annie had defied all of her expectations.

Now she takes her sister's ashes with her because there is no one else to share this afternoon with. For the first time, she is lonely in her grief.

The days are lengthened things, sprawling golden over the mountains and the smooth green valleys between. Lakes lodge in those scattered dales. If Annie were alive, would she be silent at the beauty or chattering and excited by the travel? Would she argue against this turn off the highway, taken at random? Would she shout in surprise to see her favorite ice cream's home factory, or demand to stop at the log tasting room coming up on the left?

Annie is so many ashes. Lori drives winding roads at random and does not stop until she comes on a sprawling bed and breakfast that reminds her of the Stanley Hotel, the one that inspired Stephen King to write *The Shining*. It's the same glowing white in the dusk, though much smaller, but Lori imagines it could hold ghosts. A lake stretches to her left, visible despite trees and distance. She sees lights, a house on the far side, something beautiful and modern and big if she can see it from this far away. The biting flies and mosquitoes swarm too thick to bother with sitting on the large, wraparound porch, so once she checks in she walks up the creaking stairs, down the wall-papered hallway, and into the small room with its floral comforter and odd, 1970s pastels. The mattress is all coils and springs. Lori sets Annie up in front of the mirror and lies down on the bed, thinking of the road, thinking of how green the world is, thinking of the glimpse of hidden houses in trees and real estate costs in this strange, mountainous state, of how similar it might seem to rural Texas and how impossibly different it is, the dysphoria of America. Such a large, sprawling country, this homeland, full of such difference. She is glad she can show it to Annie, for in the moments before she sleeps, she almost seems to smell her sister, to feel her warmth.

Lori dreams.

She dreams of Annie at the kitchen table of their home. Her hair has grown long. It lies like an animal in her lap, a coiled weight of brown curls. Lori cannot bring herself to touch her.

"Why are you here?" Lori asks, the way a question sits on the lips in dream, whole, undissected by words.

"Stay away from the lake," Annie says. Her lips don't move. They can't. Lori is remembering the casket, the funeral, and it is a storm in the middle of her chest, a howling. It wipes away the makeup that keeps her sister looking alive. It makes those eyes dead.

Lori wakes in the morning. She eats stale bagels with flavorless jam. The woman who keeps the books is waspish, and berates a girl working for her for some mistake there in the entryway, where everyone can hear. Lori is numb. She keeps looking for Annie out of the corner of her eye, though she shudders at the thought of seeing her with her glued lips, with her white-filmed eyes. It is all too easy to imagine her among the kitschy clutter of the bed and breakfast, the deep red carpet and antlers and fake flowers.

Lori goes upstairs and stares at the urn, its white marble face, its golden nameplate. *Annabelle Leigh Adams.* Tall, block letters. Should she let her go? Leave her here to haunt this dying building? Lori considers it for only the sparest moment.

Then she picks up the urn and her small bag of toiletries and clothes, slipping it inside for the trip to the car. There are more roads to drive.

The lake glistens in the light as she leaves, tiny waves kicking and shimmering on its surface.

THE FIFTH WIFE

The fifth wife was named Mary. She was a mathematics teacher, before Ethan found her in a coffee shop on the border of New York. She kept tutoring after they married, up until the day that she died. Her books are in the library still, all theories of quadratic equations and how to calculate the circumference of a circle. Her students, of which there were two, were told she was sick. They would need to find a new tutor. Ethan sent the emails, and the students didn't question them. Maybe they were relieved. Mary had been a distant presence to them after all, someone they saw once a week to talk about something they didn't much like.

Mary's previous relationships had not been good ones. She was the kind of nice, mousey woman who attracts domineering men like flies to honey. It was easy for Ethan to be what she needed. For her, he did not dress in suits and ties. He wore nice sweaters, glasses with thick frames, and mussed his hair. Mary thought that his name was Frank, and that he fixed computers. Both of these things intrigued her. The large house in the woods, the fortune - these were just a pleasant surprise.

They were married in spring. The flowers that Mary chose were carnations. She ordered pinks and whites, but all of the flowers came red as blood. Not being superstitious, Mary ignored the blood red flowers and the way her skin pimpled when she walked down the staircase of the foyer to meet Ethan. Her elderly father was the only one in attendance from her family. His eyes were rheumy with age, and he did not see the way Mary shivered, or the secret, cruel smile Ethan hid before he shook his hand. He was only happy for his daughter, who had found happiness.

Ethan did not love Mary. There was no requirement for him to love her, though it was very necessary for her to love him. By the time that Ethan met her, he was already adept at feigning affection, and Mary fell in love quietly, the way that a leaf slips beneath the water.

There is a scar on Ethan's thumb that Mary gave him, a white crescent in the meat of his palm. The last taste in her mouth was the copper of his blood. Mary was peaceful, nurturing and gentle, but she did not die peacefully. She does not rest peacefully, at Evergreen.

 5

Lori makes it back to Burlington two nights later. There are flowers on her doorstep. For a wonder, they have not been touched by her hallmates. Not for the first time, she thinks about looking for a new apartment. It shouldn't surprise her that her possessions have not been vandalized, but that's what cheap rent will do for you.

Lori unlocks the door, carrying the flowers inside. They are not lilies, thank goodness. She cannot stand the smell of lilies, not since the funeral service. Instead, Ethan has left her roses, such a dark red that the edges of their petals seem to blend into black. Her eyes cannot seem to leave them, and the scent they give off is intoxicating after the stale smoke smell of the hall. She places them on the small kitchen table, where some sunlight can reach them. This is the only room with windows.

There is no note amongst the flowers. When Lori slept with Ethan, she did it because she knew that it was time, even if she wasn't ready. If she wanted to keep him, she needed to acquiesce. Just as then, Lori knows that she has a choice. If she forgives this vanishing, she will be making a commitment to share her life. Maybe not forever—she's not ready for forever, not yet. But surely for now.

If she does not forgive it, Ethan will leave. It is a certainty in her gut. She will lose this one human connection. Perhaps it would be a relief. It is strange to feel alive again, to feel something besides the overwhelming numbness of Annie's death. She clenches her fist on the table, staring at the roses.

Then she gets out her phone, and types out a message to Ethan.

They get takeout and a hotel room. Lori has forgotten what comfort feels like but the soft, clean sheets remind her. The shower is clear glass, the bathroom larger than her own. She leads Ethan into the room, strips him of his clothes, fingers sure on the buttons. He groans when her hands touch his skin, his lips hot on hers.

Their food grows cold.

In the bed, later, eating lo mein with chopsticks, Lori studies Ethan. He studies her back. They've exchanged few words in this encounter. Lori didn't mind before. Now she does. Now she looks at this man and wonders why he has come back. The hotel room hammers in what she already knows: Ethan has money. She doesn't know where he lives, or what he does for a living, vague references to stocks and business trips to New York aside. Lori has not had the luxury of casual relationships. There was always Annie to consider. Now, she is not sure she knows how to do this.

"What are you thinking?" he asks her. She smiles despite herself.

"Trying to figure out how long you will stick around," she says. Not the kind of thing you usually say to someone the second time you've slept with them, but Lori has little to lose.

Ethan looks serious.

"Are you upset that I left on a trip and didn't tell you?" he asks. Lori shrugs, takes another bite of food. He is sitting up, and suddenly she feels uncomfortable in her hotel bathrobe.

"You're not my keeper, Lori," he says. It's said gently, but Lori is stung. She sits up. Looks for her clothes. This was a mistake.

"What are you doing?"

"I'm going home," she says. Thinks, longingly, of their house in San Antonio, of Annie. What would her sister say?

"Aren't you overreacting a little?" Ethan says mildly. "I didn't mean to upset you."

Lori sits back, looking Ethan in the eye. It feels vulnerable, uncomfortable, and her stomach twists, but she doesn't look away.

"I am not good at casual relationships," she tells him. "I never have been. There was always my sister, before."

"Tell me about her," he says. He's never moved from his spot on the bed. He sits so still, watching with those piercing blue eyes, his short brown hair in disarray and wet from their time in the shower. Lori bites her lip under that gaze. The urge to touch him again comes upon her suddenly, struggles against her desire to flee. It's a roiling in her gut, an impossible conflict. One feeling must defeat the other.

What would Annie do?

Annie would love.

"Annie. Her name was Annie," Lori says.

A nnie loved many things.

She loved the smell of pavement after it rained, which she swore smelled like home. Lori has different associations of their childhood before they had been separated, so she isn't sure which home Annie referred to. Maybe none of them. When Lori thinks of New England, of Massachusetts, she thinks of cold. She thinks of long, endless nights, and snow so deep you might vanish down inside it, staring up at the sky as if from the bottom of a well, everything silent and still. She thinks, even, of their birth mother, Hannah the stranger, chunky highlights in her artificially straight hair and shaking fingers wrapping around a cigarette like it was a lifeline.

Annie was too young to remember Hannah sending them away, or maybe the trauma of loss was too great. She didn't really remember New England. Annie's first memories were of a city. Lori has her file, and Annie had read it. She had lived in Boston for a while before the family that had adopted her had moved to Philadelphia and taken her along. She remembered little of it, but the smell of pavement and exhaust, the noise of traffic and the lights at night. There were whole years of her childhood that Annie did not speak of because she couldn't.

The family had been killed in a car wreck, and Annie spent two weeks in the hospital with a head injury. She forgot the collision, she forgot her adopted brother, she forgot the names of her adopted parents. But she cried sometimes for no reason, and the amnesia affected her schooling. Words blurred on paper, numbers were static but had no context. When a new family took her in she drew skyscrapers on the walls of their home in crayon and did not speak. Her foster parents gave her up.

After that, Annie bounced from family to family for two years. She turned ten, then eleven, then twelve in different houses, with different people. She became too old to inspire pity.

Lori's family had not been so afflicted by fate. She grew up in comfort if not in warmth, with a good education, with food in her belly, with toys. The couple she called Mom and Dad lived on the outskirts of Boston. When she turned thirteen, she asked her new parents for information about her mother and the sister she barely remembered. They told her no.

Lori can still remember that moment of betrayal. How her adopted mother, Ruth, had looked at her with her short blonde bob and a gimlet gleam in her eye and said, "Your mother was trash. She gave you up because she couldn't even take care of herself. I'll not have you turn out like her." Roger, her father, just shrugged and yielded to Ruth on everything. There was no help there.

It was five more years before Lori could break Ruth's hold on her life. She didn't care about finding Hannah, not really. Hannah had given her up with shaking fingers, and Lori was not ready to forgive that, not at eighteen. She wanted Annie.

And she found her.

"When Annie first saw me, she knew me instantly," Lori says, "and I loved her from the moment I saw her. If you held up pictures of me at the same age next to her, you might think we were the same child." She's lying back on the hotel bed, Ethan propped next to her. The food is boxed up and forgotten on the bedside table. In another room, barely heard through the walls, a television mumbles. She can hear it only because of the silence that holds the room between her statements. It's a silence she wants to cling to.

"The last family who got her specialized in children with trauma, and it was because of them that she could even function when I found her. My parents had required a sealed adoption. I didn't have anywhere to look until I turned eighteen." She longs for something to do with her hands.

"Then what?" Ethan asks when she is silent too long. Lori clears her throat.

"I took her. It took me another year. She was fourteen and hardly spoke at all. They had her in remedial classes in the school because they thought she had a speech impediment." Lori snorted. "Annie could chat a squirrel out of a tree. She needed stability. The family had been working with her, and they made some progress, but she needed more than that. She needed me."

And that was the crux of it. Annie had needed Lori, and Lori had been there. For fourteen years she had been there.

Lori remembers walking into that house. There were seven children there, the parents a man and a woman in their sixties who owned a farm out in rural Pennsylvania. The kids split their time between school and farm work. Annie was in charge of feeding the chickens. When Lori walked in the front door, with its pile of shoes alongside the entrance and the smell of coffee brewing, she had been nervous. Her hands had clenched, just as they are doing now. Annie was in the living room, watching a cartoon. She had looked up at Lori with big brown eyes, her curly hair pulled back in a frizzy braid. There was a moment of pure connection between them, a moment when Lori felt her heart drop out of her chest.

"You're Lori," Annie said. "You're going to take care of me now."

"Yes," Lori told her. "Yes, that's right."

6

Ethan does not disappear again, not for a long time.

They pass months in the same pattern. Ethan does not go back to his house out in the country, but stays in a hotel in Burlington. When he comes back on the ferry, Lori meets him. They go to dinner. Ethan pays. She eats at every restaurant in town. Everything is exceptional. People in Vermont like their food.

The hotel bed is much better than her own. Lori tangles the sheets with her legs wrapped around Ethan's waist and the smell of him in her nose, man and sweat and expensive cologne. She sleeps without dreams. Each night is a sinking into blackness, a release that she did not know she was missing. There is Ethan, the living, breathing presence of him, wrapped around her like shelter. There is darkness and rest.

It is on the ferry one night, sitting at the top on a bench seat looking out over the black water to the lights on the New York shore, that she realizes she loves him. Her body feels warm, light, to think of seeing him again. Lori has never felt such a lightness. The engines thrum in her bones as the ferry docks, and she watches the cars roll off and the cars roll on. Exhaust bites at her lungs. There is his black Mercedes-Benz, sleek and gleaming in the middle of the pack. It parks, and he exits. His eyes find hers. She feels speared by that gaze, and now it is an intimate sensation, not a fearful one.

Ethan straightens his suit, walks around to the stairs. Lori has to still herself. She wants to jump up and welcome him at the top of the staircase. She wants to embrace him right there in front of everyone, without reservations. To say, "This is mine."

Instead, Ethan comes to sit beside her, smiling. He kisses her lightly on the forehead, wraps his arm around her, and she leans into him for the ride back to Vermont.

That night, in the hotel bed after Ethan has gone to sleep, Lori grapples with the idea of love. Annie had loved her and she had loved Annie, but Annie still left. She feels safe with Ethan there beside her, but for how long?

The doubts are nasty, vicious things. She does not want them. She does not want to feel the barbs of loss already, when this love is so new. But she does. Lori cannot help it. She cannot help but think on how inevitable loss is. Life has taught her too well. All things die. Either she will leave Ethan or he will leave her, one way or another, and the grief of it echoes to her from that imagined future. Her eyes well with tears. She does not brush them away. Ethan is sleeping, and he will want to know why, and what would she say?

Lori sits with the grief in the darkness and does not say a word.

7

E than has never explained to her what he does exactly. He works as an investment banker, a finance man, but Lori does not think he needs to work. He spends time in Montreal and Albany and, further away, in Manhattan. When he comes home and talks to her about that work, which is rarely, he uses terms that bore her near to tears. When she told him that, he laughed and agreed it was boring. He doesn't talk about it much anymore, except to tell her when he will be gone on work-related excursions.

Lori, on the other hand, is not so affluent. The meager income from Lori's cafe job has not allowed her to add to what little she had left over from Texas. She has considered moving out of her apartment with its odor of cigarettes, but since she is currently only spending about three nights of the week there she finds it hard to justify a newer, nicer place. In any case, winter comes on before she can manage, grasping everything in an icy fist.

It's been years since Lori experienced a northern winter. Now, in the first week of November, with the holiday months looming over her, Lori realizes she is not prepared. She goes out shopping for leggings, thick sweaters, wool hats, anything to stand between her and the cold. Ethan is off in New York somewhere. The streets are strung with lights already, which bothers her. She keeps looking for marigolds and ofrendas. There has been frost on her windows and icy rain, once. She walks on the bricked width of Church Street, ducks from warm shop to warm shop, looking for layers to add to her closet. She uses her credit card—she'll figure out paying things off later.

Lori is thin, though she's fleshed out now that Ethan makes her eat. Grief had whittled her down to skin and bone. She's started running again, but she hasn't tried any of Vermont's famous hikes. In the outdoor store, a huge, brightly lit space with shiny wooden floors, she fingers lycra and soft wool dresses. Snowshoes and traction webbing feature prominently in displays, along with puffy winter coats like marshmallows, hand warmers, thermal underwear and impossibly thick socks. All of the colors are bright, futuristic after the quaint street outside. Lori browses, unsure of what she will need. Her eyes return again and again to a pair of waterproof, insulated boots, to the ice cleats, to the coats. It's all so expensive, but Lori needs to broaden her horizons. Her body, her mind, they both want something more stimulating than the bubble she has wrapped around herself. She can't rely on Ethan to entertain her all the time.

So she buys them, the boots, the cleats, the coat. She adds a pair of socks for good measure.

The next morning Lori goes into work and asks her boss about hiking.

Christine is older than Lori, though not by much. She has curly hair, like Lori's, but it's turning a steely gray, and her eyes are dark blue. Christine lived in Texas herself for a little while, in Austin. This explains her obsession with green chile salsa, which she lathers on her sweet potato tacos as if the heat cannot touch her. Lori is more of a red salsa person herself, and if she ate as much of the stuff as Christine does she is pretty sure she would turn into a weeping, red mess.

Business is slow, with everyone up on the main drag doing early Christmas shopping. It's not quite lunch, but Christine opens the place so she's been up since well before dawn. The winter light is sort of tenuous, like it's not sure it's supposed to be shining. Nothing like the light in Texas. The sun always knows exactly where it means to be there, even on cloudy days. For once, Lori thinks of it with nostalgia.

"You want to go hiking? The trails are already iced over by now." Christine takes a long pull of her cappuccino. It's just the two of them. The closing girl hasn't come in yet.

"I bought some boots," Lori says.

"Have you ever been hiking?" Christine asks. "I don't mean in Texas."

Lori twists her lips instead of touching her hair, which is what she wants to do. Touching your hair means you have to go back and wash your hands again, and her skin is dry already.

"Not yet," she admits. The last dregs of summer were too long, too hard. She was lucky to get out of bed. Only a sense of stubborn obligation kept her moving.

"Well, don't go alone," Christine says. "The woods up here can get you turned around fast, if you're not familiar. In the summer you might live long enough to find your way out. The winter, not so much."

Lori sighs and picks up a rag to have something to do with her hands. She wipes down the counter.

"I just don't want to be cooped up anymore," she says.

Christine casts her a pitying glance. Lori has never been exactly sure how much Christine knows or guesses about her reasons for moving up here alone, what story Christine tells about Lori's exodus from Texas. For that matter, she realizes, she doesn't know why Christine left either. Now's not the time to ask.

"Why don't you make that man of yours take you?" Christine demands, waggling her eyebrows.

Lori blushes, of all things. She feels like a girl.

"He's got you lit up like a Christmas tree," Christine says, laughing. "When do I get to meet him?"

Lori smiles uneasily. Ethan is so private, and their relationship is so new. He's never come to visit her at the cafe, though he knows where she works.

"I don't know," she says. "Maybe he'll stop by." She tries to imagine Ethan and Christine in a room together and fails.

"Have you made plans for the holidays yet? Going to meet the family?" Christine's tone is half teasing.

"Actually," Lori says, her smile becoming more honest, "he invited me out to his place for Thanksgiving. He promises it will be a night I won't forget."

"Guess I'll find someone else to help with the Christmas lights, then," Christine says over her shoulder. She's putting up dishes, and she doesn't sound upset, but Lori frowns.

"Of course not." She runs a rag over the counter, trying to look busy even though no one's come in for an hour. It's cold and raining, which sometimes means good traffic for coffee but apparently not today. "I'll be there with bells on."

"Good," Christine says. "Can't have him stealing away my best barista."

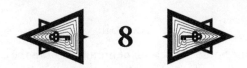

8

It's snowing when Ethan comes to pick her up for Thanksgiving dinner. Lori wears her puffy blue coat, which hangs to her knees, and shivers. She's not used to the cold yet.

Ethan has traded in his Mercedes-Benz for some monstrous black SUV which he promises will handle the snow. It snowed sometimes in San Antonio, too, but it was the exception to the rule. Lori hasn't seen snow so early for years, and the mountains of Vermont render it magical and strange. They head down the interstate, which is clear, and then get off on a local highway. Lori recognizes where they are eventually, though everything is distorted by the skimming of snow and the naked, wet gray of the trees. They are going to pass that terrible little bed and breakfast. Her fingers grasp for Annie's urn, but she left it on the table in the living room of her apartment. It has been collecting dust. Lori feels guilty, but her heart has been so light she cannot bring herself to touch it for fear of a return of her nightmares. The grief, when she thinks on it, is still a stone in her belly, a rending.

So she shoves the thoughts of her sister away, focusing on the steel blue of Caspian Lake in the monochrome world. They pass the bed and breakfast, its lights dark, and turn around the top of the lake, down into the trees. At first, it is mostly deciduous trees with bare, gray bark, but soon evergreens appear, first only a few, then many. The green is a balm after the austerity of this winter day. The heavy branches enfold them in a tunnel of silent verdigris dusted all with white. Ethan takes a turn, one she almost does not see in the dimness. Lori grips the door. The snow has begun to stick on the road.

Headlights cut through the shadows beneath the trees as they reach a simple, curved gate. It is black, and towers over the vehicle. Ethan presses a button, and the doors swing open.

"Welcome," he says, "to Evergreen."

Lori thinks, in that moment, that it is like a storybook.

The driveway takes them nearly into the lake. Lori grips the door again as the pavement dips and twists, at the last minute, away from the water. Ethan chuckles. He guides the vehicle through a second gate, with a grate and a low brick wall on either side. Past this point, the paving changes to something that looks a lot like cobbles, though the real estate agent in Lori wants to examine it further to see if it isn't just impressed concrete. The tires rumble, even with the thin skimming of snow to cushion them. Ahead, the driveway widens into a large circle, with plantings of evergreen bushes and some sculpture rendered vague in the growing dark perched on the island of soil in its center. Behind it spreads the house.

Lori realizes that she glimpsed this house before—a chance glimpse, through the briefest gap in the trees. Then, it grabbed her imagination. Now, it steals her breath. The house is a beacon of life and light in the cold, snowy night, massive and warm. It is all windows, boxy, impossible lines and golden light, though she can see the hints of more beyond, behind the trees. Evergreens frame its vastness. To their right as they enter the circle the lake sits like a mirror, waters nearly black already.

Ethan turns off the car.

"It's beautiful," Lori says, still staring, still trying to capture the details of what she is seeing.

"I'm glad you like it," Ethan says, his voice soft. "I thought you would."

E than and Lori disembark from the black SUV. The cold bites into Lori instantly. Her feet in their warm hiking boots slip on the slick ground. Ethan wraps his arm around her, catching her, and she laughs.

"I got these boots so I wouldn't slip!"

"I think you need to take them back then," Ethan jokes. They walk inside, through the entryway with its stone facade and heavy wooden doors that Lori longs to stroke. The room beyond is two stories, grandiose, filled with light and emptiness and a set of stairs that stretch up like a dream. The marble of the floor and stairway is ivory with blue-gray veins, the walls a cool dove gray. It's beautiful, if a little cold.

"This is amazing," Lori says. Ethan just smiles.

He leads her to the right, through an open arch into the wing of the house that parallels the lake. The endless wall of windows Lori saw during their approach, golden and gleaming, spreads before them now black with the weight of night. In this room is a fireplace, a dining table out of a fairytale, and a woman all in black. Her face is lined with age, her hair silver, her expression severe above her black collared shirt.

"Sir," she says, "welcome home."

Now is not the time for Lori to balk, but the idea that Ethan might have in-home waitstaff never occurred to her. She knew he was rich. But this is a different level of affluence, one that elevates him well above the household Lori grew up in, with its uppercrust desires. Ruth would be proud, if she and Ruth still spoke. Lori walks into the room, wrestling with her sudden tension. The woman takes her coat and scarf and gloves, and Ethan's as well. Ethan pulls out a chair for Lori at the beautiful table. The rug under their feet is probably worth more than the value of her car. Lori feels underdressed, though Ethan has on a sweater and jeans just like her. Lori sits down, Ethan pushes in the chair and seats himself. The woman returns with wine—a dry white, Lori's favorite kind.

"I'm sorry," Lori says, interrupting the pour of the pale golden liquid, "I didn't catch your name."

"Of course, ma'am," the woman says. "You may call me Eleanor."

Eleanor turns to Ethan's glass. Ethan smiles past her at Lori.

"Nora's been with my family for a long time. She and Paul practically raised me," Ethan says. "They'll eat later, though. I wanted this evening to be just the two of us."

"Paul?" Lori asks.

"Nora's husband," Ethan says dismissively. "He's the groundskeeper."

Lori swallows. Eleanor steps back from the table, her face impassive.

"Dinner will be ready in just a moment," she says. Lori looks down at her clean, porcelain plate, at the silver table settings and the vast, empty expanse of the table. Eleanor is gone by the time she looks up, vanishing back into the kitchen.

"Would you like to hear some music?" Ethan asks. He roots around in his pocket, sets something soothing and low to playing in the background. Lori reminds herself that she feels comfortable with Ethan, which she obviously wouldn't have to do if she felt comfortable but here they are. Eleanor reappears with bread and salads. Lori asks for bleu cheese dressing. Ethan gets balsamic vinaigrette. She cannot understand why her heart is pounding.

They've talked about the highlights of their respective days in the car and now she has nothing to say. Lori eats her salad slowly, stretching the bites. Outside, the blackness presses, except when it is broken by a flurry of white.

"You may get snowed in here," Ethan says. Lori gulps her wine. It makes a warm nest in her stomach, smooths the edges of her panic enough for her to waggle her eyebrows suggestively. Ethan laughs. Lori finds herself smiling in answer, though she can feel sweat prickling on her body from misspent adrenaline.

Eleanor returns with the turkey, stuffed and glistening, which she carves onto their plates. There is a trencher of cranberry sauce, and of gravy. There are mashed potatoes, macaroni and cheese, more soft bread and salty butter. Lori hasn't had a traditional Thanksgiving meal in years. She and Annie always had tacos for Thanksgiving. Neither of them had particularly liked Thanksgiving as a holiday, but they liked tacos. Each year they tried new toppings—pickled cabbage, teriyaki chicken, daikon, pulled pork.

For a moment, Lori can see her sister in the dark glass of the nearest window. Her face is still with death. Her eyes are black. She opens her mouth and there is a void inside, an ending.

"Lori?" Ethan asks, and Lori tears her gaze away. The insulation of the alcohol is burning from her. She smiles shakily.

"I'm sorry," she says. "What were you saying?"

"How do you like the turkey?" Ethan asks.

Lori looks down at her plate. At some point she has taken a bite, but she doesn't remember that flavor. The inside of her mouth tastes sour.

"It's good," she says, looking back up, smoothing her smile to something natural, she hopes.

She does not look at the windows again.

* * *

T he snow keeps falling throughout dinner.

Ethan has spent most of the evening telling her about the history of the house, and of the town of Greensboro, which they drove through to get here. There's a brewery he wants her to visit with him, and hiking trails—she has told him of her desire to try hiking—and they could go skiing, he says, at a resort nearby. She protests that she does not know how to ski, and he promises to teach her. The knots in her shoulders, in her stomach, are relaxing at last, though Lori still hasn't eaten much.

Dessert is pumpkin cinnamon rolls made especially for her. Lori gives them the attention they deserve, listening to Ethan with half an ear. When he mentions a tour of the house, though, she perks up.

They rise from the table, leaving their dishes. Lori brings her wine, freshly topped off by Ethan, and follows him back into the foyer. It is drafty and grandiose. She is not in the mood for it despite its beauty, and so she is glad when they step up the stairs.

"There's another stairway," Ethan is saying, "but we'll see that later."

Lori climbs the wooden stairs, the carved bannister dark and gleaming beneath her hand. They reach the top, which offers a balcony where she can review her progress, pressed against a wall of piled stones. Another set of doors greets her here, just as heavy and ostentatious as the first. The meaning is clear—she is being invited into the inner sanctum. Ethan leads her on, into the house.

Beyond is a great room. They enter on another balcony, this one of stained wood. The sudden warmth and color makes Lori inhale deeply. The great room is two stories, with black skylights speckled with snow looming above them. There is a fire in the fireplace below. There are bookshelves around the walls, and a large screen television, and plush, roomy couches. Seen from above the room looks comfortable and Lori turns towards Ethan, looking for a way down from their high vantage. To her right, a spiral staircase descends down lazily. Ethan turns her back to the left, hands warm and firm on her shoulders. There's a door against the far wall, a long catwalk's length away. Across the room from the balcony are more windows, occluded by dark. Lori wonders if there is a garden beyond. Ethan is already leading her on, so she doesn't ask. Lori expects she will get a chance to see this magnificent house in the daylight soon enough.

The hallway he leads her into has seven doors. More skylights dot the ceiling above them. Lori thinks of the heating bill and shudders, but it's beautiful. The hallway feels airy, even though the walls are a false facade of gray stone, trimmed with a light wood. Perhaps maple, she thinks. It's a different wood from the doors themselves, which remain the same dark, rich color. All of it gleams. A thick carpet runner muffles her steps.

"These are guest bedrooms," Ethan says. He gestures to an open doorway to their left. "A private living room." Lori peeks in. It has a fireplace, too, even though it's on the second floor. There's no fire lit tonight, but all of the needed materials are there.

They continue to a final set of double doors at the end of the hall. Beyond is a stairwell, with round porthole-like windows. She hesitates on the landing, looking up and down the stairs, unsure which way she should go.

"There's a gym and hot tub downstairs," Ethan says, "but we're going up." Lori turns obligingly, climbing the stairs with him behind her. At the top is a final door. Ethan reaches past her to open this door as well. Spreads his arms wide, inviting her in.

"My chamber," he says with a wry twisting of his lips.

They are in a bedroom. The bed sits in the middle of the floor, a large, canopied thing with bronze and cream draperies. The sheets are a deep red, the comforter bronze with red motes like droplets of blood. Windows surround it on two sides. Ethan reaches out and flicks off the light.

Lori watches the snow come down in the woods, smothering them. All of her anxieties at last quiet.

Ethan leads her to the bed.

THE FOURTH WIFE

The fourth wife was named Veronica. She never knew she was dying until death lay on her like a blanket. Ethan went by his own name with her, because she was beautiful and because he had almost given up on killing.

Veronica's parents called her Roni. She loved them but disliked the name. Her father was a fan of folk music. He played the guitar on Wednesdays with all of his old friends at a bar in the next valley over and Veronica went with him to sing sometimes. Not long before she died, Veronica lost both of her parents in a car accident. She never guessed that it was Ethan's fault. After all, he loved her.

And he did. Ethan loved Veronica's long black hair, her bright blue eyes. He loved the way she laughed, and how a curse word from her lips came out sharp with barbs. But in the end, he could not choose freedom in her arms, not knowing how she would look at him if she knew him for who he truly was. Never mind that he was the one who had made himself that way.

Veronica wore a small black dress to their anniversary dinner. She drank her wine red and bitter, and didn't notice the other flavors, even as her words slurred and the world faded out into nothing but bright glimpses of memory and the comfort of a place to lie down. She never knew that death was coming, and so she never feared. Her last breath left her peacefully.

The fear came after.

9

D espite everything, Lori does not spend the night at Evergreen. The snow stops at last. The forest is still and silent, wrapping them in darkness. Ethan wakes her from a doze with a kiss on her forehead.

"I'm supposed to get you home," he says. It's true, he is. Lori is supposed to be at Christine's house in the morning to help her with hanging Christmas lights. Christine has young children, and her husband uses a wheelchair. Lori didn't want her climbing on the roof alone, especially if there might be snow, so she insisted that she would make it despite Christine's doubts. She makes a sound, half disappointment, half sleep, then forces herself to roll over and hunt for her jeans. The air outside the covers is cold. She pulls her phone free of the tangle of clothes, squinting at the bright screen. To her surprise, it's only half past nine.

"Gotta love northern winters," Ethan says, then shoves her out of bed. She yelps in indignation as the cold air claims her, stumbling, and he laughs. Pulling clothes on hurriedly, Lori gives him a glare doubtless invisible in the dark. He's already leaving the warm shelter of the bed himself.

They descend the stairs. Lori pauses at the second-floor landing. Ethan leans in close behind her, his lips next to her ear.

"I'll show you the hot tub next time," he whispers, and Lori shivers at the breath on her cheek. Her body perks up to his warmth, to the presence of him, even though only a moment ago it was sated. She bites her lip and tries not to imagine throwing off her plans for the morning to explore this new possibility.

Instead, they walk back down the hall, into the foyer. The cold has gotten more severe here. Lori shivers. Eleanor, already awaiting them, hands her back her coat, her scarf and gloves. The older woman's face is impassive. Lori feels herself blushing.

"I hope you enjoyed your stay," Eleanor says. Her voice is cool.

"Of course," Lori says. "Dinner was excellent."

"Yet you ate so little."

Lori can't think of anything good to say to that, so she says nothing. Ethan says his goodbyes, and they both go outside.

"I don't think she liked me," Lori says when they are safely in the car. The dining room's lights go dark as she watches.

"Nora is just that way," Ethan says. He starts the car. "She and Paul have lost a lot. She will thaw." Lori shivers in the cold and hopes he is right.

It's a long, sleepy drive to Burlington. The car warms eventually, and Lori dozes. When Ethan drops her off at last on the street outside of her apartment, he looks tired, too. It's close to eleven.

"Are you alright to make the trip back?" Lori asks. "It's a long drive." Most of the roads are clear, but there is still a slick dusting of snow. Ethan smiles.

"Of course," he says. "See you in a few days. Have a good time tomorrow."

Lori smiles. She kisses him goodnight, her fatigue wearing on her already.

That night, Lori dreams that she is in a wood. It is all evergreen trees, foliage heavy and black in the darkness. She presses through the branches, her limbs stiff with cold, and they press back at her, holding her in place. There is a dry rustling behind her, like leaves, but she knows that is not what it is. She knows that if she turns, she will see something that should not be there. Something that should not be at all. Motion glimmers from the corner of her eye. Her body trembles. The trees, the deep, evergreen trees, will not let her go, will not let her run, they press against her skin and into her mouth until all she can taste is tree sap, and the smell fills her, and the blackness beneath the branches becomes viscous, and the cold steals her breath, and the rustling, crackling steps are the only thing she can hear—

The cold wakes her, the frigid air. Lori gasps, her heart pounding. There are tears at the corner of her eyes. She wipes at them, realizes she has lost her blanket somewhere. It was just a dream, and it is fading already. Lori paws around the bed, finds the blanket and grabs it to her. She's safe. She knows she is safe.

In the morning, she does not remember the dream at all.

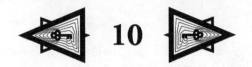

10

C hristine is pulling boxes out of the attic of her garage when Lori pulls up the next morning. The little Toyota did not want to start in the cold, which is a bitter twenty degrees. Lori can see her breath, a billowing white cloud in the morning's wan sun. The short drive was hardly enough to warm up the engine, and Lori's gloves have done little to keep the cold at bay. She's happy to get out of the icebox of the Toyota, even if the outside is not much better.

Her manager tramps down with her giant plastic bin, boots carefully searching out the fragile attic stairs. Lori hopes the box is not heavy. She sees a small array of bins in the garage as she walks up the driveway, passing Christine's own SUV. It's clear of snow, unlike Lori's car, which still sports a skimming of ice crystals in the seam of the windshield. Her night at Evergreen seems like a dream still, but the skim of snow in the grass of Christine's yard reminds her that it was real.

"Lori!" Christine calls. "You made it!"

"It's a small town," Lori says, "hard to get lost."

"Come in and let me get you some coffee," Christine says, setting down her bin and waving Lori inside. "You can meet Bill and the kids."

Lori follows Christine into her house. It is a custom ranch, mostly one level. Christine shows her into the living room, where two children under ten are playing video games on a mid-size television. The whole floor plan feels open and airy. The kitchen and dining room are gleaming, and there's coffee already on the burner. It's a local roast, of course. Christine loves her local coffees. Lori takes a mug gratefully, adds cream, and sips. She feels lethargic this morning. Likely it is just the cold.

"Bill," Christine calls, "Lori's here!"

"You don't have to bother him," Lori says. Christine gives her an amused look. A moment later, Bill glides in. He's younger than Lori expected, younger than Christine, closer to her own age. He holds out his hand.

"Lori, it's good to meet you," he says. There are laugh lines around his eyes, and his hands are calloused. She's not sure why she finds that surprising.

"It's nice to meet you," she says back, automatically. The wheelchair is sleek and black. She's never seen one like it, but she doesn't want to stare. Ruth raised her better than that, and it's one lesson that Lori is not sorry she learned. Curiosity is not always kind.

"You'll have to stay for lunch," Bill says. "I'm making anything other than tacos, at Christine's request."

Lori lifts an eyebrow. "She eats something besides tacos?" she says drily. Bill laughs.

Lori finishes her coffee regretfully. The kitchen is warm and the garage is cold, but there is work to be done. She and Christine retreat outside to sort through Christmas boxes. Lori hauls a few inside, placing them carefully against the wall and out of the kitchen walkway. One long container is full of Christmas lights, along with another smaller one. These they unpack in the garage.

Lori and Christine begin the ritual of untangling and plugging-in that accompanies any such attempt at decoration. She and Annie used to work just like this. Not for the first time, Lori misses her sister. It does not sting as much with Christine there, silently working in the brightening Vermont light.

"So," Christine says, "how was your Thanksgiving?"

Lori makes a face. "Odd, but not bad." She's thinking of Eleanor. The woman is some kind of robot. It's weird to think that she raised Ethan. He certainly didn't treat her like family, and Ethan is older than Lori by at least ten years which would make Eleanor old enough she should be retired, not waiting on Ethan hand and foot. Christine is busy untangling a net of lights, laying it out with the others. Lori has tested all of the ones they have extracted already and they all seem to work, which Christine claims is a small miracle.

"What was odd?" she asks, looking up. Lori smiles ruefully.

"He has servants," she says. She shrugs, trying not to let the discomfort of last night wrap around her. "They live there. I wasn't expecting it."

Christine gives her an incredulous face. "Did they eat dinner with you?"

"No," Lori says, feeling uneasy. She changes the subject.

"The house is huge," Lori says. "I'd guess at least ten bedrooms? And a dining room like something out of a castle. It's gorgeous."

She can't stop the wistfulness in her voice when she says that. Lori got into the business of houses because she loved them. Evergreen is beautiful, what she has seen of it, and she wants to explore it further.

"So you thought you were going to an intimate dinner with a mere mortal and got invited out to an isolated estate, huh?" Christine shakes her head. "It's like a gothic romance. Big castle in the woods, pretty little girl . . . "

"I'm no girl, not anymore," Lori says ironically.

"Girl to me!" Christine says, laughing. "What does he do to have all that money?"

"I think he inherited most of it," Lori says. "I don't really know. He travels to Montreal, I think, and to New York. He told me he was an investment banker. For startups, you know?"

Christine shakes her head, then hands Lori a newly untangled net of lights. "Test this for me?"

They break at noon for lunch. The kids have already eaten, and Bill banishes them outside as soon as Christine opens the door. It's probably for the best. Lori doesn't really understand children. Annie was quiet and nearly grown when Lori found her, and none of their friends had children. Christine's kids have blond hair, not brown, and when Lori comes in they sprint past her through the open door, out into the cold day. Lori closes the door behind them.

Bill has made spaghetti with meatballs and salad with vinaigrette. The kitchen smells amazing. Their dining room table gleams beneath her plate. Between her small breakfast and yesterday's light dinner, Lori is ravenous. She eats a whole plate of spaghetti, demolishes her salad, and seriously considers seconds. Only politeness wins out. Christine brings her more coffee.

Bill asks about their progress, nursing his own coffee, and Christine fills him in. Then conversation turns to other avenues.

"How did you end up in Vermont?" Bill asks Lori. She tenses despite herself, and takes a sip of her coffee to hide it.

"You know, just needed a change," she says.

Christine steps in. "Lori lived in Texas before," she says. "I think the winter is a surprise."

"I grew up in New England, actually," Lori says. "It's just been a long time. I had to buy a coat—mine wasn't going to cut it up here." She gestures towards the coat hanging on the back of her chair. There was no point in putting it up when they were just going out soon anyway.

"What part of New England?" Bill asks.

"Around Boston," Lori says. It's a safer topic than Texas at least. She cannot talk about Texas with a stranger. She has never told Christine why she left.

"Oh, I've got family there," Bill says. "What a small world."

Lori smiles stiffly. She's forgotten that this is why she doesn't go out, doesn't meet people. The earnestness, the idle conversation. This is everything that she cannot stand. It is like stepping through a forest laced with unexploded ordnance. Any motion could start a chain reaction, an explosion that will take you off your feet.

"Well, we'd better get back to work," Christine says, saving her.

The air outside is bitter and sharp after the soft warmth of the kitchen. Lori helps Christine wrestle the ladder from its hooks on the garage wall and set it up on the sidewalk which leads to the front of the house. It doesn't reach the bottom edge of the roof, not quite, but it gets them close enough to step across. Lori goes up, despite Christine's protests. She's lighter, and younger, and anyway that's why she came. She lays on her belly on the cold asphalt shingles and Christine hands her up the bunched string of lights. Then she scoots away, hitches herself up, and begins unrolling lights along the roof's edge.

She and Annie used to do this, at the house. It was small, though it was two stories so the roof was taller than this one. The shingles of the roof were the same tan color, though. The air was a balmy fifty degrees, and Annie had stared up at her, shouting jokes, demanding that she hurry so they could go inside out of the air she considered cold. Lori had thought it was cold, too, at the time. Now her fingers barely bend, though the air has warmed from this morning. She's taken the gloves off so she can shove little plastic hooks into the edge of the gutters, but she regrets it when her fingers fumble. At least she's most of the way done. Soon she won't even be able to feel her hands. She's not made for this weather, not anymore. The numbness of her hands reminds her of something, a gut feeling of foreboding, like a memory she can't quite hold onto. Lori shakes her head and finishes her work.

"I'm coming down," she says. Christine is below her, staring up. Lori extends one foot into the void, trying to find the top of the ladder. Christine is trying to guide her, and afterwards Lori is never quite sure how it happens, but somehow she slips. Her cold hands don't quite grab at the gutter, not that it would hold her anyway.

There is a moment of pure weightlessness. She doesn't even have time to shout, just to feel the freefall rising up in her, the clenching of her gut.

Then she hits the ground.

11

Annie sits by the bed.

Lori cannot remember how she came to be here. There is sunlight through the blinds. It is afternoon. The air feels warm the way the air has not felt in weeks, but Lori cannot remember why she thinks it should be cold. She can hear the neighborhood kids playing outside, and Annie is backlit, sitting by her bed.

"Am I sick?" Lori asks.

"You fell," Annie says. "You'll be fine in a moment."

"I don't . . . " But she does remember falling, sort of, the sensation of it anyway. It's distant, and it's over in any case. She's safe in her bed, and Annie is here.

Her sister turns her head, slightly. Lori sees the curve of her cheek in the dimness, lit by the light.

"Why aren't you listening to me, Lori? I've tried so hard to warn you."

"I don't know what you're talking about," Lori says, but memory flickers, more emotion than vision. There is an unease in her belly. The light is going out behind Annie. She can almost see her sister's face.

"It doesn't have to be this way, Lori," her sister says. "You don't have to see me this way. The fear is yours."

"I don't . . . " Lori says again, but then the light dims. There's Annie, the sharp edge of her chin, the small, upturned nose. There is something wrong with her lips. Lori stares at them.

"Lori, don't go back to Evergreen," Annie says, but her lips don't move. Lori can hear her voice but her lips don't move.

Her lips don't move, and her eyes are filmed with death.

Lori's heart stutters, once, twice. She cannot seem to get a breath.

Does Annie's face twist with grief?

"Lori, please—"

Lori opens her eyes. Her heart is pounding, and there is the taste of copper in her mouth. For a moment she cannot understand why she is staring up at a sky so washed-out blue.

"Lori!" Christine says, and her face appears. "Are you okay?"

"Yeah," she says. Her lips feel funny. She's gasping, she realizes, the breath knocked out of her by the fall. There is something important that has happened, but her mind cannot hold onto it. She tries to move, and a pounding pain shoots through her head.

"What happened?" she says. Christine helps her sit up. She can breathe again, but it feels as if she's run a mile. Her hand goes to the back of her head, where the pain is the worst. There's already a lump forming, but she can't feel any broken skin.

"You slipped. I'm so sorry," Christine says. Lori shivers.

"Let's get you out of the cold." Christine helps Lori stand. The world's a little shaky, but she doesn't feel as bad as she could feel. It wasn't that far of a drop to the ground. She must have hit her head on the sidewalk, though. There are bushes right there, but of course she landed on the sidewalk.

Inside, Bill makes a fuss and brings her an icepack and a blanket. The children have gone in the backyard to play. Lori stares at them through the dining room window, wondering why the sound of their shrieks, muffled through the glass, makes her skin crawl. Christine gives her more coffee, generously cut with cream and sugar. It's not how Lori usually takes it, but after the cold and with the peculiar hollowness of her insides Lori finds it is exactly what she wants. Bill brings a penlight to shine into her eyes.

"Should you go to the hospital?" he asks, leaning back in his wheelchair. "Your pupils are responding, and the internet tells me that is a good sign."

Lori shakes her head, and winces. "I think I'll be okay. They'll just watch me anyway." She doesn't feel nauseous, and the headache only gets bad if she moves too fast. Christine shoved some ibuprofen in her hand along with the coffee, so she is pretty sure that will go away too. Medical bills aren't something she has a big budget for right now in any case.

"Do you have a doctor in town?" Christine asks, frowning. "I'll give you a name and you can make an appointment if the headache sticks around." She writes contact information down on a piece of paper, and Lori shoves it into her jean pocket. Then she knocks back the rest of her coffee.

"Well, the lights are up," she says. "I'm sorry I worried you both, but I feel fine."

She stands. Christine stands as well. Bill rolls back out of her way, his expression concerned.

"I'd feel better if there were someone to keep an eye on you," he says. Christine nods beside him.

"I'll be fine," Lori says. She suddenly wants to be alone more than she has in days. She puts her coat back on, her scarf and hat and gloves. She doesn't even wince when she pulls the hat down over her little bump. It is tender, but Lori can take care of it at home.

She makes her excuses and leaves.

12

A few days later, when Lori has recovered and Ethan is back in town, Lori sits with him next to the fireplace in The Farmhouse, the lights glittering and low. Her belly is full of wine and steak, the heat on her skin is pure luxury. Outside the wind howls and cuts at the windows viciously. There's no storm, not yet, but it's coming.

"Do you know what today is?" Ethan asks. He's looking sleek tonight, with his hair slicked back and his black jacket. Lori shakes her head.

"What day is it?" she asks indulgently. Ethan smiles, the expression sly.

"It's our three-month anniversary," Ethan says. "Three months ago, I met you on the ferry and you lit up my life."

Lori feels herself blushing. She smiles wide enough to dimple, and it doesn't feel strange. It feels natural, to smile. It feels good, to be here, with this fire, with the hum of people in the background, with a delicious meal fading on her tongue. She sips more wine, a red tonight. The waiter returns with her dessert. He places it in front of her—a decadent chocolate torte, just as she has expected, but with one little change.

There is a ring resting softly on a single red rose petal. It is a work of art. The diamond at its center is as flawless as cut ice, the band a delicate warm gold braided back on itself, the tiny black setting stones unusual but nearly petals themselves.

"Lori," Ethan says, his voice soft. The waiter has already disappeared. Lori looks up, eyes wide. Meets his gaze, so steady. "Marry me, Lori, and move to Evergreen."

Lori, in this moment, does not think of the house. She does not even hear the name of it. Her heart is with his gaze, piercing her, the face she has come to love, the man asking her to stay with him forever. She feels giddy, joyful, proud. This is the man who has never run from her, who has cradled her, who loves her.

"Yes," she says.

She takes the ring from its bed of petals. She places it on her finger and takes Ethan's hand in hers. He brings her hand to his lips and kisses the ring on her hand. Lori licks her lips.

"Should we get dessert to go?" Ethan asks. His gaze sends heat through her. She nods. They do.

The waiter returns, a phantom in black, whisks away the dessert and Ethan's credit card, returns again only moments later. Then they are gone, into the cold night air. Lori can't even feel it. In the dark of Ethan's car, she kisses him greedily. Then he drives them to the hotel. There are flower petals already on the bed. He kisses her neck. She tangles her fingers in his hair.

There is, Lori thinks, no greater joy than to feel the warmth of someone you love.

She tells Christine two days later. They've planned a hike together despite the bitter cold. Lori has spent the morning in a daze. She and Ethan didn't leave the hotel yesterday, ordering room service and watching bad movies, talking about the future. He wants her to leave Burlington, to move in with him. He says she won't have to work—he has enough money for them both.

She repeats all this to Christine as they tramp around a little loop trail on the outskirts of Burlington. It is so cold that the water in the dirt of the path has frozen, sending up strange stalks that crunch under their feet. Lori has never seen anything like it. This whole cold world is something lovely and new.

"Are you sure?" Christine says from behind her, breaking her reverie. "You haven't known him very long, Lori."

Lori frowns. She had expected excitement. She twirls the ring on her left hand, an already reflexive gesture.

"I love him," she says simply. "I've never been able to say that about anyone before, not like this."

"If he makes you happy," Christine says, "I'm all for it."

Lori snorts. "You're the one who said I was glowing like a Christmas tree."

"That's because you were!" Christine says, laughing. She sobers. "I'm happy for you, Lori. I mean it. You deserve something good."

They walk in silence until they reach a spot that overlooks the lake. Lori stops, and Christine stops with her. The vista is beautiful, austere in the winter light. Lori smiles. She takes a deep breath of cold air. This is the beginning of the rest of her life. She's glad to have such a good friend to meet it with.

13

Ethan and Lori wait to get married until the spring. The winter is not time to try to pull together a wedding in Vermont. It seems that nearly every week a new storm blows through. Christine says that it is the worst winter she has seen in a while. Lori is glad that she doesn't need to drive to get to her job at The Laughing Fox.

Ethan gets snowed into Burlington for nearly a week in January and they spend the time mostly in bed or planning for spring. They've decided to have the wedding at Evergreen. Ethan wants something small, private, though he gives way on the guest list when Lori insists on inviting Christine. She wants to invite Hannah, too, and they're still arguing about that when Ethan takes her out to the house again on a day trip, so she can see the layout of the gardens. Even under the snow she can tell that they will be beautiful. There Lori meets Paul, Eleanor's husband. He is wiry, his hair nearly gone, his mouth pinched and sour. Lori resolves to try to like him anyway. Ethan says the beautiful roses she received were grown by Paul, so there must be something good about him.

While Ethan is talking to Paul on the front walk, Lori excuses herself to the bathroom. There is one off of the foyer, obviously for visitors, all in marble with stainless steel fixtures. She's gotten a chance to tour the house more thoroughly this visit, and the sheer size of it still surprises her. She finishes up, washing her hands in water that refuses to get warm. It is as she is walking back towards the front door that she notices another door, one she hasn't seen before. It is underneath the stairs. She would mistake it for a closet, but it's such an odd color, an indigo framed by ornate white molding with silver accents, a blue so dark it almost blends into the shadows. It's not incongruous with the rest of the space—the details of the molding match that of the guest bathroom, but that frame is an understated white, the door as gray as the walls. Meant to blend into the room, not stand apart from it. It sparks her curiosity. Lori is feeling relaxed, confident in her new life. She walks up to the door and tries the handle.

It is locked.

"What are you doing?"

Lori starts, turns. Eleanor is standing in the doorway to the dining room.

"I just wondered what this door goes to," Lori says, feeling obscurely guilty.

"That is private," Eleanor says, venom in her voice. "What is in there belongs to me and my husband. And it is none of your business."

Lori lets her hand fall. She opens her mouth—she's not sure what she will say. She doesn't get to say anything. Eleanor has already walked away. Lori swallows, and leaves the door alone. She doesn't mention the interaction to Ethan when he takes her home.

Lori does ask about Eleanor a few days later, unable to quiet the niggling voice of resentment inside her. She loves Ethan. She doesn't like Eleanor, or Paul.

"You said Eleanor and Paul raised you?" They are eating takeout on the hotel bed, debating wedding flowers. Ethan has assured her that Paul will handle them all, including the bouquet, though Lori would prefer to pick something out herself.

"Yes," Ethan says. "Why?"

"I just wondered," Lori says, trying to keep her voice casual. "Have they always lived at Evergreen?"

Ethan goes still. "No." He meets her eyes with that piercing gaze gone flat. "But they're family, Lori. Evergreen is their home."

"I didn't mean—"

"Didn't you?" Ethan says. Lori swallows, her heart thumping in her chest. "Eleanor and Paul are important to me. They were Claire's—"

Ethan breaks off. It's the first time she's seen him so agitated, and suddenly she understands why. His wife. Ethan told her he lost someone. She rolls the name around in her head. *Claire.*

The Ethan stands. Lori stands with him, pressing a palm to his chest.

"Tell me about her," she says. She's afraid he won't answer, and she wraps an arm around him, drawing him close. As if she can keep him with her.

After a long, silent moment, his arms go around her. She feels him take a deep breath, feels it sigh out.

"We grew up together," Ethan says. "Childhood sweethearts. Eleanor and Paul are her parents. They had nowhere to go once they got older. No retirement. I promised them they'd have a place."

He kisses her hair. Lori pulls back, her face flushed. She didn't know. No wonder Eleanor hates her. She almost opens her mouth to say that, but Ethan has opened up to her, has shared his pain. She doesn't want to press. Not in this moment. She resolves to work harder to like Eleanor and Paul, to accept them as family. She knows better than anyone that parents aren't perfect.

They go back to their papers and plans, and Lori doesn't protest the flowers again.

Winter trails its icy way down the spine of the world until, slowly, spring melts Vermont into mud. Lake edges thaw, birds reappear. Traffic at the cafe picks up, even as Lori gives her two weeks. She's not sure what she is going to do for a job, but an hour and a half is too long of a commute even to see Christine. She makes plans to move to Evergreen with Ethan.

And then the flowers bloom, and it is time for the wedding at last.

14

Lori spends the afternoon before her wedding packing up her little life. The apartment that she has slept in on and off for almost a year, convalescing from her sister's death, seems small and spare and beautiful in the afternoon light of spring. Through the open window, she can hear the sound of people talking in the parking lot, the growling of cars as they go by, the call of a bird. Inside, all is quiet and dim.

Grief is like a rodent in the walls. It has filled this apartment with remnants, stored in odd places. There is the blanket from Sedona, folded on the couch corner. There is the urn. There are the locks of hair cut from Annie's head when the chemo started, hidden away in a drawer. There are the shoes that are too small for Lori's feet, resting in the bottom of her closet.

Other, smaller things: A tea Annie liked that Lori brews sometimes just to smell the hint of jasmine and then pours down the sink. A picture turned facedown where Annie is smiling, her hair long before the chemo, pulled half up in a barrette, longer than it had been for her memorial service. Lori left everything in Texas. She left their furniture, their house, their cookbooks. She left her golf clubs and most of her clothes, all of her plans. She had hollowed out the space of her and filled it full of Annie. Now, at last, she will fold her sister up. She will put her away like a favorite toy outgrown. She will start life anew.

Yet she cannot get rid of the things that make her sister. The only things left of her in this world. She cannot do that.

She packs each fragment of Annie in a box, wrapped tight. The furniture was secondhand to begin with, and it will go back where it came from easily enough. This apartment was only ever a waystation. She spent more time out of it than in it. Lori tells herself she is finally ready to take a step beyond Annie's death, but she leaves nothing behind. She carries the box carefully to her little Toyota, and places it on the back seat. Movers will come tomorrow to take away everything else, a wedding gift from Ethan. She has dinner with Hannah, her biological mother, in an hour. There will be no rehearsal. The ceremony is small, and will be held at Evergreen in the afternoon.

Lori walks down to the edge of the lake, where there is a park and a concrete path through it. It's early enough in the year that the sun is still setting by seven, that she still needs her jacket. She has brought a small lock of Annie's hair with her.

"I think you would have liked it here," she says to her sister. There is a man busking on the sidewalk. There is a photographer setting up his camera to get a picture of the ferry coming in on the golden water. Yet it is as if there is no one here but Lori and the lock of hair that is all that remains of her sister. Lori pulls herself up on the brick wall by the path, just as Annie would have done. She dangles her feet over the brush and water below.

"I think you'd have liked Ethan, too," she says. "I hope you would anyway. I'm sorry I've held on so long."

She takes the hair from her pocket and leaves it on the brick wall.

"Rest well, Annie," Lori says.

I t is strange to see Hannah in Burlington, strange to have invited her and her new family to be a part of Lori's life after so many years. Hannah abandoned her, but now, older and wiser, Lori knows just how hard it is to take care of someone who completely depends on you. She and Annie had their own times when money was tight and Lori wasn't sure where the next rent payment might come from. She'd managed to land on her feet, but Annie had been old enough to feed and clothe herself, even if it had taken some time for her to come out of her shell. Once she had, Annie had even been able to help provide for the household, though she mostly worked coffee shop jobs and retail. Annie hadn't been sure what she wanted to do with life, and then, well. Then there was no life to live.

Still, Lori is not here to mourn Annie, not matter how easy it is, still, to do. She's here to marry Ethan. She's here to get to know her biological mother, after years. Ruth will come to the wedding, but Lori didn't invite her adoptive mother to this dinner. Ruth always hated Hannah. She hadn't liked Annie either. Ruth had wanted her to go to college, not run off after her damaged little sister. She'd wanted Lori to be a doctor or a lawyer or at least something besides a real estate agent who had left her agency behind and now served coffee to strangers.

This is the time, Lori knows, to mend bridges. But it is also the time to say goodbye, if those bridges are past mending. The next twenty-four hours will see which, for each of these women who have been so important to her.

She thinks Hannah will be one she mends with.

Her biological mother has come alone to a small, cozy and casual restaurant called Flatbread. It's a low-ceilinged place, the tables rough wood, the lighting dim. Lori was expecting Charles, was expecting perhaps even their new children, but it is just her and Hannah here. There is a fireplace, with a fire going despite the spring weather. The nights still get chilly, and Lori is grateful for the warmth. They order oblong, hand-tossed pizzas and Lori gets a house brewed beer. Hannah demurs. She doesn't drink anymore, she says. Lori has forgotten that Hannah drank at all, but Hannah says it like it is a chapter in her life that she regrets, like she's guilty when she looks in Lori's eyes.

They make small talk. Their food comes. As the waiter steps away from the table, items delivered, Hannah says, "I wish I could have gotten to know Annie."

Lori feels her stomach clench. She leaves her food untouched and meets Hannah's eyes.

"I know she hated me," Hannah says. Lori feels her mouth twist. She knew this would come up, but she had hoped not to speak about her sister. Annie had insisted on knowing about their mother, about the circumstances of their adoption. She'd even reached out to Hannah, once. It hadn't gone well. Hannah hadn't taken them back, hadn't dropped everything to be with them. She had a new life.

Annie could never forgive that. Lori's sister forgave so much, from so many people. But not that.

"I don't blame her," Hannah continues. She stares down at her plate. Lori forces herself to take a bite of the pizza. Flavor explodes on her tongue, but Hannah doesn't move.

"Hell is easy to find, Lori," Hannah says, looking tired. "You don't even realize you're on the path to it until you've already crossed its borders. It's just one easy step after another, one inevitable step—" she breaks off. Swallows, then takes a drink of water.

"I didn't want to lose you girls. But I couldn't be your mother anymore. I wanted Annie to understand . . . " She stops. "I'm sorry."

Lori lets the silence stretch. She wants to eat. She wants to ask Hannah questions about her new life, to get to know her at last, if not as a mother then as another woman.

"I had an alcohol problem," Hannah says, as if the silence is an invitation, not a wall. "Your dad left and I had no help and it was the only way I didn't feel like the walls were closing in. The drinking . . . " She eyes Lori's beer as if it might bite her. Lori shifts, uncomfortable. "Annie was so little, and she was fussy. Needing everything all the time. And you couldn't understand why your dad left, why he didn't take you with him, and I couldn't—" Hannah isn't even looking at her, staring at the table like she's in a confessional. Looking at some version of Lori from the past that she wants so badly to leave behind. Lori sighs out, suddenly frustrated.

"Look, Hannah," she says, "I don't care." Hannah's eyes dart back up to Lori's face finally, shock making them wide.

"What—"

"I don't care why you gave us up. I never did." It's not entirely the truth—there were moments when Lori wondered, after a fight with Ruth or, later, a particularly hard week with Annie. She resented. But she doesn't have any room for that feeling now. She softens her voice, tries to take away some of the sting. "Annie was the one who cared, Hannah, and Annie is dead. Let her rest."

Hannah looks at her. She looks old in that moment, every line on her face deepened in the firelight.

"I can't apologize to her," Hannah says at last. Her voice is broken.

"I know," Lori says. She puts her hand on Hannah's own. Pretends she can't see the tears on the other woman's cheeks.

After a while, they go back to eating dinner. Then they leave, going their separate ways with an awkward hug. Lori tries not to feel the disappointment behind her breastbone, the spikes of it pressing deep into her heart. But what she said to Hannah was true. It's time to let the past rest.

15

On the morning of her wedding, Lori has breakfast with Christine, the only person in her life who isn't weighed down with grief and bitterness besides Ethan. She and Ethan have decided traditional is best, for this day. He stayed in Evergreen, and she will drive out to meet him with all her possessions and a wedding dress.

Christine has made tacos of course, extra spicy pulled pork topped with fried eggs and salsa verde. It's messy, but they are both in old tee shirts and jeans. The window of Christine's kitchen is open wide. It's a bright place, brighter now that it is spring. Bill has taken the kids off on a pre-planned diversion for the weekend, so they are alone, which is a relief. Lori doesn't think that she could handle any unexpected personal questions after the emotional rollercoaster of the night before, no matter how benign. Christine has been working with her long enough she knows which topics are safe and which aren't.

"It go that bad?" Christine asks, laughing.

"It was rough," Lori says. "And I have my other mother to deal with today." She has told Christine about her mothers. She's even told her, vaguely, about Annie. Not everything—not even Hannah knows everything.

"What's Ruth like?" Christine asks. "You never talk about her."

"She hates Hannah," Lori says. "She hated that I went looking for Annie and didn't go to college. We don't talk much."

Lori sits back. They have mimosas, grapefruit and sparkling sweet moscato instead of the usual orange juice and champagne. Lori's never been a huge mimosa drinker, but she has to admit this variation is refreshing. She feels relaxed despite this talk of her family. The wedding planning is all done. She and Ethan applied for their marriage license last week. They're getting married.

The rest of her screwed up family doesn't matter much.

"I hope I'm not that kind of mother," Christine says, glowering. Lori laughs.

"You won't be. Ruth is one of a kind. But she'll be happy about Ethan." She would, too. Ruth had always wanted her to marry well. In this one thing at least Lori won't be a disappointment.

Talk turns to more uplifting things. Christine has helped her pick out the tablecloths and the caterer and everything else. She's gone out to Evergreen even, after Lori demanded that Ethan let her come. The gardens behind the house are gorgeous, though Eleanor and Paul are still aloof. Christine made faces at Lori behind Eleanor's back. Lori just can't call her Nora. It's the name for a nice grandmother, not that iron woman.

Ethan wanted just them at the wedding, but Lori insisted on this day being a little bit more populated than that. Eventually he acquiesced. That had been a tense time. Ethan never yells, but he becomes sharp and silent, cold as ice. Lori is certain he learned that trick from Eleanor. She's glad she didn't yield on this when she and Christine get in her Toyota and start down the road. Her hands are sweating, though she's driven this path before. Christine distracts her with music and stories about Bill and the kids. Her wedding dress hangs in its black bag behind her—black so Ethan won't see it when she arrives. It's a long drive down to Evergreen, but it seems to go by in a blink.

Ruth and Roger and Hannah won't arrive until three o'clock, when the ceremony is set to start. Lori's half siblings, Hannah's other children, won't be coming. They're home in Boston with their father. Christine helps her carry her things to the designated bedroom on the second floor. As always, the foyer is unseasonably cold. Even Christine shivers as they walk up the stairs. Then Lori leads them down the back staircase, out into the central family room and through the back doors, which open onto the large garden, bright with sunlight and blooming with roses so dusky as to appear black. There are lights strung from the trees and up the columns of the porch, and a long table set up under the overhang with a white sheet laid over it. She still has the wedding dress over her arm, and Christine has grabbed her makeup and bobby pins. There is a large white tent hidden halfway in the trees, and Lori makes her way to it with trembling knees. She never thought she would get married, and certainly not at the secluded house of her secretive millionaire boyfriend. When she thinks of Ethan like that, it nearly makes her laugh out loud, though she knows the laughter is pure nervousness.

"It's going to be perfect," Christine whispers to her as they walk through the garden and Lori smiles.

She's right. It will be perfect.

C hristine has worked a wonder.

Lori touches her hair, her face. She hasn't looked in the mirror before now, afraid of what she might see, but then the dress came out of the bag, all lace and finery, and the veil. Christine helped her climb into both and she couldn't hold herself back anymore. She looked.

She is arrested by the sight of herself. There, shimmering in the mirror, is a vision of a woman. She looks alive, healthy, glowing with joy. Her curling hair is half up, cascading onto the laced shoulders of her dress. The long sleeves make her arms slim and the veil renders her ethereal. Lori is glad she hired a photographer.

And suddenly, she is crying. One tear follows another, down the arc of her cheek, to her chin, to the fabric of her dress. It will be an absolutely beautiful ceremony. She, in the mirror, is beautiful.

Annie will never see it.

Lori presses a tissue to her eye, catching the tears, binding them away. Christine, looking on, says nothing, for which she is grateful. Outside the confines of the tent there is music and soft conversation. They will be wondering where she has gotten to, all of her small, estranged family.

"Are you ready?" Christine asks, her face concerned.

Lori smiles.

"Yes," she says.

She walks out of the tent alone.

Christine has gone ahead, joining the small audience, and Lori knows it is time when the music changes. She steps out of the tent, hearing the strains of Mozart in the air. Ethan insisted on hiring a string quartet, arguing that if he was going to have people out to Evergreen he was going to make the most of it. Lori is grateful for the lack of awkwardness that living, breathing musicians bring. There's no need to worry about a song being too long or too short. She walks between the evergreens with their soft needles cushioning her steps. She takes exactly as much time as she needs.

She sees Ruth and Roger, older than she expected. Her adopted mother is thin, her mouth pinched. She is standing beside Eleanor, and beside that woman she is frail, no matter that she has dyed her hair blonde and done her makeup well. Eleanor looks as dour as ever. Paul will be behind the arch, ready to officiate the wedding, but even without her stoic, balding husband beside her Eleanor is a presence.

Lori assures herself that it's a big house, and she's marrying Ethan, not his servants.

Hannah stands clean and pressed beside Christine. They both smile at her unabashedly. Lori smiles back. She's reached the edge of the garden now, and her gaze skates past them, searching for an arch of evergreen boughs, searching for Ethan.

And she sees him.

His tuxedo is black, his hair is slicked back, and his sharp blue gaze catches hers. Lori walks to him with the same firm steps with which she approached him all those months ago on their first date. She leaves her worries and her fears behind. She comes to the altar of her marriage with hope.

After Paul has led them in their vows and they have all retired to the long table for dinner; after the stilted conversation and the thank-yous and the tears Hannah sheds on her shoulder; after the quiet, cold leave-taking of Ruth and the clap on the back from Roger; after all of this, Ethan and Lori ascend alone to Ethan's room. The branches of the evergreens surround them on nearly all sides. The bed sits in the center, but Ethan does not go to it, not immediately. He follows Lori to the window. He pulls the veil from her hair, and the pins one by one. Lori stands and lets him undress her, lets him peel her from lace and crinoline and silk, until she stands naked before trees and sky. Then she turns to face him.

He runs a single finger down her throat, along the flat plane of her sternum, down to her navel. There is something in his eyes that she has not seen before. She cannot name what it is.

He kisses her before she can ask. The fabric of his tuxedo presses against her as he crushes her to him.

16

Spring turns into summer. Summer swells, gravid, and then shrinks. The days wane and shorten, the flame of the sun goes out and fall returns in a rush of chill air. Five months. Five months of happiness, one for each of the fragile white fingers on Lori's hand. Five months where she does not dream of her sister. Where the urn containing Annie's ashes sits in its box, beneath the detritus of her life, in the corner of Lori's room on the guest floor. She has boxed her grief away, both mentally and physically. She has packaged it tight with thick tape. She sleeps in her husband's bed, after all. This room is just storage space. Just clothes, a few books, sheets and pictures that came with the room and that she has not gotten around to changing. It is a closet for her things.

In late September, as the leaves begin to change, Lori wakes up in Ethan's bed to find it empty. She thinks little of it. He often gets up in the night, or leaves early in the morning to make his long commute to whatever city he must be in. He has not mentioned a journey, so no doubt he will be back for dinner. She gets out of bed, throws on jeans and a sweater, socks for the cold floors, pads down to the kitchen for coffee and a scone. She doesn't try to talk with Eleanor. She's gotten used to her reticence. No point in trying to break through that wall, and besides, she has Ethan to talk to, and her books. A whole lake awaits her outside, though the water is too cold now to swim. She can take out the boat like she and Ethan did in the warm summer months, the both of them tanned and relaxed in the sun. She can get in her car and drive to Burlington, stop in at the coffee shop and eat tacos with Christine. Lori is unconcerned. The library beckons, and Lori curls in her favorite chair, cracking open the book she has left on the small table. She passes hours lost in words. When she gets tired of reading, she spends some time in the small gym, then takes her lunch out by the lake. She is contemplating picking up a hobby, but isn't sure what it should be. Knitting feels too cliché. Woodworking requires tools. Gardening is taken care of by Paul, the groundskeeper. Perhaps volunteering would be a better option—there must be some nonprofit in Burlington or elsewhere that needs help. There is no need to hurry in the decision. She has all of the time in the world.

Lori walks back into the house. She uses her computer to look for volunteering opportunities, bookmarks a few. The day dwindles as she does her research, until at last Lori looks up and realizes that dark is settling in. The ferry must be nearly to the shore, she thinks, and smiles. Soon Ethan will be home to have dinner.

But Ethan doesn't come. Lori waits and waits, but the dark sinks down and, long past the time Ethan would normally return, his headlights have not pierced it. There has been no call to the house. Her cell phone, which gets spotty reception out here in any case, shows no texts or missed calls.

Her heart climbs into her throat.

She walks down to the kitchens again. The odor of chicken and red sauce reaches her. Eleanor is chopping vegetables. She looks up when Lori enters, her expression cool.

"Can I help you?"

Lori lifts a brow. Eleanor is more than cold today. It niggles, where earlier it did not.

"Did Ethan say anything about being late?" Lori asks.

"Ethan will not be home until Saturday," Eleanor says.

Lori feels confusion first, certain she has misunderstood. It is Sunday. Ethan would have said something, surely, if he was going to be gone for a week.

"Next Saturday?" she says, unable to keep the incredulity from her voice. Eleanor stills her hands, placing the knife flat on the counter.

"Yes. He told you at dinner last night." Her eyes hold a warning. Lori swallows, feeling her anger fizzle. Certainly she would remember? But Eleanor seems so sure.

"Dinner will be ready soon," says Eleanor, and picks up the knife again, in clear dismissal. Lori retreats. Her stomach is tight, her head muddled.

There is good reception in the upstairs living room. Lori goes there, stares into the empty fireplace. There is wood and kindling. She hasn't built a fire since she was a child.

She pulls out her phone, and dials Ethan's number.

The call rings to voicemail.

He does not call her back that night.

THE THIRD WIFE

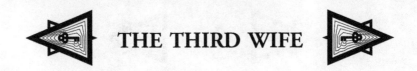

Ethan has loved all of his wives a little, though he knows that the love will only hurt. They are truly his wives. They must be. Otherwise the magic will not work. He must say the vows with love behind them.

The third wife was named Rebecca.

People get married for all sorts of reasons. Rebecca, small and blonde and spoiled, married Ethan for his money. It took a long time for her to feel something like love for him. A long time for him to tie luxury and comfort to himself so thoroughly that she could not distinguish the two. Seducing Rebecca was like weaving a web. He learned a great deal about seduction from his efforts.

Rebecca died affronted. She thought she had Ethan under control, obedient to her whims—until he drove the knife into her lung and the scream from her chest. Even as she began to bleed out, as her ribs cracked, she could not believe it.

In death she covets life. She covets Ethan.

17

The next day, Lori wakes up to the buzzing of her phone. It is 9:00 am. The sun has been up for two hours at least, but Lori did not sleep last night. She kept waiting for Ethan to call her back.

Now his name is on her phone screen. Lori answers, half asleep, before she has time to feel angry.

"Hey," she says, and Ethan chuckles. His voice is so warm, even from far away.

"Hey yourself. Sleep well?"

"Yes." She's awake now, remembering the night before. Whatever Eleanor says, Lori knows she would have remembered a conversation about him being gone for a week.

"You didn't tell me you were leaving," Lori says, unable to keep the hurt out of her voice, unable to hold herself back. Ethan is silent.

"I did," he says slowly. "I told you a few days ago."

Lori catches her breath. She feels shame wake her up, a burn in her veins. "I don't remember," she says, voice small.

There's a pause, heavy. Lori opened her mouth to apologize. She's come at this conversation all wrong. Ethan beats her to it.

"Hey look, I have a meeting to get to. Just wanted to wish you good morning." His tone is diffident, and Lori's heart constricts.

"Ethan—"

"Have a good day, Lori," he says, "I'll see you this weekend."

The call clicks off.

Lori puts the phone on the bed. The swirl of shame and anger and regret feels almost like nausea in her stomach. But it's too petty a thing for him to lie about. The kind of thing Eleanor might do, but Ethan has always been honest with her. He must have told her he was going to be gone this week. She was mistaken, and now she's made him upset.

Lori gets out of her bed—her bed, the first time she's slept in it, and it feels like a stranger's. She couldn't stand to sleep in Ethan's room without him there. It felt too much like trespassing, but this room is hers as much as anything in this house is. She walks down the hall to the room with the fireplace. The couch is leather, and there is only one blanket. She will be buying more, she decides. She'll need a place to avoid Eleanor.

The fireplace beckons. Lori kneels down next to the stone, lets the edge cut into her knees. She gets out the kindling, and the matches. She lights a spark.

It takes a while to build up the fire. She doesn't really know what she's doing. Almost, she gives up. But when the flames finally catch in the dry wood, she sits back on the couch, curled under the meager blanket, and watches them dance. Annie was cremated, just like these logs. It's the first time she's thought of her sister in weeks.

Lori gets up and walks into the bedroom. She leaves her phone on the bed. Instead, she goes to the box.

The tape is so thick. Her fingers cannot catch purchase. She needs a knife.

Lori gets back up, walks by the living room with the crackling fire, down the hall, down the stairs, and across the vast expanse of the house to the kitchen. Eleanor is there, doing whatever Eleanor does in the kitchen all day.

"I need a knife," Lori says. She is still in her pajamas, and no doubt there is soot on her hands. Normally she would get dressed before coming down. But this is supposed to be her house. She's lived here for nearly half a year. If she wants to leave her pajamas on, she very well will.

"Don't you want some breakfast, Lorelei?" Eleanor asks. Lori feels her eye twitch.

"You can make me an omelet with a side of potatoes," she says. Eleanor has never been kind to her, so Lori will no longer waste energy on kindness.

"We have scones and—"

"The knife please." Lori holds out her hand. Eleanor puts a small, sharp knife in her palm. Her face is impassive, icy and calm.

"Thank you," Lori says. She walks back up the stairs.

In her room, the box waits.

Lori slides the knife through the clear tape. It parts easily. She pulls up the flaps of the cardboard with a pop. It's a large box, too large to have failed to unpack. Avoidance only did this. Lori wastes a moment in fear, in anger with herself. Then she reaches inside.

The blanket is on top. She sets it on the carpet. It still smells like their house in San Antonio, somehow.

Below the blanket rest all of the scraps of Annie's life. Some of them, Lori decides, she will leave packed away. But the blanket, the urn, the photo—these she removes. She places the photo facedown on her bedside table, where she can look at it if she wants to, and she places the urn on the dresser, in front of the vanity mirror, where she can see it always. She takes the blanket back to the room with its fire.

She spends the day in this room, watching soap operas on the television above the mantel. When she goes down to get her breakfast, Eleanor has vanished, leaving it cold on the counter. She skips lunch, but when she goes down for dinner, there is no one. The kitchen is dark.

Lori cooks for herself, a grilled cheese sandwich with tomato soup from a carton in the refrigerator. She sits in the darkened kitchen, her chest hollow in her victory. The house feels empty without Ethan.

When she is done, Lori leaves her dishes in the sink.

* * *

B y the end of the week, Lori is a mess.

It's not the loneliness, though that is hard. She has been lonely before. It's the loneliness where no loneliness should be. It's the absence where there should be presence. It's like grieving for someone who is still alive, and it hurts more to know that he chose to leave for money. Money he already has—she's seen the kind of money Ethan can bring to bear on his problems in the year since they met and he has admitted to her that he doesn't need the job. He didn't need to leave all the months of the summer, his day trips to Montreal aside. He has an office here, attached to the bedroom. She doesn't go into the bedroom without him and the office is locked up while he's away. She tried the handle on her third day, when she began to wonder what, exactly, caused him to start treating work more seriously.

The day comes for him to return and Lori gets up. She washes her hair, puts on makeup, nice jeans, a sweater that shows off her cleavage with a little encouragement from the right bra. She wants him to want her. She wants him to have missed her as much as she missed him.

Then she goes for a walk on the lake, because she doesn't want to spend the whole day curled up on the couch waiting for him.

The air is brisk. It's well and truly fall, earlier than it would ever come further south. Last winter was bearable with Ethan courting her, but she wonders how this winter will go. It will get dark up here, so dark and cold, with only the snow and ice everywhere to keep her company.

Lori promises herself that it won't be that way. Ethan's only been gone for a week. It's not the first time he's been gone that long—he traveled often last winter, when she was still living in Burlington. She will see him more than she doesn't. The wind gusts, and she rubs her arms, wishing she had brought a coat and scarf, if only for a buffer against the wind. She'll be away from the water soon. Even as she thinks it the trail ahead of her bends. Evergreen trees wrap around her, sheltering her from the wind, though the shade brings a different kind of cold.

Lori.

Lori lifts her head, looking around. The trail is bare, the evergreen trees surrounding it packed densely. Paul maintains the trails as well as any park, and Lori doesn't fear getting lost. But anything could be hiding in the trees, a stranger come in off the road or a wild animal. Lori is not a country girl. She's heard of bears, of wolves—were those native to Vermont? She can't remember. But there are other predators she can imagine, killers in the shadows, whispering her name.

Lorelei. Lori whirls. The trees rustle and creak. She feels her heart climb into her throat, feels her lungs constrict. The hair on the back of her neck is prickling with strangeness.

Lori turns and walks back towards the lake. She can see its glimmer through the branches. Had she really come so far? The path seems to elongate, as if in a nightmare, and Lori feels as if she's been her before, in this forest with something behind her, something rustling. She's far enough away from the house that no one would hear if something happened—

There's a step on the path behind her. Lori turns, a scream rising in her throat.

It's Paul.

For a moment, Lori stands frozen, her body flushing with fear and embarrassment and confusion.

"What are you doing out here?" Paul asks gruffly. As if she's trespassing.

"I—was that you, just now?" She wants to snatch the question back as soon as it passes her lips. Paul sneers.

"Doing what? Walking?"

Lori opened her mouth, then closes it. She doesn't know how to answer. If she says she heard a voice whispering to her, Paul will think she's crazy.

"I'll head back to the house," she says after a long moment.

"You do that," Paul says.

He stands in the path, watching her, and Lori turns back towards the lake without a word. She wants to be out from under these trees, and being away from Paul is an added bonus.

It takes about a quarter hour to get back to the boathouse. She can see Ethan's car in the driveway. He's home early. Her heart leaps, and for a moment she forgets all about how angry she is.

She'll talk with him, apologize for the miscommunication. It will be alright.

When she walks in the front door, Ethan is standing in the foyer talking to Eleanor. He turns immediately when she enters, crossing the steps between them quickly and wrapping her up in his arms to crush her to him. Her lips find his without protest. It feels good to taste him again, to be wrapped in the scent of him.

"I missed you," she says. "You were gone too long."

"Show me how much you missed me," Ethan says, his grip biting. Lori pulls back, meets his eyes.

"I thought we could talk," she says. Ethan gives her a half smile, then presses his mouth to hers again, kisses her deep. When he pulls away she is breathless.

"Ethan-"

"Come to bed with me, Lori," Ethan says, his blue eyes spearing her, and Lori finds herself nodding. He takes her hand and pulls her up the stairs.

18

The day dawns cold, with a breeze that rustles the flames of leaves. It is beautiful, but Ethan is gone again. He's been gone for three days this time, another trip that was more or less unannounced. At least this time she knows when to expect him without asking. He left her a message on her phone the night he didn't come home.

Lori is counting down the days to his return. Each day she rises from bed later, her discipline flagging. There is nothing to do. The lake is too chilly for swimming. She has no cleaning to do—Paul and Eleanor take care of that. The kitchen is their demesne, great monstrosity that it is, and Lori has never really enjoyed cooking for cooking's sake. The library holds a thousand books on dry subjects like anatomy and biology and calculus, but Lori has read every text of interest. She has watched documentaries and soap operas until she thought her eyes would bleed. She has visited the gym every day for two hours. She has listened to music until her skin crawled with want of silence.

Lori wants more.

She rises late, takes a shower, gets dressed in warm sweatpants and a sweater, and wanders through the halls to count doors. It is an idle habit. Her bedroom is on the eastern side of the house, where she gets some sun from the gaps in the trees, but this late in the year the sun does not reach her until eight or nine. Soon the leaves will fall, and the time will change, so that's something. She passes her bedroom and the sitting room with a fireplace and the large, comfortable leather couch now chilly with the cold weather. There are more blankets on the couch, plain, thick, gray things she had Eleanor order. They match the room, but they're dull. Annie's blanket is back on her bed, in her room, where it will be mostly safe from the ministrations of a cleaning lady with ideas about suitable colors and patterns for blankets.

Lori walks down the hallway to the back stairwell. She pads down the wooden steps on sock feet, the sunlight catching her dark hair and throwing up hazel highlights. Eleanor is in the kitchen. Lori tries to smile. The expression feels slimy on her face.

"Is there breakfast?" she asks. She was rude to Eleanor, before, when she became demanding and left the dishes in the sink. The next day she felt guilty enough that she had almost apologized for her pettiness. Now she and Eleanor have resumed their polite, icy detente.

"Of course," says Eleanor, her face impassive. "What would you like?"

"Toast and eggs with cheese," Lori says, trying not to feel the familiar stinging anger, or the licking, fearful guilt. Eleanor's face is blank, but at least she responds when Lori speaks. At least she's another human being in this vast, increasingly cold house. Not everyone can afford to be warm.

After breakfast, and time at the gym, and another afternoon spent staring at a television, Lori decides at last to go for a walk. She hasn't walked on the paths under the trees since that day when Paul found her on the trail, but the bright curve of the lake beckons. She puts on her blue coat, and a scarf that Ethan gave her last Christmas. It makes him feel close. The foyer is as cold as it ever is, nearly an icebox, and she hurries through it, telling herself that the pebbling on her skin is just chill. Her feet hit the cobbled surface of the drive moments later, and she heads to the lakeshore, feeling the wind blow away her unease. The path by the lake dips perilously close to the water, and she takes it, her booted feet sure on the cold, damp earth. There are no voices in the woods, nothing to fear here except her own mind. Lori does not believe in ghosts. She does not believe in hauntings, except the kind you make for yourself. She was haunted by her sister, but she thought that her happiness would burn that grief away like a mist beneath the sun. Now her sun is gone. Now this house feels like a cage, a maze with her at its center, lost.

Perhaps that is why when she stares down into the water disturbed by the falling leaves, she sees a face.

Lori starts back, her heel sliding in the mud of the bank. She almost falls, but rights herself. A wind moves through the bright orange tree above her.

There is nothing in the water. Just the leaves, brown and dead, coating the lakebed. She had thought she saw something white, something diaphanous. Lori kneels down, eyes searching, her heart a deep, rapid drum in her veins. There, something brighter than the leaves. Lori does not think. She reaches into the frigid water, clutching her coat and scarf tight around her with her other hand. Her fingers grasp something hard. She draws it out.

It is a small bone.

Lori studies it, trying to determine what creature has left a bone like this. It is surprisingly smooth. Perhaps the water has protected it, or perhaps it is simply fresh. It isn't spongey and rough the way she has seen old antlers become when exposed to the elements. No matter how she looks at it she cannot guess its origin. Perhaps a squirrel, or a rabbit? Lori has little experience with bones, but she has time to spare and access to hundreds of books. She can research it. Death is something she has obsessed over for a long time, imagined and rejected over and over. Perhaps reading those books about anatomy will help her to understand it better.

She puts the bone in the pocket of her coat, glances out once more over the cold waters. With Ethan gone, the summer spent with his company seems almost a dream. Once more Lori longs to see him, to feel his warmth. But he hasn't been warm since the weather changed, she admits to herself.

Perhaps she should leave.

The thought comes from nowhere, drops into her head as if it belongs to someone else. Lori surprises herself by not rejecting it outright. It worked before, didn't it? She could drive somewhere new, become someone new. Not sit here and wait for things to fall apart. Wait to be left again.

But Lori wants to stop running. Besides all of her things are here, and Ethan, whom she thought she loved. She married him. She said a vow. Lori knows he doesn't depend on her for anything—he has all of this, after all—but she knows he still cares for her. Maybe all she needs is to pursue her own hobbies and career, her own life separate from his. That will help make these absences bearable. He can't be called on to entertain her all the time. He has his job, accounts to manage. She should have something for herself.

Lori runs her hand through her brown curls, pushing them from her face. The wind is picking up. She shivers in the cold.

The bone is a forgotten wisp of weight in her pocket as she heads back to the house.

19

I t is a relief to be back in Burlington, but Lori can't tell Christine that.
They are sitting in a little tea shop on Market Street eating salads and sand-
wiches, which is light fare considering the weather. It's been snowing out in
Greensboro, but here it's just cold and icy. Lori should have come back to Burlington over the summer, but she neglected her budding friendship with Christine despite herself. Sure, they had texted and talked on the phone, but that isn't
the same as a visit in person.

Lori had to borrow one of the SUVs to make it out. She had walked to
the garage, looking for the keys where Ethan usually hung them up. She'd just
plucked them from the wall when Paul snarled, "What are you doing?"

Lori jumped, guilty as a teenage girl with a curfew.

"I'm going out for lunch," she said after a moment. She had to press past
him to get to the car, his wrinkled, unpleasant mouth pursed as if he'd swallowed a lemon.

"How is Bill?" Lori asks, shaking off the memory. "And the kids?"

Christine smiles. "They're great. How is Ethan?"

Lori shrugs, swallows despite herself. "He travels a lot."

Christine looks at her with concern. Lori smiles, but she is aware that it is
shaky.

"So you're out there alone all the time?" Christine asks.

"I'm not alone," Lori protests, but she is. She is alone. Eleanor is cold, and
Paul makes her skin crawl. She had thought they would warm up to her, eventually. They show no signs. Christine looks at her shrewdly.

"Maybe you need a job," Christine says, leaning back.

"I've thought that," Lori says, glad to hear it from someone else's lips, "but
it's so far."

Christine nods. "It's a long commute. But you've got time, right? You can
decide what you want to do that's worth it. And if you need to come back to the
cafe for a while . . . "

"Thanks," Lori says, though her instinct is to protest. She can't justify working for Christine when it feels like charity. Besides, there are other people who
might actually need the work. She just needs to feel useful.

"I was thinking . . . " she takes a deep breath. "I might go back to school. I
never went to college." But she'd wanted to. It had been easy to write that dream
off as Ruth's when Annie was alive and she had a steady career. But a degree could
help her find a job worth the commute. She could work at the hospital, take care
of people again. Despite herself, she's finding the anatomy books pretty intriguing.

"I could register here at the University," she says, waiting for Christine to
shoot the idea down.

"You should do it," Christine says firmly and Lori feels something in her chest ease. "Whatever you do, you're going to be great at it."

They leave lunch with the usual platitudes and promises not to let it be too long before they see one another again. Lori gets in her borrowed car and drives up to the University of Vermont to see the campus. In the admissions office, she speaks with a woman about program offerings. The list is dizzying. Lori heads back to Evergreen with flyers and handouts to pore over. There's a whole college of Nursing and Health Sciences, and an advanced medical program. She has options she can contemplate. She feels more hopeful than she has in days.

That evening, Ethan comes home. He's friendly, asking her about her day, telling her about his commute, but he doesn't whisk her away to the bedroom like he has in the past. Lori feels relieved. This time she can actually talk to him, connect. They sit in the great room before the roaring fire and eat lasagna, and Lori feels at home for the first time in days. She wants to hold onto it, so it's a while before she tells Ethan about her idea to enroll in classes. He goes quiet.

"Are you unhappy here, Lori?" he asks, softly.

Lori puts down her fork. Her stomach twists. There's a tension in his voice, a warning she's heard before. Whatever response she was expecting, she knows that this is not it.

"I'm bored," she says, keeping her tone light. "I've got a ridiculous amount of free time, and I'd like to be doing something."

He studies her. There's something flat in his eyes.

"Of course," he says, and in that moment he looks so much like Eleanor it feels like a knife in her chest.

"Ethan," she begins, not sure what she will say to him. She hasn't done anything wrong, has she? She knows she hasn't.

"I don't think it's a bad idea," he says. There's a smile on his face, that little smirk he's been wearing more and more lately. "But how are you going to pay for it, Lori?"

Lori opens her mouth. Closes it. She thought—well, she thought he would pay for it. He obviously has the money. They're married, and she thought that meant that they were partners, that he would see any investment in her future as an investment in his own.

Lori is suddenly sixteen again, sitting in Ruth's living room hearing her adoptive mother call her biological family trash. Just as then, it takes a moment for it to sink in, for the full weight of the words to settle on her and squeeze the air from her lungs. She stares at Ethan blankly, feeling a numbness in her that she's only felt a few times before. A sense of being disembodied.

Lori stands, leaving her half-eaten dinner. She can't eat it, not right now. There's no way she can get financial aid with his money counting against her. Without Ethan's help—she hasn't looked at her bank account, but it's not like there will magically be more money there than there was. She needs him to support her in this.

"I can't pay for it," she says at last, her face flushed. She's proud that her voice doesn't shake. "You know that."

Ethan says nothing. His brows are furrowing. She recognizes the expression, the condescending anger.

"Ethan, what am I supposed to do here?" she demands.

"I've provided for all your needs," Ethan says stiffly. That cold anger—it's so like Eleanor's that Lori could scream. "I've given you everything, Lori. Anything you could want. I'm sorry that it's not enough for you."

Lori feels her shoulders draw in, as if she has taken a blow. She forces herself to straighten, forces her hands to unclench. She tries one last time, hating herself when her voice wobbles at last.

"Please, Ethan. Do you know what it's like being stuck here all day? You're gone all the time. Let me have this. I've got to have something to do."

"And that's exactly why I won't pay for you to go to some expensive university," Ethan says, raising his voice at last. "You don't need it. It's frivolous. Just because you didn't work for my money doesn't mean you can spend it like it's nothing."

"Is there a problem?" Eleanor's voice cuts across any reply Lori might make. Lori whirls. The old woman is staring coldly at her from the corner of the room, her nose wrinkled slightly as if in disgust. Lori feels shame boil in her, hot and nauseating.

"I'm sorry," she says, though she doesn't know why. Why is she apologizing? "Please excuse me."

She goes upstairs, to her room. Ethan does not come looking for her. She undresses and lays in her cold bed, and she keeps thinking he will knock on her door, will apologize, will invite her back into his arms. But he doesn't come, and sometime in the dark of the night Lori drifts into a restless sleep.

The next day, when she wakes up, Ethan is already gone.

20

Lori wakes from a dream and does not know where she is. The covers wrap around her like strangling vines, and the darkness is cut by broad windows on the wrong side of her bed. Moonlight shines cold and clear through the sheer curtains.

It takes a moment to remember that she is at Evergreen.

Lori sits up. The air is frigid. She pulls on a house robe, thick and warm, and fuzzy socks. She leaves the blankets turned up, to hold her warmth in she hopes. Fall is sliding into winter, and when she twitches the curtains back she sees snow falling. It's beautiful enough that Lori's heart doesn't quite fall in her chest.

Lori goes to the private bathroom in the back of her room, relieves herself, and then steps out into the hall.

The thermostat goes low at night to keep their heating costs down, which Lori approves of except when it means that getting a glass of filtered water feels like walking through the tundra. She shivers, pulling the housecoat close. Her pajamas are flannel, at least, and warm still from the heat of the bed. It doesn't seem to make much difference. She's shivering almost before she leaves her room.

She heads down the back stairs, into the great room with the fire banked and dim. It's even colder in here, with all the windows pressed against the night. Snow is still falling outside. It's hard to believe that it's been almost a year since Ethan brought her here for Thanksgiving. They haven't talked about the holidays, haven't talked about anything. After the argument about her idea to go back to school Lori didn't have the courage to bring up the future, and Ethan is gone again on one of his mysterious work trips. She's thinking about going to Massachusetts for Thanksgiving. Ethan has been invited as well, Hannah eager to continue to build on their budding relationship, but now she's not so sure that she wants him to come.

The hall to the kitchen is dark. Lori navigates it by feel. There is a nightlight in the kitchen, and she gets herself a glass of water from the dispenser on the fridge. She drains half of it, feeling the cold on her throat as a balm despite the frigid air. Then she fills it up again and starts back through the house.

It is as she is entering the great room again that she sees the light.

Lori thinks at first it is the moon, catching on a flurry of snow, but it is not that. The snow has stopped. All in the garden is still. The black trees are a firm backdrop behind the bleached landscape. Lori stops, her scalp prickling, gripped with unease. There is a light in those trees. It is not the moon. It is not a flashlight—it is too steady. Lori cannot say what it is, but she can tell that it is coming closer.

For a moment, she cannot move. She is paralyzed by the light, by an animal feeling in her belly. Her throat tightens, her hand grips the glass so hard she fears it will shatter to icy shards in her fingers. The cold climbs into her body, steals her breath.

Lori tears her eyes away and crosses to the stairs. She is shaking. The light is bright enough that she can see it casting a silvered edge on the furniture of the great room, directionless and fey. That is impossible. Lori runs up the stairs with their porthole-like windows. She does not look outside.

Her bed is still warm when she returns to it, though barely. She sets the water on the bedside table with trembling hands. Lori tells herself that it is nothing. The she turns to look for the urn, for Annie. She cannot quite make it out in the darkness. She cannot force herself back out of the blankets as if there is safety here in her bed, as if a door and her covers could save her. It takes a long time to find sleep.

Outside her window, the snow resumes.

L ori asks Paul about the light, of all people. She isn't sure why. He's only ever been gruff with her, bordering on hostile. Lori could make excuses for both him and Eleanor before—they were grieving parents, they took a while to warm up to people, she just needed to give them time—but Lori is tired of making excuses for them. Paul is a bully, but it's not like she has anyone else to ask. Perhaps she thinks he will give her an honest answer, or perhaps she's hoping that he will make fun of her enough that she gives up on the fantasy of a presence in the night.

"A light?" Paul grouses. He's shoveling the drive, and he obviously resents that she isn't. He would resent it if she tried to help, too. She learned that lesson quickly enough. "You think someone was in the woods?"

"I don't know," Lori says, already regretting approaching him. He sneers, looking her up and down.

"Seeing spirits, Lori?" he says. Eleanor likes to drag out her full name, but Paul has adopted the diminutive. Both the overdone formality and the sticky familiarity come from the same contempt. Somehow Paul's approach feels more honest. "Think there's a ghost in the trees, come to get you?"

Lori feels her lips twitch. What can she say to that? She won't tell him how her whole body drew in on itself, how everything in her felt turned upside down. He'll just torture her with it.

She's saved from answering by the sound of the gate opening, the crunching of tires in snow.

"Looks like your husband's back," Paul says, his voice gone neutral. Lori pulls in a deep breath of cold air, lets it out. She stays standing on the steps as Ethan's SUV comes down the drive and pulls up in front of her. Her heart is already raw, and now it's heavy, too. What if Ethan is cold again, and in front of Paul, who hates her?

But he steps out of the car, tosses Paul the keys, and sweeps her up into a passionate kiss.

Lori sputters, for a moment, but it feels nice. He smells of travel and himself, and she lets herself forget that there is unresolved tension between them. Lets him push her into the house, still kissing. The foyer is nearly as cold as it is outside. Ethan takes her hand and leads her up the stairs and along the catwalk, then up more stairs to his bedroom. It is unchanged, just as it has been every time she has entered it. There's nothing of her here.

That is the thought that sobers her. She pulls her hand from Ethan's. He pauses, looking at her, already loosening his tie.

"Ethan," she says, groping for something safe to say. "I missed you."

He picks up her hand again, grips it tight so she cannot slip away. He's already pulling her to him.

"I missed you," he says, and his lips are on hers and Lori decides not to fight. She decides that they can talk after. She lets him press her to the bed, lets him pull off her clothes, gives in to the weight of him.

In the bed, later, with her head on his chest, she summons her courage.

"I've been thinking about getting a job," she says. "Christine says she'll take me back at the cafe on weekends."

Ethan pulls her tighter to his chest.

"You don't need to work," he says, that warning in his voice again.

Lori pulls away. She lifts herself up on one elbow, so she can look down at his face, can impress upon him how much this means to her so that he understands.

"But I want to. I don't want to rely on you for everything." It comes out a whisper through her tightened throat, and Lori holds her breath. Ethan's blue eyes meet hers. He studies her. Then he smirks again. Lori feels anxiety rise at the familiar expression, braces herself.

"Wait until after winter," Ethan says. He tangles his hand in her hair. "You can't get out of here in that Toyota."

When he pulls her lips down to his, all she feels is relief.

21

Annie sits by the fire in the small living room which Lori has claimed as her own. She's wrapped in the blanket she bought in Sedona, and there's a mug of tea in her hands. Lori lies on the couch, facing her sister.

"Why did you have to leave?" she asks.

Annie shrugs. The scent of jasmine wafts to Lori's nose, and she wrinkles it. Annie sticks out her tongue.

"You know I was leaving anyway. It was time for me to go. I had the best life I could have, with you." She drinks her tea. Lori sighs.

"I miss you," she says.

"I know." Annie leans forward. Her eyes are clear, brown and insistent, a lighter shade than Lori's own.

"Lori, you need to get out of Evergreen. We'll help you as we can, but you need to go."

"This is the home I made when you left me," Lori says. "You left, Annie."

Her sister throws up her hands. The fire flares with her gesture, and Lori knows she is dreaming.

"Listen to me, Lori. Please listen. Let go of your grief and make a life for yourself."

"That's what I'm doing."

The daylight sears Lori's eyes. It's late. She's in Ethan's bed, alone. Behind the trees she can see Caspian Lake, glittering. She forgets sometimes, how it wraps around this property.

Lori pulls yesterday's clothes on. She and Ethan didn't leave the bed after he came home. She's not sure why he became so attentive, so manic with need. Lori feels unsettled, like the ground is shifting under her. There's something here she doesn't quite understand. She rakes a hand through hair that's grown too long and opens the door to the stairs.

Voices float up to her.

" . . . needs to be soon," says Eleanor. She sounds like steel and ice, as always. Something makes Lori pause, listening.

"I'm busy tonight," Ethan says.

"How long are you going to draw this out?" Eleanor demands. She sounds peevish now, a tone Lori has never heard her use with Ethan.

"It's not the right time."

"Because she keeps your bed warm?"

Lori draws in a sharp breath. They're talking about her.

"It's none of your business what happens in my bed, Nora." Ethan's voice is cold. Eleanor hisses something back, too low for Lori to hear, though she strains to catch the words.

"She'll be out of your hair soon enough," Ethan says.

Lori closes the door, softly. Her fingers are numb, her tongue.

Ethan is going to leave her. Lori tries to fight the certainty. She tells herself that Eleanor and Paul have poisoned his ear, but it doesn't help. The distance that she felt, the cruelty in his gaze—she pushed him too hard, she did something wrong. He doesn't want her anymore.

Lori stares at his clean, beautiful room, at the vision of the lake. She thought to make a home here. Lori makes her way back to the bed, feeling breathless. She pulls the sheets straight, and it as if she has never been there at all.

Where will she go now?

Lori doesn't cry. Instead she exits the room and starts down the steps. Ethan will be gone already and she has become adept at avoiding Eleanor. She has time to compose herself. She goes to her room, showers, dresses in good clothes. The roads are likely clear. She can probably make it back to Burlington on her own, without borrowing a vehicle with four wheel drive. That's good, because she doesn't intend to bring the vehicle back.

Lori gets her phone, intending to call Christine. There's no service. She tries to send a text. It doesn't go through. Lori puts her phone in her pocket. She can't just drop in on her friend. Perhaps she is overreacting. Lori sits on the bed and stares out over the forest, over the glimmer of the lake. The air is cold, the landscape white and frigid. No doubt the ice and snow have knocked out the cellphone tower. She sits and thinks nothing as the sun sinks closer to the horizon. The night comes on so quickly, even though she was expecting it.

Lori doesn't know why she goes back up to Ethan's bedroom as the sun begins to sink below the horizon, but she does. She sits on the bed and stares at the forest, at the lake. An eerie mist is gathering beneath the trees and frost has glazed the windows. Everything looks fragile, transient. Across the water, lights click on in the gathering shadows, small and sheltered by skeletal branches. She looks for the lights of the bed and breakfast, but it's gone dark for the winter.

It's as she sits there that she hears the office door creak open.

Lori jumps at the sound, but there is no one there. She has seen the office door open before. When things were good, she used to wake up and find Ethan working in that room. She would climb out of bed and wrap her arms around his neck and shoulders, drawing him away from his work and back to her arms. But he has always left it locked when he is gone.

The windows that wrap the bedroom continue beyond it, illuminating the office. She can see the lake from here as well. There is ice collecting on the banks, and she shivers. For a while she just stands in the door, feeling the room grow colder with night. Then Lori goes and sits at Ethan's desk.

The laptop is gone, the one that he uses for his work, but the desk is polished wood and the chair is a yielding, soft leather. She sits and stares out over the water and tries to imagine what it feels like to belong in such luxury. To command your own fate.

There is small drawer under the edge of the desk, cracked barely open. Lori catches her fingers in it idly. Ethan is her husband, but what does she know about him really? She fell into his bed and into his life, and now it seems that she will be shoved out, whatever vows they have made. She slides the drawer open an inch, another.

Inside is a brass-colored key, hung on a blue ribbon. Nothing else rests within the drawer.

Lori stares at it. She knows that there are places in this large house where she has not gone. The door under the stairs, the great grand stairs of the entryway, is the same color as this ribbon. It is never open, and yet a cold comes from it that chills to the bone. When she came too close, Eleanor warned her away. Now Lori wonders what is behind that door and why, if it is something of Eleanor's, the key is here in her husband's desk. Her hand hovers over the key for a moment. She swallows drily, and wonders why her heart pounds.

Lori pushes the drawer in. He is still her husband. That has to count for something. She has not imagined their love. She knows she hasn't.

Lori leaves the room, closing the door softly behind her.

THE SECOND WIFE

The second wife Ethan held tight as he killed her.

She was a curvy woman with brown hair and almond eyes, and her name was Jessica. Jessica had been a hairdresser before she married Ethan and moved into his big house. She had one brother, from whom she was estranged. They did not speak even on holidays. Likely, her brother still lives, somewhere, not thinking of her.

Ethan picked Jessica, as he picked all of his wives, because she would not be easily missed. But he picked Jessica especially because her almond brown eyes reminded him of Claire's. His beautiful Claire, who he loved still with all the passion of man gone mad. He did not yet know for sure what he was doing. He had read the books, books it took years to track down, old tombs of alchemy and magic made of chemicals and bones. He had robbed graves, though it could hardly be called robbing when the morticians were so well bribed. If that had been enough, Ethan would have never resorted to murder.

Jessica wore silk and cashmere, she ate from silver fork and porcelain plate. She had everything she could want, and he asked only that she be his wife. Jessica obliged. It was a life she had always dreamed of, a life of luxury after one spent barely scraping by, and she was so grateful.

On the night Ethan killed her, the night he became a murderer, Ethan listened to the bugs singing in the trees, the lapping water of the lake, until she came down to the dock to meet him. Her chestnut hair gleamed in the light from the candles he had lit, but her brown eyes were shadowed. She pressed a glass of bourbon into his hand. He put it on the railing, drew her to him.

"Do you love me?" Ethan asked his wife.

"Yes," Jessica said, leaning up to press a kiss to his mouth, her fingers sliding into his hair.

The knife entered her more easily than he had thought, thunking between her ribs, and the grip in his hair became painful. Ethan wrapped an arm around her as blood gurgled to her lips, coated his hand. He pulled the knife free and fumbled it. It bounced across the wooden deck, slipped into the lake.

Eleanor appeared from the darkness, and Paul, their faces unreadable. Jessica was gasping, a wheezing moan of sound sucking through her chest. Paul wrapped his arms around her chest, began dragging her towards the house. After a moment, Ethan went to help him, grabbing her legs. Behind him, he heard Eleanor turn on the hose, spraying the dock, spraying Jessica's blood into the lake.

Jessica hung between Ethan and Paul, too weak to fight. She was still breathing when they entered the foyer. The blue door gaped wide.

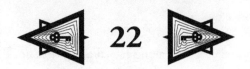

22

There is fog on the water the next morning, a thick blanket tangling the landscape in cloud. Snow is melting, running down the roof in rivulets, but it will freeze up again come nightfall. Lori wakes up, goes to the kitchen to get breakfast. She doesn't particularly want to look at Eleanor, but the woman is just as cold and aloof as ever. It's almost a relief.

Lori retires to the great room with its secret shelves. Each panel swings or slides away, leaving book upon book bare to the light. It's an odd affectation. Lori enjoyed it in the beginning, thinking it clever, but now it annoys. She still has the mystery of the bone to unravel, and her phone may not have reception but there is internet. She'll use this to distract herself, until she decides what to do.

Lori feels even more certain that she wants to pursue a medical degree, looking at these books. She needs something meaningful in her life. She needs a life outside of this house, even if her suspicions aren't true. By the light of day, with a night's sleep between her and that muttered conversation, Lori wonders again if she is jumping to irrational conclusions. A greater part of her maintains a grim sort of fatalism about her impending divorce. It was stupid to think that a fairytale like this would ever happen to someone like her. A man as rich as a prince sweeping a woman her age off her feet? A house in the woods, a life of luxury? It was naive, but she wanted something innocent and beautiful in her life.

Lori shakes her head and picks a book off the shelf at random. It won't help her to think like that.

Still, it is hard to forget the distance she feels from the man she loves, who she thought loved her. The words blur as her attention drifts. Lori flips through the pages, looking for diagrams. There, the wing of a bird, the fin of a whale, and the leg of a cat are all shown alongside the arm of a human. Lori stares, studying the shapes. This bone is something small, so perhaps it is a bird's. But Lori had heard that bird bones were hollow and fragile, and this one is thick. She has brought it down and she turns it in her fingers, staring at it. It is fluted, the length of her palm. She holds it to the diagram, comparing shapes, though none of the bones depicted are to scale.

It looks very much like the bone from a human hand. It would fit neatly in her own hand, she thinks.

Lori frowns.

The room has grown cold as she reads. Lori closes the book, restless. Perhaps she will never know where the bone comes from. There's no way a human bone would be there in the shallows of the lake. She returns the book to its shelf and closes it away.

* * *

D ays later, Lori takes a walk along the lake and tries not to think about dying. The wind blows across the water, casting sharp, white ripples of light. She has spent these days in limbo, with nothing but her thoughts for company, waiting for Ethan to return, for her suspicions to be confirmed. Dread is a constant companion. She has nothing to take her mind off of it except other, darker thoughts. The bone is smooth in her coat pocket. She knows it can't be a human bone, but it reminds her of her own mortality anyway.

She has no bones from Annie, but she has ashes. Lori wonders if she will have anyone to make such decisions for her, to come to her funeral, to keep her memory alive. Even after many months, she still grieves for her sister. It seems, standing on the shore, that she can smell the faint scent of jasmine on the wind. Annie loved the smell of that flower. It was too floral for Lori, who has always preferred roses. They have a darker, more grounded scent. But Annie loved to wear it, as lotion, as perfume when they went out. She knows the scent of jasmine is only in her memory, standing on this shore so far away, but for just a moment Lori feels close to Annie again.

And in that moment, she lets herself remember.

Annie brewed jasmine tea before she died, sweetened with just a small serving of sugar the way she always took it. Lori smelled it when she came in the kitchen door. She called for her sister, but there was no reply.

Lori sat down her keys and began sorting through the mail. There were bills to pay, bills from the hospital with numbers she didn't like to think about, and then she would need to start on dinner. She wasn't worried when her sister didn't respond. Annie slept a lot, tired from the cancer that was eating her up. It was another affirmation of the end that was coming, inevitably. Her bright sister was quiet, withdrawn. One day of laughter was followed with more days of silence. Lori cherished each and every one, desperate to keep Annie with her for one more moment.

This day of silence was the last. Lori knew that when she opened the bedroom door. Annie looked like she was sleeping, but there was an empty pill bottle next to her mug of jasmine tea. This is the secret that she has never told Ethan, that she keeps from herself except on the darkest nights. The cancer didn't take Annie. She left on her own.

She had been bright and happy again just the day before. Perhaps she had been happy to know the end was coming at last. Lori understands that, in this moment. There is a relief to embracing the loss. Standing on the shore of the lake with the pines behind her, Lori thinks of how quickly things can change. How many more times will she stand by the lake like this? She's not sure she wants to fight for more of these lonely, tired moments.

Lori clutches the bone in her pocket. She resolves, at last, to control her own fate.

Lori knew that Annie was out of options. Now, here, she finally has the distance to understand it. She can suffer through what is coming, or she can change it, like Annie did.

Lori will strive to be so strong.

23

T his is how Annie died.

She went into the kitchen on her weak legs, given strength by purpose. The sprawling San Antonio house was silent, empty. Lori was at work, selling another house to make their mortgage, and Annie was alone. Still, she was quiet as she rummaged in the cabinets where her medicines were kept. This one for pain, this one for kindling appetite, this one for keeping her alive just a bit longer. Annie read each of their names, but she already knew which one she was looking for. She clutched the bottle to her and moved with her tea and her medicine to the bedroom. She took deep breaths, fighting her panic, letting it pass through her. She counted out the pills, deliberate, cherishing each last act.

Did she think of Lori? Almost certainly. She knew what her death would do to her sister. But death was coming, either way, and she wanted to meet it on her terms. Annie lay back in her bed, the pills already in her stomach. She closed her eyes for the last time.

This is how Lori brings about the end.

She walks down the hallway that has become so familiar. Her steps are sure but quiet. She passes her bedroom with her sister's urn, and the room with the fireplace where she spends her afternoons watching television. She reaches the stairs, and climbs up.

The door to Ethan's bedroom is closed, as she left it. She steps inside. The room is cold, empty. Lori darts a glance through the windows as she closes the door behind her, then steps carefully to the office. At the door she pauses, squares her shoulders before she steps inside. She wants to know every secret of this house, of this life, before she leaves it. She wants to know what she did wrong.

Lori sits in the leather chair, just as she did the day before. She stares out over the lake. The short day is beginning to wane. Lori pulls open first one drawer, then another. She reads the names on the neat files to herself. Taxes, warranties, important documents, research. Lori pulls them out one by one. She'll need her marriage certificate, but she'll need to know enough to survive a divorce, too. So she leaves that folder for last, looking at tax returns and income. Ethan is rich. She knew that. But the numbers make her light-headed. She won't feel guilty asking for lawyer fees, anyway.

She puts the numbers aside and pulls out the last folder, spreading it wide. It takes her a moment to understand what she is seeing. Lori counts the marriage certificates with her fingertips, one, two, three, four, five. Her head spins. She reads the names to herself. Claire, Jessica, Rebecca, Veronica, Mary. Last comes Lorelei, signed by her and Ethan and Paul and their witnesses. Only Claire's certificate is stamped and certified. Only Claire's certificate has been recorded with the courthouse, the last, most important step.

Lori stares at the place where the court seal should be, disoriented. She's not married to Ethan. She never has been. The realization is like an unseen knife to the gut. They'd stood together and said their vows. Lori had married him. She had married him, brought all her self and gifted it. But no one will recognize it without a court's stamp of approval. It was a lie.

Lori leans back into the chair. Her skin crawls with some sentiment of doom. What happened to each of these women? She thinks of the bone in her coat pocket. The lights in the dark. The dreams, half-remembered, the cold in the foyer. Her breath comes fast, her heart is pounding in her chest. Every conversation, every moment of neglect, takes on new, darkened meaning.

Lori opens the drawer with the blue-ribboned key. She takes it, even though it is poison.

She has to see what is behind that door.

The foyer is empty. The cold is enough to make her glad that she has her coat. It worms its way under her clothes regardless.

Lori steps down the stairs, her feet nearly silent. The windows reveal no one in the drive. The doorway to the dining room remains empty. The key is an ice chip in her palm. She breathes shallowly through her nose, as if even the sound of her breath will give her away. She never noticed quite how many stairs there were before.

The door beneath the stairs is blue, sunken in the stone wall like a pool in the ground. Lori cannot take her eyes from it. It is a well of gravity that draws her gaze towards it as if this moment is inevitable. Lori looks once behind her, checking to make sure she is unobserved. Then, with trembling hands, she fits the key into the lock. The door sticks for a moment, then pops open. Dry, cool air rolls out. Lori slips inside and shuts the door behind her.

There are more stairs, dark and close and cold. Lori gropes for a light switch on the cold concrete wall and finds it. The click is loud in the small space. She can taste the cold in her mouth, an iron tang like blood on her tongue.

Lori starts down.

Her steps ring flatly in the still air. Lori pulls her coat tighter. This must be a basement, something entirely underground. She reaches the second door and wraps her fingers around the ice of the knob. It's so cold it seems like her skin will stick. She twists the door open.

The room is already lit, a bright space of tile and austerity. There are two long metal tables set in the tiled floor. Beyond them, strangely, are bars, and in the shadows beyond those something that looks very much like a bedroom.

Lori has time to notice those few details before movement catches her eye. At first, her mind cannot process what she sees. Something is rustling on one table, something is moving like a bird amidst dead leaves on the forest floor.

It is thin and brittle and papery skin rustles when it moves. Lori can tell that much. Her hand reaches behind her for the door handle, groping for it. She cannot find it.

Straps of leather bind the shrunken stick-thing to the tabletop. The thing moves, lifts its head. Lori's breath pants in her ears. There is a noise, rising in her throat, animal. Filmy, white eyes meet hers.

"Who?" comes a voice like the hollow of a cave, black and crawling.

The sound bursts from her then, half groan, half keen. The creature flinches.

"No, not again," it says. It pushes against its bonds. Papery, sunken flesh flakes. "Not again. I won't be part of this again."

Such a strange thing for a monster to say, and it presses on Lori's mind. She's frozen, the door handle forgotten. She is staring at the creature that was once a person. She is smelling the dry, peppery scent of it.

Rotting, fetid things make loam. But this creature has not been allowed to rot. It has withered down to nothing, dried like a bug stuck to a board, pinned in the moment of its death, forever. Living in that moment, forever.

Lori swallows. At some point, the noise she was making has dried up, too.

"What are you?" she says, her voice scratchy and hoarse. She knows the answer already. She knows in her gut, in her marrow.

"Who is there?" says the thing who was once a woman.

"My name is Lori," she says. She takes a step away from the door. The creature shivers all over, the sound crawling into Lori's ears. She shudders too, and stops. Her body feels distant. Lori knows that this is shock. It's the same feeling that took her when she found Annie in her bed, dead at last.

Lori stares, arrested, at the ruin of the face, at the gaunt limbs. Her brain says this is a doll, a human shape made of papier-mâché. Not alive. But her gut knows death. Lori has seen the dead before. She has her sister to thank for that. She knows the way the skin sinks to the skull, the way the eyes jelly and dry. Something that dead cannot move. Yet each rustle decries that fact, turns reason on its head.

"Lori. You are alone? You've found me alone?" The creature's voice is urgent. Lori can hear the traces of a woman in it, cavernous and forbidding though it may be.

"You're Claire," Lori says, wonderingly. "You're the first wife."

And Claire, the first wife, laughs a bitter laugh. It is the sound of the world coming undone.

24

This is the tale of the first wife.

Once there was a girl who fell in love with a boy on a bright summer in Vermont. It was college vacation, and Claire O'Reilly was only twenty years old when she met Ethan Locke in the Greensboro general store. He and his friends, who were all tall and thin and tanned with sunlight, were trying to buy beer with fake IDs. Of course, the owner of the store knew exactly how old Ethan was, since he and his family had been coming to their lake home every summer since he was born. Evergreen, built to hold Ethan's secrets, did not yet exist.

Claire was a few months older than Ethan, visiting her friend Molly. Molly's family was renting a vacation home nearby, and Claire had tagged along, unwilling to go home for the summer but unable to pay for an apartment on campus. The two stolen weeks with Molly's family were an oasis from the combined stressors of Claire's rigorous course load and her mother's suspicious, sharp personality. The last time Claire had gone home, Eleanor had gone through all of her things while she was out one afternoon. When Claire came back, Eleanor was cutting up her favorite party dress with scissors.

Molly was already twenty-one. She got beer easily. Before they left the store, Molly introduced Claire to Ethan and the rest of his crew. Claire didn't think much of Ethan at first. His eyes were very blue and he was beautiful, but he was shorter than his friends and laughed too loud, like he was afraid to be the butt of a joke.

He had a speedboat though, bought with his parents' money, and he invited Claire and Molly out to ride around the lake. They went along. At some point, he asked Claire for her number. She didn't expect him to call. She was just a poor girl from Holyoke, and it was obvious Ethan's family was old money, from his white, even grin to his designer swim trunks.

But he did. He called her after she had gone home to her parents' house in Massachusetts a week later, unable to put it off any longer, and he kept calling, and gradually she fell for him.

"He was kind," whispers the first wife in her halting, rustling voice. "And mom was getting worse, and I needed an escape. I can see that now, in hindsight. That I was just running away."

She and Ethan married after college. He went to work in New York City, and she followed him. They lived in a nice apartment. They did well. Ethan's family had connections, and Claire knew that she benefited from them. She didn't care. It was better than being trapped in her parents' house under her mother's sharp thumb.

Then Ethan's parents died in a car crash, and things became strange.

The money was part of it. His parents had invested well. Ethan didn't have to work anymore, and he didn't want Claire to, either. He wanted them to rebuild the summer home in Vermont to his vision, to travel the world in the winters and spend time on the lake in the summer.

"I tried to compromise," Claire tells Lori in the basement of Evergreen, and Lori hears in that cavernous voice an echo of her own frustrations, her own arguments with Ethan in this very house. It makes her head swim. "I told him I could take a leave of absence. He told me I could go back to work whenever I wanted, that he just needed time to heal. Once he had rebuilt the house, I couldn't put it off any longer. He was too insistent."

They traveled, like he wanted. And the stops Ethan picked for every trip were morbid ones. He was obsessed with death, and with what happened afterwards. They saw Indonesian funerary processions and Egyptian tombs, the crypts below Paris and the bone churches of the Czech Republic. Ethan vanished for hours or days sometimes, returning with relics or old books. Claire tried to be understanding. But eventually she demanded that they head back to Evergreen for the summer.

They'd come home, things strained between them. The day that Claire died, the day that she finally understood how twisted he had become, she and Ethan were arguing about the future. They'd taken out the boat, Ethan's idea—something relaxed, something nostalgic, and Claire went along, trying to remember the bright summer day they had met. Trying to put a finger on when Ethan's love had begun to feel less like an escape and more like a prison.

She still remembers the way the sun had looked, setting on the water.

"I told him I was going back to work, that I had already been applying for jobs," Claire says softly. "That he'd had enough time. He was angry. He grabbed my shoulder, and I shook him off and when I did—well, I slipped. I knocked my head against the side of the boat. The water was so cold."

Claire stops speaking. Lori feels a chill. She knows, already, what Claire will say next.

How many times had she thought of bringing Annie back? How many times had she thought that her sister should never have left her? It's impossible to cheat death, and yet she knows the first wife is dead. Nothing should be this broken and still live.

If she could have done what Ethan has done, would she? Lori feels the pressure in her chest and fears she knows the answer.

"He brought me back," the first wife says. Lori swallows, mouth dry. "He found a way."

"Eleanor," she says at last. "Eleanor and Paul, they knew."

"Of course they did," Claire says, bitter.

That is the moment that Lori truly understands. The other wives are dead. The man she touched, the man she loved—

"I can't—" she says, staggering back. She thinks she will vomit. The door is all that holds her up.

"Lori," Claire says, her voice implacable, "if you don't get out of here, he will feed me your heart. I will be whole for at least five years, with a new wife's heart."

"Five?" Lori chokes.

"In the spring is when it's worst," Claire says, her voice gone dreamy, "when the bulbs put up sprouts. I can hear the roots grow through the earth, if I am quiet enough. I count the springs between the hearts he feeds me."

Lori shudders, a motion that runs through her whole body like an earthquake. To hear those words, to be reminded of Claire's strangeness after hearing about her humanity, makes everything in her disconnected, uncertain.

Five years for one life. Ethan has been murdering his wives for twenty years. She remembers again the warmth of his hands, how strong they feel against her skin. Her back is still pressed to the door. She sees what she didn't before—the drain in the floor, the second, bare steel table. The saws on the wall.

For her. This room is for her. This is where he means for her to die.

Lori curls in on herself, there in the floor, curls around the twisting hook of pain in her gut. She knows its name. It is betrayal. She felt it when her mother gave them up. She felt it when Ruth forbid her from looking for Annie. She felt it when she found Annie dead in her bed.

The pain rearranges the world, throws it into sharp relief.

"You have to get out of here," the first wife whispers. "Please. I cannot stand to watch another one of you die."

25

L ori slips out from the hidden space beneath the grand staircase as if in a dream. She means to go out the front door of Evergreen, though the evening air outside is bitter cold. Her body feels leaden. Her throat aches with the desire to scream.

She forgets to take the key out of the door. She only remembers it when she sees Ethan's SUV through the windows of the foyer, lumbering down the driveway.

Lori cannot breathe. Her body turns to stone as Ethan walks to the door. She can see Paul driving the SUV away, back to the garage where her Toyota also sits. Her Toyota, whose spare keys are in her room upstairs.

The front door opens. Ethan walks in.

The sight of him is a balm, despite everything. Yet Lori feels her heart rate spike too, feels her knees try to give. She is trembling. She cannot tremble. Some last shred of self-preservation tells her that she must not show fear.

"Ethan," she says, breathy.

"Love," he says, and she almost flinches. He has already wrapped his arms around her. Why must he be so warm, smell so good? Lori relaxes into him, but then starts back.

"I need to go upstairs," she says. "I'm not feeling well."

It's not a lie. She feels as if she has a fever. Her cheeks must be flushed, her skin pale, her eyes glittering. Surely that is what it looks like.

Ethan studies her face with concern. Lori feels a scream climb in her throat when she meets his sharp blue eyes.

"What's wrong?" he asks.

"I don't know," Lori says, the words coming out of her mouth as if someone else has put them there. She's afraid he'll ask more questions, afraid that she will be forced to explain. For a moment she's afraid she will pass out from fear. She feels her eyelids flutter.

Whatever he sees seems to be enough for Ethan in this moment.

"Let me help you up the stairs," he says, solicitous.

He walks beside her up the staircase, his hand on her elbow. His grip is firm. Lori cannot think of an excuse to get away from him. Usually she wants to see him. Usually they would go up to his room, if things were good, or down to the kitchen or great room to sit and talk. Suddenly, she wants that so badly. She wants to pretend that nothing she knows is true, wants the man she married to love her, to hold her and tell her everything was a nightmare.

But her stomach twists. Lori thinks she might vomit. Ethan adjusts his grip to wrap his arm around her, and she barely stops a shudder.

Lori thinks of the marriage certificates, of the names of all the women that he has gutted. This has been a long and premeditated journey. She thinks of the whispered conversation in the stairwell. Ethan did not do this alone.

It is as if her thoughts are a summons.

"Welcome home, sir." It's Eleanor's voice. She's on the stairs above them, and Lori looks up at the woman, barely able to keep her face blank.

She has no good feelings for Eleanor, nothing to dull the bite of her terror.

"Is everything alright?" Eleanor asks, her voice lacking any real concern.

"Lori is feeling ill," Ethan says. His concern does not seem faked. Why not? Is this real? Lori takes a deep, shuddering breath. Eleanor has already stepped aside, but her gaze sharpens on Lori.

"I'm sorry to hear it," she says. "Will you need anything?"

"No, just rest," Lori says. "I think I just need to rest." Her lips are numb. It is a wonder she doesn't garble the words. How much longer can she hold this together?

"Of course," Eleanor says.

They pass her.

And then another, terrible thought strikes Lori.

Eleanor is going down the stairs.

She will see the key that Lori has left in the lock.

She will know.

"Eleanor?" Lori asks, pausing. Her heart is convulsing in her chest. She swallows.

"Yes?" Eleanor asks. Her feet have stopped on the stairs. Ethan has stopped beside her. This tableau can break in a thousand ways.

"If you could perhaps bring up some tea?" Lori says. "Something to settle my stomach."

"Of course," Eleanor says, again. Her steps downward resume.

Ethan waits for Lori to begin walking again. She takes another step up. She cannot wait to see if the task will distract Eleanor enough, cannot wait to see if the alarm will be raised. She must make it to her room. To her keys.

Lori climbs, and hopes her shaking knees will not fail her.

E than wants to help her undress, to tuck her in. Lori lets him, because she cannot think of what else to do. In her underwear and a tee shirt, she smiles a shaky smile, pulls the covers tight, and pretends to fall asleep.

Eleanor comes in with the tea, and Ethan places it on the table. Then Ethan leaves and closes the door behind him.

Lori jumps out of bed.

She puts on her thickest wool sweater, her blue jeans, her boots. She pulls the puffy winter coat back around her. The day is waning, the sun getting closer to the horizon. She won't survive long in Vermont without layers, not in the winter. Lori slings her purse over her shoulder. Then she stares for one long moment at Annie's urn.

She can't carry it with her. It's too obvious, too clear a sign she is running. Lori almost reaches for the urn anyway. She hugs herself instead, standing for an endless moment in indecision.

Her heart is pounding heavily in her chest. She has no time to grieve again. Lori cracks the door to her room, looking out. The hallway is empty, but that just means Ethan has already started ascending the stairs to his room, to his office with the papers spread everywhere and the missing blue key. The same back set of stairs she will need to go down, if she means to reach the garage.

Lori wants to run. She wants to hurtle down the hallway. But no one knows she is running yet. There's been no shout, no outcry. She reaches the door at the end of the hall, cracks it open. There is no one on the stairs.

She's gone only a few steps down when she hears Ethan's shout above her.

Lori runs.

Her steps on the stairs are clumsy, shaky things. Each one could bring ruin. But Lori keeps her feet, flying downward with all her strength. Ethan is shouting above her, but the words are blurring, too loud. Lori reaches the bottom of the stairway, sprints down the small hall to the garage door and slams through it. Paul is there. His questioning look turns into angry commands. Lori sprints past him, her hand already on her key fob. The driver door unlocks, and she closes it. Paul has nearly reached her. She presses the lock button down urgently. He grabs the handle, pulls. The door holds. He begins pounding on the glass.

Lori slams the key into the ignition.

The car starts.

The Toyota slaloms backwards, clipping Ethan's SUV. Lori doesn't stop. She whips the car into the driveway, barely missing the stone walls of the planter at its center. The car jitters on the cobbles, but the driveway is clear. Lori slams the vehicle into drive. Paul is running out of the garage, towards her. She hits the gas before he can get close. The car thrusts forward and Paul staggers back, but Lori is already turning towards the driveway. The first gate is in front of her.

Lori plows into it.

It's low, and the metal is light. It bends and tears around her, but the headlights are buffeted in the process. One goes out. It's already dark beneath the trees, but Lori can't afford to be careful. She presses the pedal to the floor, breaking the car free of the gate. The driveway dips.

The turn, that damnable turn, rises up out of the darkness beneath the evergreens. Lori screams, yanks hard on the wheel. The car goes into a spin. She hears her traction alarm beep warning.

Lori drives into the lake. Her head impacts with the steering wheel.

The water is bitter cold. It comes in through the windshield, which has cracked, is cracking. Lori's head spins. She fumbles with her seatbelt. It comes loose. Lori tries to open the door, but it won't budge. She thinks of the bone from the lake, thinks of Claire drowning, the water filling her lungs. Lori's trembling fingers find the button for the window. It won't roll down.

The water is coming in faster now. The crack in the windshield is widening. She cannot feel her fingers. Everything is too cold.

Lori leverages herself up against the seat. She kicks out at the windshield with both legs.

It shatters.

The water covers everything. Lori has time for half a breath before it floods her mouth and nose. She strikes out, blindly. Her hands find the headrest for the driver's seat. She's been pushed into the back of the car, but the water has leveled out, the current is not as strong. She swims forward, pushing off the headrest, out what she hopes is the hole the windshield made. Her lungs burn. The heavy clothes pull her down. Lori thrashes in the water.

It is as if something else possesses her, moves her limbs. Her fingers scrape mud, and something hard and sharp. Her hand wraps around it without her conscious choice. There is a blue light all around her. There are faces in the water, staring with dead eyes. She knows them, in her heart she knows them. They are the other wives. The ones like her, dead like she's about to be.

Lori slides the shape into her waistband at the small of her back, beneath her thick sweater and the sodden, heavy coat.

Hands grip her and pull her up, even as her lungs give out at last.

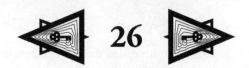

26

L ori awakens on the table, and meets the first wife's dead eyes. Claire, Lori thinks. Her name was Claire, once.

Her head hurts. Her panic is gone, but the need for it is not. She can sense that, can sense that this moment of quiet is one that should be used. Lori tries to move her arms, but her limbs feel leaden. For a moment, she fears she has been strapped down, but a wild glance shows she's still free. It's the cold and shock that steal her strength. Her clothing is wet, her hair clings to her face. Her eyes roll in her head, trying to close.

It's so cold in this room, so cold with hauntings.

It is a hand on her cheek that wakes her. It is a warmth that she did not know she could feel. It is the scent of her sister's skin, the jasmine lotion she wore.

Lori opens her eyes again. There's a sharp pressure against her back. She sits up.

The first wife is moving fitfully against her bonds, the paper rustling of her filling the small room. The door is closed.

"Annie?" Lori says. Her voice croaks. That sharp thing is still digging into the skin above her spine. She reaches back. Her hands find a smooth pommel, and Lori pulls up.

She's holding a knife.

Almost Lori drops it. She has never held a knife like it, one made so obviously for killing. The blade is sharp, and stained black.

"Keep it," the first wife says, her voice the sawing of two branches in the wind. Lori flinches. "Keep it and use it. Avenge them. Avenge us."

Lori gets off the table, or tries. Her legs shake under her, and she nearly falls, catching herself on the tabletop. She can see her breath, misting in front of her as if the room is getting colder. Lori forces her legs straight.

The door opens.

Ethan stands in the doorway. His eyes are still so blue, but they are flat now. Lori stills, her numb hand tightening on the knife.

"Lori," Ethan says. His voice is calm, resigned. "You shouldn't be up."

He walks towards her, past Claire's struggling form. Lori backs away until the wall leaves her nowhere to go. She stares into the eyes of the man she loved, looking for some trace of affection there. Is there pain? She cannot see it. She cannot see anything but ice in that gaze, now.

"Ethan. Please," she says, as if that will bring him back. As if she can summon mercy with a name.

He grimaces.

"I loved her first," he says.

Lori stands still for a shocked, unsettled moment. Her mind cannot process those words. Love? Love is what she thought to have with Ethan. It's warm arms, a fireplace in the wilderness. This room is sterile, dry air, dead flesh. It is like the way her house was empty when Annie died, and how she clung to the emptiness. There's nothing of love here, only need.

Then he reaches out. He doesn't have a weapon, but he's more than strong enough to restrain her, to pin her to the table so that she can't escape. Ethan's fingers bite into the flesh of her arm. There is no more time.

Lori cannot say, afterward, if she swings the knife or if it pulls her forward. The darkened metal slips almost gently into Ethan's stomach, angles up beneath his ribcage. He makes a small sound. It is the gasp of a mortal wound, a sucking, quiet breath. A sob rips from Lori's throat. Her body knows loss too well. It is already grieving, even as Ethan pulls her towards him, inexorable.

The knife leaves his belly and darts back, like the beak of a waterbird towards water. There is blood on Lori's hand. Ethan staggers. He pulls her down as he falls.

She lands on top of him, his warm, solid weight. The knife skitters away across the floor, trailing blood in its wake. Ethan is gasping something, his mouth moving but unable to summon air to give the words voice. Lori stares at his face, mesmerized. She cannot move from him, cannot move from the warm blood that binds him, from his struggling, futile attempts at breath as his chest rises and falls desperately. That flat gaze is gone. There is only panic there.

For a moment, his eyes focus on hers. Does she imagine regret?

Then the breath goes out of him at last, and he stills.

There is someone crying. Lori realizes it is her. Blood is seeping across the floor, has seeped into her sweater and jeans. She scrambles back, stands.

"Run," the first wife says. Lori looks up. She meets those dead eyes. Her mind is blank, a field in winter. Lori cannot think.

"What about you?" she says. The words come out of her as if through a stranger's throat. The creature on the table rattles. Again, Lori thinks of wind in dead leaves clinging to branches.

"Cut me loose," Claire says. Her rattling voice seems smoother now. There is something blurring her form, something that dulls the grotesquery of her features. Lori cannot think on it. She will not think on anything. She finds the knife where it has fallen, her fingers fumbling. She uses it to cut the wide leather straps that keep Claire still, and she does not flinch even to touch that papery skin. There is a sighing sound.

The creature that was once a woman almost seems to flutter to where Ethan lies. The blood soaks into her paper flesh, stains her lips.

When she stands, she looks nearly alive.

"Come," she says.

Lori does.

27

Claire glides across the floor. Lori cannot see her steps, she cannot hear them. The foyer is rimed with ice. Lori slips, and Claire pauses to wait for her.

Eleanor walks out of the dining room then, pulling on long rubber gloves. Her eyes go wide when she sees them, sees the blood soaking Lori's body, sees Claire unbound in the half-light and shimmering. She stops, her whole body going rigid.

"Claire," she whispers, and her face is equal parts hope and fear, a trembling, inelegant cracking of her normal mask. Lori feels like a voyeur. "What are you doing up here, Claire. Where's Ethan?"

"Where he belongs," Claire says. She steps towards Eleanor grimly.

"Claire, baby," Eleanor says, simpering, backing away. Claire keeps up her steady steps. Eleanor's face becomes a snarl. "I've done all this for you! Everything, for you!"

"I know, mother."

She crosses the remaining space between them in a blink. Her hands are around Eleanor's throat. Lori opens her mouth—to protest, to scream, she doesn't know—but there's no time. Eleanor is already falling. Her skin is blue, her body stiff and clunky and dead. Whatever sound Lori meant to utter dies in her throat.

Claire turns, the light around her fading already.

"That's all I have left," she says. "Run. Get out of here." Her body folds. She begins to collapse in on herself, and Lori feels a keening in her throat at the sight. She chokes it down. Claire is gone.

Lori turns. Her feet slip on the icy floor. The knife is a heavy weight in her fist. Her sweater clings to her body. Breath cuts in her chest. She runs out the front door, the western sun piercing her eyes with long, dying rays. The lake is purple and black before her. Lori turns away from it. The garage door is open. Lori darts inside. Her Toyota may be at the bottom of a lake, but there are other vehicles. She just needs to find the keys.

But there are no keys on the wall, there are no keys anywhere. Lori tears apart drawers of tools, sending them clattering to the concrete. She can find nothing. How far will she get on foot, soaking wet in the bitter beginnings of a Vermont winter. Even in her panic, Lori knows the answer.

There is a wisp of scent. Something makes her turn, some presence shouting in her head. She sees a shape in the doorway of the garage. She already knows who it will be.

Paul stands there with the dying sunlight painting him black. He's holding something long in his hands.

Lori is running before she realizes she has decided to, pelting towards the back of the garage and the door to the inside of the house. Behind her, Paul roars.

L ori sprints down the hall, into the great room, up the stairs. She hears Paul shouting behind her, but the panic is so loud in her ears she cannot make out the words. The knife is still in her fist, gripped tight.

There is a report like a cannon, like thunder right beside her ear. The wall beside her bucks, plaster and paint sparking off of it.

Paul has a gun.

Lori shouldn't be surprised but she is, an unpleasant pulse of adrenaline to add to the racing of her heart. The knife in her hands will not save her here. Blindly, she runs into the hallway of bedrooms. The door to her room is standing open. Annie's urn glints from the dresser, the white marble bright in the dim light. Lori doesn't think. She ducks inside the room. She can hear Paul's steps. She can feel panic rising in her throat. He's too close. She can't get out of the room.

Lori squats down beside the bed, tucking her body into a ball. It's stupid. She knows it is as soon as she has done it but her whole body is shaking with fatigue and fear. Every muscle rebels from going farther. She keeps her hands clasped in front of her, around the knife's pommel like a prayer. Keeps her head bowed. Her breath rips in and out of her chest no matter how she tries to quiet it. Ethan's blood has gone cold and tacky against her skin.

Paul steps into the room.

She knows as soon as he has, knows he is there like a pressure on her skin. Lori has never liked Paul, and now he will kill her. Now she will die in front of his gun, and she almost wishes she had never woken up on the table, that Ethan had been the one to do the deed. At least there would have been some poetry in that. She wants to believe Ethan would have been kind.

She knows Paul will not be.

He steps around the bed, and Lori looks up to the gun. The barrel is a black hole. It draws her in, and she cannot pull her gaze away.

"You killed them," Paul grinds out, and there are tears on his face. The edges of Lori's vision are going black, but she can see that he's crying.

At first, she thinks that the light behind him is a product of her panic. Lori wonders if she has died already, if her mind skipped the sound of the gun and the impact of the bullet and now she is floating in death. But Paul turns. The light filling up the room is something he can see too.

It is coming from the urn, this golden light.

Lori, she hears, and it's Annie's voice. *Now.*

Lori drives up, past the barrel of the rifle. Paul startles, pulls the trigger. The report is so loud it seems like it should stop the world.

She drives the knife into his gut.

She does not wait to see if she has killed Paul. He falls and she staggers over him, swipes the urn from the dresser. Its glow has faded, and she wonders if she imagined it.

She runs down the stairs. Through the great room, dodging furniture. The garden taunts her, but it's night now and snow is falling. She needs a phone, she needs *help*. Lori does not know how much longer she can keep moving. The familiar hallway that leads to the kitchen seems to tremble in front of her eyes. She trips just before she reaches the open doorway, as if an unseen hand has grabbed her ankle.

A report shakes the air of the hall, and shotgun pellets dig into the doorway above her head.

Lori scrambles up and runs again.

There is a stitch in her side. There is a phone on the wall. Lori almost darts towards it, but some instinct has her ducking behind the bar. Another shotgun blast pings the pots and pans, pockmarks the wall. Lori's ears ring. She stays low, running as best she can, headed for the back door and the passage that will lead to the dining room. She's not sure what she's doing at this point, except that she doesn't want to die. Paul groans behind her, but whatever damage she did isn't enough to keep him from moving.

The urn is cold and heavy in her arms, but Lori can't let it go. How many moments until she sees Annie again? She wants to keep these ashes close, so they can find one another in the beyond.

Lori bursts through the swinging kitchen door, runs down the hall. The stitch in her side has become a deep, persistent cramp. She cannot seem to catch a breath.

She reaches the dining room.

The open space of it taunts her. The last glimmers of light have caught fire to the lake, and Lori knows, suddenly and certainly, that she will die here.

She runs for the door in the glass, for the deck. The glass swings open. She feels the cold air on her face. Tastes mist on her tongue.

Pain tears through her shoulder. She hears the report, the tinkling of glass. Lori staggers. The urn falls from her arms, rolls across the deck scattering ashes. Blood begins to slide down her arm, steaming in the cold air.

Her feet move, seemingly of their own accord. She turns and she is facing Paul. He levels the shotgun in her direction. His side is drenched in blood. Lori remembers the knife, gripped so tight that her hand has gone numb. She doesn't bring it up. She doesn't do anything. She stares at Paul, at the shotgun, at the blood dripping from him and slipping the deck. He's pale, his glare baleful.

She wants to ask him why. Why this vengeance, when he has helped take so many lives? Does he think he has the right?

She doesn't get the chance.

There is light rising from the ashes. There is mist, gathering tightly into the shape of a woman, or more than one. It forms a wall in front of her. It converges on Paul.

He has time to get off one shot, before the mist swallows him. It tears through the air and into Lori's hip. She drops the knife.

28

There are five women standing around her bed in San Antonio. They are women it seems she has known all her life.

One is blonde and spare, one tall with hair as black as velvet. One is small and round with glasses to cover her ghostly eyes, and two have eyes that are brown and deep as Lori's own. The last of these brown-eyed women is Claire.

"Well, that's done, then," Claire says. She looks close to crying, and then she looks mad at herself for it. Lori reaches up her hand, touches Claire's where it rests beside her.

"It's okay to be sad," she says. Claire takes her hand and squeezes. Her fingers are icy.

The tall woman with black hair sits herself on the bed, crosses her legs.

"What a bastard," she says. "What a fucking bastard."

"Veronica," says Claire, placating.

"What?"

"She's right," sniffs the blonde. She looks like she wants a drink. Lori can commiserate with that.

"You're the wives," Lori says. "You're the ones he killed."

"Or resurrected, in Claire's case," Veronica says sardonically. Lori shudders. It all seems like a distant dream here in this warm, safe room.

"But you're not wrong," says the soft woman in glasses. "I'm Mary, dear. That's Veronica. The blonde is Rebecca and Jessica is the quiet one. Forgive her, I think her death was the hardest."

Jessica smiles.

"I gave you the knife," she says, and her voice makes Lori shiver. She doesn't want to remember the knife or the blood on her hands.

"How did I get here?" Lori says instead.

"We brought you," Claire tells her. "You've freed us. We wanted to say thank you."

Lori grimaces. "I don't deserve thanks."

"We all fell for his bullshit," Veronica says.

"Don't act like you didn't enjoy it, Veronica," Rebecca says, voice snide.

Veronica rolls her eyes. "I did say 'we' didn't I?"

"Rebecca hates Veronica because she came after," Mary says, her voice conspiratorial. There's laughter in her eyes.

"Only a little," Rebecca says, as if this is an argument they've had before.

"Ladies," Claire says. "It's time." Then she turns back to Lori.

"Thank you, Lorelei. I cannot thank you enough." She squeezes Lori's hand, and something passes between them, and Lori feels cold.

Then Claire is gone, and Jessica takes Lori's hand in hers.

"Thank you," she says, soft like waves lapping the shore, and Lori feels pain.

"Thanks," says Rebecca grudgingly, and the room begins to fade. Lori opens her mouth, but no sound passes her lips.

"Thanks for killing that bastard," says Veronica. Lori's throat is dry, her head pounds. The room is gone.

One last cold, soft grip takes hers. "Thank you, dear."

It is dark. It is cold.

Everything hurts.

Lori sucks cold breath into her lungs. Each shiver shakes her wounds, riddles her with pain. Lori moans. Her hands scrabble over the deck.

The deck. She is outside. It is night.

Now that she realizes, she can see the glimmer of stars between clouds. A cold wind pushes hair into her eyes. Her fingers are burning with the frigid air. There is ice forming in the puddles of her blood.

Lori takes a deep breath. Then she tries to sit up.

The agony is too much. She screams, a sound that tears out of her, short and sharp. Her arm gives out, and the deck rises up to meet her with a slap.

Lori takes several deep, shaking breaths. The pain rises and falls, but it never recedes low enough to let her think. The cold is stealing her strength. She grits her teeth and rolls over onto her belly.

For a while after that, she cannot move. The dark creeps along her vision in time with her pulse. There is no light on in the dining room, no light in the house. She can make out the door only by the glimmer of moonlight on glass. There's a gaping hole where the shotgun tore through, but only the lower panel is gone. The upper still reflects the sky faintly.

She's not going to make it.

The thought is a relief. Lori lets her head drop to the deck. It doesn't even seem cold anymore. Everyone in this house is dead, and she will die, too. She will finally be with Annie.

There is a scent of jasmine on the wind. There is a glow from the ashes spread around her, stained crimson-black with her blood. Lori sees it first against the backs of her eyelids, before she is able to force them open. Someone stands in front of her, too bright to see.

"Get up, Lori," Annie says. Lori feels a spark of anger. She's tried so hard. She just wants to rest.

"I can't," Lori mumbles. Her lips are numb. They don't want to shape the words.

"Yes, you can."

Lori takes a sobbing breath. She can't, she knows she can't. It's too much.

But she doesn't want to die here. She doesn't want to give up. That is what made her so angry at Annie for so long, that is what mired her in grief so deep it led her here. She thought Annie had given up, even though she knew better. Lori, though, has a chance. Annie is telling her to take it.

Lori forces herself to her feet.

The light is gone. The wind is cold. Lori's feet slide on the deck over glass and bloody ice. She staggers to the door, fumbles with the handle. She cannot feel her hands. Are her fingers blue? The handle twists. There is a tricky moment then where she fears the door has locked, until she remembers that it swings outward. She pulls, and warm air billows out. Lori staggers inside.

She bumps her hip on a chair in the dark and almost falls. The wound throbs, but she thinks it is just a graze. The shoulder is worse. She cannot move that arm, cannot lift it. She staggers on frozen legs, hand up in the dark to feel for walls. When she finds one, she leans against it and walks, puts one foot in front of the other. Her mind is blank. There is only the blackness, and the pain, and a need.

When she makes it to the kitchen at last, what seems to be hours later, she cannot quite remember what she came for. Almost, she sits down. Almost, it ends there.

But her fumbling hands have found the light. The brightness sears her eyes. The landline is perched in the far corner. Lori grits her teeth, staggers to the counter. It holds her weight as she slides towards the phone.

Lori picks it up and dials with stiff fingers the only number she can remember. "Hello?"

"Christine," she says.

"Lori? Is that you?" Christine's voice is tinny, distant. "Are you okay?"

"I need help," Lori tells her.

"Are you at Evergreen?" Christine demands, but Lori can't hear her. Nerveless fingers release the receiver. It clatters to the floor.

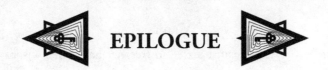

EPILOGUE

Three weeks later, Lori stands on the banks of Caspian Lake and prepares to scatter ashes.

It's her first day out of the hospital. The police have questioned her and seem to believe her claims of defense. Claire's husk of a body and the names of missing women on Ethan's marriage certificates have helped. Lori's not to leave Vermont until the investigation is closed, but they have brought no charges against her. She's been staying at Christine and Bill's house, sleeping on their couch while she recovers and figures out what comes next.

Her savior herself stands further down the shore. Christine's silvered hair glints in the light. She's looking anywhere but at Lori, trying to give her privacy even though Lori's still walking with a cane. The surgery to get the shotgun pellets out of her hip was long, and though the wound has mostly healed up, the joint is still stiff. She'll be carrying shrapnel for the rest of her life, but the doctors seem to think she'll be able to walk fine on her own eventually.

Across the lake, Lori can see Evergreen through the bare branches.

Lori and Christine have come to that same bed and breakfast. She made it down the trail to the lakeshore by leaning on Christine heavily as they navigated through the trees. Now she stands and stares at the house across the water, trying to feel something besides the harshness of her breath in her lungs.

Her lawyer, a round-faced woman who is the same age Annie was when she died, has explained that Ethan had appointed Eleanor and Paul as recipients to his fortune. Paul was dead of the knife wound Lori had given him. They'd found his body in the foyer, curled around Eleanor. He must have lived even after the wives got their spectral claws in him, though not for long. The coroner diagnosed Eleanor with sudden acute heart failure, which meant they didn't know what killed her.

Lori's lawyer assures her that no matter what happens, Lori will be paid damages from Ethan's estate. Her marriage was invalid, the certificate having never been registered with the state of Vermont. But she had believed herself married and had made decisions accordingly. There are witnesses to that, including Christine and Hannah. It isn't her fault that Ethan defrauded her.

So Lori bides her time, waiting to see what is coming. She answers the questions that her lawyer advises her to answer, and she sleeps on Christine's couch and eats with Bill and the children, and she heals. She does not think of Evergreen—or she has tried not to until now. Today, it sits on the shore, glimmering. Half of Annie's ashes are there.

The other half are in the urn slung across her shoulder, in the bag Christine has devised for it. Lori's right arm is still in a sling most of the time. She's going to have some excellent scars.

Lori props her cane against a tree to free her hand. She wishes that there could be something more poetic, more seamless. But it's time, and she knows it. It's time to let Annie rest at last. There is no more presence in these ashes. What grace they have given her is spent.

Lori tosses a handful of ashes into the wind. It carries the last remnants of her sister's body into the lake.

Later, in the car, with the empty urn beside her, Lori leans her head against the glass. She dreams of San Antonio, of Annie sitting by the window. She dreams Annie's palm in hers, dreams her sister's voice saying, *I'll see you on the other side, Lori.*

Lori slides into sleep as Annie's hand leaves hers.

THE COMFORTER

MIKE ALLEN

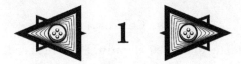

1

"**D**o you believe in Jesus?"

The rhythm of high-heeled shoes striking pavement comes to a stop.

The morning sun peers down the length of the street from its eastern end, dressing city blocks in long shadows, painting an optimistic glow across the plate glass of first floor windows. A crisp spring morning, the first without rain since the turn of the season, catches restaurants and shops still asleep, the staff that inhabits them either not yet arrived or at most milling about inside, OPEN signs unlit.

In this block, a bus depot dominates one side of the street. The other side is dominated by a not-quite mirror image, a three-story building with mock Doric columns on its facade and gargoyles along its roof that takes up far more space than the boutiques at its base seem to warrant. A man sits on the sidewalk with his back against the outer wall of the bus depot, one leg stretched out to block the progress of a slender, dark-haired woman in skinny jeans and a halter top.

"You do, doncha, baby? You believe in Him," the man says. "Can I ask you another question?" The man springs to his feet. "You got change? I'm so hungry. Help me out, baby."

The woman steps to the side. The man sidesteps too, stays in her way. He's just a little taller, much wider through the shoulders and belly, his bare arms wiry, furred with gray hair. He stretches those arms out to either side like he'll grab her up tight if she doesn't pay.

"Where you think you're going? I said I'm hungry . . . Yeah, that's right. I knew you'd do the right thing."

Tapering, graceful fingers tipped with perfectly manicured nails dig inside a tiny pouch. It doesn't have a clasp like a typical change purse. It's handmade, sealed with string threaded through cloth.

Fingers pinch tiny objects from the small pouch, which disappears. She drops what she's clutching into the cupped palm of her other hand. Colorful and reflective, they're the wrong size for coins, though they glint in the sunlight.

The woman's face twitches, her temple bulging, stretched by something underneath the skin. Leaning in close to eye her every move, the man flinches. "What was that?"

She doesn't acknowledge his question. His stare ends with a shake of the head, like he's snapping out of a daydream. She holds out her cupped hand, full of glittering trinkets that could be beads or buttons.

"What in hell is this?" He grabs her hand with both of his, peeling her fingers open. Nothing spills to the ground.

He opens his mouth. The sound he makes is not a word. A manicured hand lifts to his face. His eyes bulge. His mouth opens wider. Her fingers slide in, then her whole hand, up to the delicate wrist. Her wrist bends. Her arm continues to push down his throat, his jaw bending and folding inward as if molded from rubber.

A minute later, the man lowers to the sidewalk, places his back against the wall. The woman he waylaid has vanished.

He speaks to no one else for the rest of the day. Convoys of buses roll in and roll out of the depot bay, the advertisements that gird their flanks blocking his view every half an hour as he studies the customers who visit the shops across the street. The businesses burrowed into that neoclassical behemoth have names that ring a little too clever by half: Downhome Rave. A Whiff of Elegance. Gypsy Flair. Lights come on inside each boutique as the sun squints from the street's western end.

After the sun has set and the store lights have dimmed, a woman stands up from the place where she's been sitting on the sidewalk, brushes off a halter top and skinny jeans with perfectly manicured hands. She crosses the street to peer in through the front window of Gypsy Flair, a boutique selling the kind of clothes a woman with bohemian tastes and a wealthy husband might buy.

She is outside looking in, and then she is inside, exploring in the dark, and a few minutes later she is outside again, heels clicking as she walks away. At no point did she open a door, jimmy a lock, or break a pane of glass.

2

M addy unfolds the note.

She usually finds them stuck to the underside of her desk. She hasn't given much thought to how they adhere there, though when they come free she's never noticed glue or anything else that would make the odd-textured paper sticky. The precise little squares feel like suede, and the words at first glance look like they're stitched on in black thread, though on closer inspection the effect is more that of a tattoo. Maddy hasn't figured out how the optical illusion works.

This new one reads, in crude block letters:

how you and me are kin
my mom stole your mom's skin

She glances at the teacher, whose eyes are locked on his laptop screen. He is scowling, his goatee and shaggy dark hair giving him the look of a deeply offended beatnik, but that's just Mr. Newman's normal expression. He's a man with resting bitch face.

Her desk is strategically positioned, back corner nearest to the door. She quick-scans the rest of the class. Most are pondering the algebra questions displayed on their tablets with varying degrees of absorption or frustration. None are focused on her. She quick-grabs her bright pink backpack, stuffs this newest note into the outer pouch where she's stowed all the others.

She started getting them the day they came back from Christmas break. One came loose from the underside of the desk as she doodled in her algebra textbook, fluttered down to alight like a leaf on her bare leg. It read

found you

on one side and

i know where your parents are

on the other.

Others followed, not every day but sometimes several days in a row, always and only in this classroom, under this desk.

you should be me and i should be you
my mother will stitch us together
i like how you draw skulls draw one on the desk

With a fingertip Maddy traces the still-smudged outlines of the skull she sketched in pencil, someone else's attempt to erase it not quite finishing the job.

She hasn't figured out who is leaving the notes. Her class with Mr. Newman is second period, a group of supposedly-smart eighth graders. First period is Mr. Newman's free period. The third period class is a smaller group of advanced-placement seventh graders. She's tried hanging out late to spy, but so far as she can tell, no one sits in her desk. The little teacher's pets all cluster in the front. Later periods, she can't make it across the building in time to have a peek without being late for classes.

Whoever is making these, they know she shouldn't exist. She wants to meet them, and ask why she's alive.

3

Your mother tested you, and you failed.

You push with all your might in all directions. The box your mother has sealed you inside is the size of a large suitcase. You cannot force it open, though you are stronger than a platoon of Marines. You howl and howl with as many mouths. Like your many arms, your howls stay inside the box.

It's not your first time trapped in the box. Its walls are transparent. Your many eyes take in all the familiar sights. Above you loom the struts that support the box spring of your mother's king size bed. Below you is a carpet splotched with dark brown stains. Beside you a centipede crawls, the vibrations of your struggles causing its undulating legs to quicken their pace.

You were thinking about something else when she came into your room. It's not the first time she's caught you off guard. She demands you remain alert in all directions, outward and inward, as she has learned to be. But the last time she punished you this harshly was many months ago.

You have to understand that our kind can be hurt, she has said. *You have to understand we have weaknesses. Remember what your father used to say to you? Stay alert, stay alive.*

Your father suffered a fate worse than death at the hands of your mother. She laughs when she talks about it. She loves to talk about it. You learned to laugh with her. Any other reaction, she might coil around you like a snake made of sheets and stuff you in the box. But she hasn't talked about your father in months.

You did notice something new, though, a glitch in the lovely mask she puts so much effort into maintaining. She and you were playacting yet another family dinner, when you noticed how her face, her neck, the tawny skin across her collarbones sagged loose like wet paper. *What's wrong, mom?*

Nothing! she snapped as her skin contracted to its proper texture.

Your mother did something to fortify the box, to enchant it. There are symbols scratched into the transparent surface, you are seeing them up close and in reverse. You have no idea what they mean or how she learned them.

There is something else you have done, something that might have sparked her fury, but she doesn't know about it. She can't.

You don't know how many hours have passed. You are no longer focused on these what-ifs in any rational way. They loop through your mind as you howl.

You should not have panicked. What little air was sealed in with you escaped into the beneath. The mouths you summon gasp, the lungs bound to them burn with ever sharper starbursts of suffocation. Every second is a new death, your existence relentless agony.

You steal as much strength from those beneath as your agony-addled will allows. You howl and howl.

Whatever your mother's ulterior motives might have been, this much you know is true: you were thinking about something other than your surroundings when she came into your room.

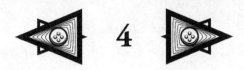

4

"**I**t'll make you a believer again, son," Hairston says. "But it won't give you nothin' to write about."

"Given all the hints you're dropping, I don't see how that could be true." When Hairston called yesterday, Aaron had suggested they meet at a coffee shop in downtown Grandy Springs, but Hairston insisted on a Shoney's at the outskirts of the town. Refused the buffet.

In front of Hairston, a black coffee steams. When it arrived, he inhaled deep. "Reminds me of the quiet mornings in the field." He still hasn't sipped from it. "Wasn't too many of those."

Hairston fought in the Korean War. The man's in his eighties, but he looks even older, the creases on his dark-skinned face quick to crumple into a mask of rage at the slightest flash of irritation, framed by his lion's mane of curly white hair. And yet his body hasn't withered. His wide shoulders and thick forearms suggest impressive muscle mass.

Aaron has delved deeper and deeper into Hairtson's story in the downtime between freelance assignments for the weekly papers. Those cowards wouldn't touch the kind of profile Aaron wants to write, but maybe he can sell it somewhere bigger. Aaron's not sure he has a book in him, but he is certain there *is* potential for a book here, an amazing one.

So far as Aaron can determine, Hairston has no permanent home. But he has a phone number that works, though its prefix matches none of those used by local carriers.

Everything about Hairston comes across as preternatural. The first time Aaron met him, sat down beside him on the bench in Spring Park, Hairston spoke before he had a chance to introduce himself. "You wanna know happened to your father? The Boneyard took him."

Aaron had heard that kind of claptrap before, crazy stories about the supposedly haunted courtyard in downtown Grandy Springs and his father's rumored obsession with it. Quick on his feet, he had decided the best way to keep Hairston talking was to play along . "What can you tell me about the Boneyard?" More claptrap had followed, a tall tale about abandoned tunnels and faceless monsters like living shadows, but Aaron got his foot in the door, and Hairston had later let him conduct multiple interviews, even write a piece for the *Owlswick Messenger*.

Aaron would never have been worth a damn as a reporter if he couldn't sweet-talk the most reluctant of sources into opening up to him. But Hairston could still, at times, be difficult. Like right now. Pondering his next verbal move, Aaron scratches at one of the scars on his cheeks. They itch at the most inopportune moments.

Unprompted, Hairston starts. "Maybe it's better that you don't remember how you got those scars."

"I *do*," Aaron protests. "We've talked about this. You told me yourself, for god's sake. I went caving and had a bad fall. I'm glad you knew where I was."

Hairston slaps the table. "Ha!" Others in the restaurant wing turn toward the noise, immediately look away.

"This isn't what you wanted to talk about, is it?" Aaron hopes he can defuse the old man. A loudly, forcefully enunciated rant about faceless shadow monsters and occult murders might well get the police called on them, and the Owlswick County Sheriff's Office isn't fond of Aaron or his subject. Hairston doesn't have an arrest record, though, astonishing given how corrupt this town consistently proves to be.

Hairston's stare drives a spike between Aaron's eyes. He fights to stay placid, and tries changing the subject. "This trip you told me about, to Hillcrest. When do you want to go?"

"Not yet," Hairston says, and at least he's quieter. "When the right time comes to me you're not going to get much warning. You sure you're okay with taking me there?"

"Absolutely, but I'd love to know when—"

"When I call you is when."

"It's just, I may need to give some sort of notice—"

"Your kind's expert at making excuses. Don't think there'll be anything to worry about there." A ferocious scowl twists Hairston's mouth, crumples his brow. "There'll be things to worry about where we're going. What's coming to Hillcrest, it's dangerous. Not for me, for *you*. Be sure to mind me while we're there. Don't need a second Boneyard." His scowl deepens.

Not for the first time, Aaron wonders why he seeks out Hairston's company so often. Though he owes the man his life. He remembers nothing about the fall that scarred his face, but Hairston missed him enough to alert rescuers.

These off-the-chain rants, too, they're just as import to this profile as the details of Hairston's military service and the relatives he left behind, the matter he discusses least of all. Aaron's grateful he has his recorder on. "I can tell this is important," he says. "I'll get you there, whatever it takes, I promise."

Hairston shocks him by putting a feverishly-warm hand over his. "You're a good man, like your father was," Hairston says. "It wasn't right, what happened to him."

Aaron's heart rate spikes hearing Hairston describe Kyle Friedrich as a good man. Throughout his childhood and adolescence, the adults he interacted with in Grandy Springs said otherwise, his mother most of all. He needs to change the subject before he reacts in a way that messes up the interview.

He jumps, despite himself, to the story Hairston keeps telling about what happened to his father. "You think there are . . . shadows there? In Hillcrest? Like the things people used to claim they saw here, in the Boneyard?"

"I don't know its full nature. Just that there's a disease and it's gonna spread," Hairston says, and finally brings his coffee to his lips, swallows. "Unless I practice a little field surgery. The world don't need another Grandy Springs."

"Field surgery? You were a medic in the war?" Aaron asks.

Hairston grins big. "I surgically inserted a few bullets."

5

A squat woman with a wide, bulging forehead sits on a folding chair in a cavernous room otherwise empty of furniture. Bare wires hang through holes in the ceiling. Crumbling drywall reveals cinderblock. Light leaks through and around the dry-rotted boards that block the high windows. Dust and mildew bathe the air.

Three people stand before her. Two are terrified. The third holds an AB-10 with its barrel aimed toward the concrete floor.

An oblong wooden box lies between the woman and her audience. It's smaller than a coffin, narrower than a steamer trunk. Carvings on its lid and sides depict densely overlapping human figures moving among formations akin to palm trees. Round objects hang in the trees and cluster under the arms of the figures. Some of those round objects have crude faces.

Behind the seated woman, a doorway with the door removed stands open in a corner, the space beyond absolute black.

The seated woman's voice is low and whisper-soft, with a pronounced Old South twang. "Y'all don't look like you're starving. Dress nice too. Why would you want to break into a dump like this? Plenty of high-class shops to plunder on the first floor if you got a hankering to steal."

The girl tries to talk first. She's tall and pretty with her straight blonde hair. "We didn't know—"

"Josey be quiet," the boy hisses. He's much older than she is, likely the mastermind of the caper.

"My lord, you college boys are the worst," the seated woman says. "Young lady, pray continue."

"We heard there was an old theater up here," Josey blurts. "We thought it was abandoned."

"It is," the woman says.

"This was all my idea," the boy says, inching forward. He's as tall as Josey and broader at the shoulders, his hair close-cropped with a fashionable curl above his brow, dressed in jeans and a black windbreaker. "I'm into urban exploring. I heard about—"

"I did not say I wanted to hear from you." The seated woman nods at her enforcer. "Here's what talking out of turn gets you."

Short, wiry, square face hard as cement, the man with the AB-10 punches Josey in the small of the back with all his might. She shrieks and crumples.

"Hey," the boy says, real soft.

The enforcer kicks the wailing girl in the ribs.

"Look what you did to her," the woman says. "Will you wait your turn now?"

The boy stares at the floor and says nothing.

The big chamber echoes with Josey's sobs. "I go by Maude," the woman says. "I have some knowledge of the history of this lost theater, which is where we are, if you haven't deduced that already. There used to be a stage, right where I'm sitting. To my left"– she points – "a piano in the wings." She points up. "They took the curtain and backdrops out long ago, but back then there was the fly tower up yonder. They had opera singers come here to sing and even some big band players. Showed moving pictures, too. At first they didn't let any coloreds in. But they needed that extra money before long, so they let 'em onto the balcony." She points to the opposite end of the chamber, where no balcony hangs, though sloppily plastered holes in the walls and ceiling, hint at what might have been. "The place still went broke. Shut down fifty years ago, and many owners since who weren't worth a damn passed this building one to the other. They gutted everything in here for its wood but never fixed it up. They even pried up the fancy old floorboards. It's a joke that the landlord got this building on the historical lists, bless his heart. The shops downstairs leave these floors alone because right now the building's grandfathered and they don't want the building inspector nosing around. Lord knows what they might have to spend to bring the building up to code if that happens. You ready to tell me more, Josey?"

During Maude's lecture, Josey gradually grows quiet. She cringes at the sound of her name.

"Urban explorers." Maude laughs and leans forward. "Why are you really up here? What brought you through that fire escape door?"

Josey looks at the boy, who keeps staring at the floor.

"He wanted to get you alone up here, away from prying eyes, no chance of getting caught, am I right? That's what boys always want, isn't it?"

The boy swallows.

"How old are you, Josey?"

She sniffs. "Fifteen." The boy clenches his jaw.

"Now how old is he?"

"Don't tell—" the boy starts. The enforcer takes a step, his boot landing a hair from Josey's outstretched fingers. She shrieks and folds her hands to her chest, curls up fetal. He rears back for another kick.

"It's okay, Bruno, I think he gets it." Maude speaks quietly, but somehow her man hears over Josey's panicked gasps of *no no no no*.

The boy, having made no move to intervene, keeps staring at the floor.

Maude speaks louder. "How old his he?"

"Tw-tw-twenty"

Maude's eyes narrow. "Only twenty? Is that the truth? Looks old enough to buy liquor, to me."

"Yes. No. Yes. His birthday is next week."

"Lordy, always the same in this sad little town. Grown man can't impress a lady his own age. What's his name, child?"

Josey's eyes squeeze shut. "Andrew."

"How long have you two been going steady?"

"Tw-two years."

"How long have you been lovers?"

A sharp intake of breath from Andrew. Bruno the enforcer raises a boot, and the boy clams up, staring a hole in that floor.

Josey never opens her eyes. "Two years." She sobs as she speaks.

"What school do you attend, Josey?"

"Willow Spring." Josey's sniffles punctuate the silence that ensues.

Maude asks, "Is that the one?"

Bruno nods. "The scent is there."

"You're certain."

Bruno nods again, with vigor.

"Well, ain't that something. Andrew, you can go." Maude's smile could be that of a grandmother favoring a beloved grandchild.

The boy turns without another word and crosses to the exit at the further end of the derelict theater, the one Bruno marched them through after he surprised them in the hall beyond the fire escape. Necking against the wall, they never saw him coming.

"Andrew don't leave me here." Josey's wail is no louder than a whisper.

"Don't worry, Andrew, she'll be fine," Maude calls. "Just wait outside, she'll be out soon." As the boy disappears she adds, "I don't think he's even gonna wait for you, darling."

"Yes he will. He'll call the police." A little louder: "You have to let me go."

"Bless your heart, no he won't. He doesn't want anybody to know what you two were doing here. He doesn't want to get caught."

Josey starts to cry. Maude ignores her. "Lordy, I miss the days when I didn't have to talk. All this yapping, it's exhausting. I'm a faithful servant, though. I always do what needs to be done and that's why I've been granted this gift."

Josey says nothing, but when she looks up, Maude reads the question in her eyes. "You, honey. You're the gift."

A sniffle. "Wh-what?"

"The fates favor my kind, when we're careful. They brought me here, where I could hide my treasures in the middle of a mother lode of human misery, and if I hadn't been right here in this pace, they could never have delivered you. Your boyfriend doesn't know it, but he's already fulfilled his life's sole purpose." Maude stands. She's not much taller than when she was sitting. Her thick ankles overflow her shoes. "Come on now, Josey. Get up."

Bruno keeps the AB-10 trained on Josey's spine. Tears have smeared mascara down her cheeks.

Josey's future drops away before her mind's eye, a yawning abyss. She thinks of the ocean cruises her parents have taken her on during the summers, the night views from the promenade deck into dark waters that fuse with clouded skies.

Standing at the rail, she's wondered more than once what it would be like to jump, whether she would simply fly forever, no boundary to stop her, a thought that both scared and thrilled her.

Now there's only fear.

"Lift the lid, please, Josey. It's not heavy."

Anticipating that it *will* be heavy, Josey lifts too hard and the lid flips away from her fingers, clatters loud on the plywood flooring. A substance glitters multi-hued in the very bottom of the box.

"Step inside," Maude says.

"I don't want to."

"It won't hurt you. Get in."

A noise from Bruno makes Josey edge closer.

"See the pretty buttons?" Maude says. "I'll let you keep a few. Just get this over with."

The objects do look like buttons, cast in many colors and shapes. Gingerly, Josey steps into the box. The buttons rustle around her ankles, though none crunch beneath her shoes. Once she's planted both feet, she shrieks. She sinks as if mired in quicksand.

Bruno set his gun down gently and steps in the box with her. He too, sinks into the bottom. He grabs Josey by the shoulders and shoves her down. She scrabbles at his arms, ripping his skin loose with her nails. No blood wells from the scrapes.

Silent, Bruno forces her all the way to the bottom of the bin. Her head disappears. Her scream fades as if falling into void. Her arms slide from his.

He lifts up something about the size and shape of a jacket and starts to unbutton it. Its blonde hood and pale sleeves flop. Once the gap spreads wide enough, Bruno brings it to his face, vanishes inside head-first.

 **6**

"Hey, Maddy, wanna play?"

That's how Lakesha greets Maddy as she shuts Mama Rochelle's front door and wipes her shoes on the mat before popping them off. No muddy shoes in the house, that's one of Rochelle's many rules, and Maddy's shoes aren't muddy but Rochelle would still tell her to leave them at the door.

Maddy had hoped she could sneak down to her room unnoticed—at least for now it's her room alone. No such luck. She knows better than to betray any disappointment, if she upsets any of the younger girls Mama Rochelle will hear about it and come knocking. She calls, "Whatcha playin' squirt?"

"Don't call me squirt," Lakesha says.

"Okay, squirrel, whatcha playin'?"

Lakesha is a foster kid like Maddy, but six years younger. Mama Rochelle's house is a split level where the front door opens onto the landing of the central staircase, and Lakesha hovers at the top of the stairs, her tiny silhouette framed by the light coming out the kitchen door. She's holding an electronic game player that's bright yellow with purple handles. "Mindeecraft," she says.

"Not sure you're saying that right," Maddy mutters with a smile.

"In the princess castle. You can play the good princess again." Lakesha loves to play the wicked witch, and Maddy's happy to let her. Maddy has a device just like Lakesha's in her room downstairs. Rochelle gives them to all her kids. They can play each other in multiplayer games without having to hook up with cords. There's something about that concept, an invisible connection binding her to others, that makes Maddy's heart pound and shudder when she lets herself dwell on it too long. She's good at not dwelling on it. It's stupid that it scares her.

"I can't, little squirrel, I got too much homework." This is a lie, which makes Lakesha's moan of disappointment like the achy wiggle of a loose tooth, but she sticks to her guns, because right now her need to be alone outweighs Lakesha's need for a big sister.

Not alone as in by herself. Alone with the notes from her desk. She got a new one today, after a whole week of silence.

"Where's everybody else, can you get some of them to play you?"

"Ashley's in her room. Prixie says she doesn't want to, she told me to leave her alone." That last bit delivered matter-of-factly.

Prixie's a year older than Lakesha, and Maddy doesn't blame her a bit, Lakesha can be pretty relentless. Ashley is eleven, just two years younger than Maddy, in her final year of elementary. She, like Maddy, has a room downstairs, and she stays in it. Rochelle always has to argue her out for meals, and at the table she keeps her eyes downcast, sullen beneath long brown bangs. Maddy's not sure how long Ashley will last, though Rochelle is working on her, like she worked on Maddy.

"Sorry, squirrel, I really can't." She hops downstairs before Lakesha can keep arguing, so she can get to her room at the end of the hall and lock it. She's really lucky she doesn't have to share it with Ashley. Rochelle has two more kids that Maddy likes to call "the twins," even though they aren't, because they have funny, rhyming names, Georgia and Porsche, a state and a car—but they're in daycare right now, too young to fend for themselves while Rochelle finishes her early morning to late afternoon shift at Peachtree Assisted Living. (Rochelle gets mad if Maddy slips and calls it a nursing home.)

She really should wait to get the notes out. She ought to wait until everyone is asleep. If Rochelle gets back from work and finds Maddy's door locked she might get worried and unlock it to see what Maddy is doing. She doesn't do that as often as she used to, thank God, but Maddy can't be too careful. Rochelle gets especially worried about Maddy, even more than Ashley, not because Maddy acts out, but because Maddy was found in a place where something terrible happened that no one understands and that she can't remember, the abandoned suburban cul-de-sac that the folks in Hillcrest call the Vanished Neighborhood.

She tried to have a heart-to-heart with Maddy about it only once, about three months after social services placed her in the house. They were sitting in plastic-webbed lawn chairs on the back deck, the sun breathing warmth against them, Maddy fighting not to squirm as the walls she maintained against the memories thinned. In the days after the police found her, even sunlight triggered alien sensations, like the heat was something solid, encasing her in a trap.

A crease had furrowed the middle of Rochelle's broad brown forehead. She'd noticed Maddy's fidgets. Her voice invited relaxation like a cozy, cool pillow. "I know you're sick of people asking you about this, so I'm not going to ask you anything. But if you ever want to talk about what happened, you can talk to me, anytime. That's all I want to make sure you know."

Maddy had already started to shake her head. "I can't. I don't remember anything."

"I know, honey," Rochelle said, but Maddy had shook her head harder.

"Honey, honey, it's okay. I didn't mean to upset you. I just wanted you to know."

Maddy holds nothing against Rochelle. Her foster mother is homemade rhubarb pie with too much sugar, which is just the right amount. She's fried chicken and microwaved pizza and quiche with spinach and bacon, a thing Maddy would never have believed she would love to eat. She's books full of amazing stories, tales of kids learning magic and having adventures that made them into heroes.

Maddy's truth about the Vanished Neighborhood skews sideways. She does remember things but she doesn't know how to put them into words. They don't make sense in any of the ways she learned to make sense of things in school.

The scene of her abduction, chatting with her mom in the front seat of the car, disrupted in a blur that whirls and strikes like a cobra. After that, more alien sensations: a burning not made of fire, a compression like she was squeezed under a thousand mattresses, every inch of her drummed upon by a pulse like the one she sometimes felt against her pillowcase when she tried to sleep, but nonstop and magnified to hammer every inch of her skin and all the tissue underneath. Vibrations as if thousands of people screamed on the other side of a window, a window she was pressed against but couldn't see through, and she was one of the people screaming, and just like she couldn't see the others, no one could see her.

Release and moonlight. A woman walking away from her, slender and dark-haired, dark-eyed. A woman who was and wasn't her mother. A woman who was stealing her mother away.

The notes offer a link to that mystery woman, a way to play a game with her. Maddy believes this even though she acknowledges the idea makes no sense. Even stranger, she takes a comfort from this irrational certainty, when her smarts tell her she should react in the exact opposite way. She shouldn't want this so badly. She shouldn't want it at all.

She locks her door and jumps with a squawk as Lakesha knocks. "Hey, Maddy! C'mon, Maddy, let me in. I'll be quiet."

"We'll play later, I promise. I gotta do homework now, I'm serious."

For all she knows, Lakesha stands sulking outside the door for the next hour. She doesn't wait to see. She unzips the pocket in her backpack that holds the notes and dumps them onto her unmade bed. They flutter out like dead leaves. The pattern they make as they alight is random, ordinary. She anticipated something more, she doesn't know why, but she's disappointed.

7

She's doing what you asked her to do.

She's tainted the same way you are, but somehow her impression in the aether is different. You don't even try to fathom it, you understand so little about yourself in the first place.

You're holed up in what would be your bedroom, were you a normal boy, though the room contains no bed, no dresser, nothing taped to the walls, no desk, a few clothes hanging in the closet that you never wear. Your mother is not home, you're on the alert and paying attention, the thrumming subliminal static that gives away her presence is far off, somewhere else in the city. In your uppermost layers you're grateful she's not near, she might seal you in the box and sink it in the reservoir if she discovers what you're up to. You'd join your father, lost somewhere deep underwater, unable to breathe, unable to die.

So far, the experiment is working. Your note to Maddy read *put all the notes together and they'll speak a new message*, bold of you because you're not at all certain this will pan out.

Maddy's presence thrums on a different frequency, without your mother's acidic burn or needle-sharp prickliness, and fainter. For months you weren't sure who the traces of otherness emanated from. If it weren't for random clumsiness, stupidly bumping into her in the hall at school while focused on someone else, the pain that seared through your layers as you recoiled, you still wouldn't be sure it was her. If she registered what you were in turn, she didn't betray any sign, hurried on oblivious.

Her presence impinges on your consciousness, a combination of unnatural warmth, the nerve-jangling pinch of a banged elbow, a shuddering of teeth pressing on aluminum foil. The surface of every note you left her absorbs her gaze and longs to squirm. You clasp the hands you've chosen, close the eyes you've chosen, will discomfort to convert to motion.

The note in Maddy's hand, the new one, reads *put all the notes together and they'll speak a new message.*

But what does that even mean? Are these squares of paper going to start crawling toward one another, hunching and stretching like worms? Are they going to bounce up and spell out words in semaphore? She lets out a single soft chuckle, annoyed, ashamed, ready to go see if Lakesha still wants to play.

One square flutters, then another. She blinks and all of them are twitching like click beetles trapped on their backs. She blinks and they have swarmed on top of each other, dry crinkled slugs crawling over one another like ants in an exposed burrow. They twist into a single mass, stretching toward the ceiling, a column of living butcher paper as tall as Maddy's arm and half as wide, fluttering and flapping, the creases up and down its form expanding at random to stretch membranes veined with words, except the letters don't resemble any alphabet she knows. Over and over the visitation tries to spell something to her, and she can almost read it, she thinks, but again and again the meaning evades her. She extends a hand and the column shrinks away—

A knock on the door practically hurls her out of her skin. "Maddy! Dinner!" It's Rochelle.

How long was she standing there gawping? The notes are gone from atop her disheveled blankets. She gasps, panics, dives to the floor.

Her backpack leans against her desk, the outer pouch zipped shut. She doesn't remember doing that. She opens the pouch to find all the notes inside as if she never emptied it out in the first place.

"Maddy, you in there?" her foster mom calls.

"I'll be right out." Relief brightens her voice.

Before she leaves, a heap of crumpled pink draws her eye back to the bed. The commotion has exposed the threadbare comforter tucked in between bedspread and sheet, the yellow and green daffodil pattern that decorates it faded to variations in gray. The comforter her mother used to tuck her under in the days before the Vanished Neighborhood. She has not thought of it in this way, as a relic of her previous life, as a leftover from her lost parent, in many, many months, and can't explain why this hits her so hard now.

At dinner, at least at the start, she's as silent and sullen as Ashley, until Rochelle's gentle razzing dislodges a smile and reels it to the surface.

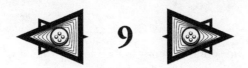

As far as Andrew is concerned, Josey's brush with death worked wonders for their relationship.

Pre-urban exploring incident, getting a blowjob out of her required Geneva Convention-level negotiating, and she'd complain about how gross it was for hours afterward. Post-incident, she volunteers without even having to be asked. If Andrew was honest with himself, he'd admit that took a lot of the fun out of it, because he got off on degrading her and that doesn't work if she's willing—but Andrew is never honest with himself.

No such self-reflection troubles him this minute. What Josey has chosen to do is so brazen it has his pulse pumping even before her hands pry his stiffening cock out from his jeans. The Chevy Tahoe his parents bought for him idles at the crest of the Petraseks' sleep climb of a driveway, in plain view of all the bright-lit windows at the front of the palatial house. If Josey's mom parts the curtains of her bedroom window—any window, really—she'll have a clear view into the SUV, where her underage daughter's unmistakable blonde perm bobs above the crotch of her just-turned-twenty-one boyfriend. She told him to sit still for his birthday present, and when he answered "Dipshit, my birthday was yesterday" she smiled back, "Part two!"

His mouth hangs open. His glazed eyes return to focus as his lips ape a grin, imagining Josey's mom watching, imaging her hand sliding down her designer slacks. The Petraseks came from old money, though that money was in the hands of a widow who'd first married a much older man, then remarried to a younger one. Josey's stepdad isn't that far from Andrew in age. Andrew's folks are rich too, new money rich, pastel McMansion in a gated county neighborhood rich. He can do what he wants to Josey short of getting her pregnant and her parents aren't going to do shit.

How is Josey doing this? When did she learn? It's like her mouth is full of tongues, pressing and lapping from every angle. He fights not to scream, it feels so good.

His orgasm is building in earnest when a pins-and-needles sensation skitters up his belly and down both legs. His cock goes numb.

She springs up. "Love you, sweetheart," she says, giving him a peck on the cheek. "Happy birthday, part two." Her voice rings the wrong timber, deep and gruff. Her kiss burns like a blowtorch. The pins and needles below flair to points of fire.

"God damn," he yells, tears streaming, but the passenger side door has already slammed behind her.

He's completely numb below the waist. The sensation of open flame searing his face dissipates fast as it struck.

"Hey," he says, meaning to shout but no louder than a whisper. "What did you do, Josey?" Even though she's already walked to the front door, an odd break in routine as before they've always entered through the mammoth garage. He looks at the figure illuminated by the outdoor lights and it's not even Josey, it's her mom, white-platinum haired and from this distance almost as pretty as her daughter. She blows him a kiss, and at that moment he doesn't even have the wits to wonder why. He can't feel his legs. And something else is wrong.

One of his hands tentatively slides toward his groin. What his fingers find— or really, what they don't find—makes him scrabble for the Tahoe's overhead light. He fights not to scream.

When agony erupts like his crotch is bursting open, like something huge and multi-limbed is burrowing out from the inside, he loses that fight.

A second locus of pain bites into the base of his brain, and he's turning the ignition, starting the Tahoe, though what he wants to do is run to the door and either scream for help or hammer Josey in the face for what she did to him. Though his nerve endings end at the phantom flesh-ripping hooks in his groin, his legs work the pedals, his hands turn the steering wheel of their own accord. He blubbers at the wheel as something else drives the Tahoe, drives his body.

Back at his own house, he does unspeakable things to his mother, his father, his little brother. He's a passenger, unable to control the monstrous forms his body takes.

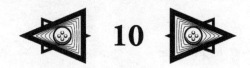

10

T he place mats, silverware, china artfully arranged on the dining table constitute a farce, as neither of you possess human appetites, yet your mother
insists. You sit across from her, you say the grace she taught you. No food dirties
the plates.

You live in a small, barren house in one of the oldest, most run-down Hillcrest neighborhoods. With so many of its rooms empty of furniture, a visitor
who walked through without encountering the inhabitants might well assume
no one lived here. The elderly man listed as the owner in city records belongs to
your mother now.

She says, "Tell me about your day, Davey."

"I spied," you say.

She regards you with the same dark eyes she had before she joined with
a monster. She's a striking woman, with her dark hair in a bob and full lips
prone to wry smiles. She looks dressed to the nines, made up for a night on
the town. It means nothing, with a thought she can make herself look however she wants.

You lack that range of flex. When you want to look like Davey, when she
demands that of you, you always end up wearing the same clothes, unless you
change, physically remove the new outfit and put one on.

Her mastery of her state borders on godlike. And yet, of late, something's
been wrong with her.

"Which face did you use and what did you see?" she asks, and when she
speaks her voice splits, a old man's voice bleeding into hers, and her mouth
splits too, fissuring at a diagonal that slashes through her lips. The moment she
stops talking the bizarre wound is gone. You know better now than to remark
upon it.

"Her name is Carolyn. She's a janitor. She lives alone. Her house is full of
dead cats. There were a few left alive, I locked them out of the house, I hope
they find someplace else to go."

You mother smirks. "I approve."

"At school hardly anyone pays her any mind. She can get in anywhere."

Your mother steeples her fingers. You know what she wants to hear, you
have a morsel ready to serve. "I took a mop bucket into the boy's locker room
and found a place to hide. There was a boy alone in there with a coach while the
teams were out practicing. There's an office in the locker room, he fucked the
boy in there."

"What did you do?"

"Watched. Remembered. Tasted the traces after they were gone, so I know
what they mean if I find them anywhere else."

"No one saw you, in any form?"

"No one."

You're not lying, but sampling the shreds of psychic aura left after that violation was an afterthought, something you nearly forgot to follow through on in your distracted state, something you needed to share with your mother to keep you out of the box under her bed. You can't afford to lose days on end again.

You watched Maddy all day, from the moment she stepped off her bus to the moment she climbed back on again. Your mother can't know that. She must never, ever, ever find out.

You watched Maddy search under her desk in Mr. Newman's room, and the sight warmed your topmost layers, but you didn't leave her a note. You don't know how to say what you want to say.

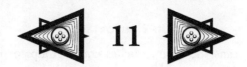

11

L unch period promises to be more of the same. Maddy reminds herself things could be worse. She hasn't been picked on in many months.

Becca's bookbag, printed deep blue with rainbow flower constellations, stands sentry in the chair across from Maddy, the rest of their corner table unoccupied. Becca's in the lunch line, her dark frizzy hair not quite contained in a pony tail that looks like it's about to slip loose, her short, slumped body further bulked in a heavy coat and sweater even though winter's well over. Maddy's not really excited to see her. They live in the same part of town, but aren't close. Becca talks compulsively about many things that Maddy really doesn't care about, but Maddy thinks that Becca knows this on some level and is just grateful not to have to eat lunch alone. It's not like Becca ever asks her what she thinks. She just talks. No harm no foul.

Becca's presence at her table helps to keep others away, and Maddy's fine with that.

When Josey pulls back the chair to Maddy's left and sits down, a lightning bolt might as well have burned a message in her lunch tray, the development is that unexpected.

Maddy's spine stiffens and her shoulders pinch together. This is prelude to a bullying, for certain. Josey's never been someone who makes a show of being a bully to impress her friends, not that Maddy knows about, but consider the odds: Josey's in ninth grade, just a couple months from graduating junior high, and Maddy's a pudgy eighth grade wallflower. Josey's tall and buxom for her age, blonde as a Viking, top class grades, a scion of old money, turns heads whatever she's wearing and carries herself like she's already high school royalty. Rumor among the distaff population is she snagged a boyfriend way older, proof in some quarters that she's already a goddess among aspiring women. Maddy thinks that's icky but she would never say it aloud because the backlash would be instant. Josey might not be a bully, but plenty of people would pick on an easy target for the chance to impress her.

"Why did you erase that skull you drew on our desk?" Josey says.

Now we're through the looking glass. Maddy has no words but "What?"

"That skull! Why'd you erase it? I thought it was ridiculously awesome."

Maddy can only stare until words practically volunteer of their own accord. "I didn't erase it." Her mind is racing. "Someone else did." She's spied on the other classes in that room and never seen Josey.

The note-maker had requested that drawing.

"So you must draw a bunch," Josey goes on. "Can I see?"

A cafeteria lady gives Becca's lunch card a swipe through the reader. Becca stuffs it back in her purse, picks up her tray laden with the latest unappetizing selection, turns and spots Josey sitting at their table. Becca's jaw drops.

Maddy quick-scans the room, catches entire groups of her fellow pupils quickly looking away, others not bothering to hide their stares.

"C'mon, show me," Josey says.

Does Josey know about the notes? Is she involved somehow? She can't imagine a more unlikely scenario, but a minute ago the notion of Josey taking an interest in her would have seemed as remote as the moon. Maddy's never seen Josey walk into Mr. Newman's classroom. But she's not there all hours of the day, is she?

Josey waves a hand in front of Maddy's face. "Hello? I'm serious. I just want a peek."

Becca walks up, her bug-eyed alarm a comical reflection of Maddy's own shock. *I hope I don't look like that*, Maddy thinks, and snaps out of her paralysis. She can hear Mama Rochelle's voice scolding, *Maybe there's more to Josey than you know.* "It's fine, sure," Maddy starts digging in her backpack. Becca sits down. Josey smiles at her, says, "Hey, Becca." A lunch period full of firsts.

Maddy has a black-and-white marbled cover composition book that she uses as a cheap sketch pad. It's about half full of doodles that she doesn't even show to Mama Rochelle. She knows what would happen if she did, she's not stupid.

Another voice in her mind hisses, *Don't trust Josey! Don't let her see!* She might laugh. She might squeal *Ew gross!* She might tell the principal that Maddy's disturbed. Maybe worse, she might love what's in those drawings.

Thinking about the notes left under her desk, Maddy teases the composition book out of her backpack.

Becca, taking her seat, sees the composition book come out and raises her eyebrows and bugs her eyes, which has the effect of turning her round, plump face into a clown mask. "I hope you've got a strong stomach," she says, though she's not looking at Josey. She's watching Maddy's hands as the cover folds open.

Becca had to beg for days before Maddy showed her those drawings, and once she saw them, she didn't like them at all. Becca doesn't quite understand the unpleasant tightening that clenches in her chest. Part of her really, really doesn't want to view those drawings again, part of her is contemplating how brainy, pretty, fashion-plate Josey gets to see Maddy's darkest secrets after asking only once.

Josey hunkers closer, eyes fever-bright as she scans the thick shadows made by ballpoint pen. "Amazeballs," she says. Becca mutters aloud, "Amazeballs? Who says that?" then remembers the risk she's taking and puts a hand over her mouth.

Josey doesn't react. She leans closer to Maddy. "May I?"

Josey touches the pages, spreads them flatter. Beneath her pink-painted nails, a furious doodle floods the paper to the edges. Faces stretch like taffy, distorted into squares, their corners tied together like handkerchiefs. Every mouth contorts in exaggerated grimace. Some eyeholes are filled in black, others contain huge and bloodshot orbs, little black veins forking like lightning strikes toward floating irises.

Page turn. A huge mouth takes up both the facing leaves of paper, the space between the upper and lower sets of teeth colored in by frenetic black scribbles, with blocky letters left white within the darkness. They spell out the words *mommy isn't that funny!?!*

Page turn. Figures that register as human only in the crudest sense—two arms, two legs, a head—are swirled into an epic spiral that funnels to a single point near the center, as if the viewer looks down into a whirlpool choked with human-shaped sheets.

"I've got an art project I'm trying to get done. It's due tomorrow and I'm just not happy with it," Josey says. "I was wondering if you could help me out."

"Um, wow, are you sure?" For the first time Maddy looks close at Josey's face. She's got everything Maddy doesn't: unblemished skin, a tiny nose, huge wide-set green eyes. Maybe there's more makeup on her cheeks than Maddy first realized, though of course it's expertly blended. A faint floral scent caresses the air between them, and there's another, stranger scent beneath, as if the crackle of a fireplace has been transmuted into candy. Maddy's nostrils flare and she lets a shudder slip before she catches herself. The underlying odor summons a vignette of her missing mother in her denim jacket, turning in the driver's seat, reaching toward her to buckle her in, wearily scolding *Hold still.*

Josey smiles ever so slightly in acknowledgment of the scrutiny, but on her face even the slight crinkle this brings to the corners of her eyes glows like a warm sunrise. "Can you come by my house tonight?"

Maddy's heart leaps, then sinks. "I don't have a ride." Mama Rochelle would never agree to this, she can't leave all the kids at home alone in the evening to give one a ride, she and Ashley had a big argument a couple months ago and Rochelle said that over and over again.

"Don't worry, my mom'll pick you up. All I have to do is tell her your address."

"That's—well—" Maddy starts, and doesn't know what to say next. *Is that what rich moms do,* she thinks, *chauffeur their little princesses wherever they want to go?* An ache accompanies the thought, as if it's imbued with longing rather than snark.

"I'm really grateful you're willing to help me, you're crazy-good at drawing."

A warmth spreads through her, touched off by the unexpected praise from someone so much further up in hierarchy, that heat precipitating as a blush that deepens as soon as she realizes she's blushing. She fidgets with her composition book, quickly flipping pages, creating a non sequitur montage of screaming faces and skulls interlocked in Escher fashion.

She steals a glance at Becca, searching for—guidance, sympathy, perhaps a reflection of her own astonishment, mutual amazement that this improbable thing is actually happening. Becca's mouth has shrunken in sullen disapproval and her eyes don't blink.

"I need to go. I should let you finish lunch," Josey says. "Just give me your address. And your cell number. My mom'll come by your house when she gets off work. She'll call first to let you know she's on the way. That ought to leave you time to do your own homework if you need it."

Becca finally speaks. "Why can't she just come straight home with you from school?" Maddy cringes inside, but at the same time, she recognizes it's a sensible question.

"I'm not going straight home. My boyfriend's picking me up." Becca's jaw drops, then snaps shut.

Josey actually gives Maddy her cell number and asks for Maddy's address again. "Text it to me." Maddy does.

"See you tonight," Josey says, and then she's gone.

Stone silence hangs between the girls in Josey's absence. Becca, instead of peppering Maddy with questions, wolfs down her lunch.

Across the cafeteria, Carolyn the janitor ties up a full trash bag and lifts it out of the can. She watches Maddy and Becca, her gaze veiled beneath crude-cut bangs.

12

C unetta settles in across the interview table from a jittery jerky strip of a frequent perp named Anton Jackson, whose street name is Hulk, hilarious because he might weigh one hundred and twenty pounds soaking wet. If he ate a four-course meal right before he got on the scale.

"Let's have the truth this time, Anton. What happened to your hand?"

"I *am* telling the truth." Hulk sounds like he's seconds from turning on the waterworks.

"What were you high on in that bar? Crystal?"

"Meth don't make me see shit," says Hulk. "Meth don't chop my fuckin' hand off without making me bleed a drop. Explain that if I'm makin' it up. Why the hell y'all arrest me anyway, I didn't do nuthin', I'm the victim here."

"Disturbing the peace," Cunetta says. "Public intoxication. Probation violation." Hulk goes sullen, lips quivering.

Cunetta has to admit, Hulk's wound or lack of one gives him the willies in an awful way. He transferred to Hillcrest PD five years ago after a decade in Grandy Springs, where some insane shit went down, stuff that he believed was real only because disbelieving could get you killed.

But he's not going to give Hulk a show of nerves.

"Listen, I'm being nice to you here. I'm just trying to make some sense out of what you're saying, so we can figure out whether or not we're gonna let you out. So I'm gonna repeat this story back to you and you tell me how you think it sounds. You spy this sweet pretty boy crying in the men's room at the Bloomer Bar, you offer to cheer him up with a handjob and he takes you up on it. You shove your hand down his shorts and he's smooth as a Ken doll. And then something grabs your hand, you say? And bites it off?"

Hulk's deeply seamed face folds in, from bug-eyed anger back to edge-of-waterworks. "Didn't bite it off. I don't know what it was. Like a bunch of needles pushin' in, but it didn't hurt the way big needles hurt. Then my hand went numb. And when I pulled my arm out my hand was just gone." For emphasis he again lifts the stump where his left hand used to be.

According to the report, Hulk had come out of the restroom shrieking like a scream queen. He didn't calm down when the police arrived. That's why he ended up in a holding cell.

"You don't believe me," Hulk sniffs, "then tell me what the fuck did this. Tell me, smart man."

Cunetta regards the stump of Hulk's wrist and can't explain what he sees. The skin wraps smooth over the knob of bone as if Hulk was born without a hand, but last time Cunetta crossed paths with him, he definitely possessed two, with skin shrunk taut and translucent around tendons and veins from a myriad of unhealthy habits but nonetheless whole and functional. Were further objective proof needed, the complete set of fingerprints on file provided it.

Cunetta maintains a bored expression, his revulsion kept subterranean. He's seen worse, he tells himself, back in Grandy Springs. Though the truth is, though he heard at least a dozen horror tales about the things that went on in the Boneyard, he never saw them himself. Except once.

Riding in the cruiser through the empty streets after 1 a.m., Cunetta heard the first of many stories from his senior partner about the monsters in the Boneyard and laughed out loud. *You are shitting me. How dumb do you think I look?*

All right, then, his partner said. *Whatever you do, don't get out of the car.*

Maybe his partner had planned it from the beginning. A few turns through downtown, and a block of vacant buildings rose on the right, and Cunetta had told himself those century-old buildings looked no different than any other wretched slum, that nothing about the glass shards in the shattered windows reminded him of teeth in a moldering skull, that the darkness behind them was just shadow, not something with thickness or the slow pulse of breath.

His partner stopped at the mouth of an alley too narrow to accommodate the cruiser. He kept the engine running. *The Boneyard's through there*, he said. *You ever go there, do it in daylight.* And he turned on the running lights so Cunetta could see the tall shadows standing in the alley, long-limbed, faceless, skeletal and glistening as if coated in oil, and Cunetta didn't need to be told twice that these creatures of living abyss had to be respected and avoided.

Whenever the Boneyard wanted something, no matter how vile, the cops didn't intervene.

He'd left those memories behind, a nightmare gladly forgotten. Hulk's inexplicable maiming, a subtler fragment from that nightmare land, brings it all slithering into the light, a black membrane glistening before his mind's eye.

Cunetta's usually quick with a sarcastic quip, but his voice quavers, a teeny hint of tectonic plates shifting, as he asks, "You been to a doctor?"

"I don't need a doctor. I need my damn hand back."

The laugh that escapes Cunetta is like a suspect on the run over open ground.

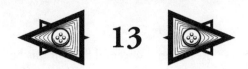
M aria draws appreciative glances as she strides across the market square. Some looks linger longer, focused on her hip-hugging skirt and its above-the-knee hemline. She maintains a wistful half-smile, meets no one's eyes directly.

She has to consciously maintain this skin, this shape, as she walks, with an effort the act has never before required. Her conscious admission of the problem swaddles a hard truth, one with sharp, serrated edges. For weeks, each venture she's made that required her to maintain a skin for an extended time has demanded ever-increasing levels of concentration to prevent a ravel.

Signals of worry bubble up from deep within her layers, from somewhere further down than her inverse-sephirothic awareness extends, down beneath all worlds where the Mystery dwells that allows her and others like her to subsist as mouths. Those dark signals drive her to walk into Gypsy Flair in broad daylight.

Across the street, a pair of rumpled, unshaven men lean against the wall beside the bus depot bay. One of them stares at her legs, not bothering to hide his admiration, grinning and nudging his grunge-mate. In the storefront window reflection, she can see how he fixates on her ass when she turns to pull open the door.

The hoop racks dangle blouses and dresses that combine a retro hippie sensibility with iterations of the little black dress. A pressure builds as Maria advances, the invisible evidence of the wards that block her from entering the empty floors above, even as the bin that once held her essence calls to her, pulls at her like a magnet. Somewhere in this store there's a chink in the armor, a crack she could squeeze through. This tantalizing sensation of weakness aches like a hard mote wedged between teeth, inaccessible by tongue or finger.

A woman who Maria recognizes from weeks of spying as the day manager stands behind the purchase counter, adjusting sparkly wares inside a glass case. Her name tag labels her Kristy. She's relatively young, in her thirties at most— or maybe a well-preserved forty. Brown hair back in a neat bun, heavy-set in a curvaceous way that would probably excite the men across the street, makeup pancaked on a little too heavy, still not quite hiding the dark circles under her eyes. If Maria had antennae they would straighten and lean in like dowsing rods in response to a whiff of addiction, something physical but not chemical.

"Hi there, welcome to Gypsy Flair," Kristy says, on script. "What can I help you with?"

Maria wants to unseam Kristy and turn her inside out for what she knows, but the rival hiding out in the space above might sense it. "I've got a strange question for you, if you don't mind."

Since the question likely won't be about merchandise, the fake smile falters a little. "Oh, I don't mind at all."

"There used to be a theater on the second floor of this building."

Kristy brightens. "Oh yes, the old Masonic Theater. This building's on the historic registry because of it."

"Do any of the shops store their inventory up there?"

Kristy's brows crease and eyes narrow in a combination of puzzlement and suspicion. Maria talks fast. "I mean, it's weird to me that you've got this historic landmark and yet it's not open to the public. I'm fascinated by local history and classic architecture and I'm wondering if there's a way to see this space."

Her smile hardening to a mask, Kristy shakes her head. "Unfortunately the cost to get it up to code so that people can go up there is just too much. I know it sounds awful—I'd like to think this city could do better, that the city council would invest or something—but the deal the building inspector made with our landlord was that so long as the upper floors stay sealed off they could lease the rest of the building commercially."

"Have you ever seen it? The theater, I mean."

Now Kristy laughs a little, the nervous titter transforming to a squeak as her eyes go wide and her lips curl back.

Maria calms herself and fixes her face, relying on the mental nature of human cattle to save the moment. Whatever sudden, gruesome transformation Kristy witnessed, she convinces herself it was a trick of the mind, her grimace subsiding back to fake smile.

"I'm serious. You're sure there's not a way up there from this store?"

Kristy laughs louder. "No. No, there isn't."

The presence, the pressure. Maria wants so badly to absorb whatever this stupid smiling mannequin might know, but she's too close to the enemy, too close. "I'm so disappointed," she says. As she turns away, her face ripples chin to forehead.

Outside, her admirers across the street have moved on.

Soon, a big dark-skinned man settles with his back against the wall, legs stretched to partially block the sidewalk. He stares into Gypsy Flair as a pair of women circle a rack and Kristy follows them, still smiling.

A man walking with crutches emerges from the bus depot, spies the squatter on the sidewalk. "Hey man, haven't seen you in ages, where you been?"

"I've been right here," the squatter says. "Where *you* been?"

14

The faceless shadows wait outside Hairston's bunker, watching. They can't touch him. They're all dead, burned away to nothing, but they're always there. Even reduced to some substance less significant than ash, their legacy haunts Grandy Springs in much the same way it haunts Hairston's skull.

Whether hallucination, memory, or reflection of some alternate dimension, they don't concern him now. With the threat they posed to this town consigned to the past, his awareness has been freed to detect new threats or seek new prey. Centered in his web, Hairston sees those pursuits as one and the same.

He stands beside the cot that has served as the receptacle for decades of restless half-sleep and peers at the curved mirror mounted on the wall that lets him see into the other rooms, and into spaces outside. It shows him visions from another town and a future time, less swathed in haze than in days before. It shows him things he will see with his own eyes. It teaches him there are monsters in the world different from the ones he intimately knows.

He hasn't dressed yet, and from his chest to the soles of his feet the fibers that infest him create phosphorescent streaks under his skin. Someday this otherworldly violation of his body will kill him, but that someday will arrive many years later than it does for anyone human. Hairston used to be human, but he entertains no illusions about what he is now. The betrayal and the blood-drenched, fiery ordeal that fused him to this state took place long ago and will never be undone. To brood upon it is to waste his energy.

The floors of the rooms that bud from Hairston's bedchamber are piled with reeking garbage. Each of those rooms contains a curved mirror like the one Hairston faces. Every room is lit by an overhead light, though anyone with a mind split open wide enough to find their way to this bunker would spot no wiring, nor would they hear the rumble of a generator.

A murky darkness spins across one of the other mirrors, like an animation made using negatives of a hurricane. Hairston's scowl deepens. Even though the mirror is in another room, he senses the disturbance like a flicker in the corner of his mind's eye. He heads into that room, kicking aside the heaped trash to get a better vantage.

Outside, phantoms wait.

15

You remove your master key from the loop on your belt. The classroom where you leave the notes for Maddy lies behind the door you open. You use your mop to push a bucket of water into the room. The teacher left moments ago, you watched him shuffle down the hallway, head down, shaggy salt-and-pepper hair curled in a mad scientist's mat. You're relieved because if he'd lingered any longer, you might have gone in anyway, and if he questioned your presence the consequences would have been drastic for you and even worse for him.

Once you lock the door, you roll the bucket to the desk where Maddy sits, lift a stubby hand palm up and will your seams to appear.

Your mother would approve of none of this. You would suffocate for weeks if she found out.

Your hand becomes a glove formed of strips fastened together by bright motes. A blink later, the motes resemble buttons, some round, some diamond-shaped, some like tiny black stars.

Carefully, with your hand that remains whole, you unfasten a square of skin from the center of your palm, detach it completely from your body. The space revealed in the hole beneath shudders in a manner that would hurt normal eyes to look at. Even you detect an unpleasant ache spreading from the depths of your borrowed eye sockets.

You fix your attention on the tiny portal into void in your palm, and something rises to the surface, like a corpse freed from the seabed, to patch the gap. A new piece of skin, drawn from those trapped in the layers..

The square of separated skin quivers between the index finger and thumb of your left hand. You focus, and a bright mote crawls out from under your thumbnail, dimming into a button molded to look like a valentine heart. The button slides onto and across the patch of skin, a planchette choreographed by your will. As it moves, it pulses red, then dims, then reddens again. Its wake leaves a visible, purpling trail. The skin etched by the planchette squirms as if it still has functional nerves.

This note is the shortest, least creative of all: *stay away from josey*

You don't know it's already too late. You will the note to curl under the desk and lie in wait, wedged tight between the grainy underside of the desktop and the horizontal support bar. From time to time during the hours that follow it trembles like a cockroach adjusting its wings.

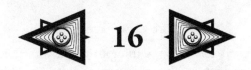

16

Josey's mom has a smile that must have cost thousands of dollars to fashion. She's as pretty as her daughter, her glossy shoulder-length hair white or platinum blonde or both and styled with beauty queen sweep. She's wearing more makeup than her daughter but her bright blue eyes draw all the attention.

Maddy's heart races at an uncomfortable tempo as she climbs into the back of the SUV—itself a beauty queen, red, spotless waxed gleam reflecting the clouds—because this is really happening, it wasn't a put on, she's really going to Josey's house. It's a little weird not riding shotgun but that's the door Josey's mom held open for her. Maddy squirms into the seat behind the driver's and buckles up.

Mama Rochelle watches from the driveway. She smiles, warm as fresh-baked bread, and gives Maddy a tiny flutter-fingered wave. Rochelle had just arrived home from day care with the not-twins when Josey's mom pulled up. *Can you carry Porsche*, Rochelle had asked as Maddy rushed up to the station wagon's driver's side door to explain who was driving that huge candy red SUV. (Whether it's Georgia or Porsche, state or car, that request always makes Maddy crack up inside, though not as much lately as the twins are getting heavier.)

In between the tasks involved in settling the twins in their room and calling sullen Ashley up from her room to help, Rochelle had flashed Maddy bits of a bright smile. Apparently she didn't share any of the trepidation that squirmed in Maddy's chest. *I'm glad she sees what you've got inside you*, Rochelle said. *The way you draw must speak really loud to something inside her. It's fine, you can go, sweetie, just call me when you're ready to come back.*

As Maddy's eyes meet hers, Rochelle brightens with that same smile. "Have a good time!" she says, and makes a *call me* gesture. Is it a trick of Maddy's mind that Mama Rochelle's smile shifts ever so slightly as she turns her gaze to Josey's mom? Eyes narrowing, a near-imperceptible downturn at the corners of the lips?

"So nice to meet you," Josey's mom calls, sounding fake as a Barbie.

"Be good," Rochelle says, a thing she always says in parting that Maddy finds really embarrassing right at that moment. The unpleasant warmth under her skin continues as she fidgets in the back seat.

She starts to imagine what a woman as rich as Josey's mom must think about these tiny, close-crammed houses in Mama Rochelle's neighborhood. All look well used, their colors muted by the passing decades, some yards already overgrown with grass or littered with toys that haven't been inside since last summer. "It's a good neighborhood," Maddy says, instantly wishing she'd stayed quiet.

"It's lovely," Josey's mom says, settling in the driver's seat. She sounds like she's been presented with a cake that's not quite to her liking. She goes on, "Thank you so much for offering to help my daughter."

The idea that Josey's mom thinks this was all Maddy's idea jars her. She wonders if that's how Josey told it to her mom, or just what her mom assumes. Maddy would never have approached Josey on her own, short of a teacher forcing her. If Josey fibbed to her mom, the fib is alarming, though flattering too in an odd way. Like Josey talked her up to her mom, made her out to be a cool artist, maybe.

For such a huge machine, the SUV's engine is eerily quiet. It prowls down Mama Rochelle's street, aimed toward the center of the city and then well beyond, to the hills full of mansions where Josey's family lives.

Josey's mom drives the speed limit, which startles Maddy because this behemoth vehicle has as many high tech displays as a spaceship, with monitor screens built into the backs of the seats and everything. Josey's mom doesn't offer to put a movie on, though.

Becca's house is three crossings up from Mama Rochelle's. When it comes in sight, Maddy spies Becca outside, bounding up her steep front yard with a rake, even though it's spring. Maybe Becca is playing witch—when she was smaller she liked to pretend the rake was a broomstick. She'd go get a real broom out of the house so Maddy could play too.

Maddy raises a hand to wave an instant before she remembers that Becca was mad at her for accepting Josey's invitation in the first place. Then an imp of the perverse takes her over and she waves hard to make sure Becca sees her. Their gazes meet. Becca spots Maddy and stops, follows her progress in the SUV but doesn't wave back.

Maddy watches Becca until she can't anymore. She's unsure whether or not she feels bad about what she's just done.

17

The digits that appear on the screen of Aaron's cellphone aren't recognizable as any kind of phone number. He knows immediately who's calling.

Despite that, he still starts his part of the conversation with a tentative "Hello?"

"I need to be in Hillcrest tomorrow," Hairston says, his voice like an Old Testament command. "Early tomorrow. You ready for that?"

For a disoriented moment, a thought takes shape that he needs to arrange for someone to watch his cats. His struggle to update his brain to his current reality almost turns physical. The same accident that knotted these awful scars onto his face put him in the hospital for weeks and during those weeks he missed rent and his shit landlord had him evicted. His ex-girlfriend Vanissa and her fiance Athenea rescued his kitties, Persephone and Prowler, and have been minding them for him without complaint, letting him visit whenever he wants, may all the gods bless them.

After the interval of silence this exercise requires, Aaron gives consent. It's almost midnight, but Hairston insists they can't wait. He gives details on where to pick him up and when.

When the call ends, Aaron regards his current apartment. With his work at the weekly newspaper reduced to part-time hours, he lives at the edge of losing this one, too. The interior decoration sense of his latest fling, Donna, who moved in with him for seven months, still surfaces through the clutter of printouts and old newspaper editions, his only consistent motif from dwelling to dwelling and relationship to relationship. Donna had a thing for Théophile-Alexandre Steinlen's cat posters, which she said would have to do since Aaron's current asshole landlord—what a run of luck he's had!—doesn't allow cats. Though apparently she didn't love cats enough to take the prints with her when she moved in with her next lover, who she was banging well before she and Aaron mutually agreed she needed to leave.

Aaron doesn't resent the posters. They're like the crisp gold coins he got to keep after washing a pile of shit down the drain.

"Goodbye, kitties," he tells them. "I'm not sure when I'm coming back."

18

The SUV ascends toward a sprawling stuccoed house perched like a crown atop the crest of a hill. The driveway curves languorously up a steep grassy slope that must be a nightmare for whomever Josey's family hires to do the mowing. To Maddy the lawn looks near vertical.

The engine of the SUV at last makes a little noise, roaring as it hauls its bulk to the peak where the terrain abruptly levels to reveal box hedges that surround the mansion like green dolmens. A garage door at least three cars wide opens to engulf the SUV, like a grouper with a brightly lit mouth preparing to suck in a smaller fish. Two more cars are parked inside, a sports coupe and a minivan. They gleam like jewelry.

"Different tools for different tasks," says Josey's mom.

"Uh huh," Maddy says, not understanding. "What kind of car is that?" She points at the coupe. "It's pretty sweet!"

"That's Josey's Jaguar. She gets to drive it if she keeps her grades up through junior high graduation."

"Wow. I'd totally stay straight A's for that!"

Josey's mom emits a wistful sigh, as if she's just emerged from a daydream. "Of course you would, you're a good girl." She puts the SUV in park. "Come on, Josey's waiting for us." She exits and waits for Maddy to join her.

Maddy pictures an illustration from the tale of the ugly duckling as she follows Josey's mom into the house, the frazzle-haired kid from the wrong side of town trailing the golden swan. Mama Rochelle would scold her for giving in so quickly to assumptions, tell her not to let this alien woman threaten her sense of self, and for that matter not to judge this woman whose load in life is so unfamiliar. *Never doubt that you've got life well in hand*, Rochelle tells her. *You're the toughest kid I've ever known.* Maddy doubts that's true, but it warms her to the core every time Rochelle says it.

The door from the garage opens, apparently by magic, Maddy doesn't see her escort click a remote control. They enter an anteroom that's like a designer airlock, with brass hooks to either side for coats and shoes and a forbidding second door of dark-stained wood set in a stucco wall. "You can leave your shoes here," Josey's mom says, though she doesn't remove her own.

Maddy hangs her sneakers side by side on the wide shoe hooks. The chance positioning of the lace loops, toes, and sole patterns gives them fretful puppy expressions, as if they're silently pleading with her not to abandoned them. *You'll be okay*, Maddy reassures them, then giggles at her own silliness.

Josey's mom smiles ever so slightly at the sound before she opens the inner door. Beyond the airlock lies a big playroom dominated by a fancy pool table with gleaming flanks and ornately curved and carved legs. Past the pool table an atoll of plush black couches forms an incomplete square, the missing side open to the largest flat screen TV Maddy has ever seen. Josey's family must host dozens of visitors at a time—or maybe they lounged in those vast couches all on their lonesome. Maddy wonders if Josey and her boyfriend spend time on those couches. She shies away from the thought, not wanting to blush in from of Josey's mom.

"This way," Josey's mom says. "Let's go to the kitchen. I've got cookies waiting." Still a duckling, Maddy follows her through a sitting room with yet another big screen TV, then down a hall that opens into a kitchen that's bigger than the room at school where the cafeteria ladies scoop out the latest mush onto trays as the kids push past.

A marble-topped bar extends out from a counter in a graceful curve and widens into a central table surrounded by tall stools. That's where Josey's mom directs Maddy to sit. Once perched on a stool, her feet don't reach the floor. She resists an impulse to kick like a baby in a highchair.

Josey's mom sets a whole pack of fancy store-bought cookies in front of her, unopened. "Help yourself. I'll go get Josey."

Until that moment, it hasn't occurred to Maddy how odd it was that Josey wasn't right there waiting when they pulled into the garage, or stepped into the playroom. Even for a rich kid, someone from a world Maddy knows only by imagination, that seems pretty damn weird.

She keeps brushing her gaze over all the shining surfaces in this immense kitchen, so spotless she wonders if Josey's family ever uses it. Appliances, cutlery, cupboards, counter tops all glisten as if freshly removed from the box and spruced up for a photo shoot. Speaking of box, she opens the cookies out of a need to do something with her hands during this awkward pause. She eats the first and second cookie with the greatest care possible, fearful she'll leave a stray crumb and violate some unspoken rule. The cookies neither look nor taste as good as the package promises. They're like sweetened cardboard.

Minutes pass. Maddy wonders if she'll violate another taboo if she clambers down from her stool and ventures out into the enticing labyrinth of surrounding rooms. She imagines opening an outsized closet door, something horrible and yet hilarious spilling out from behind it, like the corpse of a gardener or a motherlode of creepy dolls, the commotion bringing Josey's mom at a run, her glossy lips curled in a snarl, to banish Maddy from the mansion with an accusing finger and a cry of *Out, out, out!*

"Hey, so glad you came!"

Josey is standing right behind her, practically yelling in her ear. Thank goodness Maddy froze instead of springing up in surprise, she might have toppled from her stool and smashed her head open.

"Jeez!" Maddy clutches at her chest as her heart pounds a wild tattoo. "You scared me like—"

a monster vomiting its multi-limbed shape out of the back seat to tear mommy and me apart

Maddy leaves the sentence unfinished, the unbidden nightmare that flooded the theater of her mind gone as quick as it gushed forth.

Josey waves a hand in front of her face. "Yo, you okay?"

Maddy shakes herself. *Don't be such a baby,* she tells herself. "Yeah, yeah. You just startled me is all. Where's your mom?"

"She had to go run another errand."

A notion makes Maddy nervous, or rather taps into a strand of jitters flowing close to the surface. "Gone to pick up more of your friends?" Friends eager to impress Josey by stomping all over Maddy . . .

Josey smiles a quick, cold smile, exactly like her mother's. There's an embodiment of *oh how awkward* burnished into its angles, and Maddy at once recalls that Josey has never declared her a friend.

Josey gives Maddy no space to squirm from that admonishment. "My project's in my room, you ready to look at it?"

"'Course! That's all I'm here for, right?" Maddy means those words to wield an edge. Josey doesn't take the bait, maybe doesn't even care, she's immune to anything Maddy could dish out.

"I'm so grateful you're here, I really need your help. You've got like ten times the talent I do. My teacher won't cut me a break!"

Maddy suspects false flattery. "You can't be *that* bad."

"Yes I can, you'll see. Hey, bring those cookies with you, I want some. They're so good!" The most human and fallible and ridiculous thing to come out of Josey's mouth since she started talking to Maddy.

"Seriously? You've tried these? I think they're gross." Again, Josey doesn't acknowledge the bait. She troops into the hall, leaving Maddy no choice but to tuck the cookie package under an arm and follow.

Josey's return heralds the return of that strange smell, like sweetness, like cooked meat, like burning. Except Maddy realizes it didn't just reappear on the way here. She smelled it in the SUV, in the playroom, in the kitchen.

The stench has a new intensity that makes her head swim. It calls lunacy to mind, a déjà vu sensation of tremendous crushing pressure, wet and suffocating, unending in its agony, relieved with a twisting mockery of birth. She hears a girl's voice, *Mommy, don't you think it's funny?* repeated over and over.

Josey descends a set of wide, grand stairs. The vertigo adds to Maddy's nausea. She fights to keep her balance even with the plushly carpeted basement floor beneath her feet. Josey doesn't look back, thank God, as Maddy has to put a hand to a wall to keep steady.

Josey pulls open a door in that same wall, and next thing they're in her bedroom. It's as big as the garage. Maddy has never seen so many toys in one place outside of a store. Most are still in their boxes, displayed on shelves, Barbies of all sorts, pale big-busted blonde women with long, luscious hair, elegant gowns and identical smiles.

Josey has—no surprise—her own TV and game console, a set of cushion-y chairs of her own and a bed big enough to hold a pizza party for a couple dozen kids, and Maddy bets it's been used for exactly that.

Josey heads straight to what Maddy assumes is a closet door. "I have my drawings posted up in here. I tried using glow in the dark paint."

"That sounds cool!"

"It's really not. I suck. Hopefully you can help me not suck."

Maddy pushes past her into the shadowed chamber beyond, too big to be any ordinary closet.

Josey shudders violently at the incidental contact, like she's enveloped in a blizzard blast. The shuddering is more than that, though—beneath Josey's shirt, Maddy feels something sliding and twitching, a snake in spasms, as if electrocuted.

Maddy shrieks and hops away, deeper into the unlit room.

The door closes. Josey flips on the overhead light. It's a bathroom. Josey has her own private bathroom. Maddy hears a second click. Maybe Josey is flicking another switch, to turn on a vent or something.

A leathery sheet of art paper covers the mirror over the sink, two more are taped to the wall on either side, even more plaster the facing wall above the towel rack, more are taped up in the shower.

There are markings on the sheets, but Maddy wouldn't call them drawings. They're furious scratches in the paper, like epic scribbles made with a pen that's run out of ink, though at a glance they defy easy dismissal, the patterns in them arresting to the eye, not at all random.

Josey still has a hand on the doorknob, though she's facing forward, her slender arm bent at a painful angle. "I'm putting you back where you belong," she says.

The drawings rustle as if whipped by a breeze.

"What?" says Maddy.

"Maude told me how to sniff you out. You fell for it so easy, I can't believe you really don't remember what you are. Your mother must have taught you to play ignorant when she made you."

Maddy wants to say, *I don't know what you're talking about*, but her tongue won't move.

"I can't see the point, trying to hide that way, because like can tell when like is near. But what I do I know?" The timbre and pitch of Josey's voice alters syllable by syllable, sometimes deep, sometimes raspy, sometimes creaking with age, masculine in all variations. "I'm just a puppet that will never be a real boy."

The flapping pieces of not-paper and Josey's gross voice-trick split Maddy's fracturing attention. Any question she wants to ask sticks in her throat. She's too bewildered to scream.

"Once you're back with us, we'll find your mother," the man inside Josey says. Somehow, while Maddy wasn't looking, Josey drew lines all over her face. They divide her face into not quite symmetrical squares. She must have put in contacts, too, her eyes are different colors, brown in one, green in the other, instead of blue.

The lines on her face are studded with glittering lumps. Her hand has twisted around the doorknob like a wet, crumpled towel that retains the tint and texture of tanning-bed-bronzed skin. Her t-shirt and designer jeans twitch all over, as if mice cluster underneath the fabric.

"What are you doing?" Maddy's mind fastens to the notion that this is all a prank, maybe there's a hidden camera, maybe Josey's a bully after all—

A snake is crawling across the ceiling, toward the light fixture. Another extends along the wall by Josey's shoulder. Both are flat and leathery, like the drawings, which flutter frantically in a nonexistent wind.

From behind Josey's back more flattened serpents stretch, slinking across the floor, fanning out over the door, tendrils like strips of animated skin edged by glittering beads.

The drawings, too, have formed pearls along their edges, scintillating with color. Everything expands and contracts, everything curls and twists.

a shape like skins from a hundred slaughterhouse animals peeled and twined together, snaking forward between the driver and passenger seats

Maddy doesn't shriek. Instincts seared into nerve and muscle goad her to flee whatever Josey is becoming, but the drawings that are also part of Josey are snapping and stretching on the walls beside her and in the shower behind her. There's no way out unless she magically gains the strength to tear through tile and drywall.

"Panic all you want," the man inside Josey says. "You know what's coming."

Cornered, Maddy switches from flight to fight. The only way out is through Josey. She lunges forward, fingers hooked to claw Josey's face.

Josey opens out into a slobbering cyclone of writhing skin and glittering jewels. The hole her body peels apart to reveal extends outside the room, the house, the world, and it's filled with screaming multitudes. Limbs overflow the lip of the vortex, grasping arms and legs bent in triskelion curls. Tendrils of skin and raw muscle lash out, knocking Maddy off her feet, into the expanding anemone swirl.

The arms and legs fold over her. Tendrils wrap her neck, whip around her head, cover her mouth and eyes, crush her nose flat, a suffocating membrane of hot, hairy flesh. Her body lifts from the floor. Small things swarm her, she can't see but they burn like sparks and crawl like ants. They seethe over every inch of her, pierce her with needles of electricity. She relives the moment in the car when she and her mother were undone, enduring a billion points of agony. If her scream sounds through the sheath crushing her head, it's still drowned out by the howls from uncountable others, flooding her ears even though they're muffled by fleshy wrappings.

That first time, numbness replaced the agony, and she was submerged into an enormous pressure that never abated, her mind swiftly sunk beneath layers upon layers of meat, experiencing what a fossil cursed with immortality would feel, trapped inside a billion years of sediment.

This time, the needles retract as fast as they invade.

The limbs and tendrils whip away from her, tumbling her out of the vortex of limbs. She slams onto the hard tiles, hardly noticing the impact as she scrambles to her feet. The spinning maw made of body parts is retracting into midair. Within it, a storm of bright motes retreats into the hellmouth funnel, and she knows they were the tiny invaders burning into her skin the instant before.

The tunnel out of reality shrinks, large as trampoline, as a playpen, as a tire, as a hubcap. The extruding tendrils of what used to be Josey's body corkscrew and twist together, and then the phenomenon no longer resembles a fleshy whirlpool, it's a rope made of coiling worms, flailing in midair, its ends tied to nothing. Bright motes scurry all over it, their numbers rapidly dwindling as they disappear under its twitching strands.

Josey cringes away, ends up curled on the floor, hands raised to guard her face, but the thrashing rope doesn't touch her. Thinner and thinner it grows, its high-pitched wail unceasing as a tea kettle brought to tortured boil.

Josey's voice abruptly breaks through the screech. "Maddy! Oh, God, Maddy, help me!"

The rope narrows to a thread, then it's gone, thinned beyond visibility. A presence continues to vibrate, a motion that spins Maddy's head and hurts her eyes. She gags and dry heaves.

A long time passes before she gains enough control of her body to uncurl and turn her head. She breathes in long, hissing gasps, her eyes focused on the glass light fixture at the center of the ceiling, its glow burning her retinas. At last she uses the vanity drawers to pull herself up. She's alone in the bathroom, even the drawings, if that's what they were, have disappeared. There is no sign of Josey or the thing she became.

Maddy stares at herself in the bathroom mirror. The girl that looks back at her is pale and bug-eyed, shaking like she's standing naked in a winter storm. She wants to forget everything that girl has just seen. The back of her head throbs, a goose egg rising.

At last she wanders dazed through Josey's bedroom and out into the hall. No one else crosses her path or calls to her. Nothing looks familiar and she's swiftly lost.

One of the many rooms showcases a collection of fine-crafted grandfather clocks. All hands point to the same numbers, 7:34 p.m. Maddy told Mama Rochelle she'd be eating dinner at Josey's. The thought of eating makes her double over and retch.

Through the ceiling a bell chimes, muffled. She thinks it's a clock, but then it repeats, insisted and arrhythmic. A finger punching a doorbell with panicked urgency. Maddy follows the noise like bread crumbs in a labyrinth. She hesitates before each closed door, picturing a vortex of limbs yawning in wait on the other side. The doorbell continues to call.

The gap between the front room curtains exposes slices of a red sunset. The doorbell stops hammering her eardrums. The voice that calls could belong to a boy or girl. "Maddy? Are you there?"

Maddy's heart is in her throat, she can't speak around it.

"I know you got all my notes," her visitor says. "I tried to tell you not to come here. I'm sorry I wasn't quick enough. We need to get far, far away, before our mothers come looking."

Maddy opens the door.

19

R ochelle can't stop pacing. Won't stop pacing, until she comes to a decision. No text from Maddy, much less a call, and it's quarter till 11. It's the first time Maddy's been out with a school friend (if that's what Josey Petrasek is) for many months, so if she's enjoying herself Rochelle doesn't want to harsh the vibe. Maybe she's happy and she's just lost track of time. But that's not like Maddy, she's not a rebel, she'd much rather just go unnoticed than act out.

And though she doesn't live on her phone like most kids (and adults now too, let's be fair) it's not like her to ignore it. Rochelle has sent four texts and left two voicemails.

She paces back and forth in the living room, the television tuned to a rerun of *How to Get Away with Murder*, the volume low but still loud enough to mask Rochelle's words as she mutters under her breath. "Maddy's not one to make trouble. You know that because *you* were one to make trouble. Back on Lewis Street when you'd sneak out with the boys and your granma would track you down and whup you so hard she shoulda gone to jail. But she kept you outta jail. You know what she would have done about *this*."

The projects off Lewis Street were a scary place to raise a child, but they were a loving place too, full of fond memories for Rochelle, and her granma, quick to strike with a wooden spoon and quicker to smile, was the core of almost all of those memories. Her home and her mind were a whole city quadrant and many years distant from Lewis Street, but she tried to keep her granma's best lessons front and center, and one of those lessons was, if you don't know where your child is, you go and find her and bring her back.

Rochelle has her laptop set up on the dining room table—after dinner, she tallied bills and receipts, with the kids rounded up in the living room to watch *Wreck-It Ralph* again, all of them except Ashley, who shuffled downstairs for her evening sulk.

Mrs. Petrasek has a listed number, it turns out, and she's not answering her phone either. At least that gives Rochelle an address she can plug into her GPS. Maybe Mrs. Petrasek has another number, a personal cellphone that's unlisted. "Fool, you shoulda asked for it," Rochelle tells herself. Maybe she was double foolish, allowing Maddy to go off with that woman even though something about her seemed off, like she was looking at Rochelle and Maddy and the other girls the way an indoor cat watches birds through the window. At the time she'd chided herself that she shouldn't be suspicious of anyone, low or high, on account of where they come from. But she also knew, and in truth was confronted with this fact every day she reported to work at PAL, that having money didn't make people responsible, for their own bodies or the bodies of others. For all she knew Mrs. Petrasek was one of those parents who treated her kids like the people who left their dogs chained outside through snow and scorching sunshine. Only when they have that much money social services is never going to intervene to rescue their kids.

Rochelle barges into Ashley's room with its barren walls—the kid doesn't even try to act like she wants this house to be her home, has done nothing to make the room hers, not yet. Ashley protests but she's not doing anything embarrassing, just playing a game on her tablet with her headphones on, and she clearly wasn't asleep. Rochelle cuts her off. "I gotta go out and get Maddy. You get upstairs and mind the young ones until I get back."

Ashley smiles for once, but not for a good reason. "Is Maddy in trouble?"

Rochelle reminds herself that beggars can't be choosers. "It's none of your concern, okay?" Ashley's smile converts to her standard glower. Rochelle adds a spoonful of sugar. "I'll tell you what's in it for you. I've been saving a box of Samoas for your birthday, but you can have it tonight if you do this right for me."

Ashley's love for Samoas makes for the only positive avenue of communication she's established with the kid. Rochelle does have a box she's been saving, because Ashley's birthday is next month. Bribing Ashley is not the way Rochelle wants to do things but these are desperate times, and wow, the girl is smiling again.

About half an hour later the minivan's engine strains up the Petrasek's steep driveway, the angle of her headlights failing to render the strip of asphalt as much more than a band of shadow in the grass. Rochelle's heart pounds at a profoundly unhealthy pace as she contemplates the downhill slide that would ensue if she let the van drift into the grass.

Neither her van nor her heart gives out and she reaches the crest, almost swerving into the bushes that stand sentry around the mansion because the place is cast in darkness. No outside lights on, curtains drawn, which she can only tell because some light is on somewhere deep inside the house, granting the windows the faintest of radium glows. She pictures a ghost standing in a hall, eyes shining, and curses her overactive imagination.

She gets out of the van, manages to find the front walk, rings the doorbell, beats on the front door first with the fancy door knocker, then her fist. Nothing. She tries calling Maddy again.

Maybe her own brain punks her, or maybe it's a super-sense that activates because a foster mother is still a mother, but she could swear she hears Maddy's generic I-don't-care-it's-just-a-phone ringtone, muffled within a millimeter of its life, somewhere inside this massive monument to someone's excessive inheritance. The call goes to voicemail, she hangs up and calls again, starts to pace to the left, where she thinks the sound is coming from. A motion detector light comes on, and she's grateful for it because she won't trip as she circles the house. There's a backyard that's fenced off and a gate that's not locked. She lets herself in. More motion detectors blaze.

The back of the mansion is ludicrous. Tennis court, covered pool, a patio that could host a tiny nation. She can't hear the ringtone at all, so she heads back to the front door. She rounds the corner of the house at the same time rolling blue lights appear at the bottom of the driveway. She counts the police cruisers as they ascend, one, two, three, complete overkill, kill being the word that sticks in her mind. She's a woman, short and round, not too scary to most, but she's a black woman outside a rich white woman's house and she can guess how this is going to go.

The cops would never have arrived this fast at Lewis Street. Hell, not even in the mixed middle class neighborhood where Rochelle lives now. She tells herself to breathe slowly, not to raise her voice, not to make any quick moves. Her heart pounds at a rhythm her body can't quite get a handle on.

The all-too-thinkable happens. "Police! Put your hands above your head!"

She does all the things they yell at her to do. "My daughter's missing," she says, calm as she can. She's face down on the ground, arms wrenched behind her back and handcuffed. The officers aren't listening.

20

Maria makes no effort to find her missing child. She contemplates the translucent underbed box, which has held Davey inside for countless hours. She's placed it atop her bed. She sits beside it, nude, her skin a lattice of exposed seams. Her bare thigh presses against its side scratched with letters from an ancient alphabet, her fingers rest lightly on the cold surface of its lid, as if she might detect residue from its frequent prisoner, and through that contact find guidance.

She thinks of herself as Maria still, though the shreds within her of the sad creature that started all of this, the late unlamented Lenahan, supply knowledge that this retention of a name and consistent appearance results from an involuntary consequence. The Maria from the Vanished Neighborhood had a strong sense of self, a willful personality that has parasitically entwined with the hungry intelligence that drives her impulses.

This parasite permitted, even insisted upon Davey's independence. That part of her could not bear the thought of his tiny cries lost among the shrieking multitudes folded into the layers. When she at last dropped the charade of motherhood and unmade him, instead of fastening his skin and sins into the quilt, she segregated him, made him a separate, weaker being, something that could still play the part of pupil and son.

She regards this fact with dispassion, neither satisfaction nor regret. Lenahan indulged in a similar arrangement, as had predecessors before him. Over the centuries the predators could not help but assume traits of the prey.

The hand on the box is no longer Maria's hand. It's lighter-skinned, thick and meaty, its fingernails ragged. She did not will that fragment to the surface.

She has no heartbeat, no pulse to quicken. Maria's hand from her former life, brown and supple, supplants the escapee.

She reflects briefly on her predecessor, the pathetic boy whose short, sad tenure as the mind that guided the quilt links her back to Lenahan. The boy left the box of button motes behind, and lost all control in a matter of days. Perhaps the tenacity that kept her sovereign for so long has only slowed the rot and delayed the inevitable.

Despite the reminder that she has more pressing problems than Davey's dereliction, she turns her attention inward, to the infinite layers of flesh and agony for which she serves as curator and mouth. The roots that anchor Davey in these layers are as mobile as hers, and even an hours-long search can only be precursory. She finds no trace.

When the dawn comes, she washes, dresses, stands before the bathroom mirror and applies makeup. She hasn't aged since she became the quilt. She remains what crude men call a cougar. Many such men howl silently within her, their limbs, their eyes stripped away forever.

For a moment, the lower half of her face glowers, skin dark brown, jaw square and bristled with stubble. Heavy lips curl open in a rictus of surprise. Bright blue eyes widen where dark, sultry eyes had been.

Another blink, and her seamless beauty returns, remains steadfast as she studies herself closely. At last she smirks before fetching her purse from the bedroom and heading out into the day.

21

A ri Newman glances at the classroom clock. Only fifteen minutes to go before first period ends and he has to open the door to students.

He's sorted his transparencies for the day for all six classes and tucked them into separate files. He decides with a sigh that he needs to go through them again because one misplaced page could mean a disastrous disruption. He sighs again because he has to work with transparencies.

Thanks to the ultra-stingy city council and an ignorant school board applying cuts the way a toddler wields a hatchet, he's stuck using an ancient, embarrassingly outmoded overhead projector this semester because the laptop-run projector any decent school system would provide died last semester and still hasn't been replaced.

The reminders he sends via email haven't produced results. Neither have complaints made in person at school and county administration offices. He's convinced that if a leaky roof was pouring water onto his desk, he'd be told to buy a year's worth of buckets at his own expense and shamed if he complained.

Teaching is hard enough without so-called state of the art equipment going on the fritz. Every day he catches at least one student playing a game or snapchatting on their supposedly hack-proof school issue tablets. He fails to catch dozens upon dozens more, he's certain of that.

He's wondered more than once what these kids who've never been taught cursive writing will do when the inevitable nuclear apocalypse destroys the internet. The monster in the White House and the monster in Pyongyang are going to pull the triggers any minute. Probably immediately after one of his students did something amazing enough to finally convince him he'd chosen the right career.

Ari made his mother, a life-long fourth grade teacher, deliriously happy when he earned his B.Ed. Five years into this job, he still wondered if he'd made a huge mistake. Whenever the function of his ongoing efforts approached a mathematical limit remotely resembling pride in his work, variables large and small cropped up to undermine that result. Case in point, a mouse must have taken up residence in the classroom sometime during the night, the sporadic rustling sound increasingly more annoying.

Half an hour ago he dug his phone out of his jacket and sent an email to maintenance. If that noise continues after class starts—and of course it will—he might as well give up, even though his second period seventh graders are supposedly the precocious ones. Precocious, yes, mature, no. The distraction will be too much, his commands to ignore it will go unheard.

The rustling resumes, louder. An empty desk at the back of the room shifts.

Ari recoils so hard his chair capsizes behind him. He manages to gain his feet instead of falling, in the process spilling half of his carefully arranged folders and their wobbling contents into the floor.

A rapid pattering against a solid surface, as if a bird is trapped inside a box. The desk—it's the one nearest the door—slides a foot sideways and two feet backward. "Jesus!" Ari shouts.

He has the self-possession to open the door into the hall before dashing to the desk. Hoping he'll free whatever animal is trapped underneath so that it will flee the classroom, he flips it over.

A piece of paper flutters up from the underside of the desk and spirals to the checkered floor, where it twitches and flaps like a moth on its back.

He stares dumbfounded, then decides it must have a small motor of some sort attached. It's a nonsensical assumption but one that makes sense in the moment. He bends to pick it up. It burrows into his palm, spraying his blood across the tiles. Pain shreds through the center of his forearm, as if someone shoved a vibrating knife blade deep between the bones of his wrist, which bulges, flesh displaced in a moving lump big as an egg that disappears under the blue cuff of his dress shirt. The thing boring through the center of his arm feels armed with many piercing mouthparts, a cluster of horseflies attacking muscle and bone, biting in all directions. Ari's shriek is raw and endless. He's collapsed, slamming his arm on the floor, trying to kill the thing inside.

Blood bursts from his elbow, staining his shirt, before the blood-slicked creature tears its way out through skin and cloth. A funny bone tingle times a thousand surges up and down Ari's arm before it goes numb.

The creature unfolds on the floor, once again a flat piece of paper, now soaked in blood. It flaps like an insect wing, sliding and swerving, and in doing so spells out a word in wet red smears. *Run.*

Ari's scream peters out as he regards the word and the object that wrote it. Even with his arm ruined by the inexplicable, he insists to himself the pattern is random, it spells nothing, his mind is trying to impose a message where none exists.

As if lifted by a burst of wind, the paper flies into the hall with the speed of an attacking yellowjacket.

22

The pallet beneath the overpass stinks. Maddy registers the stench first, of accumulated weeks of sweat, urine and filth, before she recognizes that something else on the pallet with her is shifting its weight, it's that motion that woke her.

She doesn't understand where she is, why it smells so badly, what makes the thunderous rhythmic clunking, why she's fully dressed, why curtains provide no shelter from the sun's eye.

A dark-haired boy sits cross-legged on the other side of the mattress. His eyes are squinched shut, his teeth bared, his hands raised, fingers curled into claws. He shudders again, at the edge of seizure.

Maddy remembers.

They've taken shelter beneath an overpass that crosses Miner's Creek at the city's southernmost edge, where the creek's wide enough to pass for a river. A concrete incline rises from the creek's bank to the ledge where the mattress and blankets were stowed. The pylons that hold up the center of the overpass rise from the other side of the creek. The underside of the bridge hangs barely five feet above Maddy's head. Thuds like distant hammer blows echo each time a vehicle crosses the bridge, she can hear the whoosh of their passage.

The boy, Davey, shudders again. She calls his name. His eyelids snap open. "He found it. I didn't want him to. I didn't want to do that."

Maddy sits up. "Who found what?"

"Nothing," he says. "It's nothing. I was . . . dreaming, sorry." Davey's not frightening to look at. Small, waif-thin, in a shirt with horizontal strips like Ernie from Sesame Street, tan corduroy pants that pull up at the ankles to expose white socks. His eyes, though—his gaze is unnerving, his irises seem to float in their sockets as if they're not really attached and might slide off.

"You have dreams?" Davey showed her, last night, what he is. She saw the hidden seams in his skin and the bright buttons that hold him together. He showed her the filthy old homeless man who used to sleep on this mattress. The old man continued talking with Davey's high voice, before the boy-form reappeared. He said Maddy's real mother is trapped inside the being that used to be his mother, the way the old man is trapped inside him. He told Maddy that she used to be trapped, too, but his mother let her go. He asked her what happened with Josey. She struggled to shape the horrors into words.

"Something like dreams," Davey says.

Above them both the traffic whooshes and thumps with increasing frequency, the noises arriving with blurred edges, dying in soft echoes.

The blankets, which she pulled over herself during the night, might once have been blue. They're gray with stains. She shoves them away and surreptitiously inspects her bare arms for signs of bug bites, snorts in relief when she finds none.

"I've been thinking about the things Josey said to you," says Davey. "Maybe she, or whoever that was, thought you were *me*."

A vision of Josey expanding into a hungry spiral of raw flesh and grasping limbs. Maddy looses a single nervous laugh. "That makes no sense. We don't look anything alike. Plus, you know, I'm a girl. And she knew who I was."

"I mean it in a different way. When it told you it was going to use you to find your mother, it meant *my* mother."

Maddy paraphrases Davey's note. "Your mother stole my mother's skin." She should be afraid of him, but he's told her that he can't hurt her, that if he tries to touch her what happened to Josey will happen to him. *When she tried to take you back into the quilt, there was a reaction, I felt it. I think, because my mom cast you out whole, I don't think she meant for this to happen, but now the quilt can't take you back. I can feel that inside me, it's like when magnets repel.* His words would be nonsense except she understands exactly what he means because she'd lived it all. As they walked the deserted night streets toward the underpass, he'd flinch away if her steps happened to bring her close to him. Even if he wasn't looking at her.

Davey goes on, "It's not about how you look. You were part of it once. The thing mom is. The quilt. The layers. The thing I'm part of. I've learned how to hide what I am. Mom made me learn. But I bet you didn't even know that you had anything you needed to hide."

Maddy remembers sitting in the street in the middle of the Vanished Neighborhood, her mind a chaos of slithering flesh, a slender woman standing over her, speaking to her, walking away with all the regal poise of a queen of Hell.

"How do you know, really?" she says. "I remember your mom. You weren't there."

"When my mom made me, she shared her memory of how she made you. I don't think she meant to. She had you on her mind, what she did when she cast you out, what she wanted to do different with me, and I was part of her then, so I saw it all. She's never talked about you, ever. But I never forgot. That I had a sister."

Maddy hugs her knees to her chest. He called her that last night, too: *sister*. "But I'm not one of you. I can't—I can't do that shit you do. I can't kill people."

Davey's gaze wanders. "You killed Josey." He says it like *the sky is blue*.

She wants to shout, *I did not!* She wants to shout, *I didn't mean to!* But what he says is fact, not accusation.

"I tried to warn you not to go with Josey," says Davey. "I tried to leave you a note, because I thought there was time. I should have just told you. I'm sorry."

The burble of the creek provides a soothing counterpoint, a false positive. She doesn't know what to say to his apology, because it means he was watching when Josey approached her. Has been watching her the entire time, using the eyes of other people.

She has endured worse. She has been abducted, turned inside out and unfastened into a thousand pieces, then remade. She's lived among kids who shrank from her and mocked her as if she were the monster. When the monsters were hidden all around her. A wave of darkness sinks through her. "Are there more like Josey?"

"Has to be. Something made her."

Hope springs eternal. "Will your mom . . . will our mom . . . fight them?"

Davey starts shaking. He could be a beetle, trapped on its back, fruitlessly buzzing its wings.

"What?"

"When my mom gets mad at me she puts me in a box that she keeps under her bed. I can't breathe and it hurts so bad. She leaves me in there for days." His gaze meets hers. "She'd do it to you too if she could." The description strikes Maddy as ridiculous. She tamps down an impulse to laugh. He goes on, "We need to get away from here. From Hillcrest. Far away. From my mom. From the others like Josey."

Running away, for real, maybe forever. For the thousandth time Maddy misses the weight of her cellphone in her back pants pocket. "I wanna tell my foster mom I'm okay."

His unnerving eyes don't blink, it's like they move separate from his shuddering body. "I don't have a phone."

"I know, you told me. We can ask someone. Someone will help—"

His lips don't movie, but a grotesque high-pitched whine emanates from him, from many different throats at once, from mouths she can't see. The noise coalesces into a word. *nnnnnnnnNNNOOO*

She wants to yell back at him, but her mind has filled with the mutilated funnel that bloomed from Josey's body. He's shaking his head, speaking in his high voice, his usual voice. "We can't trust anyone. We can't let anyone know where we are."

Different species of fear overrun her fear of what he is. "How are we going to get anywhere without talking to anyone? We can't just walk!" She takes a huge, wheezing breath. "I'm hungry—how are we even going to eat?" She manages to sit on her next question, *Does something like you even eat?* "I want to go home."

He shakes his head harder. His strange eyes grow wider. "You don't understand. That stuff you told me about, that Josey did, that was nothing. Nothing compared to what my mother can do. She's closer now, I can feel that. We have to keep moving. We have to."

She cuts him off. "Okay, okay. So what do we do now?"

The silence stretches. Davey's eyes don't blink. She wishes he'd pretend to be human long enough to set her at ease. Finally he stands. "C'mon."

"Where are we going?"

"Away from *her*."

23

R ochelle shares a cell with a tiny blonde woman who won't stop crying.
Early on, she tried to engage the woman, whose name she still doesn't
know, in some kind of conversation, but the little blonde hissed like a cornered
cat, and, Rochelle can't be completely sure, but those syllables sure sounded like
a racist epithet. Rochelle might look like a tame ball of fluff, but she damn well
knows she could pound the face on that little minx to hamburger without so
much as scabbing her knuckles. Her plan to bring Maddy back has already tak-
en every possible Murphy's Law-determined twist and she's certain that beating
up the little white girl would make things a thousand times worse, so she lets
it go. Blondie at least keeps to herself, but the constant sniffling still threatens
to drive Rochelle to distraction. That's not the only thing—an unpleasant anti-
septic reek fails to mask an even more unpleasant stench, like a long unflushed
toilet.

No alternatives for conversation. The cell across from them is empty, as
is the cell catty-corner to the left, as best as Rochelle can tell through the bars
and heavy mesh. She and Blondie are in the cell furthest from the thick pod
door—the cells, about eight in total, are not unlike bathroom stalls, and damn
near as tiny, but divided by cinderblock walls so the front view is the only view.
She can't remember if she saw anyone else besides Blondie when the deputies
marched her in. An occasional murmur has suggested to her that the women's
pod might indeed have other occupants. She lacks the urge to put the notion
to the test. She saves her energy. She told the cops over and over that she was
trying to find her daughter, that her daughter was missing. They told her to shut
up and cooperate and put her in here. She's going to give them hell, but first
she has to get out from under their power. She remembers all too well the black
woman who died in her cell in Texas, the painfully phony "suicide" cited as the
cause. Virginia's not so different from Texas. She can't lose her head.

When the deputies come to collect Blondie, Rochelle has no idea of the
time. The police took her phone along with the rest of her possessions and
clothes when they booked her. She hasn't slept a wink, hasn't even dozed, lying
on that upper cot mounted in the wall is like lying on concrete and her mind
runs a mile a minute.

As the deputies put Blondie in shackles, Rochelle stands, expecting the
same treatment. "Sit down," says a deputy, a black woman of a size and height
with Rochelle.

"What? Why?"

"You're not being arraigned," snaps the other deputy, a little smaller than
her partner, with short, slicked back red hair. "Sit down!"

Rochelle complies. "I want to call a lawyer."

"You used your phone call last night," the redhead says.

"My daughter is missing. What are you doing to find her?"

"You just hold your horses," says her partner. "Relax. We'll come get you when it's time to talk."

"About what?"

The redhead glares. Her partner shakes her head once in warning. "Just wait."

They did let her have that phone call last night after they took her finger-prints and mugshot and made her change into the goddamn orange jail jump-suit. She called Nadiya, her friend and fellow foster parent, who has a key to her house and always has her back. "What's going on?" Nadiya asked after she accepted the call.

"A terrible, terrible misunderstanding, and I'm going to tear some people a new one when it's all over. But I need your help now, and I need you to promise you won't say anything to social services."

After a long silence, "I promise. Of course."

"Can you take in the kids, just for tonight? Maddy's gone out, and I can't find her. Ashley's watching the young ones and I don't trust her to mind them a full night by herself."

Nadiya was well familiar with Ashley's attitude. "You got it. And you take care of yourself."

Nadiya's tone left a dozen questions unasked, but she wasn't going to push for answers yet, for which Rochelle was eternally grateful. "I'll call again tomor-row, as soon as they'll let me."

And they still haven't allowed it. Blondie doesn't come back, and neither do the deputies. Rochelle closes her eyes and concentrates on the sound and sensa-tion of her own breathing, hoping maybe if she blanks her mind sleep will find her, help her fast forward to the end of the nightmare.

No such luck.

24

Aaron can't imagine even trying to get shut-eye, not with Hairston in the passenger seat. If he didn't know better, he'd swear a static energy sloughs off the old man, one that agitates the soul instead of the skin.

He craves a nap, though. He took the exit to Hillcrest at 5 a.m. and for the next two hours turned his Buick down one random street after another on Hairston's demand. His passenger wasn't following a map, didn't even bring one. *Turn here. Left, left. Now right.* If they ended up in a cul-de-sac, *Back out, try again, this is the right way.* At one point Aaron made the mistake of asking whether Hairston could tell him the name of the bar they were looking for. *You think if I knew that we'd be doing this?* he snarled back.

They crossed a bridge over railroad tracks and rolled through the middle of a modest-sized downtown with the morning sun in their eyes. *Stop!* Hairston hollered. Aaron stopped the brakes mid-street, the Buick frozen with a bus station on one side and a row of darkened boutiques on the other. Seconds passed. Hairston's bushy white brows lowered, glaring at one of the shops. Aaron kept checking the rear view mirror, amazed no cars had pulled up behind him to honk their horns. Finally Hairston said, *Not here, keep going.* A slender Latina woman in blue-hued business attire rounded a corner from a side street, heels clicking toward the bus station bay, as Aaron stomped the gas.

Strange to see a woman so dolled up on a street where nothing's open, Aaron thought, but he kept the thought to himself.

At last, as they trundled along a three-lane road, left and right and center turn lane, Hairston pointed at a low brown and tan building and said, *This is it. This is where it happens. Park!*

They're in a corner of the front parking lot. Aaron can't stop yawning. The damnable scars on his cheeks itch. When he pops the driver's side door to get out and stretch his legs, Hairston says nothing.

Called Hillcrest Inn, the establishment definitely ain't no inn. He can see pool tables and a U-shaped bar through the plate glass, one panel of which sports a sloppily patched crack. He goes back to the Buick, cracks open the door. "It doesn't open until noon."

"We're gonna wait then."

Better not to argue. Probably fine. Traffic whooshes by, no one seems to pay them any particular notice. Maybe during those hours he could sweet-talk Hairston into sharing more about his decades before and after he came to Grandy Springs, maybe even get him talking about Korea. But Aaron's head feels like any available space in his skull has been stuffed with wire mesh. He'll have to latch his eyelids open with hooks to keep from nodding off while Hairston speaks, unless he gets some coffee in his system or *something*. There's a fast food restaurant open across the street about a hundred yards in what's likely south, judging by the position of the sun. "I'm hungry," he says. "I'll get some breakfast for us. What do you want?"

Hairston rolls his eyes, sighs, settles back in his seat. "You eat a big breakfast, you're gonna regret it later. Your world gets turned over, it'll turn your stomach too."

Aaron chooses to ignore that advice, to his later regret.

25

The man settling on the sidewalk outside the bus depot has broad shoulders and deep brown skin, wisps of white hair that leave his scalp bald, uneven stubble muting his cheeks and chin. He fidgets as he stares at the boutique across the street. The air is cool but sweat beads his forehead.

It's only a Wednesday, but pedestrians still flow thick on both sides of a street sluggish with lunch hour traffic.

A tiny, wasp-waisted woman in a pantsuit stops by the homeless man's feet and gasps, one hand covering her mouth, reducing her face to wide, mascara-ringed eyes. Though her fingers she says, "Oh my god, what's wrong with you?"

The center cannot hold. The features of the man's face won't stay still. Small green eyes, then blue, then deep brown. A luscious, freckled mouth beneath a ginger mustache, then bigger, darker lips surrounded by even darker skin. In fact every bit of exposed skin has devolved into patchwork, no two squares shaded alike.

"I dunno, ma'am," the man says. "Do you believe in Jesus?"

He stretches and folds, and where he sat, a woman rises. For an instant she holds a single shape, a slender Latina, large dark eyes narrowed in a venomous stare. When she reaches her full height she continues to stretch, for an instant returned to the scruffy homeless man, looming over the teeny, gape-mouthed passerby. "Answer me, ma'am."

The little woman tucks her head and runs, her sensible flats pitching off her feet. The man stops in the act of reaching for her, arrested by the sight of his hands. Seams divide the fingers, the palms. A seam in his left hand parts, revealing smooth pale skin underneath.

Five more onlookers, stalled in their progress, hover within reach of the homeless man's right arm. A white man in a gray suit and salt-and-pepper crew cut, physique thick in every dimension. A short, skinny couple, him with a goatee, paused in the pushing of a baby carriage, her with short straight hair, staring over sunglasses. A teen girl with a denim jacket over a half-shirt that exposes a midriff still plump with baby fat.

The mesmerizing prospect of the unraveling man before them, and the false security of the herd, prevents them from bolting like the tiny woman did, reduces them to rubberneckers.

He turns to them as if he were a street preacher and they had all gathered to listen. The rasping voice doesn't come from the mouth on his face, but one that has opened in his throat. "I need ten cents so I can get a beer. Just ten damn cents. Why in hell can't you people just give me ten goddamn cents? Don't lie to me and tell me you don't have change!"

At the same time another voice speaks, like there's a second mouth hidden inside the first, hooked up to independent vocal chords. A woman's voice. "I wasn't a bad person. I sinned but I was never cruel. I never wanted to tear anyone to pieces. I just need to live."

A large hairy arm springs from that dual mouth like a chameleon's tongue, grabs the man with the crew cut by the sag of fat at the front of his neck.

The knot of onlookers flies apart, screaming. A second arm erupts from under the swelling figure's shirt, stuffs its fifteen-fingered hand down the pants of the crew-cut man's suit. The block of his square head slumps squishy like an emptying sand bag. His mouth opens. "Let's go shopping," says a woman's voice from somewhere deep in his guts. Two huge figures tangled together and slowly fusing into one, they waltz into the street.

A car screeches short and honks its horn, the blare joined an instant later by the scream of the driver, a two-part disharmony in reaction to the protean thing spinning past the bumper in grotesque do-si-do.

By the time the avant-garde duo fully cross the street they resemble a single person with an arm too many. This extra arm pulls open the boutique door.

The sales clerk approaches, smiling, not noticing at first how the figure's face is struggling to assume a final shape, how its empty eyes are windows into a fluttering void. As dark eyes rise up to fill the holes, the clerk's smile falters, but not completely, her mind unable to fully process what she's witnessing.

"I need to get to the second floor." The figure speaks in several voices at once. "I know there's a way. I can feel it."

In the back office, manager Kristy watches a lesbian porn video on her monitor. Her hunched shoulders straighten with a jolt as a wail pierces through the office door from the sales floor, cut off abrupt as a customer hang-up.

Kristy rushes to the door and locks it, backtracks to the landline on her desk, the video still playing in the background, flesh on flesh in soft focus. She grabs the receiver without looking and drops it, all her focus on the wide, white, leathery ribbon sliding in from under the door, crossing the tasteful blue rug like a haunted snakeskin. It thickens like a hose filling with water.

The small of her back against the front of her desk, she kicks at the ribbon and it coils around her ankle, tearing open her hose to grope around and up her leg, a warm, fleshy, supple tube. Her face contorts in a soundless shriek. More ribbons are invading through the gap under the door, a half dozen, two dozen, scores. In seconds the office fills to the ceiling. Crushed beneath an avalanche of skin, Kristy's lungs burn, the sensation of suffocation unceasing even as her limbs and head detach. The flip of the switch under the desk that trips the silent alarm happens by sheer accident.

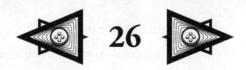

26

C unetta parks the cruiser by the curb where First Street crosses Hartwell Avenue, with the front of the Gypsy Flair boutique visible at his ten o'clock. Foley, his partner, gets out on the passenger side. Cunetta scans for citizens that might need to be cleared from the scene, but the sidewalk around Gypsy Flair is strangely free of pedestrians.

As Cunetta steps out, another cruiser rolls past on Hartwell, lights and siren off, heading to the other end of the block. The day smells of asphalt and spiced meat from the Venezuelan restaurant two doors down. A trio of cars trundle by on First in the other lane, apparently oblivious to Cunetta standing there. Typical.

At the intersection of Hartwell and Second, the other cruiser makes an impressively tight mid-street U-turn, pulls up beside a fire hydrant near the bus station bay. Spillman, the driver, gets out first, followed by Diego, an Odd Couple team if there ever was one, Spillman is pale and lanky and there's a droop to his shoulders and his eyelids, Diego is squat and built like a barrel, her hair pulled back in a ponytail that looks severe enough to stretch her scalp. Stand them together, Diego barely comes up to Spillman's chest.

Right now another cruiser should be parking a block south at Second and Santoro, where the officers could access the back of the store. The whole lot of them are about to converge on Gypsy Flair, guns holstered until they get a view inside the store.

Foley crosses the intersection, hand floating near his Glock, so close as to make the possibilities on his mind way too damn obvious. Cunetta makes a mental note to correct his junior partner after they assess the threat.

Cunetta's radio hisses—Tripp and Gearhardt checking in, already positioned at the shop's back entrance, awaiting further word.

Dispatch received an automated message minutes before, robbery in progress, no follow up call to cancel from a live human being. For all they know, an accountant bumped a switch under a desk with her knee. The security companies that sell these systems swear they're klutz proof, but mistakes happen. Sometimes the causes aren't even human error. A loose wire and a rain leak or even a sharp change in temperature can do the trick. Unlikely, as this spring day there's no rain and a breeze adds just the right seasoning to the early afternoon warmth.

Diego and Spillman cross to the boutique, Diego making up for her short stature and Spillman's beanpole height by taking extra-quick steps that remind Cunetta of a tiny dog's bouncy trot.

The pincer of brown uniforms closes as the four of them stand before the glass store front. No orange card posted in the glass door warns them of a false alarm. Inside, the brightly lit sales floor offers an assortment of tastefully eccentric and colorful dresses. No sign of any people.

Cunetta puts his hand on the grip of his gun and pushes open the door. "POLICE!" No one answers. He draws his Glock, and the others follow suit as they file in behind, Diego last, muttering into her radio, letting Tripp and Gearhardt and Dispatch know what they've seen so far.

None of the officers shudder at the chill that gives Cunetta goosebumps. It's not cold inside the store, not a physical chill. Of all the times to remember the Boneyard, this might be the worst. He'd returned to that courtyard once in broad daylight, and what he felt then—as he eyed the crude stick figure graffiti, the odd shadows where nothing obvious stood to cast them, the rotten slum facades that surrounded the courtyard like multi-floor mausoleums, the busted out windows dark as gullets, the sensation of a presence close-by, unseen, predatory—he feels it now.

They spread out in a quick sweep, finding no one hiding under racks or in the changing booths. No blood stains the carpets. Behind the checkout counter the door to the back room stands ajar. Through they go.

The next door on the left, behind which presumably lies the office where the safe is kept, turns out to be locked. The larger room beyond is divided by shelf racks stacked in surprisingly slapdash fashion with the long, flat boxes that hold clothes. Plenty of good hiding places there. Before Cunetta can say anything, Spillman takes point , advancing into the inventory room with Diego shuffling behind him.

A band of light shines from under the locked office door. Knocking and shouting produces no reaction. The door's ancient wood is flimsy enough that it bows under Cunetta's fist. Giving thanks that the landlords haven't seen fit to renovate in the decades since the first floor of this building was converted to commercial use, he plants his left foot and kicks hard beside the lock with his right. A hole splinters wide open. Beyond, the office is empty.

Foley, bushy eyebrows raised in bewilderment, voices Cunetta's thought. "Where the hell did they all go?"

"Come look at this," shouts Spillman, his voice way too deep for his reed-thin frame.

Cunetta nods to Foley. "Let Gearhardt and Tripp in, I'll see what he found." Foley, bless him, doesn't balk at being bossed around.

An aisle between two tall shelf racks ends in a shattered mess, chunks of plaster heaped on the cement floor. A big gap torn through the drywall reveals the frame of an old door not unlike the one Cunetta just put his foot through. Sealed inside the wall for decades, this door's been torn from its hinges, the raw daggers of its shattered boards strewn against the left-hand rack.

In the cavity made by this forcefully excavated exit, Cunetta spies the bottom step of a narrow stairwell going up. It's been hidden within the wall all this time, then, a relic of the days when the vacant upper stories were used for a theater and the town's black citizens had to take a separate staircase up to the balcony.

The stairwell, barely wide enough to accommodate one body, ascends leftward and up, into darkness.

Spillman opens his mouth, but Cunetta raises a finger to hush him. A chorus of female voices carries down from above, no words distinct enough to decipher.

27

Two women face each other, one sitting, one standing. Between them lies a wooden box large enough to fit a man inside. The box has no lid. A soft hiss like shifting gravel rises from its depths.

No light reaches them. Neither woman has need of light to see.

The seated woman, Maude, leans forward on the folding chair that serves her as throne. "Took you long enough, sweet thing."

Maria twitches. Her body maintains an approximation of her usual shape, but all of her features, eyes, lips, hair, skin, are shifting from second to second, her countenance just shy of a blur. It takes effort to speak but she manages. "You're the one Lenahan made."

"Them things you stole from the box, they're dying," Maude says. "The ones left with me, they want their kin back with every ounce of will they have. You've been feeling that for weeks, honey. I know it."

Maria speaks with several mouths simultaneously, the sentences overlapping. "I didn't steal anything. *I know what you were trying to do.* That shit happened on your sorry watch. *You brought the box to the city as bait.* I joined the quilt and the quilt loves me. *To draw me out.* The layers love me. *And you blocked my way back.* The buttons you lost are mine now. *So you could starve me out, keep me from the box, till I got weak.* And these will be too. *Till I was easy pickings.* And *you'll* be *nothing.* Finders *keepers—*"

"Losers weepers," Maude finishes. "You know who my master was, you've got him inside you. He was a *fool,* thought he was a *god,* started to play with his food instead of eating it. The kid that undid him was even worse. But you're the biggest fool of all, if you ever thought you were in control of anything."

Maria's flesh flaps with constant motion, her frame swaying forward, tugged toward the large bin with its strange carvings by the gravity of like siren-calling to like. The buttons in the bin surge toward her, surge again, fall.

All Maria's mouths vocalize in unison. "What you say doesn't matter. All this time you've kept watch over the bin, but I'm still so much stronger than you, little pet." Her body expands, sheets of skin unfurling behind her like a thousand capes. The buttons in the bin froth at the lip of the box, hungry children beating at the rail of their playpen.

Maude stands, her chair toppling behind her like a man shot. "I've never tried to fight what I really am." She steps into the box. The living buttons surge up her body like fleas.

Maria's form fountains upward in a geyser of flesh that comes hammering down.

28

The stairway hidden in the wall is so narrow the officers can only ascend one at a time. Tripp is first up, illuminating the way with the flashlight mounted on his Glock. Barrel-chested Gearhardt goes next, and he has to take the stairs in a sideways shuffle to avoid getting stuck. Cunetta goes after him, Diego at his back breathing fast and too loud.

The sounds above make little sense. Dozens of soft things dragged across a gritty floor. The grating of something heavy and wooden. Hands slapping on concrete.

The stairwell stretches higher than seems reasonable, perhaps further proof of its original purpose, that it leads to a balcony that no longer exists.

Tripp turns his head and his light to the right to peer through an opening hardly more than six feet tall and two feet wide, its edges cracked ragged. Whatever smashed its way into the stairwell smashed its way out, too. Cunetta unconsciously holds his breath, his every instinct expecting Tripp to die right at this moment, his flashlight making him a perfect target. Even if he weren't poking his head out the hole, that wall won't shield him from bullets.

The slapping sounds stop.

Tripp squeezes through, shuffles off to one side. Gearhardt goes through next, breaking more drywall loose as he forces his wide torso through the gap.

His mishap makes Cunetta's exit easier. Pieces of the shattered wall crunch under his shoes. Moving in a crouch, Cunetta hurries forward into an immense, vacant space. The size of the chamber startles him, though he's been vaguely aware for years that a gutted theater filled the building's upper floors, sealed off from the first floor shops as a building code compromise that saved the landlords from an expensive renovation. It's an odd fact for him to retain about his adopted city, as he's never been to a play in his adult life.

Diego, Foley and Spillman clamber in behind him. Cunetta clicks on his own Glock-mounted flashlight. The others do the same.

Their accumulated beams sweep across a wide curtain drawn across a low stage at the far end of the enormous room. The curtain ripples, motions that can't possibly be caused by air current. At Cunetta's two o'clock, the edge of the curtain twitches, as if something pushed at it from behind.

Foley sees it at the same time and starts toward it at speed. In a split second, Cunetta weighs what to do, whether to bellow *POLICE! FREEZE!* before Foley reaches the curtain, decides to let Foley make that call—even as he reflexively raises a hand, wanting to warn Foley to stop, no need to be so eager, but his partner, focused on the target, doesn't notice the gesture.

Foley reaches the curtain, pulls back the edge. He neither shouts nor speaks. His flashlight goes out.

"Foley! Foley! What's going on?" Cunetta aims his own light at the spot where his partner ducked behind the curtain, finds no sign Foley was ever there. The other four officers shine their lights on the same spot. The texture of the curtain is like no cloth Cunetta's ever seen, dun and leathery, divided into squares of different shades, fastened together with an astonishing variety of buttons. As big as the curtain is, there must be thousands of them.

"FOLEY!"

The remaining officers all shout at once, waving their flashlights and guns.

All along the curtain's width and height, small slits open to expose glistening orbs. Cunetta instantly assumes that the mix of darkness, uneven illumination and adrenaline has concocted a mirage, because it's not at all rational to accept that constellations of eyes have opened all over the buttoned-together squares of leathery fabric.

A flash of memory disrupts Cunetta's focus, a nightmare that plagued him back in Grandy Springs, when he was still married. Waking up in the middle of the night to find the bedroom crowded with tar-black, eyeless forms, human in shape but in no other way, more than a dozen standing shoulder to shoulder around the bed as he stared bug-eyed and tongue-tied and his wife slept on oblivious. A hand would reach toward his face, and he'd wake up again, wife still oblivious, the room empty. In the months before divorce, he came to resent her freedom from this nightmare most of all.

In a moment the nightmare will end. He cannot accept that he's awake, even though he knows better than all the other cops in the Hillcrest P.D. that the world can contain horrors that beggar even the most overactive imagination. It doesn't stop with the glistening shadow creatures he left behind in the Boneyard. It doesn't begin with Hulk's missing hand. He came to Hillcrest long enough ago that the city's own tale of mystery and horror still bled fresh: the houses left empty in the Vanished Neighborhood, that little girl left behind in the street, repeating delusional claims like a living corpse reading a live report from Hell, *I was nothing but skin just like my mom and dad but I could still scream.*

Did she scream like barrel-chested Gearhardt, who fires his Glock as he topples to the floor?

At the same time, at Cunetta's four o'clock, Diego opens fire at the violently billowing curtain, the pops from her Glock weirdly muffled, like firecrackers exploding under a smothering mattress. Cunetta swings the beam of his flashlight across the chamber as it floods with nonsensical shapes. He finds Spillman, whose beanpole frame is absurdly truncated, sunk from the waist down into an undulating, leathery carpet animated like the surface of a wind-blown lake.

Needles prick Cunetta's legs and they go numb from the knees down.

A glance at his feet reveals clusters of eyes looking back at him. Cunetta gasps, the sound rising to a rough howl as he registers his legs are submerged up to mid-thigh in the field of stares. Ornate motes leap up his body like fleas made of jewelry as a sensation of nerves deadening bores up past his hips and through the core of his Kevlar-clad belly.

A hole opens in the floor at his one o'clock. It's Gearhardt's mouth, stretching into a soundless scream, the sum of his features unmistakable for a second longer, until his eyes float away to join the thousands of others that stud this still-expanding blanket of flesh.

A hand flaps in his peripheral vision and it's Tripp at his nine o'clock, submerged chest deep in the chaos that has engulfed them all. As their gazes meet Tripp comes apart, his arms flowing away from his shoulders, his head stretching and flattening into the curtain.

Spillman too is chest deep in the monster, Diego is neck deep, her teeth bared in a petrified rictus. A switch flips inside Cunetta and he accepts that he will never wake up. He squeezes the trigger of his Glock and blood and brains blow out the back of Diego's head. Spillman gargles as Cunetta's next shot goes through his throat, but the next gets him right in the eye and his head snaps back, mouth open as if he's trying to catch a snowflake.

The living carpet doesn't absorb Diego's head, it tumbles free across the swells of flesh. As Cunetta's chest goes numb, he burns the roof of his mouth with the friction-hot end of the Glock's barrel and feeds himself metal and fire.

earhardt's voice crackles in Dispatcher Jeppsen's headset. "That's right, Dispatch, all our radios went out at the same time, I can't explain why. Cunetta, Diego and Spillman still can't get theirs to work."

"Can you put Cunetta on?" Something about this declaration of all clear is giving Jeppsen the willies. Six officers having trouble with their radios all at once. In terms of unlikely coincidences, this one brings down a giant hammer and rings Jeppsen's bullshit bell hard. Gearhardt's solid, so far as she knows, unlikely to screw up protocols, but Cunetta's the senior officer on the scene.

"Negative, he's still in the store talking with the manager, Dispatch. They're trying to work out why the alarm went off."

Jeppsen glances over at her supervisor, Haysome, seated at the bank of computer monitors to her left. He's sipping from a coffee mug that reads ADORABLE BADASS. He sets down the mug, proffers Jeppsen a puzzled frown.

"No one with a working radio went with him?" Jeppsen asks.

The next voice she hears is that of Tripp, Gearhardt's partner. "Beverly, honey, everything is fine. But we figure we'd better come back to the station and switch out our faulty radios till shift's over. That sound alright to you?"

Haysome grabs his own headset. "Officer Tripp, that's way out of line. You're gonna be explaining yourself to the Chief."

Jeppsen clams up out of sheer shock, cheeks flushing deep red. She and Tripp went to high school together. He was a slender, well-toned athlete, she was a plump girl with a crush, he knew it and took advantage of her, calling her his "home base" when he was between girlfriends. He's never spoken to her this way since she started work in the dispatch center, never acted as if they had any history, always professional smiles with no attempt to engage deeper, and that has always been more than fine with her.

She wants to spew rage and profanity over the channel at him. Even though he provoked it, she'd be fired on the spot.

Gearhardt comes back on as if his partner never spoke. "We'll be there in ten to exchange our radios. Dispatch, can you confirm whether Rochelle Turner is still in custody?"

Jeppsen, still furious, exchanges glances with her supervisor, whose gray eyebrows have lowered in a puzzled frown. Word of Turner's arrest got around the department. The foster mother of Madeleine Bowes, a.k.a. the girl found at the Vanished Neighborhood. Caught trying to break into a house in north Hillcrest, where all the old money lives in hilltop mansions. Swearing up and down her Maddy was missing, charged at the scene with resisting arrest. The chief didn't want to give her a chance to post bail, not just yet. Whether or not the Bowes girl was really missing, who knew, not uncommon for foster kids to run away—but the Petrasek family was definitely M.I.A.

"10-4," says Haysome. "Why do you want to know? Is there a connection to the call you're on?"

"I'll talk to you about it when we're 10-25."

Jeppsen vows, no matter what Haysome might think, that she has every right to let Tripp have it once he returns to the station and she's going to do so, she's not going to let him get away with belittling her this way.

Fifteen minutes later, through the glass paneling of the dispatch center, she spies Gearhardt walking up. He's alone.

When Gearhardt leaves, heading for the chief's office, then the jail, the dispatch center is empty.

30

A ndrew steps down from his dad's Ford Focus into the parking lot of a bar he's never visited before, Hillcrest Inn on Shenandoah Valley Road. He gets to drive his dad's SUV because his parents can't object anymore in the place where they now exist.

Not that he's in a state to gloat. He hasn't slept for many days. He can't control where he goes, his legs are not his own and the remainder of his nervous system can be hijacked to any degree at any time. His swollen innards grate with a sharp ache, as if one wrong step will cause him to split from tailbone to crotch and spill his intestines down the insides of his jeans.

He's made several trips like this one, goaded by the gift Josey left him, going where the parasitic urges direct him. The things inside him hunger for recruits. His panic helped the first one escape, that sad looking addict that tried to grope him. The parasitic layers punished him for letting the creep get away. Since then, he hasn't fought their desires. He won't fight them this time either.

A squadron of motorcycles leans in majestic formation, filling the parking spots closest to the front door. Andrew lurches inside, the tinted glass muffling the afternoon sun as the door shuts behind him,

There's a small crowd in leather vests, half bellied up to the U-shaped bar, scattered among the stools, reminding Andrew of a lower jaw with teeth missing. The other half of the biker bunch surrounds one of the pool tables. Just days ago Andrew would have been scared to walk among these people, with their wiry arms and tattoos and glances that assess and contemptuously dismiss a soft, indulged rich boy. But that's not what he is now.

Beyond that table, at a booth underneath a window, an old black man looks up with a sharp snap of shaggy head to eyeball Andrew. The old man's white mane frames a face carved from basalt.

Andrew lurches, his gait entirely without grace, practically stumbling in the direction of the pool table. Layers shift in his overloaded, overheated belly. A picture coalesces in his head, of a broad-shouldered, denim-jacketed giant of a fellow with cigarette in mouth, salt-and-pepper hair, pool cue in hand. A man that one of the parasites hopes to find. The eyes in his head don't spy such a person anywhere inside the Hillcrest Inn; neither do the eyes elsewhere on his body.

The black man barks an order. "Aaron, get over here!"

His command appears to be aimed at a short fellow who manages to be handsome despite a head that's a bit too big for his body. Said fellow, Aaron, leaning on the bar, waiting to get the bartender's attention, half-turns toward the shout, startled. "You said you didn't want anything—"

Clearly the wrong response. "You stupid jackass, get over here, now!"

A couple of the bikers at the pool table chuckle at the drama. One mutters under his breath, loud enough for Andrew to hear, "Massa says you better move, bitch."

Aaron follows the black man's gaze, regards Andrew, his square-jawed features contorting in crumple-browed puzzlement that gradually gives way to alarm, lips parting, eyes widening. The black man, too, stares at Andrew, upper lip curled in repulsion.

Whoever these men are, the hunger in Andrew doesn't hunger for them. But it will devour them nonetheless.

A couple more steps bring him right up to the men and women clustered at the pool table. A fellow with a trucker's cap, Wolverine side-burns and bare arms knotted with muscle straightens up and moves to obstruct his path. "Boy, you need something?"

What will be will be, but the part of Andrew that's a helpless passenger gasps at an unexpected distraction. Andrew isn't sure how the black man's name, John Hairston, has come to be in his mind, or how he can hear Hairston speak without the man's mouth moving. *I see what kind of thing you are. You're a hole full of corpses. A hole that needs to be closed.*

The man in the trucking cap squints and frowns, caught between different strains of concern. "Do you need help? Or do you need me to help you out the door?" His entire party watching now, five men and three women of varying ages, all hard-bitten, white-skinned, stained by cigarette smoke and dried out with the premature aging brought on by harsh living.

The part of Andrew that experiences fear must still have some input over the rest of his body because the skin he can feel slicks with sweat. His face flushes hot. The pain threatening to split his crotch fades as he grows numb below the belt, and he knows what that means, but this intensifying warmth, that's new.

"Y'all get out of here," Hairston shouts, his voice sounding in the room and Andrew's head at the same time.

Trucker man twists his neck in the black man's direction with vehement indignation, way more than he's demonstrated to Andrew. One of his fellows yells, "What the hell's your problem, y'old freak?"

Warmer and warmer.

Aaron reaches Hairston's table. Hairston whispers something, but Andrew hears it somehow, the link straight into his mind still live. "If we live through this, you're gonna be a believer. Get that window open."

Aaron does a startled double take. Trucking cap puts a hand on Andrew's shoulder. "Boy, you need to answer."

Andrew groans as openings full of teeth appear all down the lower half of his body, muffled under his jeans and flannel shirt.

"Quit starin' and get the window open," says Hairston to Aaron.

Trucker hat is staring at the hand he placed on Andrew's shoulder, as ornate buttons swarm over it, etching seams up his forearm. He's almost certainly discovered he can't take his hand away, if he's even trying. He may not be, as other parts of Andrew have already reached out to touch him. A bridge of flesh has sprouted from under Andrew's shirt and stuffed its tendril down the front of trucker hat's pants, and more bright button motes are crossing the bridge.

Warmer and warmer.

A woman on the other side of the pool table picks up that there's something funny about trucker hat's stance. "Pete, what's wrong? Let that kid go."

The worst part of the condition Josey inflicted on him: that he's fully aware, independent of the things using his body to work mischief. The layers are filling Pete even as his friend tries to get his attention. Andrew wants to scream, because there's more sensation than just the expansion of the quilt folds. Heat sparks and spikes as if dozens of matches are striking inside him, somewhere an impossible distance away and at the same time immediately assaulting his nerves.

"What the fuck—?" says the burly giant to Pete's right. Perhaps he's noticed the way Pete shudders as the motes crawl up his neck, invading his stubble, scaling his face.

Long flaps of loose skin curl out from under Andrew's shirt. The bubbling fabric of his jeans splits open, unleashing twists of flesh that inflate into gape-mouth faces and grasping hands. One of the women screams, and Andrew screams with her.

The young man at the back table, Aaron, screams something too, and Andrew doesn't hear that clearly, but he catches Hairston's response, still carbon copied straight to his brain. "Break the glass, genius . . . shit, get down!"

The burly giant pulls a pistol, a beat behind two of his compatriots at the bar. Membranes of skin billow like windblown curtains from Andrew's waist, arms sprouting from them like time lapse branches on fast forward. His torso remains intact atop the fleshy chaos, a buoy bobbing atop a geyser of body parts. He raises his hands in a futile warning, his arms drenched in sweat as an oven's heat bakes him from the inside.

The bullets that pass through his lungs and belly and neck also burn, steel-hard punches with a red-hot poker that would flatten him if he weren't attached by flesh and bone to a monster. As much as they hurt, as much as he wishes they would kill him, they have no lasting effect.

A tide of convulsing flesh pours out from the nether spaces where the layers reside, spilling over the pool table, upending and smashing chairs before avalanching over the bar. This isn't how this usually goes, usually the layers urge Andrew to isolate a new recruit before they consume him. The forces he's enslaved to are as panicked as he is. The gang around the pool table succumbs in an instant to the bloodless dismemberment enabled by the glimmering buttons, heads still shrieking as they detach and flatten, the sounds muffled only when mouths submerge into the layers. One bottle-blonde woman escapes their fate as friendly fire blows blood and brains out the back of her head.

No such mercy for Andrew. Hot impacts shred his neck and his view of the chaos in the room flips as his head ends up dangling upside down from the strip of his neck that remains, but he doesn't bleed and he doesn't die.

The bar patrons, the staff, don't stand a chance, but as their screams subside, more rise from the captives trapped in the layers. They share their agony with Andrew. His insides are being cooked, layer after layer of living skin pressed against a hot burner. "Stop!" he yells, though he can't draw air to project his voice. "Stop!"

The mass of gasping mouths, bulging eyes, flailing limbs that fills the Hillcrest Inn blackens and smolders in a thousand places. Some of those parts are newly part of the quilt, taken from those unlucky enough to be in the bar when Andrew staggered in, equally subject to the encroaching fire.

His head happens to flop in the right direction and he can see how the extensions of his possessed self that flow too near Aaron and Hairston erupt in blistering embers and immediately shrink back.

The window Aaron has been charged with opening was painted shut long ago, but he swings a chair at the glass, again, again, and this time it shatters. Hairston stares straight at Andrew, his voice carrying again without his mouth moving. "I'm a gateway too, motherfucker."

Andrew experiences a moment of eureka: he's up against someone who also contains the inexplicable within, a different inexplicable from the monstrous thing that operates through him.

Molten lead flows between the infinite spaces where his intestines should have been. His world is an agony he can't escape.

Andrew's mouth opens wide in a soundless scream, his almost-detached head still hardwired into miles and miles of shrieking nerves.

Hairston's voice in Andrew's ear. "Nothing I can do to save you. Any of you. But I can end it. Fire purges everything."

31

T he hours stretch to days, it seems, as Rochelle waits for deliverance. When it comes, its approach gives her no comfort. For one, it's not a pair of female deputies who arrive to escort her from her cell, but a lone male police officer. The silver name tag on his blue uniform reads B.R. GEARHARDT. He's big, his protective vest makes him look like a walking oil drum with a buzz-cut block of a head mounted on top.

As he regards her through the mesh, Rochelle tries not to betray how her heart's in her mouth. "Have you found my daughter?"

"She's not your daughter." Gearhardt has a voice like a bull moose. "You're her foster mother."

"She might as well be my daughter." Rochelle fights to keep her voice from rising in pitch and volume. "Have you done anything to find her? Anything at all?"

"We're looking for her now," he says. "I had to pull some strings and hook some buttons in the right buttonholes, but we're ready to help. There's an officer headed to your house right now, in case she came back home while you were away. Too bad you didn't stay put and call us in the first place."

Rochelle doesn't even want to admit to herself that she took matters into her own hands because she didn't want word getting out that she'd lost track of one of her fosters. Maybe it's too late to salvage things now. But maybe not.

"I didn't call the police because I didn't think I needed the police. Last I saw Maddy she got into a car with Josey Petrasek's mother. I went over there because no one was answering the phone. I just thought they might not be paying attention. That's a big house, you know, maybe they were just in another room. But they weren't there at all. Have you found them?"

"We haven't found Maddy."

"Are you gonna let me out?"

His face might as well be carved from wood. "Maybe. If you can answer a few questions." Yet he's fitting a key in the square of metal that contains the lock, sliding the door aside. "Be nice and we'll discuss that option."

Rochelle backs up to the cots, mounted one above the other in the wall. "Where are we going?"

"Nowhere," Gearhardt says. He squeezes through the entrance sideways. He's wide enough that there's no way around him. "At least not for now."

"What questions?" Rochelle contemplates whether screaming will bring help or get her killed. "I'll answer all the questions you've got, just ask away."

There's something wrong with Gearhardt's face. He's not sweating, he's not smiling or grimacing, but seams have appeared around his eyes and mouth and across his broad, blunt forehead that weren't there before. And glimmering beads. Of different colors, lined up along the seams. "Lord have mercy," Rochelle says.

The cop's head lowers and his mouth opens in a wide, hang-jawed grin, the kind you see on a psycho killer in a movie. But what's revealed behind his parted lips is not teeth and tongue but another mouth, like he's a costume and someone inside is wearing him.

Rochelle screams loud and long but she already understands there's no help coming.

The thing wearing Gearhardt widens its eyes and stretches its mouth in mockery and it lurches forward, advancing past the sink and toilet. Then it falters backward. Its upper and lower lips split vertically and the mouth behind them curls up in a grimace and shrieks as a tongue of bright flame curls out.

Rochelle scrambles backward onto the lower cot and against the wall.

Her brain breaks completely. First the Gearhardt thing is uncoiling like every part of it is a living, slithering roll of skin unwinding, the single shriek it emits multiplying into a thousand. The next second, a fireball floods the cell. The next second, nothing, no smoke, no flames, no cop or monster pretending to be a cop.

The smell of burned hair overwhelms. Her hands, her forearms, reflexively drawn up to shield her face, are terrifyingly red and raw and blistered. The sheets of the cot smolder.

The cell door remains open. Rochelle makes a run for it, ignoring the cries from her nerve endings as her body starts to register the damage from the freak blast. "Help!" she rasps. "Anyone?"

The jail pod gate also stands open. No one responds to her calls.

32

The police cruiser veers off the road, three blocks shy of Mama Rochelle's house, and rolls down the sloping front yard of Becca's home. It crosses the cobblestone front walk that leads visitors to the porch, rolls right over the tidy garden, crushing bushes and flowers, and smashes through the wall.

Becca's father is asleep when the cruiser lands on top of him. He works third shift in a plastics factory, sweeping his arm through a dangerous hot press to pluck parts for medical equipment out of molds. He resigned himself long ago to the risk of dismemberment from the elbow down for the sake of steady income. The possibility of being pinned under a running car engine has never even crossed his mind.

The cruiser smashes through the window over his bed and drops in at angle, tilting the bed so his head bounces off the transmission before the bumper crushes his thighs into the mattress, his hips pressed up against the underside of the radiator, the oil pan pressing his gut up into his diaphragm.

Becca sits on the living room coach watching Netflix cartoons when the shattering of glass and the crunch of splintered wood and smashed drywall interrupts. She freezes until her father's wheezing screams begin. More screams follow, a chorus loud as thunder—it sounds like a thousand people are howling their last in her parents' bedroom.

She throws the door open to find a bashed up police car where her parents' bed should be.

A nightmare fills the car's cab, a writhing morass of loose skin, glistening muscle, flailing limbs, rotating faster and faster around an impossible opening, a cyclone shaft that drains into nowhere. It's like one of Maddy's creepy sketches roaring into violent life. The screams of multitudes pour out from this narrowing funnel, and elongated flames lick from its walls. A stench assaults Becca, smoke and a grotesque swell of burning meat. As she gags, her eyes play a bewildering trick—motes like white embers shine out within the whirling flesh and fire, and then those motes hurtle into the depths of the contracting tunnel like a hyperspace special effect.

Spinning flesh, agonized shrieks, sickening smell all vanish, leaving behind the car's rumbling engine and her father's feeble cries for help. Becca spies his legs for the first time, jutting from under the front bumper.

When she calls 911, it rings and rings and rings and no one picks up at the other end. It will take hours for distracted city authorities to comprehend that an entire shift of police officers and dispatchers has gone missing.

33

You raise your hand like you're a kid in class, hoping Maddy will understand your gesture and stop walking. "Something's wrong," you say. "Something's really fucked up."

Maddy pops her eyes comically and holds her nose. "You think?" The field the two of you are crossing reeks of manure.

You and Maddy have walked for miles. It's a wonder no one has waylaid your progress, tried to question you or Maddy. Obviously neither of you rated an Amber Alert.

You could drive, some parts of you nestled in the layers know how, but if it went wrong it could bring a lot of attention, and Maddy told you she didn't want you to hurt anyone else. Whatever she is, she's much more human than you, affected by things like smells and uncomfortable surfaces and displays of cruelty. You don't want to drive her away. And you have reason to be afraid of her, though you aren't.

Soon after leaving the overpass, the two of you sat in a park and dined on fast food breakfasts you stole using Carolyn's form. Two kids wandering in the open during school hours could draw attention, and so could an adult wandering with a young girl. Lucky you, there's a park path parallel to a big creek that's not much used because it runs through rundown neighborhoods. That got you as far as the Hillcrest Mall, once all hustle and bustle, now half empty. Maddy argued with you about going inside. *You don't want me to go in then you stop me*, she said. You couldn't. The worst didn't happen, though. None of the elderly mall walkers making use of all that empty space seemed to care that the two of you were there. You comprehend the adult world enough to suspect that no one's looking for Maddy, no urgent news alerts, which could mean something's gone wrong back at her home, but you're not going to say anything because she'll bolt straight back to Mama Rochelle and what's waiting might only look like her.

You left her wandering in a lonely secondhand clothing store so you could hunt for a lunch. It was for her, you didn't need one. As the homeless man you crossed the parking lot, acting on a stolen memory. You asked the gruff old man running the sausage stand in front of the big box hardware store if he'd spare a dog to help out a fellow man. He did, bless his soul. The hot dog had cooled considerably by the time you got it to Maddy. She wolfed it down.

You've walked and walked some more, along residential streets, through crude woodland paths, over fences and across hilly pastures, the sun disappearing behind clouds and blazing out again.

You haven't shared with Maddy that you have no plan. You only have wants.

You've wanted to get away from your mother and her suffocating box. You've wanted to find your sibling, to recruit her to your cause. Some part of you, maybe the part that's still Davey, dreamed you'd have a peer. An ally in the fight against the world. Against you mother. Some part of you believed that if you doubled yourself, you'd never again suffer the lonely agony of your mother's sealed box.

She's not a double. She's out of your reach. Touching her is death. Something in you whispers, *try it, try it*, not in another voice but in your own.

You do have direction of a sort. Your instinct is to get away from your mother, from that sensation of her presence that makes you itch deep. Over the years you've come to sense the nearness of her collective presence like radiation from a node of hell. You have let that sensation propel you and you have felt the radiation dim another fraction with each step you take.

Beyond that you've got no firm ideas on how to travel, how to live, where exactly to go. If—no, *when*—Maddy questions your choices, the sham of your decisiveness will peel open, but, so far, despite her snark, she's following where you lead.

Except something is wrong. Something new. Something warm.

"What are you even talking about?" she asks. "*Everything* is fucked up."

"No, that's not what I mean," you say. You don't have the words to explain the disturbances you feel, emanating from somewhere both well outside and deep inside you.

A continent is shifting, lava trickling, threatening flood.

Maddy reaches the top of the grassy slope you're ascending and stops. "Whoa! Cows. Lots of them. Wow, they're huge."

Despite the heated queasiness rising from below, you laugh. "What?" Then you see them. Huge black beasts, as big as any car, the massive furred barrels of their bodies improbably mounted on the comical stilts of their legs. Ears twitching in agitation, they watch you with eyes like black marbles, empty of soul.

Maddy moves closer, an arm held out to touch one of the beasts. It shifts its weight on those spindles, eyes widening enough to show whites.

"Be careful!" The irony, that if you touch Maddy the reaction could kill you, or worse—yet if these stupid animals stampeded and trampled, you would survive and Maddy would likely die. Unless your mother's act of expelling Maddy from the layers instilled even more surprises.

She still tries to pet the cow, which shuffles two quick steps sideways. Maddy laughs, not seeing how the others are rolling their eyes, the way they teeter as if winding up to a run.

You start to scold her, but a different threat commands your attention. That abstract notion of lava flow grows less abstract by the second. Echoes reach you of screams, the shrills of pure fear from forest creatures fleeing a primordial fire.

"Stop," you say. "Stop a second. Something's happening."

"Yeah, cows are happening," Maddy says. "I can't believe this, you're not even human and you're scared of cows. That's pathetic. Wait, what are you doing?"

The warmth filling you brings no comfort.

You clutch at your chest, your face, pacing in a tight circle. "Something bad is happening," you say. Howls of distant agony vibrate inside your skin. Somewhere, somehow, the layers are on fire. Should that fire spread you don't know how to escape it. You are tethered to the kindling.

"Stop that, it's gross," Maddy says.

"I don't understand what's happening!" Your panic could be your own or it could be amplifications of the fear shrieking through the layers. Your grip on the fluttering spark of self your mother granted you, the thing that keeps you Davey by default, falters. You no longer notice the agitation of the cattle or Maddy's own cries of alarm at the animals' bleats and bellows. The heat and grit of smoke stuffs your interstices. Hooves kick up clods of grass and moist dirt.

Outside yourself half-lives trapped in the layers are burning alive, their fear and pain boiling up into you like magma forcing open a crack in the crust. The force killing them is following through the crack, heat rising, oven elements reddening in the spaces where the old Davey, the real Davey, contained muscle and bone.

"Get away, Maddy! Get away!" you shout through three, seven, thirteen mouths. You can see that she doesn't obey, that she's disgusted and mesmerized by what's happening to your body. What's trapped inside you is trying to flee, a futile folly, but the shape of Davey can no longer dam the outward flow. Arms radiate out from you in all directions, grasping for nonexistent lifebuoys, for rungs to climb away from the fire. The words from your many mouths blur to raw screams.

Like a bay door slammed down on concrete, a force intercedes between you and the surging lava. Something with power on a level you've never encountered has carved through the infinite layers of flesh and pain and sheered off the mass afflicted by fire, repelling it into the region outside time and mind where it will consume itself and shrivel to nothing. The falling away relieves you of that heat, replaced with a familiar presence that radiates a sickness all its own.

The endless lengths of nerves that tie you into the remaining layers convey an image to your mind, a slender form of vaguely bipedal outline, standing in a box proportioned like a coffin but smaller, swarming all over with tiny crawling motes—the parasites, the buttons—congealing in thick, ever-shifting clumps, the way bees form a beard on a beekeeper.

She is radiating the strength of a dark sun, severing through the layers by the thousands to protect herself from the fire, and in the process, the big brown eyes that are truly hers open somewhere in the mass and focus on you. And her voice says, *There you are.*

You shout with a hundred voices, *"Maddy run!"*

 **34**

I n the car, Hairston grabs the dashboard and digs his fingers so hard into the plastic that it cracks, arching his back and grimacing as if he's just taken a bullet.

The gesture so startles Aaron that he jerks the wheel.

What follows he observes with a strange calm. The outcome of the next few seconds will depend on factors completely beyond his control. His car does a donut in the middle of the Interstate, tires screeching, the grill missing the jersey wall by inches, going for a second spin as an 18-wheeler bears down on them, this time the left rear passenger side slamming into the concrete barrier, the Buick coming to a stop facing the wrong way in the passing lane as the truck veers partway onto the shoulder and blares past. Incredibly there's no traffic immediately behind it and Aaron stomps the gas, making a U-turn that takes them off the shoulder and into the new-mowed grass.

"Fuck!" he shouts as his car comes to rest. "Are you alright?"

Hairston raises his hands and glares at Aaron from between his splayed fingers. All of his fingernails have split, rivulets of blood wind down from the cuticles.

"It fought back," Hairston says. "The cursed thing fought back."

"What fought back?" Aaron saw the flailing flesh of the monster incinerate. There was nothing left to fight back. There couldn't be. It has to be over.

"Turn around," Hairston growls.

It has to be over, because Aaron wants the world to give him an opening, a chance to convince himself that he witnessed nothing, that reality did not unhinge its jaw and vomit up monsters inside the Hillcrest Inn. That the man who rides beside him did not summon the fires of Hell in return.

"Turn the fuck around!" Hairston points further down the interstate, where there's a median crossover of the kind used by ambulances and state troopers. "Take that there turn and go back to Hillcrest. We have to go back. Now!"

35

"*M*addy run!*"
Maddy almost obeys.

Davey seethes as if he's made of coils of animate mummy-wrappings, a boy-shaped spindle of snakes. The cows have scattered, their meaty masses vanished over grassy hills.

About ten yards separate them. Maddy would have a good head start if she ran but in a race against the kind of creature he is she's not at all sure she could win. Yet if he caught her—he's told her that if she touches him what happened to Josey will happen to him. She can't be sure it's true until she tries it. A part of her desperately wants to and if she's honest with herself it's this desire even more than concern for her brother in misery that keeps her from bolting. "What's happening to you?" She hates how shrill she sounds. "Tell me!"

Davey's body elongates upward. "She found me!" he wails. His eyes emerge from the chaos of his face, but they are darker, larger. He swells and ripples as if inflated from inside by cyclone-force winds. His outlines recede and sharpen. A woman stands in his place. Tall and slender, in jeans, sneakers and a sweater, hair dark as her eyes.

The woman smiles. "I remember you. Do you remember me?"

That voice. *I gave you back everything I could. Maybe I'll see you again. When you're older.*

Maddy folds her arms over her stomach and hunches down like she's trying to curl into a ball and vanish. She crouches, shivering, the same way she once shivered in the street, watching a monster in the shape of a woman as it strolled off into the night. Leaving her alone in the Vanished Neighborhood, where police would find her many hours later, crouched in the exact same spot, muttering, *Mommy, don't you think it was funny?*

"She swallowed the spider to catch the fly," the woman says, sing-song. "I don't know why she swallowed that fly. Perhaps she'll die."

The world around Maddy contracts to gray, her heart pounding, the rest of her trapped in stasis. That song. It's her long-lost mother's song, a little ditty she sang in a chirpy voice to make her daughter laugh, her tone stripping out all the morbidity.

Davey's notes: *my mom stole your mom's skin*

"Maddy, what have you been doing with my son? He won't tell me."

The only thing that keeps Maddy from collapsing and curling up like a pillbug is a paralysis of stupefaction. Davey's pathetic transformation instilled more pity than fear despite its violence, but this woman, standing as casual as if she had been the one walking by Maddy's side this whole day, encases Maddy's mind in ice, her voice unmistakably the same as that of Maddy's long-lost mother as she calls Maddy's name again. With a smile pleasant as a late sunrise she bends and leans, putting the gaze from her large brown eyes level with Maddy's own. She waves. "Hello?" Smile fading to a cockeyed smirk, she hums the song again. *There was an old lady that swallowed a fly. . .*

"Mom," Maddy whispers. Ice cracks, adrenaline bubbling out through it, and her nerves retake command. She wants to puke but she doesn't. She could run, but holds her place and pose. "Is my mom in there? With Davey? Have you got her in there?"

The woman tips her head back, regards Maddy with eyes half-lidded. Above, ordinary clouds drift beneath an unremarkable sky. A shift in air current brings a waft of manure like a sick punchline. Nausea rises in response and it's all Maddy can do to keep from retching.

"I've missed you so much."

The last time Maddy heard that voice, she had just finished watching a musical in elementary school about a smart little girl who didn't want to share. The play made her laugh so hard, she couldn't stop telling her mommy how funny she thought it was. They got in the car, and she wanted to know if her mommy thought it was funny too, and her mommy kept telling her what to do—*Maddy, don't be silly. Hold still, damn it. Hold still.*—instead of answering her question. She kept asking, while a thing with no shape of its own hid in the back seat, letting a few seconds pass, enough for Maddy and her mom to buckle in, before it slithered forward.

The change unfolded too quick for Maddy to follow, as if the woman standing in front of her had always been curly-haired, blonde, blue-eyed, her broad faced etched with seams of worry that all too rarely yielded a fragile smile. Her outfit has altered, her jeans faded and flared into bell-bottoms, her denim jacket unsnapped, exposing the image on her T-shirt, two young girls, one blonde, one brunette, staring at a candle flame.

Maddy trembles.

"Oh my god, look at you," her mom says. "I'm so sorry. I'm sorry you've been alone so long."

The treacherous surge of longing, of hope, counter to all rational thought, pulls her to run toward her mother, not away. Maddy tries hard, so hard, to keep her head, to remember that much-missed face hides an all-devouring funnel of flesh.

The mommy in front of her is all smiles as she takes a step and opens her arms. "Honey, come here. Let me make it up to you. For everything."

It takes no stretch to imagine a caress from those hands would match the ones from memory, palms warm, fingertips cold. *I need you to warm 'em up,* she'd say when Maddy whined at the chill touch. *You're so warm, you're my hot water bottle.*

"Hey, you know, your father is here, too. I can have him speak if you want to hear his voice."

The spell breaks. Even after all these years, Maddy remembers how frightened her mom had been of her dad, though she's foggy as to the reasons. She just recalls the tension in her mommy's wiry frame, the bulges of muscle at the corners of her jaw, when he came up in conversation, heightened tenfold when he paid a visit. Even then Maddy could tell something was wrong, the way her beleaguered mother would, maybe without even meaning to, shift to maintain the maximum distance possible between herself and her ex-lover in the tiny rooms of the modular home where they lived. And how her mom would stiffen when he closed that distance.

Maddy's surge of elation sours into stinging hot pain behind her eyes. It seeps into her chest, threatens to clench her throat. She gives that pain an angry shove to stop herself from producing tears for the monster's enjoyment. Unfrozen, the question at the top of her mind comes loose. "What did you do to Davey?"

36

There are things your mother doesn't know, but you can't keep them from her for long. Once she has you back in the box, whatever form it takes, she will never let you out again.

37

Maddy asks again, louder. "What did you do to Davey?"

"Nothing," says the thing pretending to be Maddy's mother. "He's right here."

"Maddy, touch her."

She isn't sure where the second voice came from. Her not-mother keeps on talking. "I've missed you so much. You were in here with me once. She let you out because I begged her to, because you were too young. She agreed with me because she's a mother herself. But I've been so lonely without you."

Again, a whisper. *"Maddy please."* Davey.

"You'll never be lonely again. Your father is here and so many others and they will all love you. Remember that blanket you loved so much, the one with the daffodils, it'll be like you're all wrapped up in it, like a comforter made from warm hands. We have so many hands to hold you. We'll hug you and it'll last forever."

A flap of flesh droops out from under the hem of her mother's jacket, about the same size and shape as a hip flask. The flap has a mouth, it's been speaking at the same time as Maddy's mom, who doesn't seem to notice. As Maddy stares, the flap swells, eyeholes open below the mouth, eyes inflate to fill them. It's Davey, his face upside-down. "Do what she wants," he pleads. "Let her touch you." The flap of his inverted head contracts and bulges. He coughs out a long twist of skin.

"C'mon, sweetie," Maddy's mom says, bending with her arms held out. "Let me scoop you up."

Maddy isn't sure who she is obeying as she starts forward. The twist of skin protruding from Davey's mouth unfurls, the pale scars and tangles of veins revealed there spelling out *KILL US*.

Maddy's mom lunges forward to grab her, and as she's lifted Maddy shrieks and kicks her legs, sure she's been tricked.

Her mom says, "There you gooooo—" and her mouth continues to stretch in a grotesquely elongated oval, her lips at last folding over and peeling back like a sausage rind, exposing membranes beneath that are also splitting and peeling back, opening a hole so deep that it descends beneath the wholesome pasture grass, plummeting into the earth and at the same time somewhere outside it. Human howls by the thousands rise from the pit.

"Don't let go!" wails Davey, his squeak barely audible above the din.

Below her a glittering exodus rains into the void, bright motes leaping like burning fleas to escape her.

"Don't let go!"

But the hands clutching Maddy do let go and her grip slips and she's falling. She screams as she falls. An object like a hard pillow shoves her and she lands half on ground, half on a shuddering strip of flesh that proves to be the grotesque lip of a hellmouth, a roughly circular sphincter wide as a station wagon, orifice for an abyss filled with shrieks of human agony.

On contact with her the ledge of flesh splits and recoils. As the cartilaginous tissue parts a face appears in the gap, Davey's face, peering up at her with desperate dark eyes. He opens his mouth to speak or scream but his features peel off like wet wallpaper, leaving a rudimentary skull behind that melts to paste even as it becomes visible, button-motes bursting out of its crevices and falling away. His dark eyes remain an instant longer, flattening into large buttons that scuttle away like frightened cockroaches.

The hellmouth contracts inward and down, the turf folds in over it. Maddy lies on her belly in an empty pasture, grass tickling her face, the stink of manure overwhelming.

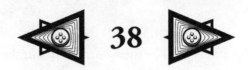

38

Maddy sets foot on Mama Rochelle's driveway somewhere between midnight and the witching hour, her bedraggled form emerging into the pool of illumination made by the squat brick lamppost that stands sentry at the front of the yard, her clothes and face shaded with dirt.

Rochelle must be home, her light blue minivan with its rust spots sits cozy in the driveway, cast in chiaroscuro by the light angling from the lamppost. Maddy aches from sole to scalp, or she would dash to the door and pound on it. She doesn't know how she'll explain where she's been or what she's seen and she doesn't care.

She angles across the grass toward the front walk, reduced to a silhouette in the patch of darkness that's just out of reach of both lamppost and porch light.

The front door of the house opens inward, the screen door creaks outward. "Mama," Maddy calls, quickening her step. The motion detector mounted between the second-floor windows clicks and an even brighter light joins the chorus, granting a golden gloss to the sleek flow of dark hair that crowns the woman on the concrete stoop.

Maddy freezes. She's making tiny noises, part gasp, part groan, in between panicked inhales.

"You called me mama," says Davey's mother. "I guess that's fitting."

A terrible notion blooms in Maddy's brain. She holds her ground, and if she sheds tears, they are tears of rage.

"I never regretted letting you go, until today," the woman says. "Now I know how much of a mistake it was." She sounds calm, up until she says *mistake*, then her voice cracks. "There's a price for what you did to my son."

"He wanted to get away from you, far away, more than anything else in the whole wide world," Maddy says. "Where's Mama Rochelle?"

The woman hasn't let the screen door shut. She pushes it so it creaks wider. "Won't you come in?"

"Where's Mama Rochelle?"

"Come inside, I'll show you."

"No I won't. What have you done to her?" Though Maddy knows. "Where are her kids? Where are my sisters?"

"I'll let them all go," the woman says, "all of them, if you kill yourself."

"If—" It's like Maddy's tongue lodges in her throat, her breath stoppered. She wants to laugh and shout to the hidden camera crew that must exist that they can come out now, the joke's over. If there's a hidden camera, it's manned by demons, and they're the ones laughing.

The significance of that string of words won't come into focus, and yet her eyes burn, her breath wheezes fast, she's hitching and sniffling, and her heartbeat rushes faster, too fast, painfully fast, like it's a machine overloading.

"Think what I'm offering. If I let them out, I can't hurt them again, just like I can't hurt you anymore. They'll never know what happened to them. But after what you did—I can't tolerate that, and you know too much, and I can't allow *that*."

I can't hurt you anymore. It's a lie, though. The thing hiding in the back seat has taken her family again, torn a new hole, a deeper pain than Maddy has ever felt in a life riddled with never-healing wounds.

It's not done hurting Maddy. It will never be done.

"Just do what I want," the monster says, not commanding, but syrup-sweet. "I'll help you make it painless—"

In the distance, an engine roar, a car tearing through the neighborhoods at high speed, the shriek of rubber sliding on asphalt. Dogs bark in response.

Maddy finds her words. "You let them all go!" Across the street, a light turns on behind a shaded window. The engine roar grows louder.

The woman withdraws a step, holding the screen door like a shield against Maddy. "If you want that, you need to calm down and do what I—"

"You took everything from me!"

Maddy springs and grabs the edge of the door before the woman can jerk it shut.

She hurtles forward even as the woman's body unfurls into a monstrous curtain of tooth-filled mouths.

Maddy leaps, hands curled into claws. Teeth press in like knives, all over her body, their piercing pressure withdrawn the same instant they strike. She strikes at the same time and as her nails rake strips from the curtain of flesh it rips apart, opening before her in a whirlpool of skin and blood, large enough to swallow a bus.

She falls in. A thousand hands grab for her, trying to expel her, disintegrating at the moment of contact. She lands on a slimy surface, too uneven to be called a floor. She scrambles forward because the surface contracts away from whatever part of her touches it. To move in any direction other than down she must crawl like a mole in a tunnel, she made a terrible mistake and she can't take it back, she can't stop moving for even a second or she'll fall forever.

Hands swarm her as she thrashes and advances. Their owners could be pleading for help or lashing out at her with intent to pluck out her eyes, shred her skin, pound her into bloody paste. They keep her fully surrounded, a churning surface of blows and caresses that retract at the last second, fleshy gloves immediately unraveled and just as quickly replaced by new outspread palms or bunched fists, which too peel away, immediately replaced by more, the cycle unending, the fleshy ground collapsing under each lurch no matter how fast she moves, her nightmare exit from the world inevitable, unstoppable.

A man shouts and somehow the noise forces its way through the din of disintegrating souls to make itself known. There's no room in what's left of Maddy's mind to contemplate how this is possible. He talks with a stentorian authority, every syllable a command, but Maddy's panicked perpetual flight flays the words to nonsense.

Rochelle is screaming Maddy's name. Prixie is screeching in agony. The twins are bawling. Lakesha squeals like she's being boiled alive. Ashley laughs, nonstop cruelty, *your gonna die you dumb bitch you're going to be eaten alive ha ha ha ha ha.* The man shouts at Maddy to stop listening, *it's all tricks don't listen don't believe a word it lies.*

The comforter of warm hands her mother promised. It tries and tries to weave itself around her and shreds to pieces even as it forms. The bed it purports to cover keeps tearing open underneath her, dropping her down amid the monsters underneath. *Mommy, do you think this is funny? Stop it mommy stop it STOP IT*

A woman's hand grabs her right wrist, its light brown skin blotched with blisters and blighted by red and peeling skin, horrific burns that will scar in moonscape furrows. A man's hand grabs her left wrist, its near-black skin barely concealing a fire inside, an inferno of hatred and worse, a strain of unnatural life that worms through its veins and winds fibers through its meat, a force that was never meant to exist in this world. Even as this mismatched pair lifts her out of the pit, she cannot tell whether they're real.

ABOUT THE AUTHORS

World Fantasy Award-winning writer **C. S. E. Cooney** is the author of *Desdemona and the Deep*, and *Bone Swans: Stories*. She has narrated over a hundred audiobooks—including her own—and has produced three albums as the singer/songwriter Brimstone Rhine. Her poetry collection *How to Flirt in Faerieland and Other Wild Rhymes* includes "The Sea-King's Second Bride," which won the Rhysling Award for best long-form verse in speculative poetry. Her short stories and poems can be found in numerous anthologies and magazines: most recently Jonathan Strahan's *Book of Dragons*, and Ellen Datlow's *Mad Hatters and March Hares: All New Stories from the World of Lewis Carroll's Alice in Wonderland*. Learn more online at csecooney.com.

About her story, she wrote: "Indispensable to the writing of 'The Twice-Drowned Saint' were Carlos Hernandez (who can take a weird angel and make them so much weirder), Robert Peterson (new friend and ice-climbing expert: all mistakes in the text are my own), Magill Foote (for his insights into early cinema), the Infernal Harpies (Caitlyn Paxson, Tiffany Trent, Ysabeau Wilce, Nicole Kornher-Stace, Jessica P. Wick, Patty Templeton, and Amal El-Mohtar) for their constant support, my RAMP writing group (Joel Derfner, Liz Duffy Adams, Delia Sherman, Ellen Kushner, and again, my beloved Carlos) for cheerleading the early draft, my mother Sita, unfailingly enthusiastic about all my literary endeavors, and the Erewhon Salon, where I debuted the first chapter. And thank you, Mike Allen, for the invitation to write what I'd always meant to get to 'one day' and the encouragement to finish it in a more or less timely manner."

Jessica P. Wick is a writer and freelance editor living in Rhode Island. She enjoys rambling through graveyards and writing by candlelight. She will take her shoes off to walk through some truly freezing surf. You can follow her at instagram: foamlyre, twitter: lunelyre, or jessicapwick.com.

About "An Unkindness," she shared, "This is dedicated to Jeremy Wick."

Amanda J. McGee is a mapmaker by day and a writer by night. She has degrees from Hollins University and Virginia Tech, where she studied languages, politics, and infrastructure. She is the author of the epic fantasy series *The Creation Saga*, one half of the podcast *Pop Fizz!*, and blogs weekly on books, movies, anime, and writing advice.

When not writing, she can be found in the garden. She lives in Southwest Virginia with the love of her life, two fluffy cats, and a plethora of plants. You can find out more on her website at amandajmcgee.com.

About the origins of "Viridian," she wrote: "Special thanks to my parents for giving me a cassette tape of *Bluebeard* which I listened to over and over as a child. In retrospect, that was probably not the best fairytale for an eleven-year-old girl, but alright, I guess. I wouldn't have been inspired to write this story without internalizing at a young age the idea that human men are monsters. Luckily, I've since learned this is only true a certain percentage of the time.

"Thanks also to my husband who decided that we were going to Vermont for our honeymoon. I am very glad that you are not a 'Bluebeard.' To the humans who influenced the settings of this book, willingly or otherwise, by providing us many places to stay in Vermont, thank you again. Some of the places in this story are real places where I laid my head, but you should find them on your own if you want to experience them. I cannot promise that you will be haunted there.

"Lastly, to my Patreon supporters, for supporting this story in its original iteration and reading the early scenes as they came out. Thanks, friends. I got this far because of you."

 Nebula, Shirley Jackson and two-time World Fantasy award finalist **Mike Allen** wears many hats. As editor and publisher of the Mythic Delirium Books Books imprint, he helmed *Mythic Delirium* magazine and the five volumes in the *Clockwork Phoenix* anthology series. His own short stories have been gathered in three collections: *Unseaming*, *The Spider Tapestries* and the forthcoming *Aftermath of an Industrial Accident*. He's won the Rhysling Award for poetry three times, and his most recent collection of verse, *Hungry Constellations*, was a Suzette Haden Elgin Award nominee. A dark fantasy novel, *The Black Fire Concerto*, appeared in 2013.

For more than a decade he's worked as the arts and culture columnist for the daily newspaper in Roanoke, Va., where he and his wife Anita live with a cat so full of trouble she's named Pandora. You can follow Mike's exploits as a writer at descentintolight.com, as an editor at mythicdelirium.com, and all at once on Twitter at @mythicdelirium.

Here's what he has to share about "The Comforter" and *A Sinister Quartet*: "It's all Scott Nicolay's fault, really. Though I mean that in the best possible way.

"Scott and his significant other Anya Martin also wear a lot of hats, among them co-founders of the Outer Dark Symposium on the Greater Weird. I attended the first of these wonderful gatherings in Atlanta, Georgia in 2017, and during on of many conversations with Scott, I mentioned that I have ideas for a third installment in my series of horror tales that begins with 'The Button Bin' and continues with 'The Quiltmaker.'

"(As an aside: 'The Comforter' ties into not just the nightmare world of 'The Button Bin,' but to my stories 'Gutter' in *Unseaming*, 'Nolens Volens' in Scott Gable and C. Dombrowski's stunning anthology *Nowhereville*, and 'The Sun Saw,' forthcoming in Joe Pulver's anthology *The Leaves of a Necronomicon* and my own collection *Aftermath of an Industrial Accident*. There are references even to places mentioned in my dark fantasy 'The Hiker's Tale.')

"Be that as it may: Scott came back at me with an idea for publishing this new installment as a limited edition chapbook. Later, the idea evolved into something akin to one of those old Ace Doubles. I reached out to C. S. E. Cooney to see if she'd be interested in providing the flip side (or maybe the front side!) of this double book, and she was game. Additional lagniappe: her potential offering, 'The Twice-Drowned Saint,' had ties to previous stories of her own -- 'Godmother Lizard,' published at *Black Gate*, and 'Life on the Sun,' another *Black Gate* special that became the opening novella in her collection *Bone Swans*, which I published through Mythic Delirium Books and which went on to beat incredible odds and win the World Fantasy Award.

"For reasons too complex to go into, and for which Scott is blameless, this proposed double chapbook never happened, though obviously 'The Comforter' and 'The Twice-Drowned Saint' both existed in various stages of draft. Pondering new projects to follow up Mythic Delirium's 2019 offerings, *Snow White Learns Witchcraft* by Theodora Goss and *The History of Soul 2065* by Barbara Krasnoff, I realized the answer was right in front of me.

"The book became a much more straightforward compilation of novellas (actually a short novel in Claire Cooney's case.) You could say Cooney and I each brought a friends to the table (though we're all friends here.) Claire brought Jessica P. Wick's 'An Unkindess' to my attention at about the same time I read a draft of Amanda J. McGee's 'Viridian,' and a duet became a quartet.

"I want to thank my fellow authors for going along with this book's madcap schedule. I want to additionally thank Amanda McGee, Jeffrey Thomas, and my wife Anita for the invaluable feedback they gave me on 'The Comforter'; Anita additionally provided invaluable insights on the project as a whole. My gratitude goes out as well to Jason Wren for his surprisingly timely art and to designer Brett Masse for his amazing hustle and talent (and thanks to Patty Templeton for introducing me to Brett, high-five!) And I'll raise a glass one more time to Scott, who sparked it all."